GOD EMPEROR OF DUNE

GOD EMPEROR OF
DUNE

Frank Herbert

The right of Frank Herbert to be identified as the author
of this work has been asserted by him in accordance
with the Copyright, Designs and Patents Act 1988.

First published in Great Britain in 1981 by
Victor Gollancz

This edition published in Great Britain in 2003
by Gollancz

An imprint of the Orion Publishing Group
Orion House, 5 Upper St Martin's Lane,
London WC2H 9EA

5 7 9 10 8 6

A CIP catalogue record for this book
is available from the British Library

ISBN 13: 978 0 575 07506 1
ISBN 10: 0 575 07506 6

Printed and bound in Great Britain by
Clays Ltd, St Ives plc

The Orion Publishing Group's policy is to use papers that
are natural, renewable and recyclable products and
made from wood grown in sustainable forests. The logging
and manufacturing processes are expected to conform to
the environmental regulations of the country of origin.

www.orionbooks.co.uk

PROLOGUE

Excerpt from the speech by Hadi Benotto announcing the discoveries at Dar-es-Balat on the planet of Rakis:

It not only is my pleasure to announce to you this morning our discovery of this marvellous storehouse containing, among other things, a monumental collection of manuscripts inscribed on ridulian crystal paper, but I also take pride in giving you our arguments for the authenticity of our discoveries, to tell you why we believe we have uncovered the original journals of Leto II, the God Emperor.

First, let me recall to you the historical treasure which we all know by the name of *The Stolen Journals*, those volumes of known antiquity which over the centuries have been so valuable in helping us to understand our ancestors. As you all know, *The Stolen Journals* were deciphered by the Spacing Guild, and the method of the Guild Key was employed to translate these newly discovered volumes. No one denies the antiquity of the Guild Key and it, *and it alone*, translates these volumes.

Second, these volumes were printed by an Ixian dictatel of truly ancient make. *The Stolen Journals* leave no doubt that this was in fact the method employed by Leto II to record his historical observations.

Third, and we believe that this is equal in portent to the actual discovery, there is the storehouse itself. The repository for these *journals* is an undoubted Ixian artifact of such primitive and yet marvellous construction that it is sure to throw new light on the historical epoch known as "The Scattering". As was to be expected, the storehouse was invisible. It was buried far deeper than myth and the Oral

1

History had led us to expect and it emitted and absorbed radiation to simulate the natural character of its surroundings, a mechanical mimesis which is not surprising of itself. What has surprised our engineers, however, is the way this was done with the most rudimentary and truly primitive mechanical skills.

I can see that some of you are as excited by this as we were. We believe we are looking at the first Ixian Globe, the no-room from which all such devices evolved. If it is not actually the first, we believe it must be *one* of the first and embodying the same principles as the first.

Let me address your obvious curiosity by assuring you that we will take you on a brief tour of the storehouse presently. We will ask only that you maintain silence while within the storehouse because our engineers and other specialists are still at work there unravelling the mysteries.

Which brings me to my fourth point, and this may well be the capstone of our discoveries. It is with emotions difficult to describe that I reveal to you now another discovery at this site—namely, actual oral recordings which are labelled as having been made by Leto II in the voice of his father, Paul-Muad'Dib. Since authenticated recordings of the God Emperor are lodged in the Bene Gesserit Archives, we have sent a sampling of our recordings, all of which were made on an ancient microbubble system, to the Sisterhood with a formal request that they conduct a comparison test. We have little doubt that the recordings will be authenticated.

Now, please turn your attention to the translated excerpts which were handed to you as you entered. Let me take this opportunity to apologize for their weight. I have heard some of you joking about that. We used ordinary paper for a practical reason—economy. The original volumes are inscribed in symbols so small that they must be magnified substantially before they can be read. In fact, it requires more than forty ordinary volumes of the type you now hold just to reprint the contents of one of the ridulian crystal originals.

If the projector—yes. We are now projecting part of an original page on to the screen at your left. This is from the first page of the first volume. Our translation is on the screens to the right. I call your attention to the internal evidence, the poetic vanity of the words as well as the meaning derived from the translation. The style conveys a personality which is identifiable and consistent. We believe that this could only have been written by someone who had the direct experience of ancestral memories, by someone labouring to share that extraordinary experience of previous lives in a way that could be understood by those not so gifted.

Look now at the actual meaning content. All of the references accord with everything history has told us about the one person whom we believe is the only person who could have written such an account.

We have another surprise for you now. I have taken the liberty of inviting the well-known poet, Rebeth Vreeb, to share the platform with us this morning and to read from this first page a short passage of our translation. It is our observation that, even in translation, these words take on a different character when read aloud. We want to share with you a truly extraordinary quality which we have discovered in these volumes.

Ladies and gentlemen, please welcome Rebeth Vreeb.

From the reading by Rebeth Vreeb:

I assure you that I am the book of fate.

Questions are my enemies. For my questions explode! Answers leap up like a frightened flock, blackening the sky of my inescapable memories. Not one answer, not one suffices.

What prisms flash when I enter the terrible field of my past. I am a chip of shattered flint enclosed in a box. The box gyrates and quakes. I am tossed about in a storm of mysteries. And when the box opens, I return to this presence like a stranger in a primitive land.

Slowly (slowly, I say) I relearn my name.

But that is not to know myself!

This person of my name, this Leto who is the second of that calling, finds other voices in his mind, other names and other places. Oh, I promise you (as I have been promised) that I answer to but a single name. If you say, "Leto", I respond. Sufferance makes this true, sufferance and one thing more:

I hold the threads!

All of them are mine. Let me but imagine a topic—say . . . *men who have died by the sword*—and I have them in all of their gore, every image intact, every moan, every grimace.

Joys of motherhood, I think, and the birthing beds are mine. Serial baby smiles and the sweet cooings of new generations. The first walkings of the toddlers and the first victories of youths brought forth for me to share. They tumble one upon another until I can see little else but sameness and repetition.

"Keep it all intact," I warn myself.

Who can deny the value of such experiences, the worth of learning through which I view each new instant?

Ahhh, but it's the past.

Don't you understand?

It's only the past!

This morning I was born in a yurt at the edge of a horse-plain in a land of a planet which no longer exists. Tomorrow I will be born someone else in another place. I have not yet chosen. This morning, though—ahh, this life! When my eyes had learned to focus, I looked out at sunshine on trampled grass and I saw vigorous people going about the sweet activities of their lives. Where . . . oh where has all of that vigour gone?

—The Stolen Journals

The three people running northward through moon shadows in the Forbidden Forest were strung out along almost half a kilometre. The last runner in the line ran less than a hundred metres ahead of the pursuing D-wolves. The animals could be heard yelping and panting in their eagerness, the way they do when they have the prey in sight.

With First Moon almost directly overhead, it was quite light in the forest and, although these were the higher latitudes of Arrakis, it was still warm from the heat of a summer day. The nightly drift of air from the Last Desert of the Sareer carried resin smells and the damp exhalations of the duff underfoot. Now and again, a breeze from the Kynes Sea beyond the Sareer drifted across the runners' tracks with hints of salt and fishes.

By a quirk of fate, the last runner was called Ulot which in the Fremen tongue means *Beloved Straggler*. Ulot was short in stature and with a tendency to fat which had placed

5

an extra dieting burden on him in training for this venture. Even when slimmed down for their desperate run, his face remained round, the large brown eyes vulnerable in that suggestion of too much flesh.

To Ulot it was obvious that he could not run much farther. He panted and wheezed. Occasionally, he staggered. But he did not call out to his companions. He knew they could not help him. All of them had taken the same oath, knowing they had no defences except the old virtues and Fremen loyalties. This remained true even though everything that once had been Fremen had now a museum quality—rote recitals learned from Museum Fremen.

It was Fremen loyalty that kept Ulot silent in the full awareness of his doom. A fine display of the ancient qualities, and rather pitiful when none of the runners had any but book knowledge and the legends of the Oral History about the virtues they aped.

The D-wolves ran close behind Ulot, giant grey figures almost man-height at the shoulders. They leaped and whined in their eagerness, heads lifted, eyes focused on the moon-betrayed figure of their quarry.

A root caught Ulot's left foot and he almost fell. This gave him renewed energy. He put on a burst of speed, gaining perhaps a wolf-length on his pursuers. His arms pumped. He breathed noisily through his open mouth.

The D-wolves did not change pace. They were silver shadows which went flick-flick through the loud green smells of their forest. They knew they had won. It was a familiar experience.

Again, Ulot stumbled. He caught his balance against a sapling and continued his panting flight, gasping, his legs trembling in rebellion against these demands. No energy remained for another burst of speed.

One of the D-wolves, a large female, moved out on Ulot's left flank. She swerved inward and leaped across his path. Giant fangs ripped Ulot's shoulder and staggered him but he did not fall. The pungency of blood was added to the forest smells. A smaller male caught his right hip and at last

6

Ulot fell, screaming. The pack pounced and his screams were cut off in abrupt finality.

Not stopping to feed, the D-wolves again took up the chase. Their noses probed the forest floor and the vagrant eddies in the air, scenting the warm tracery of two more running humans.

The next runner in the line was named Kwuteg, an old and honourable name on Arrakis, a name from the Dune times. An ancestor had served Sietch Tabr as Master of the Death Stills, but that was more than three thousand years lost in a past which many no longer believed. Kwuteg ran with the long strides of a tall and slender body which seemed perfectly fitted to such exertion. Long black hair streamed back from his aquiline features. As with his companions, he wore a black running suit of tightly knitted cotton. It revealed the workings of his buttocks and stringy thighs, the deep and steady rhythm of his breathing. Only his pace, which was markedly slow for Kwuteg, betrayed the fact that he had injured his right knee coming down from the man-made precipices which girdled the God Emperor's Citadel fortress in the Sareer.

Kwuteg heard Ulot's screams, the abrupt and potent silence, then the renewed chase-yelps of the D-wolves. He tried not to let his mind create the image of another friend being slain by Leto's monster guardians but imagination worked its sorcery on him. Kwuteg thought a curse against the tyrant but wasted no breath to voice it. There remained a chance that he could reach the sanctuary of the Idaho River. Kwuteg knew what his friends thought about him— even Siona. He had always been known as a conservative. Even as a child he had saved his energy until it counted most, parcelling out his reserves like a miser.

In spite of the injured knee, Kwuteg increased his pace. He knew the river was near. His injury had gone beyond agony into a steady flame which filled his entire leg and side with its burning. He knew the limits of his endurance. He knew also that Siona should be almost at the water. The fastest runner of them all, she carried the sealed packet ‗

7

and, in it, the things they had stolen from the fortress in the Sareer. Kwuteg focused his thoughts on that packet as he ran.

Save it, Siona! Use it to destroy him!

The eager whining of the D-wolves penetrated Kwuteg's consciousness. They were too close. He knew then that he would not escape.

But Siona must escape!

He risked a backward glance and saw one of the wolves move to flank him. The pattern of their attack plan imprinted itself on his awareness. As the flanking wolf leaped Kwuteg also leaped. Placing a tree between himself and the pack, he ducked beneath the flanking wolf, grasped one of its hind legs in both hands and, without stopping, whirled the captive wolf as a flail which scattered the others. Finding the creature not as heavy as he had expected, almost welcoming the change of action, he flailed his living bludgeon at the attackers in a dervish whirl which brought two of them down in a crash of skulls. But he could not guard every side. A lean male caught him in the back, hurling him against a tree and he lost his bludgeon.

"Go!" he screamed.

The pack bored in and Kwuteg caught the throat of the lean male in his teeth. He bit down with every gramme of his final desperation. Wolf blood spurted over his face, blinding him. Rolling without any knowledge of where he went, Kwuteg grappled another wolf. Part of the pack dissolved into a yelping, whirling mob, some turning against their own injured. Most of the pack remained intent on the quarry, though. Teeth ripped Kwuteg's throat from both sides.

Siona, too, had heard Ulot scream, then the unmistakable silence followed by the yelping of the pack as the wolves resumed the chase. Such anger filled her that she felt she might explode with it. Ulot had been included in this venture because of his analytical ability, his way of seeing a whole from only a few parts. It had been Ulot who, taking the inevitable magnifier from his kit, had examined

8

the two strange volumes they had found in with the Citadel's plans.

"I think it's a cipher," Ulot had said.

And Radi, poor Radi who had been the first of their team to die . . . Radi had said, "We can't afford the extra weight. Throw them away."

Ulot had objected: "Unimportant things aren't concealed this way."

Kwuteg had joined Radi. "We came for the Citadel plans and we have them. Those things are too heavy."

But Siona had agreed with Ulot. "I will carry them."

That had ended the argument.

Poor Ulot.

They had all known him as the worst runner in the team. Ulot was slow in most things, but the clarity of his mind could not be denied.

He is trustworthy.

Ulot *had been* trustworthy.

Siona mastered her anger and used its energy to increase her pace. Trees whipped past her in the moonlight. She had entered that timeless void of the running when there was nothing else but her own movements, her own body doing what it had been conditioned to do.

Men thought her beautiful when she ran. Siona knew this. Her long dark hair was tied tightly to keep it from whipping in the wind of her passage. She had accused Kwuteg of foolishness when he had refused to copy her style.

Where is Kwuteg?

Her hair was not like Kwuteg's. It was that deep brown which is sometimes confused with black, but is not truly black, not like Kwuteg's at all.

In the way genes occasionally do, her features copied those of a long dead ancestor: gently oval and with a generous mouth, eyes of alert awareness above a small nose. Her body had grown lanky from years of running, but it sent strong sexual signals to the males around her.

Where is Kwuteg?

The wolf pack had fallen silent and this filled her with alarm. They had done that before bringing down Radi. It had been the same when they got Setuse.

She told herself the silence could mean other things. Kwuteg, too, was silent . . . and strong. The injury had not appeared to bother him too much.

Siona began to feel pain in her chest, the gasping-to-come which she knew well from the long kilometres of training. Perspiration still poured down her body under the thin black running garment. The kit with its precious contents sealed against the river passage ahead rode high on her back. She thought about the Citadel charts folded there.

Where does Leto hide his hoard of spice?

It had to be somewhere within the Citadel. It had to be. Somewhere in the charts there would be a clue. The melange-spice for which the Bene Gesserit, the Guild and all the others hungered . . . that was a prize worth this risk.

And those two cryptic volumes. Kwuteg had been right in one thing. Ridulian crystal paper was heavy. But she shared Ulot's excitement. Something important was concealed in those lines of cipher.

Once more the eager chase-yelps of the wolves sounded in the forest behind her.

Run, Kwuteg! Run!

Now, just ahead of her through the trees, she could see the wide cleared strip which bordered the Idaho River. She glimpsed moon brightness on water beyond the clearing.

Run, Kwuteg!

She longed for a sound from Kwuteg, any sound. Only the two of them remained now from the eleven who had started the run. Nine had paid for this venture with their lives: *Radi, Aline, Ulot, Setuse, Inineg, Onemao, Hutye, Memar and Oala.*

Siona thought their names and with each sent a silent prayer to the old gods, not to the tyrant Leto. Especially, she prayed to Shai-Hulud.

I pray to Shai-Hulud who lives in the sand.

Abruptly, she was out of the forest and on to the moon-bright stretch of mowed ground along the river. Straight ahead beyond a narrow shingle of beach, the water beckoned to her. The beach was silver against the oily flow.

A loud yell from back in the trees almost made her falter. She recognized Kwuteg's voice above the wild wolf sounds. Kwuteg called out to her without name, an unmistakable cry with one word containing countless conversations—a message of death and life.

"Go!"

The pack sounds took on a terrible commotion of frenzied yelps, but nothing more from Kwuteg. She knew then how Kwuteg was spending the last energies of his life.

Delaying them to help me escape.

Obeying Kwuteg's cry, she dashed to the river's edge and plunged headfirst into the water. The river was a freezing shock after the heat of the run. It stunned her for a moment and she floundered outward, struggling to swim and regain her breath. The precious kit floated and bumped against the back of her head.

The Idaho River was not wide here, no more than fifty metres, a gently sweeping curve with sandy indentations fringed by roots and shelving banks of lush reeds and grass where the water refused to stay in the straight lines Leto's engineers had designed. Siona was strengthened by the knowledge that the D-wolves had been conditioned to stop at the water. Their territorial boundaries had been drawn, the river on this side and the desert wall on the other side. Still, she swam the last few metres underwater and surfaced in the shadows of a cutbank before turning and looking back.

The wolf pack stood ranged along the bank, all except one which had come down to the river's edge. It leaned forward with its forefeet almost into the flow. She heard it whine.

Siona knew the wolf saw her. No doubt of that. D-wolves were noted for their keen eyesight. There were Gaze

Hounds in the ancestry of Leto's forest guardians and he bred the wolves for their eyesight. She wondered if this once the wolves might break through their conditioning. They were mostly sight-hunters. If that one wolf at the river's edge should enter the water, all might follow. Siona held her breath. She felt the dragging of exhaustion. They had come almost thirty kilometres, the last half of it with the D-wolves close behind.

The wolf at the river's edge whined once more then leaped back up to its companions. At some silent signal they turned and loped into the forest.

Siona knew where they would go. D-wolves were allowed to eat anything they brought down in the Forbidden Forest. Everyone knew this. It was why the wolves roamed the forest—the guardians of the Sareer.

"You'll pay for this, Leto," she whispered. It was a low sound, her voice, very close to the quiet rustling of the water against the reeds just behind her. "You'll pay for Ulot, for Kwuteg and for all the others. You'll pay."

She pushed outward gently and drifted with the current until her feet met the first shelving of a narrow beach. Slowly, her body dragged down by fatigue, she climbed from the water and paused to check that the sealed contents of her kit had remained dry. The seal was unbroken. She stared at it a moment in the moonlight, then lifted her gaze to the forest wall across the river.

The price we paid. Ten dear friends.

Tears glimmered in her eyes, but she had the stuff of the ancient Fremen and her tears were few. The venture across the river, directly through the forest while the wolves patrolled the northern boundaries, then across the Last Desert of the Sareer and over the Citadel's ramparts—all of this already was assuming dream proportions in her mind . . . even the flight from the wolves which she had anticipated because it was a certainty that the guardian pack would cross the track of the invaders and be waiting . . . all a dream. It was the past.

I escaped.

She stored the kit with its sealed packet and fastened it once more against her back.

I have broken through your defences, Leto.

Siona thought then about the cryptic volumes. She felt certain that something hidden in those lines of cipher would open the way for her revenge.

I will destroy you, Leto!

Not *We will destroy you!* That was not Siona's way. She would do it herself.

She turned and strode toward the orchards beyond the river's mowed border. As she walked she repeated her oath, adding to it aloud the old Fremen formula which included her full name:

"Siona Ibn Fuad al-Seyefa Atreides it is who curses you, Leto. You will pay in full!"

The following is from the Hadi Benotto translation of the volumes discovered at Dar-es-Balat:

I was born Leto Atreides II more than three thousand standard years ago, measuring from the moment when I cause these words to be printed. My father was Paul-Muad'Dib. My mother was his Fremen consort, Chani. My maternal grandmother was Faroula, a noted herbalist among the Fremen. My paternal grandmother was Jessica, a product of the Bene Gesserit breeding scheme in their search for a male who could share the powers of the Sisterhood's Reverend Mothers. My maternal grandfather was Liet-Kynes, the planetologist who organized the ecological transformation of Arrakis. My paternal grandfather was *The* Atreides, descendant of the House of Atreus and tracing his ancestry directly back to the Greek original.

Enough of these begats!

My paternal grandfather died as many good Greeks did, attemping to kill his mortal enemy, the old Baron Vladimir Harkonnen. Both of them rest uncomfortably now in my ancestral memories. Even my father is not content. I have done what he feared to do and now his shade must share in the consequences.

The Golden Path demands it. And what is the Golden Path? you ask. It is the survival of humankind, nothing more nor less. We who have prescience, we who know the pitfalls in our human futures, this has always been our responsibility.

Survival.

How you feel about this—your petty woes and joys, even your agonies and raptures—seldom concerns us. My father had this power. I have it stronger. We can peer now and again through the veils of Time.

This planet of Arrakis from which I direct my multi-galactic empire is no longer what it was in the days when it was known as Dune. In those days the entire planet was a desert. Now, there is just this little remnant, my Sareer. No longer does the giant sandworm roam free, producing the spice melange. The spice! Dune was noteworthy only as the source of melange, *the only source*. What an extraordinary substance. No laboratory has ever been able to duplicate it. And it is the most valuable substance humankind has ever found.

Without melange to ignite the linear prescience of Guild Navigators, people cross the parsecs of space only at a snail's crawl. Without melange, the Bene Gesserit cannot endow Truthsayers or Reverend Mothers. Without the geriatric properties of melange, people live and die according to the ancient measure—no more than a hundred years or so. Now, the only spice is held in Guild and Bene Gesserit storehouses, a few small hoards among the remnants of the Great Houses, and my gigantic hoard which they all covet. How they would like to raid me! But they don't dare. They know I would destroy it all before surrendering it.

No. They come hat in hand and petition me for melange. I dole it out as a reward and hold it back as punishment. How they hate that.

It is my power, I tell them. It is my gift.

14

With it, I create Peace. They have had more than three thousand years of Leto's Peace. It is an enforced tranquillity which humankind knew only for the briefest periods before my ascendancy. Lest you have forgotten, study Leto's Peace once more in these, my journals.

I began this account in the first year of my stewardship, in the first throes of my metamorphosis when I was still mostly human, even visibly so. The sandtrout skin which I accepted (and my father refused) and which gave me greatly amplified strength plus virtual immunity from conventional attack and aging—that skin still covered a form recognizably human: two legs, two arms, a human face framed in the scrolled folds of the sandtrout.

Ahhh, that face! I still have it—the only human skin I expose to the universe. All the rest of my flesh has remained covered by the linked bodies of those tiny deep sand vectors which one day can become giant sandworms.

As they will . . . someday.

I often think about my final metamorphosis, that *likeness of death*. I know the way it must come but I do not know the moment or the other players. This is the one thing I cannot know. I only know whether the Golden Path continues or ends. As I cause these words to be recorded, the Golden Path continues and for that, at least, I am content.

I no longer feel the sandtrout cilia probing my flesh, encapsulating the water of my body within their placental barriers. We are virtually one body now, they my skin and I the force which moves the whole . . . most of the time.

At this writing, the *whole* could be considered rather gross. I am what could be called a pre-worm. My body is about seven metres long and somewhat more than two metres in diameter, ribbed for most of its length, with my Atreides face positioned man-height at one end, the arms and hands (still quite recognizable as human) just below. My legs and feet? Well, they are mostly atrophied. Just flippers, really, and they have wandered back along my body. The whole of me weighs approximately five old tons.

15

These items I append because I know they will have historical interest.

How do I carry this weight around? Mostly on my Royal Cart which is of Ixian manufacture. You are shocked? People invariably hated and feared the Ixians even more than they hated and feared me. Better the devil you know. And who knows what the Ixians might manufacture or invent? Who knows?

I certainly don't. Not all of it.

But I have a certain sympathy for the Ixians. They believe so strongly in their technology, their science, their machines. Because we believe (no matter the content) we understand each other, the Ixians and I. They make many devices for me and think they earn my gratitude thus. These very words you are reading were printed by an Ixian device, a dictatel it is called. If I cast my thoughts in a particular mode, the dictatel is activated. I merely think in this mode and the words are printed for me on ridulian crystal sheets only one molecule thick. Sometimes I order copies printed on material of lesser permanence. It was two of these latter types that were stolen from me by Siona.

Isn't she fascinating, my Siona? As you come to understand her importance to me, you may even question whether I really would have let her die there in the forest. Have no doubt about it. Death is a very personal thing. I will seldom interfere with it. Never in the case of someone who must be tested as Siona requires. I could let her die at any stage. After all, I could bring up a new candidate in very little time as I measure time.

She fascinates even me, though. I watched her there in the forest. Through my Ixian devices I watched her, wondering why I had not anticipated this venture. But Siona is . . . Siona. That is why I made no move to stop the wolves. It would have been wrong to do that. The D-wolves are but an extension of my purpose and my purpose is to be the greatest predator ever known.

—The Journals of Leto II

The following brief dialogue is credited to a manuscript source called "The Welbeck Fragment". The reputed author is Siona Atreides. The participants are Siona herself and her father, Moneo, who was (as all the histories tell us) a major-domo and chief aide to Leto II. It is dated at a time when Siona was still in her teens and was being visited by her father at her quarters in the Fish Speaker school at the Festival City of Onn, a major population centre on the planet now known as Rakis. According to the manuscript identification papers, Moneo had visited his daughter secretly to warn her that she risked destruction.

SIONA: How have you survived with him for so long a time, father? He kills those who are close to him. Everyone knows that.

MONEO: No! You are wrong. He kills no one.

SIONA: You needn't lie about him.

MONEO: I mean it. He kills no one.

SIONA: Then how do you account for the known deaths?

MONEO: It is the worm that kills. The worm of God. Leto lives in the bosom of God but he kills no one.

SIONA: Then how do you survive?

MONEO: I can recognize the worm. I can see it in his face and in his movements. I know when Shai-Hulud approaches.

SIONA: He is not Shai-Hulud!

MONEO: Well, that's what they called the worm in the Fremen days.

SIONA: I've read about that. But he is not the God of the desert.

MONEO: Be quiet, you foolish girl! You know nothing of such things.

SIONA: I know that you are a coward.

MONEO: How little you know. You have never stood where I have stood and seen it in his eyes, in the movements of his hands.

SIONA: What do you do when the worm approaches?

MONEO: I leave.

SIONA: That's prudent. He has killed nine Duncan Idahos that we know about for sure.

MONEO: I tell you he kills no one!

SIONA: What's the difference? Leto or worm, they are one body now.

MONEO: But they are two separate beings—Leto the Emperor and the worm who is God.

SIONA: You're mad!

MONEO: Perhaps. But I do serve God.

I am the most ardent people-watcher who ever lived. I watch them inside me and outside. Past and present can mingle with odd impositions in me. And as the metamorphosis continues in my flesh wonderful things happen to my senses. It's as though I sensed everything in close-up. I have extremely acute hearing and vision plus a sense of smell extraordinarily discriminating. I can detect and identify pheromones at three parts per million. I know. I have tested it. You cannot hide very much from my senses. I think it would horrify you what I can detect by smell alone. Your pheromones tell me what you are doing or are prepared to do. And gesture and posture! I stared for half a day once at an old man sitting on a bench in Arrakeen. He was a fifth-generation descendant of Stilgar the Naib and did not even know it. I studied the angle of his neck, the skin flaps below his chin, the cracked lips and moistness about his nostrils, the pores behind his ears, the wisps of grey hair which crept from beneath the hood of his antique still-suit. Not once did he detect that he was being watched. Hah! Stilgar would have known it in a second or two. But this old man was just waiting for someone who never came. He got up finally and tottered off. He was very stiff after all of that sitting. I knew I would never see him in the flesh again. He was that near death and his water was sure to be wasted. Well, that no longer mattered.

—The Stolen Journals

Leto thought it the most interesting place in the universe, this place where he awaited the arrival of his current

Duncan Idaho. By most human standards, it was a gigantic space, the core of an elaborate series of catacombs beneath his Citadel. Radiating chambers thirty metres high and twenty metres wide ran like spokes from the hub where he waited. His cart had been positioned at the centre of the hub in a domed and circular chamber four hundred metres in diameter and one hundred metres high at its tallest point above him.

He found these dimensions reassuring.

It was early afternoon at the Citadel, but the only light in his chamber came from the random drifting of a few suspensor-borne glowglobes tuned into low orange. The light did not penetrate far into the spokes, but Leto's memories told him the exact position of everything there—the water, the bones, the dust of his ancestors and of the Atreides who had lived and died since the Dune times. All of them were here plus a few containers of melange to create the illusion that this was all of his hoard should it ever come to such an extreme.

Leto knew why the Duncan was coming. Idaho had learned that the Tleilaxu were making another Duncan, another ghola created to the specifications demanded by the God Emperor. This Duncan feared that he was being replaced after almost sixty years of service. It was always something of that nature which began the subversion of the Duncans. A Guild envoy had waited upon Leto earlier to warn that the Ixians had delivered a lasgun to this Duncan.

Leto chuckled. The Guild remained extremely sensitive to anything which might threaten their slender supply of spice. They were terrified at the thought that Leto was the last link with the sandworms which had produced the original stockpiles of melange.

If I die away from water there will be no more spice, not ever.

That was the Guild's fear. And their historian-accountants assured them Leto sat on the largest store of melange in the universe. The knowledge made the Guild almost reliable as allies.

While he waited, Leto did the hand and finger exercises of his Bene Gesserit inheritance. The hands were his pride. Beneath a grey membrane of sandtrout skin, their long digits and opposable thumbs could be used much as any human hands. The almost useless flippers which once had been his feet and legs were more inconvenience than shame. He could crawl, roll and toss his body with astonishing speed, but he sometimes fell on the flippers and there was pain.

What was delaying the Duncan?

Leto imagined the man vacillating, staring out of a window across the fluid horizon of the Sareer. The air was alive with heat today. Before descending to the crypt, Leto had seen a mirage in the southwest. The heat-mirror tipped and flashed an image across the sand, showing him a band of Museum Fremen trudging past a Display Sietch for the edification of tourists.

It was cool in the crypt, always cool, the illumination always low. Tunnel spokes were dark holes sloping upward and downward in gentle gradients to accommodate the Royal Cart. Some tunnels extended beyond false walls for many kilometres, passages Leto had created for himself with Ixian tools—feeding tunnels and secret ways.

As he contemplated the coming interview, a sense of nervousness began to grow in Leto. He found this an interesting emotion, one he had been known to enjoy. Leto knew that he had grown reasonably fond of the current Duncan. There was a reservoir of hope in Leto that the man would survive the coming interview. Sometimes they did. There was little likelihood the Duncan posed a mortal threat, although this had to be left to such chance as existed. Leto had tried to explain this to one of the earlier Duncans . . . right here in this room.

"You will think it strange that I, with my powers, can speak of luck and chance," Leto had said.

The Duncan had been angry. "You leave nothing to chance! I know you!"

"How naive. Chance is the nature of our universe."

20

"Not chance! Mischief. And you're the author of mischief!"

"Excellent, Duncan! Mischief is a most profound pleasure. It's in the ways we deal with mischief that we sharpen creativity."

"You're not even human anymore!" Oh, how angry the Duncan had been.

Leto had found this accusation irritating, like a grain of sand in an eye. He held on to the remnants of his once-human self with a grimness which could not be denied, although irritation was the closest he could come to anger.

"Your life is becoming a cliché," Leto had accused.

Whereupon the Duncan had produced a small explosive from the folds of his uniform robe. What a surprise!

Leto loved surprises, even nasty ones.

It is something I did not predict! And he said as much to the Duncan who had stood there oddly undecided now that decision was absolutely demanded of him.

"This could kill you," the Duncan said.

"I'm sorry, Duncan. It will do a small amount of injury, no more."

"But you said you didn't predict this!" The Duncan's voice had grown shrill.

"Duncan, Duncan, it is absolute prediction which equals death to me. How unutterably boring death is."

At the last instant, the Duncan had tried to throw the explosive to one side, but the material in it had been unstable and it had gone off too soon. The Duncan had died. Ahh, well—the Tleilaxu always had another in their axlotl tanks.

One of the drifting glowglobes above Leto began to blink. Excitement gripped him. Moneo's signal! Faithful Moneo had alerted his God Emperor that the Duncan was descending to the crypt.

The door to the human lift between two spoked passages in the northwest arc of the hub swung open. The Duncan strode forth, a small figure at that distance, but Leto's eyes discerned even tiny details—a wrinkle on the uniform

21

elbow which said the man had been leaning somewhere, chin in hand. Yes, there were still the marks of his hand on the chin. The Duncan's odour preceded him: the man was high on his own adrenalin.

Leto remained silent while the Duncan approached, observing details. The Duncan still walked with the spring of youth despite all of his long service. He could thank a minimal ingestion of melange for that. The man wore the old Atreides uniform, black with a golden hawk at the left breast. An interesting statement, that: "I serve the honour of the *old* Atreides!" His hair was still the black cap of karakul, the features fixed in stony sharpness with high cheekbones.

The Tleilaxu make their gholas well, Leto thought.

The Duncan carried a thin briefcase woven of dark brown fibres, one he had carried for many years. It usually contained the material upon which he based his reports, but today it bulged with some heavier weight.

The Ixian lasgun.

Idaho kept his attention on Leto's face as he walked. The face remained disconcertingly Atreides, lean features with eyes of total blue which the nervous felt as a physical intrusion. It lurked deep within a grey cowl of sandtrout skin which, Idaho knew, could roll forward protectively in a flickering reflex—a faceblink rather than an eyeblink. The skin was pink within its grey frame. It was difficult avoiding the thought that Leto's face was an obscenity, a lost bit of humanity trapped in something alien.

Stopping only six paces from the Royal Cart, Idaho did not attempt to conceal his angry determination. He did not even think about whether Leto knew of the lasgun. This Imperium had wandered too far from the old Atreides morality, had become an impersonal juggernaut which crushed the innocent in its path. It had to be ended!

"I have come to talk to you about Siona and other matters," Idaho said. He brought the case into position where he could withdraw the lasgun easily.

"Very well." Leto's voice was full of boredom.

"Siona was the only one who escaped, but she still has a base of rebel companions."

"You think I don't know this?"

"I know your dangerous tolerance for rebels! What I don't know is the contents of that package she stole."

"Oh, that. She has the complete plans for the Citadel."

For just a moment, Idaho was Leto's Guard Commander, deeply shocked at such a breach of security.

"You let her escape with that?"

"No, you did."

Idaho recoiled from this accusation. Slowly, the newly resolved assassin in him regained ascendancy.

"Is that all she got?" Idaho asked.

"I had two volumes, copies of my journal, in with the charts. She stole the copies."

Idaho studied Leto's immobile face. "What is in these journals? Sometimes you say it's a diary, sometimes a history."

"A bit of both. You might even call it a textbook."

"Does it bother you that she took these volumes?"

Leto allowed himself a soft smile which Idaho accepted as a negative answer. A momentary tension rippled through Leto's body then as Idaho reached into the slim case. Would it be the weapon or the reports? Although the core of his body possessed a powerful resistance to heat, Leto knew that some of his flesh was vulnerable to a lasgun, especially the face.

Idaho brought a report from his case and, even before he began reading from it, the signals were obvious to Leto. Idaho was seeking answers, not providing information. Idaho wanted justification for a course of action already chosen.

"We have discovered a cult of Alia on Giedi Prime," Idaho said.

Leto remained silent while Idaho recounted the details. *How boring.* Leto let his thoughts wander. The worshippers of his father's long-dead sister served these days only to provide occasional amusement. The Duncans predictably saw such activity as a kind of underground threat.

Idaho finished reading. His agents were thorough, no denying it. Boringly thorough.

"This is nothing more than a revival of Isis," Leto said. "My priests and priestesses will have some sport suppressing this cult and its followers."

Idaho shook his head as though responding to a voice within it.

"The Bene Gesserit knew about the cult," he said.

Now *that* interested Leto.

"The Sisterhood has never forgiven me for taking their breeding programme away from them," he said.

"This has nothing to do with breeding."

Leto concealed mild amusement. The Duncans were always so sensitive on the subject of breeding, although some of them occasionally stood at stud.

"I see," Leto said. "Well, the Bene Gesserit are all more than a little insane, but madness represents a chaotic reservoir of surprises. Some surprises can be valuable."

"I fail to see any value in this."

"Do you think the Sisterhood was behind this cult?" Leto asked.

"I do."

"Explain."

"They had a shrine. They called it 'The Shrine of the Crysknife'."

"Did they now?"

"And their chief priestess was called 'The Keeper of Jessica's Light'. Does that suggest anything?"

"It's lovely!" Leto did not try to conceal his amusement.

"What is lovely about it?"

"They unite my grandmother and my aunt into a single goddess."

Idaho shook his head slowly from side to side, not understanding.

Leto permitted himself a small internal pause, less than a blink. The grandmother-within did not particularly care for this Giedi Prime cult. He was required to wall off her memories and her identity.

"What do you suppose was the purpose of this cult?" Leto asked.

"Obvious. A competing religion to undermine your authority."

"That's too simple. Whatever else they may be, the Bene Gesserit are not simpletons."

Idaho waited for an explanation.

"They want more spice!" Leto said. "More Reverend Mothers."

"So they annoy you until you buy them off?"

"I am disappointed in you, Duncan."

Idaho merely stared up at Leto, who contrived a sigh, a complicated gesture no longer intrinsic to his new form. The Duncans usually were brighter, but Leto supposed that this one's plot had clouded his alertness.

"They chose Giedi Prime as their home," Leto said. "What does that suggest?"

"It was a Harkonnen stronghold, but that's ancient history."

"Your sister died there, a victim of the Harkonnens. It is right that the Harkonnens and Giedi Prime be united in your thoughts. Why did you not mention this earlier?"

"I didn't think it was important."

Leto drew his mouth into a tight line. The reference to his sister had troubled the Duncan. The man knew *intellectually* that he was only the latest in a long line of fleshly revivals, all products of the Tleilaxu axlotl tanks and taken from the original cells at that. The Duncan could not escape his revived memories. He knew that the Atreides had rescued him from Harkonnen bondage.

And whatever else I may be, Leto thought, *I am still Atreides.*

"What're you trying to say?" Idaho demanded.

Leto decided that a shout was required. He let it be a loud one: "The Harkonnens were spice hoarders!"

Idaho recoiled a full step.

25

Leto continued in a lower voice: "There's an undiscovered melange hoard on Giedi Prime. The Sisterhood was trying to winkle it out with their religious tricks as a cover."

Idaho was abashed. Once it was spoken, the answer appeared obvious.

And I missed it, he thought.

Leto's shout had shaken him back into his role as Commander of the Royal Guard. Idaho knew about the economics of the empire, simplified in the extreme: no interest charges permitted; cash on the barrel head. The only coinage bore a likeness of Leto's cowled face: The God Emperor. But it was all based on the spice, a substance whose value, though enormous, kept increasing. A man could carry the price of an entire planet in his hand luggage.

"Control the coinage and the courts. Let the rabble have the rest," Leto thought. Old Jacob Broom said it and Leto could hear the old man chortling within. *"Things haven't changed all that much, Jacob."*

Idaho took a deep breath. "The Bureau of the Faith should be notified immediately."

Leto remained silent.

Taking this as a cue to continue, Idaho went on with his reports, but Leto listened with only a fraction of his awareness. It was like a monitoring circuit which only recorded Idaho's words and actions with but an occasional intensification for an internal comment:

And *now* he wants to talk about the Tleilaxu.

That is dangerous ground for you, Duncan.

But this opened up a new avenue for Leto's reflection.

The wily Tleilaxu still produce my Duncans from the original cells. They do a religiously forbidden thing and we both know it. I do not permit the artificial manipulation of human genetics. But the Tleilaxu have learned how I treasure the Duncans as the captains of my Guard. I do not think they suspect the amusement value in this. It amuses me that a river now bears the Idaho name where once it was a mountain. That mountain no longer exists. We brought it

26

down to get material for the high walls which girdle my Sareer.

Of course, the Tleilaxu know that I occasionally breed the Duncans back into my own programme. The Duncans represent mongrel strength . . . and much more. Every fire must have its damper.

It was my intent to breed this one with Siona, but that may not be possible now.

Hah! He says he wants me to "crack down" on the Tleilaxu. Why will he not ask it straight out? "Are you preparing to replace me?"

I am tempted to tell him.

Once more, Idaho's hand went into the slender pouch. Leto's introspective monitoring did not miss a beat.

The lasgun or more reports? It is more reports.

The Duncan remains wary. He wants not only the assurance that I am ignorant of his intent but more "proofs" that I am unworthy of his loyalty. He hesitates in a prolonged fashion. He always has. I have told him enough times that I will not use my prescience to predict the moment of my exit from this ancient form. But he doubts. He always was a doubter.

This cavernous chamber drinks up his voice and, were it not for my sensitivity, the dankness here would mask the chemical evidence of his fears. I fade his voice out of immediate awareness. What a bore this Duncan has become. He is recounting the history, the history of Siona's rebellion, no doubt leading up to personal admonitions about her latest escapade.

"It's not an ordinary rebellion," he says.

That brings me back! Fool. All rebellions are ordinary and an ultimate bore. They are copied out of the same pattern, one much like another. The driving force is adrenalin addiction and the desire to gain personal power. All rebels are closet aristocrats. That's why I can convert them so easily.

Why do the Duncans never really hear me when I tell them about this? I have had the argument with this very Duncan.

27

It was one of our earliest confrontations right here in the crypt.

"The art of government requires that you never give up the initiative to radical elements," he said.

How pedantic. Radicals crop up in every generation and you must not try to prevent this. That's what he means by "give up the initiative". He wants to crush them, suppress them, control them, prevent them. He is living proof that there is little difference between the police mind and the military mind.

I told him, "Radicals are only to be feared when you try to suppress them. You must demonstrate that you will use the best of what they offer."

"They are dangerous. They are dangerous!" He thinks that by repeating he creates some kind of truth.

Slowly, step by step, I lead him through my method and he even gives the appearance of listening.

"This is their weakness, Duncan. Radicals always see matters in terms which are too simple—black and white, good and evil, them and us. By addressing complex matters in that way, they rip open a passage for chaos. The art of government, as you call it, is the mastery of chaos."

"No one can deal with every surprise."

"Surprise? Who's talking about surprise? Chaos is no surprise. It has predictable characteristics. For one thing, it carries away order and strengthens the forces at the extremes."

"Isn't that what radicals are trying to do? Aren't they trying to shake things up so they can grab control?"

"That's what they think they're doing. Actually, they're creating new extremists, new radicals and they are continuing the old process."

"What about a radical who sees the complexities and comes at you that way?"

"That's no radical. That's a rival for leadership."

"But what do you do?"

"You co-opt them or kill them. That's how the struggle for leadership originated, at the grunt level."

28

"Yes, but what about messiahs?"

"Like my father?"

The Duncan does not like this question. He knows that in a very special way I am my father. He knows I can speak with my father's voice and persona, that the memories are precise, never edited and inescapable.

Reluctantly, he says: "Well . . . if you want."

"Duncan, I am all of them and I know. There has never been a truly selfless rebel, just hypocrites—conscious hypocrites or unconscious hypocrites, it's all the same."

That stirs up a small hornets' nest among my ancestral memories. Some of them have never given up the belief that they and they alone held the key to all of humankind's problems. Well, in that, they are like me. I can sympathize even while I tell them that failure is its own demonstration.

I am forced to block them off, though. There's no sense dwelling on them. They now are little more than poignant reminders . . . as is this Duncan who stands in front of me with his lasgun . . .

Great Gods below! He has caught me napping. He has the lasgun in his hand and it is pointed at my face.

"You, Duncan? Have you betrayed me, too?"

Et tu, Brute?

Every fibre of Leto's awareness came to full alert. He could feel his body twitching. The worm-flesh had a will of its own.

Idaho spoke with derision: "Tell me, Leto: How many times must I pay the debt of loyalty?"

Leto recognized the inner question: "How many of me have there been?" The Duncans always wanted to know this. Every Duncan asked it and no answer satisfied. They doubted.

In his saddest Muad'Dib voice, Leto asked: "Do you take no pride in my admiration, Duncan? Haven't you ever wondered what it is about you that makes me desire you as my constant companion through the centuries?"

"You know me to be the ultimate fool!"

"Duncan!"

29

The voice of an angry Muad'Dib could always be counted on to shatter Idaho. Despite the fact that Idaho knew no Bene Gesserit had ever mastered the powers of Voice as Leto had mastered them, it was predictable that he would dance to this one voice. The lasgun wavered in his hand.

That was enough. Leto was off the cart in a hurtling roll. Idaho had never seen him leave the cart this way, had not even suspected it could happen. For Leto, there were only two requirements—a real threat which the worm-body could sense and the release of that body. The rest was automatic and the speed of it always astonished even Leto.

The lasgun was his major concern. It could scratch him badly, but few understood the abilities of the pre-worm body to deal with heat.

Leto struck Idaho while rolling and the lasgun was deflected as it was fired. One of the useless flippers which had been Leto's legs and feet sent a shocking burst of sensations crashing into his awareness. For an instant, there was only pain. But the worm-body was free to act and reflexes ignited a violent paroxysm of flopping. Leto heard bones cracking. The lasgun was thrown far across the floor of the crypt by a spasmodic jerk of Idaho's hand.

Rolling off Idaho, Leto poised himself for a renewed attack but there was no need. The injured flipper still sent pain signals and he sensed that the tip of the flipper had been burned away. The sandtrout skin already had sealed the wound. The pain had eased to an ugly throbbing.

Idaho stirred. There could be little doubt that he had been mortally injured. His chest was visibly crushed. There was obvious agony when he tried to breathe, but he opened his eyes and stared up at Leto.

The persistence of these mortal possessions! Leto thought.

"Siona," Idaho gasped.

Leto saw the life leave him then.

Interesting, Leto thought. *Is it possible that this Duncan and Siona . . . No! This Duncan always displayed a true*

30

sneering disdain for Siona's foolishness.

Leto climbed back on to the Royal Cart. That had been a close one. There could be little doubt that the Duncan had been aiming for the *brain*. Leto was always aware that his hands and feet were vulnerable, but he had allowed no one to learn that what had once been his brain was no longer directly associated with his face. It was not even a brain of human dimensions anymore, but had spread in nodal congeries throughout his body. He had told this to no one but his journals.

> *Oh, the landscapes I have seen! And the people! The far wanderings of the Fremen and all the rest of it. Even back through the myths to Terra. Oh, the lessons in astronomy and intrigue, the migrations, the dishevelled flights, the leg-aching and lung-aching runs through so many nights on all of those cosmic specks where we have defended our transient possession. I tell you we are a marvel and my memories leave no doubt of this.*

> **—The Stolen Journals**

The woman working at the small wall desk was too big for the narrow chair on which she perched. Outside, it was mid-morning, but in this windowless room deep beneath the city of Onn there was but a single glowglobe high in a corner. It had been tuned to warm yellow but the light failed to dispel the grey utility of the small room. Walls and ceilings were covered by identical rectangular panels of dull grey metal.

There was only one other piece of furniture, a narrow cot with a thin pallet covered by a featureless grey blanket. It was obvious that neither piece of furniture had been designed for the occupant.

She wore a one-piece pyjama suit of dark blue which stretched tightly across her wide shoulders as she hunched over the desk. The glowglobe illuminated closely cropped blonde hair and the right side of her face, emphasizing the square block of jaw. The jaw moved with silent words as her thick fingers carefully depressed the keys of a thin keyboard on the desk. She handled the machine with a deference which had originated as awe and moved reluctantly into fearsome excitement. Long familiarity with the machine had eliminated neither emotion.

As she wrote, words appeared on a screen concealed within the wall rectangle exposed by the downward folding of the desk.

"Siona continues actions which predict violent attack on Your Holy Person," she wrote. "Siona remains unswerving in her avowed purpose. She told me today that she will give copies of the stolen books to groups whose loyalty to You cannot be trusted. The named recipients are the Bene Gesserit, the Guild and the Ixians. She says the books contain Your enciphered words and, by this gift, she seeks help in translating Your Holy Words.

"Lord, I do not know what great revelations may be concealed on those pages, but if they contain anything of threat to Your Holy Person I beg You to relieve me from my vow of obedience to Siona. I do not understand why You made me take this vow but I fear it.

"I remain Your worshipful servant, Nayla."

The chair creaked as Nayla sat back and thought about her words. The room fell into the almost soundless withdrawal of thick insulation. There was only Nayla's faint breathing and a distant throbbing of machinery felt more in the floor than in the air.

Nayla stared at her message on the screen. Destined only for the eyes of the God Emperor, it required more than holy truthfulness. It demanded a deep candour which she found draining. Presently, she nodded and pressed the key which would encode the words and prepare them for transmission. Bowing her head, she prayed silently before concealing the desk within the wall. These actions, she knew, transmitted the message. God himself had implanted a physical device within her head, swearing her to secrecy and warning her that there might come a time when he would speak to her through the thing within her skull. He had never done this. She suspected that Ixians had fashioned the device. It had possessed some of their *look*. But God Himself had done this thing and she could ignore the suspicion that there might be a *computer* in it, that it might be prohibited by the Great Convention.

"Make no device in the likeness of the mind!"

Nayla shuddered. She stood then and moved her chair to its regular position beside the cot. Her heavy, muscular body strained against the thin blue garment. There was a steady deliberation about her, the actions of someone constantly adjusting to great physical strength. She turned at the cot and studied the place where the desk had been. There was only a rectangular grey panel like all the others. No bit of lint, no strand of hair, nothing caught there to reveal the panel's secret.

Nayla took a deep, restorative breath and let herself out of the room's only door into a grey passage dimly lighted by widely spaced white glowglobes. The machinery sounds were louder here. She turned left and a few minutes later was with Siona in a somewhat larger room, a table at its centre upon which things stolen from the Citadel had been arranged. Two silvery glowglobes illuminated the scene—Siona seated at the table with an assistant named Topri standing beside her.

Nayla nurtured grudging admiration for Siona, but Topri, there was a man worthy of nothing except active dislike. He was a nervous fat man with bulging green eyes, a pug nose and thin lips above a dimpled chin. Topri squeaked when he spoke.

"Look here, Nayla! Look what Siona has found pressed between the pages of these two books."

Nayla closed and locked the room's single door.

"You talk too much, Topri," Nayla said. "You're a blurter. How could you know if I was alone in the passage?"

Topri paled. An angry scowl settled on to his face.

"I'm afraid she's right," Siona said. "What made you think I wanted Nayla to know about my discovery?"

"You trust her with everything!"

Siona turned her attention to Nayla. "Do you know why I trust you, Nayla?" The question was asked in a flat, unemotional voice.

Nayla put down a sudden surge of fear. Had Siona discovered her secret?

Have I failed my Lord?

"Have you no response to my question?" Siona asked.

"Have I ever given you cause to do otherwise?" Nayla asked.

"That's not a sufficient cause for trust," Siona said. "There's no such thing as perfection—not in human or machine."

"Then why *do* you trust me?"

"Your words and your actions always agree. It's a marvellous quality. For instance, you don't like Topri and you never try to conceal your dislike."

Nayla glanced at Topri, who cleared his throat.

"I don't trust him," Nayla said.

The words popped into her mind and out of her mouth without reflection. Only after she had spoken did Nayla realize the true core of her dislike: Topri would betray anyone for personal gain.

Has he found me out?

Still scowling, Topri said, "I am not going to stand here and accept your abuse." He started to leave but Siona held up a restraining hand. Topri hesitated.

"Although we speak the old Fremen words and swear our loyalty to each other, that is not what holds us together," Siona said. "Everything is based on performance. That is all I measure. Do you understand, both of you?"

Topri nodded automatically, but Nayla shook her head from side to side.

Siona smiled up at her. "You don't always agree with my decisions, do you, Nayla?"

"No." The word was forced from her.

"And you have never tried to conceal your disagreement, yet you always obey me. Why?"

"That is what I have sworn to do."

"But I have said this is not enough."

Nayla knew she was perspiring, knew this was revealing, but she could not move. *What am I to do? I swore to God that I would obey Siona but I cannot tell her this.*

"You must answer my question," Siona said. "I command it."

Nayla caught her breath. This was the dilemma she had most feared. There was no way out. She said a silent prayer and spoke in a low voice.

"I have sworn to God that I will obey you."

Siona clapped her hands in glee and laughed.

"I knew it!"

Topri chuckled.

"Shut up, Topri," Siona said. "I am trying to teach *you* a lesson. You don't believe in anything, not even in yourself."

"But I . . ."

"Be still, I say! Nayla believes. I believe. This is what holds us together. Belief."

Topri was astonished. "Belief? You believe in . . ."

"Not in the God Emperor, you fool! We believe that a higher power will settle with the tyrant Worm. We are that higher power."

Nayla took a trembling breath.

"It's all right, Nayla," Siona said. "I don't care where you draw your strength, just as long as you believe."

Nayla managed a smile, then grinned. She had never been more profoundly stirred by the wisdom of her Lord. *I may speak the truth and it works only for my God!*

"Let me show you what I've found in these books," Siona said. She gestured at some sheets of ordinary paper on the table. "Pressed between the pages."

Nayla stepped around the table and looked down at it.

"First, there's this." Siona held up an object which Nayla

35

had not noticed. It was a thin strand of something . . . and what appeared to be a . . .

"A flower?" Nayla asked.

"This was between two pages of paper. On the paper was written this."

Siona leaned over the table and read: "A strand of Ghanima's hair with a starflower blossom which she once brought me."

Looking up at Nayla, Siona said: "Our God Emperor is revealed as a sentimentalist. That is a weakness I had not expected."

"Ghanima?" Nayla asked.

"His sister! Remember your Oral History."

"Oh . . . oh, yes. The Prayer to Ghanima."

"Now, listen to this." Siona took up another sheet of paper and read from it.

> "The sand beach as grey as a dead cheek,
> A green tideflow reflects cloud ripples;
> I stand on the dark wet edge.
> Cold foam cleanses my toes.
> I smell driftwood smoke."

Again, Siona looked up at Nayla. "This is identified as 'Words I wrote when told of Ghani's death.' What do you think of that?"

"He . . . he loved his sister."

"Yes! He is *capable* of love. Oh, yes! We have him now."

Sometimes I indulge myself in safaris which no other being may take. I strike inward along the axis of my memories. Like a schoolchild reporting on a vacation trip, I take up my subject. Let it be . . . female intellectuals! I course backward into the ocean which is my ancestors. I am a great winged fish in the depths. The mouth of my awareness opens and I scoop them up! Sometimes . . . sometimes I hunt out specific persons recorded in our histories. What a private joy to relive the life of such a one while I mock the academic pretensions which supposedly formed a biography.

—**The Stolen Journals**

Moneo descended to the crypt with sad resignation. There was no escaping the duties required of him now. The God Emperor required a small pasage of time to grieve the loss of another Duncan . . . but then life went on . . . and on . . .

The lift slid silently downward with its superb Ixian dependability. Once, just once, the God Emperor had cried out to his majordomo: "Moneo! Sometimes I think *you* were made by the Ixians!"

Moneo felt the lift stop. The door opened and he looked out across the crypt at the shadowy bulk on the Royal Cart. There was no indication that Leto had noticed the arrival. Moneo sighed and began the long walk through the echoing gloom. There was a body on the floor near the cart. No need for *déjà vu*. This was merely familiar.

Once, in Moneo's early days of service, Leto had said: "You don't like this place, Moneo. I can see that."

"No, Lord."

With just a little prodding of memory, Moneo could hear his own voice in that naive past. And the voice of the God Emperor responding:

"You don't think of a mausoleum as a comforting place, Moneo. I find it a source of infinite strength."

Moneo remembered that he had been anxious to get off this topic. "Yes, Lord."

Leto had persisted: "There are only a few of my ancestors here. The water of Muad'Dib is here. Ghani and Harq al-Ada are here, of course, but they're not *my* ancestors. No, if there's any true crypt of *my* ancestors, *I* am that crypt. This is mostly the Duncans and the products of my breeding programme. You'll be here someday."

Moneo found that these memories had slowed his pace. He sighed and moved a bit faster. Leto could be violently impatient on occasion but there was still no sign from him. Moneo did not take this to mean that his approach went unobserved.

Leto lay with his eyes closed and only his other senses to record Moneo's progress across the crypt. Thoughts of

37

Siona had been occupying Leto's attention.

Siona is my ardent enemy, he thought. *I do not need Nayla's words to confirm this. Siona is a woman of action. She lives on the surface of enormous energies which fill me with fantasies of delight. I cannot contemplate those living energies without a feeling of ecstasy. They are my reasons for being, the justification for everything I have ever done . . . even for the corpse of this foolish Duncan in front of me now.*

Leto's ears told him that Moneo had not yet crossed half the distance to the Royal Cart. The man moved slower and slower, then picked up his pace.

What a gift Moneo has given me in this daughter, Leto thought. *Siona is fresh and precious. She is the* new *while I am a collection of the obsolete, a relic of the damned, of the lost and strayed. I am the waylaid pieces of history which sank out of sight in all of our pasts. Such an accumulation of riffraff has never before been imagined.*

Leto paraded the past within him then to let them observe what had happened in the crypt.

The minutiae are mine!

Siona, though . . . Siona was like a clean slate upon which great things might yet be written.

I guard that slate with infinite care. I am preparing it, cleansing it.

What did the Duncan mean when he called out her name?

Moneo approached the cart diffidently yet consummately aware. Surely Leto did not sleep.

Leto opened his eyes and looked down as Moneo came to a stop near the corpse. At this moment, Leto found the majordomo a delight to observe. Moneo wore a white Atreides uniform with no insignia, a subtle comment. His face, almost as well known as Leto's, was all the insignia he needed. Moneo waited patiently. There was no change of expression on his flat, even features. His thick, sandy hair lay in a neat, equally divided part. Deep within his grey eyes there was that look of directness which went with knowledge of great personal power. It was a look which he

modified only in the God Emperor's presence, and sometimes not even there. Not once did he glance toward the
body on the crypt's floor.

When Leto continued silent, Moneo cleared his throat,
then: "I am saddened, Lord."

Exquisite! Leto thought. *He knows I feel true remorse
about the Duncans. Moneo has seen their records and has
seen enough of them dead. He knows that only nineteen
Duncans died what people usually refer to as natural deaths.*

"He had an Ixian lasgun," Leto said.

Moneo's gaze went directly to the gun on the floor of the
crypt off to his left, demonstrating that he already had seen
it. He returned his attention to Leto, sweeping a glance
down the length of the great body.

"You are injured, Lord?"

"Inconsequential."

"But he hurt you."

"Those flippers are useless to me. They will be entirely
gone within another two hundred years."

"I will dispose of the Duncan's body personally, Lord,"
Moneo said. "Is there . . ."

"The piece of me he burned away is entirely ash. We will
let it blow away. This is a fitting place for ashes."

"As my Lord says."

"Before you dispose of the body, disable the lasgun and
keep it where I can present it to the Ixian ambassador. As
for the Guildsman who warned us about it, present him
personally with ten grammes of spice. Oh—and our
priestesses on Giedi Prime should be alerted to a hidden
store of melange there, probably old Harkonnen contraband."

"What do you wish done with it when it's found,
Lord?"

"Use a bit of it to pay the Tleilaxu for the new ghola. The
rest of it can go into our stores here in the crypt."

"Lord." Moneo acknowledged the orders with a nod, a
gesture which was not quite a bow. His gaze met Leto's.

Leto smiled. He thought: *We both know that Moneo will*

not leave without addressing directly the matter which most concerns us.

"I have seen the report on Siona," Moneo said.

Leto's smile widened. Moneo was such a pleasure in these moments. His words conveyed many things which did not require open discussion between them. His words and actions were in precise alignment, carried on the mutual awareness that he, of course, spied on everything. Now, there was a natural concern for his daughter, but he wished it understood that his concern for the God Emperor remained paramount. From his own traverse through a similar evolution, Moneo knew with precision the delicate nature of Siona's present fortunes.

"Have I not created her, Moneo?" Leto asked. "Have I not controlled the conditions of her ancestry and her up-bringing?"

"She is my only daughter, my only child, Lord."

"In a way she reminds me of Harq al-Ada," Leto said. "There doesn't appear to be much of Ghani in her, although that has to be there. Perhaps she harks back to our ancestors in the Sisterhood's breeding programme."

"Why do you say that, Lord?"

Leto reflected. Was there need for Moneo to know this peculiar thing about his daughter? Siona could fade from the prescient view at times. The Golden Path remained, but Siona faded. Yet . . . she was not prescient. She was a unique phenomenon . . . and if she survived. Leto decided he would not cloud Moneo's efficiency with unnecessary information.

"Remember your own past," Leto said.

"Indeed, Lord! And she has such a potential, so much more than I ever had. But that makes her dangerous, too."

"And she will not listen to you," Leto said.

"No, but I have an agent in her rebellion."

That will be Topri, Leto thought.

It required no prescience to know that Moneo would have an agent in place. Ever since the death of Siona's mother, Leto had known with increasing sureness the course of Moneo's actions. Nayla's suspicions pinpointed Topri. And now, Moneo paraded his fears and actions, offering them as the price of his daughter's continued safety.

How unfortunate he had fathered only the one child on that mother.

"Recall how I treated you in similar circumstances," Leto said. "You know the demands of the Golden Path as well as I do."

"But I was young and foolish, Lord."

"Young and brash, never foolish."

Moneo managed a tight smile at this compliment, his thoughts leaning more and more toward the belief that he now understood Leto's intentions. *The dangers, though!*

Feeding his belief, Leto said: "You know how much I enjoy surprises."

That is true, Leto thought. *Moneo does know it. But even while Siona surprises me she reminds me of what I fear most—the sameness and boredom which could break the Golden Path. Look at how boredom put me temporarily in the Duncan's power! Siona is the contrast by which I know my deepest fears. Moneo's concern for me is well grounded.*

"My agent will continue to watch her new companions, Lord," Moneo said. "I do not like them."

"Her companions? I myself had such companions once long ago."

"Rebellious, Lord? You?" Moneo was genuinely surprised.

"Have I not proved a friend of rebellion?"

"But Lord . . ."

"The aberrations of our past are more numerous than you may think!"

"Yes, Lord." Moneo was abashed, yet still curious. And he knew that the God Emperor sometimes waxed loquacious after the death of a Duncan. "You must have seen many rebellions, Lord."

Involuntarily, Leto's thoughts sank into the memories aroused by these words.

41

"Ahhh, Moneo," he muttered. "My travels in the ancestral mazes have memorized uncounted places and events which I never desire to see repeated."

"I can imagine your inward travels, Lord."

"No, you cannot. I have seen peoples and planets in such numbers that they lose meaning even in imagination. Ohhh, the landscapes I have passed. The calligraphy of alien roads glimpsed from space and imprinted upon my innermost sight. The eroded sculpture of canyons and cliffs and galaxies has imprinted upon me the certain knowledge that I am a mote."

"Not you, Lord. Certainly not you."

"Less than a mote! I have seen people and their fruitless societies in such repetitive posturings that their nonsense fills me with boredom, do you hear?"

"I did not mean to anger my Lord." Moneo spoke meekly.

"You don't anger me. Sometimes you irritate me, that is the extent of it. You cannot imagine what I have seen— caliphs and mjeeds, rakahs, rajas and bashars, kings and emperors, primitos and presidents—I've seen them all. Feudal chieftains, every one. Every one a little pharaoh."

"Forgive my presumption, Lord."

"Damn the Romans!" Leto cried.

He spoke it inwardly to his ancestors: *Damn the Romans!*

Their laughter drove him from the inward arena.

"I don't understand, Lord," Moneo ventured.

"That's true. You don't understand. The Romans broadcast the pharaonic disease like grain farmers scattering the seeds of next season's harvest—Caesars, Kaisers, Tsars, Imperators, Caseris . . . Palatos . . . damned pharaohs!"

"My knowledge does not encompass all of those titles, Lord."

"I may be the last of the lot, Moneo. Pray that this is so."

"Whatever my Lord commands."

Leto stared down at the man. "We are myth-killers, you and I, Moneo. That's the dream we share. I assure you from a God's Olympian perch that government is a shared myth. When the myth dies the government dies."

"Thus you have taught me, Lord."

"That man-machine, the Army, created our present dream, my friend."

Moneo cleared his throat.

Leto recognized the small signs of the majordomo's impatience.

Moneo understands about armies. He knows it was a fool's dream that armies were the basic instrument of governance.

As Leto continued silent, Moneo crossed to the lasgun and retrieved it from the crypt's cold floor. He began disabling it.

Leto watched him, thinking how this tiny scene encapsulated the essence of the Army myth. The Army fostered technology because the power of machines appeared so obvious to the short-sighted.

That lasgun is no more than a machine. But all machines fail or are superseded. Still, the Army worships at the shrine of such things—both fascinated and fearful. Look at how people fear the Ixians! In its guts, the Army knows it is the Sorcerer's Apprentice. It unleashes technology and never again can the magic be stuffed back into the bottle.

I teach them another magic.

Leto spoke to the hordes within then:

"You see? Moneo has disabled the deadly instrument. A connection broken here, a small capsule crushed there."

Leto sniffed. He smelled the esters of a preservative oil riding on the stink of Moneo's perspiration.

Still speaking inwardly, Leto said: *"But the genie is not dead. Technology breeds anarchy. It distributes these tools at random. And with them goes the provocation for violence. The ability to make and use savage destroyers falls inevitably into the hands of smaller and smaller groups until at last the group is a single individual."*

Moneo returned to a point below Leto, holding the disabled lasgun casually in his right hand. "There is talk on

43

Parella and the planets of Dan about another jihad against such things as this."

Moneo lifted the lasgun and smiled, signalling that he knew the paradox in such empty dreams.

Leto closed his eyes. The hordes within wanted to argue, but he shut them off, thinking: *Jihads create armies. The Butlerian Jihad tried to rid our universe of machines which simulate the mind of man. The Butlerians left armies in their wake and the Ixians still make questionable devices . . . for which I thank them. What is anathema? The motivation to ravage, no matter the instruments.*

"It happened," he muttered.

"Lord?"

Leto opened his eyes. "I will go to my tower," he said. "I must have more time to mourn my Duncan."

"The new one is already on his way here," Moneo said.

> *You, the first person to encounter my chronicles for at least four thousand years, beware. Do not feel honoured by your primacy in reading the revelations of my Ixian storehouse. You will find much pain in it. Other than the few glimpses required to assure me that the Golden Path continued, I never wanted to peer beyond those four millennia. Therefore, I am not sure what the events in my journals may signify to your times. I only know that my journals have suffered oblivion and that the events which I recount have undoubtedly been submitted to historical distortion for eons. I assure you that the ability to view our futures can become a bore. Even to be thought of as a god, as I certainly was, can become ultimately boring. It has occurred to me more than once that holy boredom is good and sufficient reason for the invention of free will.*

> —**Inscription over the storehouse entrance, Dar-es-Balat**

I am Duncan Idaho.

That was about all he wanted to know for sure. He did not like the Tleilaxu explanations, their *stories*. But then

44

the Tleilaxu had always been feared. Disbelieved and feared.

They had brought him down to the planet on a small Guild shuttle, arriving at the dusk line with a green glimmer of sun corona along the horizon as they dipped into the shadow. The spaceport had not looked at all like anything he remembered. It was larger and with a ring of strange buildings.

"Are you sure this is Dune?" he had asked.

"Arrakis," his Tleilaxu escort had corrected him.

They had sped him in a sealed groundcar to this building somewhere within a city they called Onn, giving the *"n"* sound a strange rising nasal inflection. The room in which they left him was about three metres square, a cube really. There was no sign of glowglobes, but the place was filled with warm yellow light.

I am a ghola, he told himself.

That had been a shock, but he had to believe it. To find himself living when he knew he had died, that was proof enough. The Tleilaxu had taken cells from his dead flesh and they had grown a bud in one of their axlotl tanks. That bud had become this body in a process which had made him feel at first an alien in his own flesh.

He looked down at the body. It was clothed in dark brown trousers and jacket of a coarse weave which irritated his skin. Sandals protected his feet. Except for the body, that was all they had given him, a parsimony which said something about the real Tleilaxu character.

There was no furniture in the room. They had let him in through a single door which had no handle on the inside. He looked up at the ceiling and around at the walls, at the door. Despite the featureless character of the place, he felt that he was being watched.

"Women of the Imperial Guard will come for you," they had said. Then they had gone away, smiling slyly among themselves.

Women *of the Imperial Guard?*

The Tleilaxu escort had taken sadistic delight in exposing

45

their shape-changing abilities. He had not known from one minute to the next what new form the plastic flow of their flesh would present.

Damned Face Dancers!

They had known all about him, of course, had known how much the Shape Changers disgusted him.

What could he trust if it came from Face Dancers? Very little. Could anything they said be believed?

My name. I know my name.

And he had his memories. They had shocked the identity back into him. Gholas were supposed to be incapable of recovering the original identity. But the Tleilaxu had done it and he was forced to believe because he understood how it had been done.

In the beginning, he knew, there had been the fully formed ghola, adult flesh without name or memories—a palimpsest upon which the Tleilaxu could write almost anything they wished.

"You are Ghola," they had said. That had been his only name for a long time. Ghola had been taken like a malleable infant and conditioned to kill a particular man—a man so like the original Paul-Muad'Dib he had served and adored that Idaho now suspected it might have been another ghola. But if that were true, where had they obtained the original cells?

Something in the Idaho cells had rebelled at killing an Atreides. He had found himself standing with a knife in one hand, the bound form of the pseudo-Paul staring up at him in angry terror.

Memories had gushed into his awareness. He remembered Ghola and he remembered Duncan Idaho.

I am Duncan Idaho, swordmaster of the Atreides.

He clung to this memory as he stood in the yellow room.

I died defending Paul and his mother in a cave sietch beneath the sands of Dune. I have been returned to that planet but Dune is no more. Now it is only Arrakis.

He had read the truncated history which the Tleilaxu provided, but he did not believe it. *More than thirty-five hundred years?* Who could believe his flesh existed after such a time? Except . . . with Tleilaxu it was possible. He had to believe his own senses.

"There have been many of you," his instructors had said.

"How many?"

"The Lord Leto will provide that information."

The Lord Leto?

The Tleilaxu history said this Lord Leto was Leto II, grandson of the Leto whom Idaho had served with fanatical devotion. But this second Leto (so the history said) had become something . . . something so strange that Idaho despaired of understanding the transformation.

How could a human slowly turn into a sandworm? How could any thinking creature live more than three thousand years? Not even the wildest projections of geriatric spice allowed such a lifespan.

Leto II, the God Emperor?

The Tleilaxu history was not to be believed!

Idaho remembered a strange child—twins really: Leto and Ghanima, Paul's children, the children of Chani who had died delivering them. The Tleilaxu history said Ghanima had died after a relatively normal life, but the God Emperor Leto lived on and on and on . . .

"He is a tyrant," Idaho's instructors had said. "He has ordered us to produce you from our axlotl tanks and to send you into his service. We do not know what has happened to your predecessor."

And here I am.

Once more, Idaho let his gaze wander around the featureless walls and ceiling.

The faint sound of voices intruded upon his awareness. He looked at the door. The voices were muted but at least one of them sounded female.

Women of the Imperial Guard?

The door swung inward on noiseless hinges. Two women entered. The first thing to catch his attention was the fact that one of the women wore a mask, a cibus hood of shapeless, light-drinking black. She would see him clearly

47

through the hood, he knew, but her features would never reveal themselves, not even to the most subtle instruments of penetration. The hood said that the Ixians or their inheritors were still at work in the Imperium. Both women wore one-piece uniforms of rich blue with the Atreides hawk in red braid at the left breast.

Idaho studied them as they closed the door and faced him.

The masked woman had a blocky, powerful body. She moved with the deceptive care of a professional muscle fanatic. The other woman was graceful and slender with almond eyes in sharp, high-boned features. Idaho had the feeling that he had seen her somewhere but he could not fix the memory. Both women carried needle knives in hip sheaths. Something about their movements told Idaho these women would be extremely competent with such weapons.

The slender one spoke first.

"My name is Luli. Let me be the first to address you as Commander. My companion must remain anonymous. Our Lord Leto has commanded it. You may address her as Friend."

"Commander?" he asked.

"It is the Lord Leto's wish that you command his Royal Guard," Luli said.

"That so? Let's go and talk to him about it."

"Oh, no!" Luli was visibly shocked. "The Lord Leto will summon you when it is time. For now, he wishes us to make you comfortable and happy."

"And I must obey?"

Luli merely shook her head in puzzlement.

"Am I a slave?" Idaho asked.

Luli relaxed and smiled. "By no means. It's just that the Lord Leto has many great concerns which require his personal attention. He must make time for you. He sent us because he was concerned about his Duncan Idaho. You have been a long time in the hands of the dirty Tleilaxu."

Dirty Tleilaxu, Idaho thought.

48

That, at least, had not changed.

He was concerned, though, by a particular reference in Luli's explanation.

"*His* Duncan Idaho?"

"Are you not an Atreides warrior?" Luli asked.

She had him there. Idaho nodded, turning his head slightly to stare at the enigmatic masked woman.

"Why are you masked?"

"It must not be known that I serve the Lord Leto," she said. Her voice was a pleasant contralto but Idaho suspected that this, too, was masked by the cibus hood.

"Then why are you here?"

"The Lord Leto trusts me to determine if you have been tampered with by the dirty Tleilaxu."

Idaho tried to swallow in a suddenly dry throat. This thought had occurred to him several times aboard the Guild transport. If the Tleilaxu could condition a ghola to attempt the murder of a dear friend, what else might they plant in the psyche of the regrown flesh?

"I see that you have thought about this," the masked woman said.

"Are you a mentat?" Idaho asked.

"Oh, no!" Luli interrupted. "The Lord Leto does not permit the training of mentats."

Idaho glanced at Luli, then returned his attention to the masked woman. *No mentats.* The Tleilaxu history had not mentioned that interesting fact. Why would Leto prohibit mentats? Surely, the human mind trained in the superabilities of computation still had its uses. The Tleilaxu had assured him that the Great Convention remained in force and that mechanical computers were still anathema. Surely, these women would know that the Atreides themselves had used mentats.

"What is your opinion?" the masked woman asked. "Have the dirty Tleilaxu tampered with your psyche?"

"I don't . . . think so."

"But you are not certain?"

"No."

"Do not fear, Commander Idaho," she said. "We have ways of making sure and ways of dealing with such problems should they arise. The dirty Tleilaxu have tried it only once and they paid dearly for their mistake."

"That's reassuring. Did the Lord Leto send me any messages?"

Luli spoke up: "He told us to assure you that he still loves you as the Atreides have always loved you." She was obviously awed by her own words.

Idaho relaxed slightly. As an old Atreides hand, superbly trained by them, he had found it easy to determine several things from this encounter. These two had been heavily conditioned to a fanatic obedience. If a cibus mask could hide the identity of that woman, there had to be many more whose bodies were very similar. All of this spoke of dangers around Leto which still required the old and subtle services of spies and an imaginative arsenal of weapons.

Luli looked at her companion. "What say you, Friend?"

"He may be brought to the Citadel," the masked woman said. "This is not a good place. Tleilaxu have been here."

"A warm bath and change of clothing would be pleasant," Idaho said.

Luli continued to look at her Friend. "You are certain?"

"The wisdom of the Lord cannot be questioned," the masked woman said.

Idaho did not like the sound of fanaticism in this *Friend's* voice, but he felt secure in the integrity of the Atreides. They could appear cynical and cruel to outsiders and enemies, but to their own people they were just and they were loyal. Above all else, the Atreides were loyal to their own.

And I am one of theirs, Idaho thought. *But what happened to the* me *that I am replacing?* He felt strongly that these two would not answer this question.

But Leto will.

"Shall we go?" he asked. "I'm anxious to wash the stink of the dirty Tleilaxu off me."

Luli grinned at him.

"Come. I shall bathe you myself."

> *Enemies strengthen you.*
>   *Allies weaken.*
>   *I tell you this in the hope that it will help you understand why I act as I do in the full knowledge that great forces accumulate in my empire with but one wish—the wish to destroy me. You who read these words may know full well what actually happened but I doubt that you understand it.*
>
> **—The Stolen Journals**

The ceremony of "Showing" by which the rebels began their meetings dragged on interminably for Siona. She sat in the front row and looked everywhere but at Topri who was conducting the ceremony only a few paces away. This room in the service burrows beneath Onn was one they had never used before but it was so like all of their other meeting places that it could have been used as a standard model.

Rebel Meeting Room—Class B, she thought.

It was officially designated as a storage chamber and the fixed glowglobes could not be tuned away from their blank white glaring. The room was about thirty paces long and slightly less in width. It could be reached only through a labyrinthine series of similar chambers, one of which was conveniently stocked with a supply of stiff folding chairs intended for the small sleeping chambers of the service personnel. Nineteen of Siona's fellow rebels now occupied these chairs around her, with a few empty for any late-comers who might still make the meeting.

The time had been set between the midnight and morning shifts to mask the flow of extra people in the service warrens. Most of the rebels wore energy-worker disguises—thin grey disposable trousers and jackets. Some

51

few, including Siona, were garbed in the green of machinery inspectors.

Topri's voice was an insistent monotone in the room. He did not squeak at all while conducting the ceremony. In fact, Siona had to admit he was rather good at it, especially with new recruits. Since Nayla's flat statement that she did not trust the man, though, Siona had looked at Topri in a different way. Nayla could speak with a cutting naiveté which pulled away masks. And there were things that Siona had learned about Topri since that confrontation.

Siona turned at last and looked at the man. The cold silvery light did not help Topri's pale skin. He used a copy of a crysknife in the ceremony, a contraband copy bought from the Museum Fremen. Siona recalled the transaction as she looked at the blade in Topri's hands. It had been Topri's idea and she had thought it a good one at the time. He had led her to the rendezvous in a hovel on the city's outskirts, leaving Onn just at dusk. They had waited well into the night until darkness could mask the Museum Fremen's coming. Fremen were not supposed to leave their sietch quarters without a special dispensation from the God Emperor.

She had almost given up on him when the Fremen arrived slipping in out of the night, his escort left behind to guard the door. Topri and Siona had been waiting on a crude bench against a dank wall of the absolutely plain room. The only light had come from a dim yellow torch supported on a stick driven into the crumbling mud wall.

The Fremen's first words had filled Siona with misgivings.

"Have you brought the money?"

Both Topri and Siona had risen at his entry. Topri did not appear bothered by the question. He tapped the pouch beneath his robe, making it jingle.

"I have the money right here."

The Fremen was a wizened figure, crabbed and bent, wearing a copy of the old Fremen robes and some glistening garment underneath, probably their version of a stillsuit.

52

His hood was drawn forward, shading his features. The torchlight sent shadows dancing across his face.

He peered first at Topri, then at Siona, before removing an object wrapped in cloth from beneath his robe.

"It is a true copy but it is made of plastic," he said. "It will not cut cold grease."

He pulled the blade from its wrappings then and held it up.

Siona, who had seen crysknives only in museums and in the rare old visual recordings of her family's archives, had found herself oddly gripped by the sight of the blade in this setting. She felt something atavistic working on her and imagined this poor Museum Fremen with his plastic crysknife as a real Fremen of the old days. The thing he held was suddenly a silver-bladed crysknife shimmering in the yellow shadows.

"I guarantee the authenticity of the blade from which we copied it," the Fremen said. He spoke in a low voice, somehow made menacing by its lack of emphasis.

Siona heard it then, the way he carried his venom in a sleeve of soft vowels and she was suddenly alerted.

"Try treachery and we will hunt you down like vermin," she said.

Topri shot a startled glance at her.

The Museum Fremen appeared to shrivel, drawing in upon himself. The blade trembled in his hand, but his gnome fingers still curled inward around it as though clasping a throat.

"Treachery, Lady? Oh, no. But it occurred to us that we asked too little for this copy. Poor as it is, making it and selling it this way puts us in dreadful peril."

Siona glared at him, thinking of the old Fremen words from the Oral History: *"Once you acquire a marketplace soul, the* suk *is the totality of existence."*

"How much do you want?" she demanded.

He named a sum twice his original figure.

Topri gasped.

Siona looked at Topri. "Do you have that much?"

"Not quite, but we agreed on . . ."

"Give him what you have, all of it," Siona said.

"All of it?"

"Isn't that what I said? Every coin in that bag." She faced the Museum Fremen. "You will accept this payment." It was not a question and the old man heard her correctly. He wrapped the blade in its cloth and passed it to her.

Topri handed over the pouch of coins, muttering under his breath.

Siona addressed herself to the Museum Fremen. "We know your name. You are Teishar, aide to Garun of Tuono. You have a *suk* mentality and you make me shudder at what Fremen have become."

"Lady, we all have to live," he protested.

"You are not alive," she said. "Be gone!"

Teishar had turned and scurried away, clutching the money pouch close to his chest.

Memory of that night did not sit well in Siona's mind as she watched Topri wave the crysknife copy in their rebel ceremony. *We're no better than Teishar*, she thought. *A copy is worse than nothing*. Topri brandished the stupid blade over his head as he neared the ceremony's conclusion.

Siona looked away from him and stared at Nayla seated off to her left. Nayla was looking first in one direction and now another. She paid special attention to the new cadre of recruits at the back of the room. Nayla did not give her trust easily. Siona wrinkled her nose as a stirring of the air brought the smell of lubricants. The depths of Onn always smelled dangerously *mechanical*! She sniffed. And this room! She did not like their meeting place. It could easily be a trap. Guards could seal off the outer corridors and send in armed searchers. This could be too easily the place where their rebellion ended. Siona was made doubly uneasy by the fact that this room had been Topri's choice.

One of Ulot's few mistakes, she thought. Poor dead Ulot had approved Topri's admission to the rebellion.

"He is a minor functionary in city services," Ulot had

explained. "Topri can find us many useful places to meet and arm ourselves."

Topri had reached almost the end of his ceremony. He placed the knife in an ornate case and put the case on the floor beside him.

"My face is my pledge," he said. He turned his profile to the room, first one side and then the other. "I show my face that you may know me anywhere and know that I am one of you."

Stupid ceremony, Siona thought.

But she dared not break the pattern of it. And when Topri pulled a black gauze mask from a pocket and placed it over his head, she took out her own mask and donned it. Everyone in the room did the same thing. There was a stirring around the room now. Most of the people here had been alerted that Topri had brought a special visitor. Siona secured her mask's tie behind her neck. She was anxious to see this visitor.

Topri moved to the room's one door. There was a clattering bustle as everyone stood and the chairs were folded and stacked against the wall opposite the door. At a signal from Siona, Topri tapped three times on the door panel, waited for a two-count, then tapped four times.

The door opened and a tall man in a dark brown official singlet slipped into the room. He wore no mask, his face open for all of them to see—thin and imperious with a narrow mouth, a skinny blade of a nose, dark brown eyes deeply set under bushy brows. It was a face recognized by most of the room's occupants.

"My friends," Topri said, "I present Iyo Kobat, Ambassador from Ix."

"Ex-Ambassador," Kobat said. His voice was guttural and tightly controlled. He took a position with his back to the wall facing the masked people in the room. "I have this day received orders from our God Emperor to leave Arrakis in disgrace."

"Why?"

Siona snapped the question at him without formality.

55

Kobat jerked his head around, a quick movement which fixed his gaze on her masked face. "There has been an attempt on the God Emperor's life. He traced the weapon to me."

Siona's companions opened a space between her and the ex-Ambassador, clearly signalling that they deferred to her.

"Then why didn't he kill you?" she demanded.

"I think he is telling me that I am not worth killing. There is also the fact that he uses me now to carry a message to Ix."

"What message?" Siona moved through the cleared space to stop within two paces of Kobat. She recognized the sexual alertness in him as he studied her body.

"You are Moneo's daughter," he said.

Soundless tension exploded across the room. Why did he reveal that he recognized her? Who else did he recognize here? Kobat did not appear the fool. Why had he done this?

"Your body, your voice and your manner are well known here in Onn," he said. "That mask is a foolishness."

She ripped the mask from her head and smiled at him. "I agree. Now answer my question."

Siona heard Nayla move up close on her left; two more aides chosen by Nayla came up beside her.

Siona saw the moment of realization come over Kobat— his death if he failed to satisfy her demands. His voice did not lose its tight control but he spoke slower, choosing his words more carefully.

"The God Emperor has told me that he knows about an agreement between Ix and the Guild. We are attempting to make a mechanical amplifier of . . . those Guild navigational talents which presently rely on melange."

"In this room we call him the Worm," Siona said. "What would your Ixian machine do?"

"You are aware that Guild Navigators require the spice before they can *see* the safe path to traverse?"

"You would replace the navigators with a machine?"

"It may be possible."

"What message do you carry to your people concerning this machine?"

"I am to tell my people that they may continue the project only if they send him daily reports on their progress."

She shook her head. "He needs no such reports! That's a stupid message."

Kobat swallowed, no longer concealing nervousness.

"The Guild and the Sisterhood are excited by our project," he said. "They are participating."

Siona nodded once. "And they pay for their participation by sharing spice with Ix."

Kobat glared at her. "It's expensive work and we need the spice for comparative testing by Guild Navigators."

"It is a lie and a cheat," she said. "Your device will never work and the Worm knows it."

"How dare you accuse us of . . ."

"Be still! I have just told you the real message. The Worm is telling you Ixians to continue cheating the Guild and the Bene Gesserit. It amuses him."

"It could work!" Kobat insisted.

She merely smiled at him. "Who tried to kill the Worm?"

"Duncan Idaho."

Nayla gasped. There were other small signs of surprise around the room, a frown, an indrawn breath.

"Is Idaho dead?" Siona asked.

"I presume so, but the . . . ahh, Worm refuses to confirm it."

"Why do you presume him dead?"

"The Tleilaxu have sent another Idaho ghola."

"I see."

Siona turned and signalled to Nayla who went to the side of the room and returned with a slim package wrapped in pink Suk paper, the kind of paper shopkeepers used to enclose small purchases. Nayla handed the package to Siona.

"This is the price of our silence," Siona said, extending

the package to Kobat. "This is why Topri was permitted to bring you here tonight."

Kobat took the package without removing his attention from her face.

"Silence?" he asked.

"We undertake not to inform the Guild and Sisterhood that you are cheating them."

"We are not cheat . . ."

"Don't be a fool!"

Kobat tried to swallow in a dry throat. Her meaning had become plain to him: true or not, if the rebellion spread such a story it would be believed. It was "common sense" as Topri was fond of saying.

Siona glanced at Topri who stood just behind Kobat. No one joined this rebellion for reasons of "common sense". Did Topri not realize that his "common sense" might betray him? She turned her attention to Kobat.

"What's in this package?" he asked.

Something in the way he asked it told Siona he already knew.

"That is something I am sending to Ix. You will take it there for me. That is copies of two volumes we removed from the Worm's fortress."

Kobat stared down at the package in his hands. It was obvious that he wanted to drop the thing, that his venture into rebellion had loaded him with a burden more deadly than he had expected. He shot a scowling glance at Topri which said as though he had spoken it: *"Why didn't you warn me?"*

"What. . . ." He brought his gaze back to Siona, cleared his throat. "What's in these . . . volumes?"

"Your people may tell us that. We think they are the Worm's own words, written in a cipher which we cannot read."

"What makes you think we . . ."

"You Ixians are clever at such things."

"And if we fail?"

She shrugged. "We will not blame you for that. However, should you use those volumes for any other purpose or fail to report a success fully . . ."

"How can anyone be sure we . . ."

"We will not depend only on you. Others will get copies. I think the Sisterhood and the Guild will not hesitate to try deciphering those volumes."

Kobat slipped the package under his arm and pressed it against his body.

"What makes you think the . . . the Worm doesn't know about your intentions . . . even about this meeting?"

"I think he knows many such things, that he may even know who took those volumes. My father believes he is truly prescient."

"Your father believes the Oral History!"

"Everyone in this room believes it. The Oral History does not disagree with the Formal History on important matters."

"Then why doesn't the Worm act against you?"

She pointed to the package under Kobat's arm. "Perhaps the answer is in there."

"Or you and these cryptic volumes are no real threat to him!" Kobat was not concealing his anger. He did not like being forced into decisions.

"Perhaps. Tell me why you mentioned the Oral History."

Once more, Kobat heard the menace.

"It says the Worm is incapable of human emotions."

"That is not the reason," she said. "You will get one more chance to tell me the reason."

Nayla moved two steps closer to Kobat.

"I . . . I was told to review the Oral History before coming here, that your people . . ." He shrugged.

"That we chant it?"

"Yes."

"Who told you this?"

Kobat swallowed, cast a fearful glance at Topri, then back to Siona.

"Topri?" Siona asked.

"I thought it would help him to understand us," Topri said.

"And you told him the name of your leader," Siona said.

"He already knew!" Topri's voice had found its squeak.

"What particular parts of the Oral History were you told to review?" Siona asked.

"The . . . uhhh, the Atreides line."

"And now you think you know why people join me in rebellion."

"The Oral History tells exactly how he treats everyone in the Atreides line!" Kobat said.

"He gives us a little rope and then he hauls us in?" Siona asked. Her voice was deceptively flat.

"That's what he did with your own father," Kobat said.

"And now he's letting *me* play at rebellion?"

"I'm just a messenger," Kobat said. "If you kill me, who will carry your message?"

"Or the message of the Worm," Siona said.

Kobat remained silent.

"I do not think you understand the Oral History," Siona said. "I think also you do not know the Worm very well, nor do you understand his messages."

Kobat's face flushed with anger. "What's to prevent you from becoming like all the rest of the Atreides, a nice obedient part of . . ." Kobat broke off, aware suddenly of what anger had made him say.

"Just another recruit for the Worm's inner circle," Siona said. "Just like the Duncan Idahos?"

She turned and looked at Nayla. The two aides, Anouk and Taw, became suddenly alert, but Nayla remained impassive.

Siona nodded once to Nayla.

As they were sworn to do, Anouk and Taw moved to positions blocking the door. Nayla went around to stand at Topri's shoulder.

"What's . . . what's happening?" Topri asked.

"We wish to know everything of importance that the

ex-Ambassador can share with us," Siona said. "We want the entire message."

Topri began to tremble. Perspiration started from Kobat's forehead. He glanced once at Topri, then returned his attention to Siona. That one glance was like a veil pulled aside for Siona to peer into the relationship between these two.

She smiled. This merely confirmed what she had already learned.

Kobat became very still.

"You may begin," Siona said.

"I . . . what do you . . ."

"The Worm gave you a private message for your masters. I will hear it."

"He . . . he wants an extension for his cart."

"Then he expects to grow longer. What else?"

"We are to send him a large supply of ridulian crystal paper."

"For what purpose?"

"He never explains his demands."

"This smacks of things he forbids to others," she said.

Kobat spoke bitterly. "He never forbids himself anything!"

"Have you made forbidden toys for him?"

"I do not know."

He's lying, she thought, but she chose not to pursue this. It was enough to know the existence of another chink in the Worm's armour.

"Who will replace you?" Siona asked.

"They are sending a niece of Malky," Kobat said. "You may remember that he . . ."

"We remember Malky," she said. "Why does a niece of Malky become the new Ambassador?"

"I don't know. But it was ordered even before the Go . . . the Worm dismissed me."

"Her name?"

"Hwi Noree."

"We will cultivate Hwi Noree," Siona said. "You were

61

not worth cultivating. This Hwi Noree may be something else. When do you return to Ix?"

"Immediately after the Festival, the first Guild ship."

"What will you tell your masters?"

"About what?"

"My message!"

"They will do as you ask."

"I know. You may go, ex-Ambassador Kobat."

Kobat almost collided with the door guards in his haste to leave. Topri made to follow him, but Nayla caught Topri's arm and held him. Topri swept a fearful glance across Nayla's muscular body, then looked at Siona, who waited for the door to shut behind Kobat before speaking.

"The message was not merely to the Ixians but to us as well," she said. "The Worm challenges us and tells us the rules of the combat."

Topri tried to wrest his arm from Nayla's grip. "What do you . . ."

"Topri!" Siona said. "I, too, can send a message. Tell my father to inform the Worm that we accept."

Nayla released his arm. Topri rubbed the place where she had gripped him. "Surely you don't . . ."

"Leave while you can and never come back," Siona said.

"You can't possibly mean that you sus . . ."

"I told you to leave! You are clumsy, Topri. I have been in the Fish Speaker schools for most of my life. They taught me to recognize clumsiness."

"Kobat is leaving. What harm was there in . . ."

"He not only knew me, he knew what I had stolen from the Citadel! But he did *not* know that I would send that package to Ix with him. Your actions have told me that the Worm wants me to send those volumes to Ix!"

Topri backed away from Siona toward the door. Anouk and Taw opened a passage for him, swung the door wide. Siona followed him with her voice.

"Do not argue that it was the Worm who spoke of me and my package to Kobat! The Worm does not send clumsy messages. Tell him I said that!"

Some say I have no conscience. How false they are, even to themselves. I am the only conscience which has ever existed. As wine retains the perfume of its cask, I retain the essence of my most ancient genesis, and that is the seed of conscience. That is what makes me holy. I am God because I am the only one who really knows his heredity!

—The Stolen Journals

The Inquisitors of Ix having assembled in the Grand Palais with the candidate for Ambassador to the Court of the Lord Leto, the following questions and answers were recorded:

INQUISITOR: You indicate that you wish to speak to us of the Lord Leto's motives. Speak.

HWI NOREE: Your Formal Analyses do not satisfy the questions I would raise.

INQUISITOR: What questions?

HWI NOREE: I ask myself what would motivate the Lord Leto to accept this hideous transformation, this worm-body, this loss of his humanity? You suggest merely that he did it for power and for long life.

INQUISITOR: Are those not enough?

HWI NOREE: Ask yourselves if one of you would make such payment for so paltry a return?

INQUISITOR: From your infinite wisdom then, tell us why the Lord Leto chose to become a worm.

HWI NOREE: Does anyone here doubt his ability to predict the future?

INQUISITOR: Now then! Is that not payment enough for his transformation?

HWI NOREE: But he already had the prescient ability as did his father before him. No! I propose that he made this desperate choice because he saw in our future something that only such a sacrifice would prevent.

INQUISITOR: What was this peculiar thing which only he saw in our future?

HWI NOREE: I do not know but I propose to discover it.

INQUISITOR: You make the tyrant appear a selfless servant of the people!

HWI NOREE: Was that not a prominent characteristic of his Atreides family?

INQUISITOR: So the official histories would have us believe.

HWI NOREE: The Oral History affirms it.

INQUISITOR: What other good character would you give to the tyrant Worm?

HWI NOREE: *Good* character, sirra?

INQUISITOR: Character, then?

HWI NOREE: My Uncle Malky often said that the Lord Leto was given to moods of great tolerance for selected companions.

INQUISITOR: Other companions he executes for no apparent reason.

HWI NOREE: I think there are reasons and my Uncle Malky deduced some of those reasons.

INQUISITOR: Give us one such deduction.

HWI NOREE: Clumsy threats to his person.

INQUISITOR: *Clumsy* threats now!

HWI NOREE: And he does not tolerate pretensions. Recall the execution of the historians and the destruction of their works.

INQUISITOR: He does not want the truth known!

HWI NOREE: He told my Uncle Malky that they lied about the past. And mark you! Who would know this better than he? We all know the subject of his introversion.

INQUISITOR: What proof have we that all of his ancestors live in him?

HWI NOREE: I will not enter that bootless argument. I will merely say that I believe it on the evidence of my Uncle Malky's belief, and his reasons for that belief.

INQUISITOR: We have read your uncle's reports and interpret them otherwise. Malky was overly fond of the Worm.

HWI NOREE: My uncle accounted him the most supremely artful diplomat in the Empire, a master conversationalist and expert in any subject you could name.

INQUISITOR: Did your uncle not speak of the Worm's brutality?

HWI NOREE: My uncle judged him ultimately civilized.

INQUISITOR: I asked about brutality.

HWI NOREE: Capable of brutality, yes.

INQUISITOR: Your uncle feared him.

HWI NOREE: The Lord Leto lacks all innocence and naiveté. He is to be feared only when he pretends these traits. *That* was what my uncle said.

INQUISITOR: Those were his words, yes.

HWI NOREE: More than that! Malky said: "The Lord Leto delights in the surprising genius and diversity of humankind. He is my favourite companion."

INQUISITOR: Giving us the benefit of your supreme wisdom, how do you interpret these words of your uncle?

HWI NOREE: Do not mock me!

INQUISITOR: We do not mock. We seek enlightenment.

HWI NOREE: These words of Malky and many other things that he wrote directly to me, suggest that the Lord Leto is always seeking after newness and originality but that he is wary of the destructive potential in such things. So my uncle believed.

INQUISITOR: Is there more which you wish to add to these beliefs which you share with your uncle?

HWI NOREE: I see no point in adding to what I've already said. I am sorry to have wasted the Inquisitors' time.

INQUISITOR: But you have not wasted our time. You are confirmed as Ambassador to the Court of Lord Leto, the God Emperor of the known universe.

You must remember that I have at my internal demand every expertise known to our history. This is the fund of energy I draw upon when I address the mentality of war. If you have not heard the moaning cries of the wounded and the dying you do not know about war. I have heard those cries in such numbers that they haunt me. I have cried out myself in the aftermath of battle. I have suffered wounds in every epoch— wounds from fist and club and rock, from shell-studded limb and bronze sword, from the mace and the cannon, from arrows and lasguns and the silent smothering of atomic dust, from biological invasions which blacken the tongue and drown the lungs, from the swift gush of flame and the silent working of slow poisons . . . and more I will not recount! I have seen and felt them all. To those who dare ask why I behave as I do, I say: With my memories, I can do nothing else. I am not a coward and once I was human.

—The Stolen Journals

In the warm season when the satellite weather controllers were forced to contend with winds across the great seas, evening often saw rainfall at the edges of the Sareer. Moneo, coming in from one of his periodic inspections of the Citadel's perimeter, was caught in a sudden shower. Night fell before he reached shelter. A Fish Speaker guard helped him out of his damp cloak at the south portal. She was a heavyset, blocky woman with a square face, a type Leto favoured for his guardians.

"Those damned weather controllers should be made to shape up," she said as she handed him his damp cloak.

Moneo gave her a curt nod before beginning the climb to his quarters. All of the Fish Speaker guards knew the God Emperor's aversion to moisture, but none of them made Moneo's distinction.

It is the Worm who hates water, Moneo thought. *Shai-Hulud hungers for Dune.*

In his quarters, Moneo dried himself and changed to dry clothing before descending to the crypt. There was no point in inviting the Worm's antagonism. Uninterrupted conversation with Leto was required now, plain talk about the impending peregrination to the Festival City of Onn.

Leaning against a wall of the descending lift, Moneo closed his eyes. Immediately, fatigue swept over him. He knew he had not slept enough in days and there was no let up in sight. He envied Leto's apparent freedom from the need for sleep. A few hours of semi-repose a month appeared to be sufficient for the God Emperor.

The smell of the crypt and the stopping of the lift jarred Moneo from his catnap. He opened his eyes and looked out at the God Emperor on his cart in the centre of the great chamber. Moneo composed himself and strode out for the familiar long walk into the terrible presence. As expected, Leto appeared alert. That, at least, was a good sign.

Leto had heard the lift approaching and saw Moneo awaken. The man looked tired and that was understandable. The peregrination to Onn was at hand with all of the tiresome business of off-planet visitors, the ritual with the Fish Speakers, the new ambassadors, the changing of the Imperial Guard, the retirements and the appointments, and now a new Duncan Idaho ghola to fit into the smooth working of the Imperial apparatus. Moneo was occupied with mounting details and he was beginning to show his age.

Let me see, Leto thought. *Moneo will be one hundred and eighteen years old in the week after our return from Onn.*

The man could live many times that long if he would take the spice, but he refused. Leto had no doubt of the reason. Moneo had entered that peculiar human state where he longed for death. He lingered now only to see Siona installed in the Royal service, the next director of the Imperial Society of Fish Speakers.

My houris, as Malky used to call them.

And Moneo knew it was Leto's intention to breed Siona with a Duncan. It was time.

Moneo stopped two paces from the cart and looked up at Leto. Something in his eyes reminded Leto of the look on the face of a pagan priest in the Terran times, a crafty supplication at the familiar shrine.

"Lord, you have spent many hours observing the new Duncan," Moneo said. "Have the Tleilaxu tampered with his cells or his psyche?"

"He is untainted."

A deep sigh shook Moneo. There was no pleasure in it.

"You object to his use as a stud?" Leto asked.

"I find it peculiar to think of him as both an ancestor and the father of my descendants."

"But he gives me access to a first-generation cross between an older human form and the current products of my breeding programme. Siona is twenty-one generations removed from such a cross."

"I fail to see the purpose. The Duncans are slower and less alert than anyone in your Guard."

"I am not looking for good segregant offspring, Moneo. Did you think me unaware of the progression geometrics dictated by the laws which govern my breeding programme?"

"I have seen your stock book, Lord."

"Then you know that I keep track of the recessives and weed them out. The key genetic dominants are my concern."

"And the mutations, Lord?" There was a sly note in Moneo's voice which caused Leto to study the man intently.

"We will not discuss that subject, Moneo."

Leto watched Moneo pull back into his cautious shell.

How extremely sensitive he is to my moods, Leto thought. *I do believe he has some of my abilities there, although they operate at an unconscious level. His question suggests that he may even suspect what we have achieved in Siona.*

Testing this, Leto said: "It is clear to me that you do not yet understand what I hope to achieve in my breeding programme."

Moneo brightened. "My Lord knows I try to fathom the rules of it."

"Laws tend to be temporary over the long haul, Moneo. There is no such thing as rule-governed creativity."

"But Lord, you yourself speak of laws which govern your breeding programme."

"What have I just said to you, Moneo? Trying to find rules for creation is like trying to separate mind from body."

"But something is evolving, Lord. I know it in myself!"

He knows it in himself! Dear Moneo. He is so close.

"Why do you always seek after absolutely derivative translations, Moneo?"

"I have heard you speak of *transformational evolution*, Lord. That is the label on your stock book. But what of surprise . . ."

"Moneo! Rules change with each surprise."

"Lord, have you no improvement of the human stock in mind?"

Leto glared down at him, thinking: *If I use the key word now will he understand? Perhaps . . .*

"I am a predator, Moneo."

"Pred . . ." Moneo broke off and shook his head. He knew the meaning of the word, he thought, but the word itself shocked him. Was the God Emperor joking?

"Predator, Lord?"

"The predator improves the stock."

"How can this be, Lord? You do not hate us."

"You disappoint me, Moneo. The predator does not hate its prey."

"Predators kill, Lord."

"I kill but I do not hate. Prey assuages hunger. Prey is good."

Moneo peered up at Leto's face in its grey cowl.

Have I missed the approach of the Worm? Moneo wondered.

Fearfully, Moneo looked for the signs. There were no tremors in the giant body, no glazing of the eyes, no twisting of the useless flippers.

"For what do you hunger, Lord?" Moneo ventured.

"For a humankind which can make truly long-term decisions. Do you know the key to that ability, Moneo?"

"You have said it many times, Lord. It is the ability to change your mind."

"Change, yes. And do you know what I mean by long-term?"

"For you, it must be measured in millennia, Lord."

"Moneo, even my thousands of years are but a puny blip against infinity."

"But your perspective must be different from mine, Lord."

"In the view of infinity, any defined long-term is short-term."

"Then are there no rules at all, Lord?" Moneo's voice conveyed a faint hint of hysteria.

Leto smiled to ease the man's tensions. "Perhaps one. Short-term decisions tend to fail in the long-term."

Moneo shook his head in frustration. "But, Lord, your perspective is . . ."

"Time runs out for any finite observer. There are no closed systems. Even I only stretch the finite matrix."

Moneo jerked his attention from Leto's face and peered into the distances of the mausoleum corridors. *I will be here someday. The Golden Path may continue, but I will end.* That was not important, of course. Only the Golden Path which he could sense in unbroken continuity, only *that* mattered. He returned his attention to Leto, but not to the all-blue eyes. Was there truly a predator lurking in that gross body?

"You do not understand the function of a predator," Leto said.

The words shocked Moneo because they smacked of mind-reading. He lifted his gaze to Leto's eyes.

"You know *intellectually* that even I will suffer a kind of death someday," Leto said. "But you do not believe it."

"How can I believe what I will never see?"

Moneo had never felt more lonely and fearful. What was the God Emperor doing? *I came down here to discuss the problems of the peregrination . . . and to find out about his intentions toward Siona. Does he toy with me?*

"Let us talk about Siona," Leto said.

Mind-reading again!

"When will you test her, Lord?" The question had been waiting in the front of his awareness all this time, but now that he had spoken it, Moneo feared it.

"Soon."

"Forgive me, Lord, but surely you know how much I fear for the well-being of my only child."

"Others have survived the test, Moneo. You did."

Moneo gulped, remembering how he had been sensitized to the Golden Path.

"My mother prepared me. Siona has no mother."

"She has the Fish Speakers. She has yóu."

"Accidents happen, Lord."

Tears sprang into Moneo's eyes.

Leto looked away from him, thinking: *He is torn by his loyalty to me and his love of Siona. How poignant it is, this concern for an offspring. Can he not see that all of humankind is my only child?*

Returning his attention to Moneo, Leto said: "You are right to observe that accidents happen even in my universe. Does this teach you anything?"

"Lord, just this once couldn't you . . ."

"Moneo! Surely you do not ask me to delegate authority to a weak administrator?"

Moneo recoiled one step. "No, Lord. Of course not."

"Then trust Siona's strength."

Moneo squared his shoulders. "I will do what I must."

"Siona must be awakened to her duties as an Atreides."

"Yes, of course, Lord."

"Is that not our commitment, Moneo?"

"I do not deny it, Lord. When will you introduce her to the new Duncan?"

"The test comes first."

Moneo looked down at the cold floor of the crypt.

He stares at the floor so often, Leto thought. *What can he possibly see there? Is it the millennial tracks of my cart? Ahhh, no—it is into the depths that he peers, into the realms of treasure and mystery which he expects to enter soon.*

Once more, Moneo lifted his gaze to Leto's face. "I hope she will like the Duncan's company, Lord."

"Be assured of it. The Tleilaxu have brought him to me in the undistorted image."

"That is reassuring, Lord."

"No doubt you have noted that his genotype is remarkably attractive to females."

"That has been my observation, Lord."

"There's something about those gently observant eyes, those strong features and that black-goat hair which positively melts the female psyche."

"As you say, Lord."

"You know he's with the Fish Speakers right now?"

"I was informed, Lord."

Leto smiled. Of course Moneo was informed. "They will bring him to me soon for his first view of the God Emperor."

"I have inspected the viewing room personally, Lord. Everything is in readiness."

"Sometimes I think you wish to weaken me, Moneo. Leave some of these details for me."

Moneo tried to conceal a constriction of fear. He bowed and backed away. "Yes, Lord, but there are some things which I must do."

Turning, he hurried away. It was not until he was ascending in the lift that Moneo realized he had left without being dismissed.

He must know how tired I am. He will forgive.

> *Your Lord knows very well what is in your heart. Your soul suffices this day as a reckoner against you. I need no witnesses. You do not listen to your soul, but listen instead to your anger and your rage.*

> **—Lord Leto to a Penitent, from the Oral History**

The following assessment of the state of the Empire in the year 3508 of the reign of the Lord Leto is taken from The Welbeck Abridgment. The original is in the Chapter House Archives of the Bene Gesserit Order. A comparison reveals that the deletions do not subtract from the essential accuracy of this account.

In the name of our Sacred Order and its unbroken Sisterhood, this accounting has been judged reliable and worthy of entry into the Chronicles of the Chapter House.

Sisters Chenoeh and Tawsuoko have returned safely from Arrakis to report confirmation of the long-suspected execution of the nine historians who disappeared into his Citadel in the year 2116 of Lord Leto's reign. The Sisters report that the nine were rendered unconscious, then burned on pyres of their own published works. This conforms exactly with the stories which spread across the Empire at the time. The accounts of that time were judged to have originated with Lord Leto himself.

Sisters Chenoeh and Tawsuoko bring the handwritten records of an eyewitness account which says that when Lord Leto was petitioned by other historians seeking word of their fellows, Lord Leto said:

"They were destroyed because they lied pretentiously. Have no fear that my wrath will fall upon you because of your innocent mistakes. I am not overly fond of creating martyrs. Martyrs tend to set dramatic events adrift in human affairs. Drama is one of the targets of my predation. Tremble only if you build false accounts and stand pridefully upon them. Go now and do not speak of this."

Internal evidence of the handwritten account identifies its author as Ikonicre, Lord Leto's majordomo in the year 2116.

Attention is called to Lord Leto's use of the word *predation*. This is highly suggestive in view of theories advanced by Reverend Mother Syaksa that the God Emperor views himself as a predator in the *natural* sense.

Sister Chenoeh was invited to accompany the Fish

73

Speakers in an entourage which accompanied one of Lord Leto's infrequent peregrinations. At one point, she was invited to trot beside the Royal Cart and converse with the Lord Leto himself. She reports the exchange as follows:

The Lord Leto said: "Here on the Royal Road I sometimes feel that I stand on battlements protecting myself against invaders."

Sister Chenoeh said: "No one attacks you here, Lord."

The Lord Leto said: "You Bene Gesserit assail me on all sides. Even now, you seek to suborn my Fish Speakers."

Sister Chenoeh says that she steeled herself for death, but the God Emperor merely stopped his cart and looked across her at his entourage. She says the others stopped and waited on the road in well-trained passivity, all of them at a respectful distance.

The Lord Leto said, "There is my little multitude and they tell me everything. Do not deny my accusation."

Sister Chenoeh said, "I do not deny it."

The Lord Leto looked at her then and said, "Have no fear for your person. It is my wish that you report my words in your Chapter House."

Sister Chenoeh says she could see then that the Lord Leto knew all about her, about her mission, her special training as an oral recorder, everything. "He was like a Reverend Mother," she said. "I could hide nothing from him."

The Lord Leto then commanded her, "Look toward my Festival City and tell me what you see."

Sister Chenoeh looked toward Onn and said, "I see the city in the distance. It is beautiful in this morning light. There is your forest on the right. It has so many greens in it I could spend all day describing them. On the left and all around the city there are the houses and the gardens of your servitors. Some of them look very rich and some look very poor."

The Lord Leto said, "We have cluttered this landscape! Trees are a clutter. Houses, gardens . . . You cannot exult at new mysteries in such a landscape."

Sister Chenoeh, emboldened by Lord Leto's assurances, asked, "Does the Lord truly want mysteries?"

The Lord Leto said, "There is no outward spiritual freedom in such a landscape. Do you not see it? You have no open universe here with which to share. Everything is closures—doors, latches, locks!"

Sister Chenoeh asked, "Has mankind no longer any need for privacy and protection?"

The Lord Leto said, "When you return, tell your Sisters that I will restore the outward view. Such a landscape as this one turns you inward in search for whatever freedom your spirits can find within. Most humans are not strong enough to find freedom within."

Sister Chenoeh said, "I will report your words accurately, Lord."

The Lord Leto said, "See that you do. Tell your Sisters also that the Bene Gesserit of all people should know the dangers of breeding for a particular characteristic, of seeking a defined genetic goal."

Sister Chenoeh says this was an obvious reference to the Lord Leto's father, Paul Atreides. Let it be noted that our breeding programme achieved the Kwisatz Haderach one generation early. In becoming Muad'Dib, the leader of the Fremen, Paul Atreides escaped from our control. There is no doubt that he was a male with the powers of a Reverend Mother and other powers for which humankind still is paying a heavy price. As the Lord Leto said:

"You got the unexpected. You got me, the wild card. And I have achieved Siona."

The Lord Leto refused to elaborate on this reference to the daughter of his majordomo, Moneo. The matter is being investigated.

In other matters of concern to the Chapter House, our investigators have supplied information on:

THE FISH SPEAKERS: The Lord Leto's female legions have elected their representatives to attend the Decennial Festival on Arrakis. Three representatives will attend from each planetary garrison. *(See attached list of those chosen.)* As usual, no adult males will attend, not even consorts of Fish Speaker officers. The consort list has changed very little in this reporting period. We have appended the new names with geneological information where available. Note that only two of the names can be starred as descendants of the Duncan Idaho gholas. We can add nothing new to our speculations about his use of the gholas in his breeding programme.

None of our efforts to form an alliance between Fish Speakers and Bene Gesserit succeeded during this period. Lord Leto continues to increase certain garrison sizes. He also continues to emphasize the alternative missions of the Fish Speakers, de-emphasizing their military missions. This has had the expected result of increasing local admiration and respect *and gratitude* for the presence of the Fish Speaker garrisons. *(See attached list for garrisons which were increased in size. Editor's note: The only pertinent garrisons were those on the home planets of the Bene Gesserit, Ixians and Tleilaxu. Spacing Guild monitors were not increased.)*

PRIESTHOOD: Except for the few natural deaths and replacements which are listed in attachments, there have been no significant changes. Those consorts and officers delegated to perform the ritual duties remain few, their powers abridged by continuing requirement for consultation with Arrakis before taking any important action. It is the opinion of the Reverend Mother Syaksa and some others that the religious character of the Fish Speakers is slowly being devolved.

BREEDING PROGRAMME: Other than the unexplained reference to Siona and to our failure with his father, we have nothing significant to add to our continued monitoring of the Lord Leto's breeding programme. There is evidence of a certain randomness in his plan which is reinforced by the Lord Leto's statement about *genetic goals*, but we cannot be certain that he was truthful with Sister Chenoeh. We call your attention to the many instances where he has either lied or changed directions dramatically and without warning.

The Lord Leto continues to prohibit our participation in his breeding programme. His monitors from our Fish Speaker garrison remain adamant in "weeding out" our births to which they object. Only by the most stringent controls were we able to maintain the level of Reverend Mothers during this reporting period. Our protests are not answered. In response to a direct question from Sister Chenoeh, the Lord Leto said:

"Be thankful for what you have."

This warning is duly noted here. We have transmitted a gracious letter of thankfulness to the Lord Leto.

ECONOMICS: The Chapter House continues to maintain its solvency but the measures of conservation cannot be eased. In fact, as a precaution, certain new measures will be instituted in the next reporting period. These include a reduction in the ritual uses of melange and an increase in the rates charged for our usual services. We expect to double the fees for the schooling of Great House females across the next four reporting periods. You are hereby charged to begin preparing your arguments in defence of this action.

The Lord Leto has denied our petition for an increase in our melange allotment. No reason was given.

Our relationship with the Combine Honnete Ober Advancer Mercantiles remains on a sound footing. CHOAM has accomplished in the preceding period a regional cartel in Star Jewels, a project whereby we gained a substantial return through our advisory and bargaining functions. The ongoing profits from this arrangement should more than offset our losses on Giedi Prime. The Giedi Prime investment has been written off.

GREAT HOUSES: Thirty-one former Great Houses suffered economic disaster in this reporting period. Only six managed to maintain House Minor status. *(See attached list.)* This continues the general trend noted over the past thousand years where the once Great Houses melt gradually into the background. It is to be noted that the six who averted total disaster were all heavy investors in CHOAM and that five of these six were deeply involved in the Star Jewel project. The lone exception held a diversified portfolio, including a substantial investment in antique whale fur from Caladan.

(Our ponji rice reserves were increased almost two-fold in this period at the expense of our whale fur holdings. The reasons for this decision will be reviewed in the next period.)

FAMILY LIFE: As has been observed by our investigators over the preceding two thousand years, the homogenization of family life continues unabated. The exceptions are those you would expect: the Guild, the Fish Speakers, the Royal Courtiers, the shape-changing Face Dancers of the Tleilaxu (who are still mules despite all efforts to change that condition), and our own situation, of course.

It is to be noted that familial conditions grow more and more similar no matter the planet of residence, a circumstance which cannot be attributed to accident. We are seeing here the emergence of a portion of the Lord Leto's grand design. Even the poorest families are well fed, yes, but the circumstances of daily life grow increasingly static.

We remind you of a statement from the Lord Leto which was reported here almost eight generations ago:

"I am the only spectacle remaining in the Empire."

Reverend Mother Syaksa has proposed a theoretical explanation for this trend, a theory which many of us are beginning to share. RM Syaksa attributes to Lord Leto a motive based on the concept of hydraulic despotism. As you know, hydraulic despotism is possible only when a substance or condition upon which life in general absolutely depends can be controlled by a relatively small

78

and centralized force. The concept of hydraulic despotism originated when the flow of irrigation water increased local human populations to a demand level of absolute dependence. When the water was shut off, people died in large numbers.

This phenomenon has been repeated many times in human history, not only with water and the products of arable land, but with hydrocarbon fuels such as petroleum and coal which were controlled through pipelines and other distribution networks. At one time, when distribution of electricity was only through complicated mazes of lines strung across the landscape, even this energy resource fell into the role of a hydraulic-despotism substance.

RM Syaksa proposes that the Lord Leto is building the Empire toward an even greater dependence upon melange. It is worth noting that the aging process can be called a disease for which melange is the specific treatment, although not a cure. RM Syaksa proposes that the Lord Leto may even go so far as introducing a new disease which can only be suppressed by melange. Although this may appear far-fetched, it should not be discarded out of hand. Stranger things have happened, and we should not overlook the role of syphilis in early human history.

TRANSPORT/GUILD: The three-mode transportation system once peculiar to Arrakis (that is, on foot with heavy loads relegated to suspensor-borne pallets, in the air via ornithopter, or off-planet by Guild Transport) is coming to dominate more and more planets of the Empire. Ix is the primary exception.

We attribute this in part to planetary devolution into sedentary and static lifestyles. And partly it is the attempt to copy the pattern of Arrakis. The generalized aversion to things Ixian plays no small part in this trend. There is also the fact that the Fish Speakers promote this pattern to reduce their work in maintaining order.

Over the Guild's part in this trend hangs the absolute dependence of the Guild Navigators upon melange. We are, therefore, keeping a close watch upon the joint effort of Guild and Ix to develop a mechanical substitute for the Navigators' predictive talents. Without melange or some other means of projecting a Heighliner's course, every translight Guild voyage risks disaster. Although we are not very sanguine about this Guild-Ixian project, there is always the possibility and we shall report on this as conditions warrant.

THE GOD EMPEROR: Other than some small increments of growth, we note little change in the bodily characteristics of the Lord Leto. A rumoured aversion to water has not been confirmed, although the use of water as a barrier against the original sandworms of Dune is well documented in our records, as is the *water-death* by which Fremen killed a small worm to produce the spice essence employed in their orgies.

There is considerable evidence for the belief that the Lord Leto has increased his surveillance of Ix, possibly because of the Guild-Ixian project. Certainly, success in that project would reduce his hold upon the Empire.

He continues to do business with Ix, ordering replacement parts for his Royal Cart.

A new ghola Duncan Idaho has been sent to the Lord Leto by the Tleilaxu. This makes it certain that the previous ghola is dead, although the manner of his death is not known. We call your attention to previous indications that the Lord Leto himself has killed some of his gholas.

There is increasing evidence that the Lord Leto employs computers. If he is, in fact, defying his own prohibitions and the proscriptions of the Butlerian Jihad, the possession of proof by us could increase our influence over him, possibly even to the extent of certain joint ventures which we have long contemplated. Sovereign control of our breeding programme is still a primary concern. We will continue our investigation with, however, the following caveat:

As with every report preceding this one, we must address the Lord Leto's prescience. There is no doubt that his ability to predict future events, an oracular ability much more powerful than that of any ancestor, is still the mainstay of his political control.

We do not defy it!

It is our belief that he knows every important action we take far in advance of the event. We guide ourselves, therefore, by the rule that we will not knowingly threaten either his person or such of his grand plan as we can discern. Our address to him will continue to be:

"Tell us if we threaten you that we may desist."

And:

"Tell us of your grand plan that we may help."

He has provided no new answers to either question during this period.

THE IXIANS: Other than the Guild-Ix project, there is little of significance to report. Ix is sending a new Ambassador to the Court of the Lord Leto, one Hwi Noree, a niece of the Malky who once was reputed to be such a boon companion of the God Emperor. The reason for the choice of replacement is not known, although there is a small body of evidence that this Hwi Noree was bred for a specific purpose, possibly as the Ixian representative at the Court. We have reason to believe that Malky also was genetically designed with that official context in mind.

We will continue to investigate.

THE MUSEUM FREMEN: These degenerate relics of the once proud warriors continue to function as our major source of reliable information about affairs on Arrakis. They represent a major budget item for our next reporting period because their demands for payment are increasing and we dare not antagonize them.

It is interesting to note that although their lives bear little resemblance to that of their ancestors, their performance of Fremen rituals and their ability to ape Fremen ways remains flawless. We attribute this to Fish Speaker influence upon Fremen training.

THE TLEILAXU: We do not expect the new ghola of Duncan Idaho to provide any surprises. The Tleilaxu continue to be much chastened by the Lord Leto's reaction to their one attempt at changing the cellular nature and the psyche of the original.

A recent envoy from the Tleilaxu renewed their attempts to entice us into a joint venture, the avowed purpose being the production of a totally female society without the need for males. For all of the obvious reasons, including our distrust of everything Tleilaxu, we responded with our usual polite negative. Our Embassy to the Lord Leto's Decennial Festival will make a full report of this to him.

Respectfully submitted:

The Reverend Mothers Syaksa, Yitob, Mamulut, Eknekosk and Akeli.

> *Odd as it may seem, great struggles such as the one you can see emerging from my journals are not always visible to the participants. Much depends on what people dream in the secrecy of their hearts. I have always been as concerned with the shaping of dreams as with the shaping of actions. Between the lines of my journals is the struggle with humankind's view of itself—a sweaty contest on a field where motives from our darkest past can well up out of an unconscious reservoir and become events with which we not only must live but contend. It is the hydra-headed monster which always attacks from your blind side. I pray, therefore, that when you have traversed my portion of the Golden Path you no longer will be innocent children dancing to music you cannot hear.*

—**The Stolen Journals**

Nayla moved in a steady, plodding pace as she climbed the circular stairs to the God Emperor's audience chamber atop the Citadel's south tower. Each time she traversed the southwest arc of the tower, the narrow slitted windows drew dust-defined golden lines across her path. She knew that the central wall beside her confined a lift of Ixian make large enough to carry her Lord's bulk to the upper chamber, certainly large enough to hold her relatively smaller body, but she did not resent the fact that she was required to use the stairs.

The breeze through the open slits brought her the burnt-flint smell of blown sand. The low-lying sun ignited the light of red mineral flakes in the inner wall, ruby matches glowing there. Now and then she cast a glance through a slitted window at the dunes. Never once did she pause to admire the things to be seen around her.

"You have heroic patience, Nayla," the Lord had once told her.

Remembrance of those words warmed Nayla now.

Within the tower, Leto followed Nayla's progress up the long circular stairs that spiralled around the Ixian tube. Her progress was transmitted to him by an Ixian device which projected her approaching image quarter-size on to a region of three-dimensional focus directly in front of his eyes.

How precisely she moves, he thought.

The precision, he knew, came from a passionate simplicity.

She wore her Fish Speaker blues and a cape-robe without the hawk at the breast. Once past the guard station at the foot of the tower, she had thrown back the cibus mask he required her to wear on these personal visits. Her blocky, muscular body was like that of many others among his guardians, but her face was like no other in all of his memory—almost square with a mouth so wide it seemed to extend around the cheeks, an illusion caused by deep creases at the corners. Her eyes were pale green, the closely cropped hair like old ivory. Her forehead added to the square effect, almost flat with pale eyebrows which often went unnoticed because of the compelling eyes. The nose was a straight, shallow line which terminated close to the thin-lipped mouth.

When Nayla spoke, her great jaws opened and closed like those of some primordial animal. Her strength, known to few outside the corps of Fish Speakers, was legendary there. Leto had seen her lift a one-hundred-kilo man with one hand. Her presence on Arrakis had been arranged originally without Moneo's intervention, although the majordomo knew Leto employed his Fish Speakers as secret agents.

Leto turned his head away from the plodding image and looked out of the wide opening beside him at the desert to the south. The colours of the distant rocks danced in his awareness—brown, gold, a deep amber. There was a line of pink on a faraway cliff the exact hue of an egret's feathers. Egrets did not exist anymore except in Leto's memory, but he could place that pale pastel ribbon of stone against an inner eye and it was as though the extinct bird flew past him.

The climb, he knew, should be starting to tire even Nayla. She paused at last to rest, stopping at a point two steps past the three-quarter mark, precisely the place where she rested every time. It was part of her precision, one of the reasons he had brought her back from the distant garrison on Seprek.

A Dune hawk floated past the opening beside Leto, only a few wing lengths from the tower wall. Its attention was held on the shadows at the base of the Citadel. Small animals sometimes emerged there, Leto knew. Dimly on the horizon beyond the hawk's path he could see a line of clouds.

What a strange thing those were to the Old Fremen in him: clouds on Arrakis and rain and open water.

Leto reminded the inner voices: *Except for this last desert, my Sareer, the remodelling of Dune into verdant Arrakis has gone on remorselessly since the first days of my rule.*

The influence of geography on history went mostly unrecognized, Leto thought. Humans tended to look more at the influence of history on geography.

Who owns this river passage? This verdant valley? This peninsula? This planet?

None of us.

Nayla was climbing once more, her gaze fixed upward on the stairs she must traverse. Leto's thoughts locked on her.

In many ways she is the most useful assistant I have ever had. I am her God. She worships me quite unquestioningly. Even when I playfully attack her faith, she takes this merely as testing. She knows herself superior to any test.

When he had sent her to the rebellion and had told her to obey Siona in all things, she did not question. When Nayla doubted, even when she framed her doubts in words, her own thoughts were enough to restore faith . . . or had been enough. Recent messages, however, made it clear that Nayla required the Holy Presence to rebuild her inner strength.

Leto recalled that first conversation with Nayla, the woman trembling in her eagerness to please.

"Even if Siona sends you to kill me, you must obey. She must never learn that you serve me."

"No one can kill you, Lord."

"But you must obey Siona."

"Of course, Lord. That is your command."

"You must obey her in all things."

"I will do it, Lord."

Another test. Nayla does not question my tests. She treats them as flea bites. Her Lord commands? Nayla obeys. I must not let anything change that relationship.

She would have made a superb Shadout in the old days, Leto thought. It was one of the reasons he had given Nayla a crysknife, a real one preserved from Sietch Tabr. It had belonged to one of Stilgar's wives. Nayla wore it in a concealed sheath beneath her robes, more a talisman than a weapon. He had given it to her in the original ritual, a ceremony which had surprised him by evoking emotions he had thought forever buried.

"This is the tooth of Shai-Hulud."

He had extended the blade to her on his silver-skinned hands.

"Take it and you become part of both past and future. Soil it and the past will give you no future."

Nayla had accepted the blade, then the sheath.

"Draw the blood of a finger," Leto had commanded.

Nayla had obeyed.

"Sheath the blade. Never remove it without drawing blood."

Again, Nayla had obeyed.

As Leto watched the three-dimensional image of Nayla's approach, his reflections on that old ceremony were touched by sadness. Unless fixed in the old Fremen way, the blade would grow increasingly brittle and useless. It would keep its crysknife shape throughout Nayla's life, but little longer.

I have thrown away a bit of the past.

How sad it was that the Shadout of old had become today's Fish Speaker. And a true crysknife had been used to bind a servant more strongly to her master. He knew that some thought his Fish Speakers were really priestesses—Leto's answer to the Bene Gesserit.

He creates another religion, the Bene Gesserit said.

Nonsense! I have not created a religion. I am the religion!

Nayla entered the tower sanctuary and stood three paces from Leto's cart, her gaze lowered in proper subservience.

Still in his memories, Leto said: "Look at me, woman!"

She obeyed.

"I have created a holy obscenity!" he said. "This religion built around my person disgusts me!"

"Yes, Lord."

Nayla's green eyes on the gilded cushions of her cheeks stared out at him without questioning, without comprehension, without the need of either response.

If I sent her out to collect the stars, she would go and she would attempt it. She thinks I am testing her again. I do believe she could anger me.

86

"This damnable religion should end with me!" Leto shouted. "Why should I want to loose a religion upon my people? Religions wreck from within—Empires and individuals alike! It's all the same."

"Yes, Lord."

"Religions create radicals and fanatics like you!"

"Thank you, Lord."

The short-lived pseudo-rage sank back out of sight into the depths of his memories. Nothing dented the hard surface of Nayla's faith.

"Topri has reported to me through Moneo," Leto said. "Tell me about this Topri."

"Topri is a worm."

"Isn't that what you call me when you're among the rebels?"

"I obey my Lord in everything."

Touché!

"Topri is not worth cultivating then?" Leto asked.

"Siona assessed him correctly. He is clumsy. He says things which others will repeat, thus exposing his hand in the matter. Within seconds after Kobat began to speak she had confirmation that Topri was a spy."

Everyone agrees, even Moneo, Leto thought. *Topri is not a good spy.*

The agreement amused Leto. The petty machinations muddied water which remained completely transparent to him. The performers, however, still suited his designs.

"Siona does not suspect you?" Leto asked.

"I am not clumsy."

"Do you know why I summoned you?"

"To test my faith."

Ahhh, Nayla. How little you know of testing.

"I want your assessment of Siona. I want to see it on your face and see it in your movements and hear it in your voice," Leto said. "Is she ready?"

"The Fish Speakers need that one, Lord. Why do you risk losing her?"

"Forcing the issue is the surest way of losing what I treasure most in her," Leto said. "She must come to me with all of her strengths intact."

Nayla lowered her gaze. "As my Lord commands."

Leto recognized the response. It was a Nayla reaction to whatever she failed to understand.

"Will she survive the test, Nayla?"

"As my Lord describes the test . . ." Nayla lifted her gaze to Leto's face, shrugged. "I do not know, Lord. Certainly, she is strong. She was the only one to survive the wolves. But she is ruled by hate."

"Quite naturally. Tell me, Nayla, what will she do with the things she stole from me?"

"Did Topri not inform you about the books which they say contain Your Sacred Words?"

Odd how she can capitalize words with only her voice, Leto thought. He spoke curtly.

"Yes, yes. The Ixians have a copy and soon the Guild and Sisterhood as well will be hard at work on them."

"What are those books, Lord?"

"They are my words for my people. I want them to be read. What I want to know is what Siona has said about the Citadel charts she took."

"She says there is a great hoard of melange beneath Your Citadel, Lord, and the charts will reveal it."

"The charts will not reveal it. Will she tunnel?"

"She seeks Ixian tools for that."

"Ix will not provide them."

"Is there such a hoard of spice, Lord?"

"Yes."

"There is a story about how Your hoard is defended, Lord. That Arrakis itself would be destroyed if anyone tried to steal Your melange. Is it true?"

"Yes. And that would shatter the Empire. Nothing would survive—not Guild or Sisterhood, not Ix or Tleilaxu, not even the Fish Speakers."

She shuddered, then: "I will not let Siona try to get Your Spice."

"Nayla! I command you to obey Siona in everything. Is this how you serve me?"

"Lord?" She stood in fear of his anger, closer to a loss of faith than he had ever seen her. It was the crisis he had created, knowing how it must end. Slowly, Nayla relaxed. He could see the shape of her thought as though she had laid it out for him in illuminated words.

The ultimate test!

"You will return to Siona and guard her life with your own," Leto said. "That is the task I set for you and that you accepted. It is why you were chosen. It is why you carry a blade from Stilgar's household."

Her right hand went to the crysknife concealed beneath her robe.

How sure it is, Leto thought, *that a weapon can lock a person into a predictable pattern of behaviour.*

He stared with fascination at Nayla's rigid body. Her eyes were empty of everything except adoration.

The ultimate rhetorical despotism . . . and I despise it!

"Go then!" he barked.

Nayla turned and fled the Holy Presence.

Is it worth this? Leto wondered.

But Nayla had told him what he needed to know. Nayla had renewed her faith and revealed with accuracy the thing which Leto could not find in Siona's fading image. Nayla's instincts were to be trusted.

Siona has reached that explosive moment which I require.

The Duncans always think it odd that I choose women for combat forces, but my Fish Speakers are a temporary army in every sense. While they can be violent and vicious, women are profoundly different from men in their dedication to battle. The cradle of genesis ultimately predisposes them to behaviour more protective of life. They have proved to be the best keepers of the Golden Path. I reinforce this in my design for their training. They are set aside for a time from ordinary routines. I give them special sharings which they can look back upon with pleasure for the rest of their lives. They come of age in the company of their sisters in preparation for events more profound. What you share in such companionship always prepares you for greater things. The haze of nostalgia covers their days among their sisters, making those days into something different than they were. That's the way today changes history. All contemporaries do not inhabit the same time. The past is always changing, but few realize it.

—The Stolen Journals

After sending word to the Fish Speakers, Leto descended to the crypt in the late evening. He had found it best to begin the first interview with a new Duncan Idaho in a darkened room where the ghola could hear Leto describe himself before actually seeing the pre-worm body. There was a small side room carved in black stone off the central rotunda of the crypt which suited this requirement. The chamber was large enough to accommodate Leto on his cart, but the ceiling was low. Illumination came from hidden glowglobes which he controlled. There was only the one door, but it was in two segments—one swinging wide to admit the Royal Cart, the other a small portal in human dimensions.

Leto rolled his Royal Cart into the chamber, sealed the large portal and opened the smaller one. He composed himself then for the ordeal.

Boredom was an increasing problem. The pattern of the Tleilaxu gholas had become boringly repetitive. Once,

Leto had sent word warning the Tleilaxu to send no more Duncans, but they had known they could disobey him in this thing.

Sometimes I think they do it just to keep disobedience alive!

The Tleilaxu relied on an important thing which they knew protected them in other matters.

The presence of a Duncan pleases the Paul Atreides in me.

As Leto had explained it to Moneo in the majordomo's first days at the Citadel:

"The Duncans must come to me with much more than Tleilaxu preparation. You must see to it that my houris gentle the Duncans and that the women answer *some* of his questions."

"Which questions may they answer, Lord?"

"They know."

Moneo had, of course, learned all about this procedure over the years.

Leto heard Moneo's voice outside the darkened room, then the sound of the Fish Speaker escort and the hesitantly distinctive footsteps of the new ghola.

"Through that door," Moneo said. "It will be dark inside and we will close the door behind you. Stop just inside and wait for the Lord Leto to speak."

"Why will it be dark?" The Duncan's voice was full of aggressive misgivings.

"He will explain."

Idaho was thrust into the room and the door was sealed behind him.

Leto knew what the ghola saw—only shadows among shadows and blackness where not even the source of a voice could be fixed. As usual, Leto brought the Paul-Muad'Dib voice into play.

"It pleases me to see you again, Duncan."

"I can't see you!"

Idaho was a warrior and the warrior attacks. This reassured Leto that the ghola was a fully restored original. The morality play by which the Tleilaxu reawakened a ghola's pre-death memories always left some uncertainties in the gholas' minds. Some of the Duncans believed they had threatened a real Paul-Muad'Dib. This one carried such illusions.

"I hear Paul's voice but I can't see him," Idaho said. He didn't try to conceal the frustrations, let them all come out in his voice.

Why was an Atreides playing this stupid game? Paul was truly dead in some long-ago and this was Leto, the carrier of Paul's resurrected memories . . . and the memories of many others if the Tleilaxu stories were to be believed.

"You have been told that you are only the latest in a long line of duplicates," Leto said.

"I have none of those memories."

Leto recognized hysteria in the Duncan, barely covered by the warrior bravado. The cursed Tleilaxu post-tank restoration tactics had produced the usual mental chaos. This Duncan had arrived in a state of near shock, strongly suspecting he was insane. Leto knew that the most subtle powers of reassurance would be required now to soothe the poor fellow. This would be emotionally draining for both of them.

"There have been many changes, Duncan," Leto said. "One thing, though, does not change. I am still Atreides."

"They said your body is . . ."

"Yes, that has changed."

"The damned Tleilaxu! They tried to make me kill someone I . . . well, he looked like you. I suddenly remembered who I was and there was this . . . Could that have been a Muad'Dib ghola?"

"A Face Dancer mimic, I assure you."

"He looked and talked so much like . . . Are you sure?"

"An actor, no more. Did he survive?"

"Of course! That's how they wakened my memories. They explained the whole damned thing. Is it true?"

"It's true, Duncan. I detest it, but I permit it for the pleasure of your company."

The potential victims always survive, Leto thought. *At*

92

least for the Duncans I see. There have been slips, the fake Paul slain and the Duncans wasted. But there are always more cells carefully preserved from the original.

"What about your body?" Idaho demanded.

Muad'Dib could be retired now; Leto resumed his usual voice. "I accepted the sandtrout as my skin. They have been changing me ever since."

"Why?"

"I will explain that in due course."

"The Tleilaxu said you look like a sandworm."

"What did my Fish Speakers say?"

"They said you're God. Why do you call them Fish Speakers?"

"An old conceit. The first priestesses spoke to fish in their dreams. They learned valuable things that way."

"How do you know?"

"I *am* those women . . . and everything that came before and after them."

Leto heard the dry swallowing in Idaho's throat, then: "I see why the darkness. You're giving me time to adjust."

"You always were quick, Duncan."

Except when you were slow.

"How long have you been changing?"

"More than thirty-five hundred years."

"Then what the Tleilaxu told me is true."

"They seldom dare to lie anymore."

"That's a long time."

"Very long."

"The Tleilaxu have . . . copied me many times?"

"Many."

It's time you asked how many, Duncan.

"How many of me?"

"I will let you see the records for yourself."

And so it starts, Leto thought.

This exchange always appeared to satisfy the Duncans, but there was no escaping the nature of the question:

"How many of me?"

The Duncans made no distinctions of the flesh even

93

though no mutual memories passed between gholas of the same stock.

"I remember my death," Idaho said. "Harkonnen blades, lots of them trying to get at you and Jessica."

Leto restored the Muad'Dib voice for momentary play: "I was there, Duncan."

"I'm a replacement, is that right?" Idaho asked.

"That's right," Leto said.

"How did the other . . . me . . . I mean, how did he die?"

"All flesh wears out, Duncan. It's in the records."

Leto waited patiently, wondering how long it would be until the tamed history failed to satisfy this Duncan.

"What do you really look like?" Idaho asked. "What's this sandworm body the Tleilaxu described?"

"It will make sandworms of sorts someday. It's already far down the road of metamorphosis."

"What do you mean *of sorts*?"

"It will have more ganglia. It will be aware."

"Can't we have some light? I'd like to see you."

Leto commanded the floodlights. Brilliant illumination filled the room. The black walls and the lighting had been arranged to focus the illumination on Leto, every visible detail revealed.

Idaho swept his gaze along the faceted silvery-grey body, noted the beginnings of a sandworm's ribbed sections, the sinuous flexings . . . the small protuberances which had once been feet and legs, one of them somewhat shorter than the other. He brought his attention back to the well-defined arms and hands and finally lifted his attention to the cowled face with its pink skin almost lost in the immensity, a ridiculous extrusion on such a body.

"Well, Duncan," Leto said. "You were warned."

Idaho gestured mutely toward the pre-worm body.

Leto asked it for him: "Why?"

Idaho nodded.

"I'm still Atreides, Duncan, and I assure you with all the honour of that name, there were compelling reasons."

94

"What could possibly . . ."

"You will learn in time."

Idaho merely shook his head from side to side.

"It's not a pleasant revelation," Leto said. "It requires that you learn other things first. Trust the word of an Atreides."

Over the centuries, Leto had found that this invocation of Idaho's profound loyalties to all things Atreides dampened the immediate wellspring of personal questions. Once more, the formula worked.

"So I'm to serve the Atreides again," Idaho said. "That sounds familiar. Is it?"

"In many ways, old friend."

"Old to you, maybe, but not to me. How will I serve?"

"Didn't my Fish Speakers tell you?"

"They said I would command your elite Guard, a force chosen from among them. I don't understand that. An army of *women*?"

"I need a trusted companion who can command my Guard. You object?"

"Why women?"

"There are behavioural differences between the sexes which make women extremely valuable in this role."

"You're not answering my question."

"You think them inadequate?"

"Some of them looked pretty tough, but . . ."

"Others were, ahhh, *soft* with you?"

Idaho blushed.

Leto found this a charming reaction. The Duncans were among the few humans of these times who could do this. It was understandable, a product of the Duncans' early training, their sense of personal honour—very chivalrous.

"I don't see why you trust women to protect you," Idaho said. The blood slowly receded from his cheeks. He glared at Leto.

"But I have always trusted them as I trust you—with my life."

"What do we protect you from?"

"Moneo and my Fish Speakers will bring you up to date."

Idaho shifted from one foot to the other, his body swaying in a heartbeat rhythm. He stared around the small room, his eyes not focusing. With the abruptness of sudden decision, he returned his attention to Leto.

"What do I call you?"

It was the sign of acceptance for which Leto had been waiting. "Will Lord Leto do?"

"Yes . . . m'Lord." Idaho stared directly into Leto's Fremen-blue eyes. "Is it true what your Fish Speakers say—you have . . . memories of . . ."

"We're all here, Duncan." Leto spoke it in the voice of his paternal grandfather, then:

"Even the women are here, Duncan." It was the voice of Jessica, Leto's paternal grandmother.

"You knew them well," Leto said. "And they know you."

Idaho inhaled a slow, trembling breath. "That will take a little getting used to."

"My own initial reaction exactly," Leto said.

An explosion of laughter shook Idaho, and Leto thought it more than the weak jest deserved, but he remained silent.

Presently, Idaho said: "Your Fish Speakers were *supposed* to put me in a good mood, weren't they?"

"Did they succeed?"

Idaho studied Leto's face, recognizing the distinctive Atreides features.

"You Atreides always did know me too well," Idaho said.

"That's better," Leto said. "You're beginning to accept that I'm not just one Atreides. I'm all of them."

"Paul said that once."

"So I did!" As much as the original personality could be conveyed by tone and accent, it was Muad 'Dib speaking.

Idaho gulped, looked away at the room's door.

96

"You've taken something away from us," he said. "I can feel it. Those women . . . Moneo . . ."

Us against you, Leto thought. *The Duncans always choose the human side.*

Idaho returned his attention to Leto's face. "What have you given us in exchange?"

"Throughout the Empire, Leto's Peace!"

"And I can see that everyone's delightfully happy! That's why you need a personal guard."

Leto smiled. "My peace is actually enforced tranquillity. Humans have a long history of reacting against tranquillity."

"So you give us the Fish Speakers."

"And a hierarchy you can identify without any mistakes."

"A female army," Idaho muttered.

"The ultimate male-enticing force," Leto said. "Sex always was a way of subduing the aggressive male."

"Is that what they do?"

"They prevent or ameliorate excesses which could lead to more painful violence."

"And you let them believe you're a god. I don't think I like this."

"The curse of holiness is as offensive to me as it is to you!"

Idaho frowned. It was not the response he had expected.

"What kind of game are you playing, *Lord* Leto?"

"A very old one but with new rules."

"Your rules!"

"Would you rather I turned it all back to CHOAM and Landsraad and the Great Houses?"

"The Tleilaxu say there is no more Landsraad. You don't allow any real self-rule."

"Well then, I could step aside for the Bene Gesserit. Or maybe the Ixians or the Tleilaxu? Would you like me to find another Baron Harkonnnen to assume power over the Empire? Say the word, Duncan, and I'll abdicate!"

Under this avalanche of meanings, Idaho again shook his head from side to side.

"In the wrong hands," Leto said, "monolithic centralized power is a dangerous and volatile instrument."

"And your hands are the right ones?"

"I'm not certain about my hands, but I will tell you, Duncan, I'm certain about the hands of those who've gone before me. I *know* them."

Idaho turned his back on Leto.

What a fascinating, ultimately human gesture, Leto thought. *Rejection coupled to acceptance of his vulnerability.*

Leto spoke to Idaho's back.

"You object quite rightly that I use people without their full knowledge and consent."

Idaho turned his profile to Leto, then turned his head to look up at the cowled face, cocking his head forward a bit to peer into the all-blue eyes.

He is studying me, Leto thought, *but he has only the face to measure me by.*

The Atreides had taught their people to know the subtle signals of face and body, and Idaho was good at it, but the realization could be seen coming over him: he was over his depth here.

Idaho cleared his throat. "What's the worst thing you would ask of me?"

How like a Duncan! Leto thought. This one was a classic. Idaho would give his loyalty to an Atreides, to the guardian of his oath, but he sent a signal that he would not go beyond the personal limits of his own morality.

"You will be asked to guard me by whatever means necessary, and you will be asked to guard my secret."

"What secret?"

"That I am vulnerable."

"That you're not God?"

"Not in that ultimate sense."

"Your Fish Speakers talk about rebels."

"They exist."

"Why?"

"They are young and I have not convinced them that my way is better. It's very difficult convincing the young of anything. They're born knowing so much."

"I never before heard an Atreides sneer at the young that way."

"Perhaps it's because I'm so much older—old compounded by old. And my task gets more difficult with each passing generation."

"What is your task?"

"You will come to understand it as we go along."

"What happens if I fail you? Do your women eliminate me?"

"I try not to burden the Fish Speakers with guilt."

"But you would burden me?"

"If you accept it."

"If I find that you're worse than the Harkonnens I'll turn against you."

How like a Duncan. They measure all evil against the Harkonnens. How little they know of evil.

Leto said: "The Baron ate whole planets, Duncan. What could be worse than that?"

"Eating the Empire."

"I am pregnant with my Empire. I'll die giving birth to it."

"If I could believe that . . ."

"Will you command my Guard?"

"Why me?"

"You're the best."

"Dangerous work, I'd imagine. Is that how my predecessors died, doing your dangerous work?"

"Some of them."

"I wish I had the memories of those others!"

"You couldn't have and still be the original."

"I want to learn about them, though."

"You will."

"So the Atreides still need a sharp knife?"

"We have jobs that only a Duncan Idaho can do."

"You say . . . we . . ." Idaho swallowed, looked at the door, then at Leto's face.

Leto spoke to him as Muad'Dib would have, but still in the Leto-voice.

"When we climbed to Sietch Tabr for the last time together, you had my loyalty then and I had yours. Nothing of that has really changed."

"That was your father."

"That was me!" Paul-Muad'Dib's voice of command coming from Leto's bulk always shocked the gholas.

Idaho whispered: "All of you . . . in that one . . . body . . ." He broke off.

Leto remained silent. This was the decision moment.

Presently, Idaho permitted himself that devil-may-care grin for which he had been so well known. "Then I will speak to the first Leto and to Paul, the ones who know me best. Use me well, for I did love you."

Leto closed his eyes. Such words always distressed him. He knew it was love to which he was most vulnerable.

Moneo, who had been listening, came to the rescue. He entered and said: "Lord, shall I take Duncan Idaho to the guards he will command?"

"Yes." The one word was all that Leto could manage.

Moneo took Idaho's arm and led him away.

Good Moneo, Leto thought. *So good. He knows me so well, but I despair of his ever understanding me.*

> *I know the evil of my ancestors because I am those people. The balance is delicate in the extreme. I know that few of you who read my words have ever thought about your ancestors this way. It has not occurred to you that your ancestors were survivors and that the survival itself sometimes involved savage decisions, a kind of wanton brutality which civilized humankind works very hard to suppress. What price will you pay for that suppression? Will you accept your own extinction?*

—The Stolen Journals

As he dressed for his first morning of Fish Speaker command, Idaho tried to shake off a nightmare. It had awakened him twice and both times he had gone out on to the balcony to stare up at the stars, the dream still roaring in his head.

Women . . . weaponless women in black armour . . . rushing at him with the hoarse, mindless shouting of a mob . . . waving hands moist with red blood . . . and as they swarmed over him, their mouths opened to display terrible fangs!

In that moment, he awoke.

Morning light did little to dispel the effects of the nightmare.

They had provided him with a room in the north tower. The balcony looked out over a vista of dunes to a distant cliff with what appeared to be a mud-hut village at its base.

Idaho buttoned his tunic as he stared at the scene.

Why does Leto choose only women for his army?

Several comely Fish Speakers had offered to spend the night with their new commander, but Idaho had rejected them.

It was not like the Atreides to use sex as a persuader!

He looked down at his clothing: a black uniform with golden piping, a red hawk at the left breast. That, at least, was familiar. No insignia of rank.

"They know your face," Moneo had said.

Strange little man, Moneo.

This thought brought Idaho up short. Reflection told him that Moneo was not little. *Very controlled, yes, but no shorter than I am.* Moneo appeared drawn into himself, though . . . collected.

Idaho glanced around his room—sybaritic in its attention to comfort—soft cushions, appliances concealed behind panels of brown polished wood. The bath was an ornate display of pastel blue tiles with a combination bath and shower in which at least six people could bathe at the same time. The whole place invited self-indulgence. These were quarters where you could let your senses indulge in remembered pleasures.

"Clever," Idaho whispered.

A gentle tapping on his door was followed by a female voice saying: "Commander? Moneo is here."

Idaho glanced out at the sunburnt colours on the distant cliff.

"Commander?" The voice was a bit louder.

"Come in," Idaho called.

Moneo entered, closing the door behind him. He wore tunic and trousers of chalk white which forced the eyes to concentrate on his face. Moneo glanced once around the room.

"So this is where they put you. Those damned women! I suppose they thought they were being kind, but they ought to know better."

"How do you know what I like?" Idaho demanded. Even as he asked it, he realized it was a foolish question.

I'm not the first Duncan Idaho that Moneo has seen.

Moneo merely smiled and shrugged.

"I did not mean to offend you, Commander. Will you keep these quarters, then?"

"I like the view."

"But not the furnishings." It was a statement.

"Those can be changed," Idaho said.

"I will see to it."

"I suppose you're here to explain my duties."

"As much as I can. I know how strange everything must appear to you at first. This civilization is profoundly different from the one you knew."

"I can see that. How did my . . . predecessor die?"

Moneo shrugged. It appeared to be his standard gesture, but there was nothing self-effacing about it.

"He was not fast enough to escape the consequences of a decision he had made," Moneo said.

"Be specific."

Moneo sighed. The Duncans were always like this—so demanding.

102

"The rebellion killed him. Do you wish the details?"

"Would they be useful to me?"

"No."

"I'll want a complete briefing on this rebellion today, but first: Why are there no men in Leto's army?"

"He has you."

"You know what I mean."

"He has a curious theory about armies. I have discussed it with him on many occasions. But do you not want to breakfast before I explain?"

"Can't we have both at the same time?"

Moneo turned toward the door and called out a single word: "Now!"

The effect was immediate and fascinating to Idaho. A troop of young Fish Speakers swarmed into the room. Two of them took a folding table and chairs from behind a panel and placed them on the balcony. Others set the table for two people. More brought food—fresh fruit, hot rolls and a steaming drink which smelled faintly of spice and caffeine. It was all done with a swift and silent efficiency which spoke of long practice. They left as they had come, without a word.

Idaho found himself seated across from Moneo at the table within a minute after the start of this curious performance.

"Every morning like that?" Idaho asked.

"Only if you wish it."

Idaho sampled the drink: melange-coffee. He recognized the fruit, the soft Caladan melon called *paradan*.

My favourite.

"You know me pretty well," Idaho said.

Moneo smiled. "We've had some practice. Now, about your question."

"And Leto's curious theory."

"Yes. He says that the all-male army was too dangerous to its civilian support base."

"That's crazy! Without the army there would've been no . . ."

"I know the argument. But he says that the male army was a survival of the screening function delegated to the non-breeding males in the prehistoric pack. He says it was a curiously consistent fact that it was always the older males who sent the younger males into battle."

"What does that mean, *screening function*?"

"The ones who were always out on the dangerous perimeter protecting the core of breeding males, females and the young. The ones who first encountered the predator."

"How is that dangerous to the . . . civilians?"

Idaho took a bite of the melon, found it ripened perfectly.

"The Lord Leto says that when it was denied an external enemy, the all-male army always turned against its own population. Always."

"Contending for the females?"

"Perhaps. He obviously does not believe, however, that it was *that* simple."

"I don't find this a curious theory."

"You have not heard all of it."

"There's more?"

"Oh, yes. He says that the all-male army has a strong tendency toward homosexual activities."

Idaho glared across the table at Moneo. "I never . . ."

"Of course not. He is speaking about sublimation, about deflected energies and all the rest of it."

"The rest of what?" Idaho was prickly with anger at what he saw as an attack on his male self-image.

"Adolescent attitudes, just boys together, jokes designed purely to cause pain, loyalty only to your pack-mates . . . things of that nature."

Idaho spoke coldly. "What's your opinion?"

"I remind myself . . ." Moneo turned and spoke while looking out at the view. ". . . of something which he has said and which I am sure is true. He is every soldier in human history. He offered to parade for me a series of examples—famous military figures who were frozen in adolescence. I declined the offer. I have read my history with care and have recognized this characteristic for myself."

Moneo turned and looked directly into Idaho's eyes.

"Think about it, Commander."

Idaho prided himself on self-honesty and this hit him. Cults of youth and adolescence preserved in the military? It had the ring of truth. There were examples in his own experience . . .

Moneo nodded. "The homosexual, latent or otherwise, who maintains that condition for reasons which could be called purely psychological, tends to indulge in pain-causing behaviour—seeking it for himself and inflicting it upon others. Lord Leto says this goes back to the testing behaviour in the prehistoric pack."

"You believe him?"

"I do."

Idaho took a bite of the melon. It had lost its sweet savour. He swallowed and put down his spoon.

"I will have to think about this," Idaho said.

"Of course."

"You're not eating," Idaho said.

"I was up before dawn and ate then." Moneo gestured at his plate. "The women continually try to tempt me."

"Do they ever succeed?"

"Occasionally."

"You're right. I find his theory curious. Is there more to it?"

"Ohhh, he says that when it breaks out of the adolescent-homosexual restraints, the male army is essentially rapist. Rape is often murderous and that's not survival behaviour."

Idaho scowled.

A tight smile flitted across Moneo's mouth. "Lord Leto says that only Atreides discipline and moral restraints prevented some of the worst excesses in your times."

A deep sigh shook Idaho.

Moneo sat back, thinking of a thing the God Emperor

had once said: *"No matter how much we ask after the truth, self-awareness is often unpleasant. We do not feel kindly toward the Truthsayer."*

"Those damned Atreides!" Idaho said.

"I am Atreides," Moneo said.

"What?" Idaho was shocked.

"His breeding programme," Moneo said. "I'm sure the Tleilaxu mentioned it. I am directly descended from the mating of his sister and Harq al-Ada."

Idaho leaned toward him. "Then tell me, Atreides, how are women better soldiers than men?"

"They find it easier to mature."

Idaho shook his head in bewilderment.

"They have a compelling physical way of moving from adolescence into maturity," Moneo said. "As Lord Leto says, 'Carry a baby in you for nine months and that changes you.'"

Idaho sat back. "What does he know about it?"

Moneo merely stared at him until Idaho recalled the multitude in Leto—both male and female. The realization plunged over Idaho. Moneo saw it, recalling a comment of the God Emperor's: *"Your words brand him with the look you want him to have."*

As the silence continued, Moneo cleared his throat. Presently, he said: "The immensity of the Lord Leto's memories has been known to stop my tongue, too."

"Is he being honest with us?" Idaho asked.

"I believe him."

"But he does so many . . . I mean, take this breeding programme. How long has that been going on?"

"From the very first. From the day he took it away from the Bene Gesserit."

"What does he want from it?"

"I wish I knew."

"But you're . . ."

"An Atreides and his chief aide, yes."

"You haven't convinced me that a female army is best."

"They continue the species."

106

At last, Idaho's frustration and anger had an object. "Is that what I was doing with them that first night—breeding?"

"Possibly. The Fish Speakers take no precautions against pregnancy."

"Damn him! I'm not some animal he can move from stall to stall like a . . . like a . . ."

"Like a stud?"

"Yes!"

"But the Lord Leto refuses to follow the Tleilaxu pattern of gene surgery and artificial insemination."

"What have the Tleilaxu got to . . ."

"They are the object lesson. Even I can see that. Their Face Dancers are mules, closer to a colony organism than to humans."

"Those others of . . . me . . . were any of them his studs?"

"Some. You have descendants."

"Who?"

"I am one."

Idaho stared into Moneo's eyes, lost suddenly in a tangle of relationships. Idaho found the relationships impossible to understand. Moneo obviously was so much older than . . . *But I am* . . . Which of them was truly the older? Which the ancestor and which the descendant?

"I sometimes have trouble with this myself," Moneo said. "If it helps, the Lord Leto assures me that you are not my descendant, not in any ordinary sense. However, you may well father some of my descendants."

Idaho shook his head from side to side.

"Sometimes I think only the God Emperor himself can understand these things," Moneo said.

"That's another thing!" Idaho said. "This god business."

"The Lord Leto says he has created a holy obscenity."

This was not the response Idaho had expected. *What did I expect? A defence of the Lord Leto?*

"Holy obscenity," Moneo repeated. The words rolled from his tongue with a strange sense of gloating in them.

Idaho focused a probing stare on Moneo. *He hates his God Emperor! No . . . he fears him. But don't we always hate what we fear?*

"Why do you believe in him?" Idaho demanded.

"You ask if I share in the popular religion?"

"No! Does he?"

"I think so."

"Why? Why do you think so?"

"Because he says he wishes to create no more Face Dancers. He insists that his human stock, once it has been paired, breeds in the way it has always bred."

"What the hell does that have to do with it?"

"You asked me what he believes in. I think he believes in chance. I think that's his God."

"That's superstition!"

"Considering the circumstances of the Empire, a very daring superstition."

Idaho glared at Moneo. "You damned Atreides," he muttered. "You'll dare anything!"

Moneo noted that there was dislike mixed with admiration in Idaho's voice.

The Duncans always begin that way.

What is the most profound difference between us, between you and me? You already know it. It's these ancestral memories. Mine come at me in the full glare of awareness. Yours work from your blind side. Some call it instinct or fate. The memories apply their leverages to each of us—on what we think and what we do. You think you are immune to such influences? I am Galileo. I stand here and tell you: "Yet it moves." That which moves can exert its force in ways no mortal power ever before dared stem. I am here to dare this.

—The Stolen Journals

"When she was a child she watched me, remember? When she thought I was not aware, Siona watched me like the desert hawk which circles above the lair of its prey. You yourself mentioned it."

Leto rolled his body a quarter turn on his cart while speaking. This brought his cowled face close to that of Moneo, who trotted beside the cart.

It was barely dawn on the desert road which followed the high artificial ridge from the Citadel in the Sareer to the Festival City. The road from the desert ran laser-beam straight until it reached this point where it curved widely and dipped into terraced canyons before crossing the Idaho River. The air was full of thick mists from the river tumbling in its distant clamour, but Leto had opened the bubble cover which sealed the front of his cart. The moisture made his worm-self tingle with vague distress, but there was the smell of sweet desert growth in the mist and his human nostrils savoured it. He ordered the cortège to stop.

"Why are we stopping, Lord?" Moneo asked.

Leto did not answer. The cart creaked as he heaved his bulk into an arching curve which lifted his head and allowed him to look across the Forbidden Forest to the Kynes Sea glistening silver far off to the right. He turned left and there were the remains of the Shield Wall, a sinuous low shadow in the morning light. The ridge here had been raised almost two thousand metres to enclose the Sareer and limit airborne moisture there. From his vantage, Leto could see the distant notch where he had caused the Festival City of Onn to be built.

"It is a whim which stops me," Leto said.

"Shouldn't we cross the bridge before resting?" Moneo asked.

"I am not resting."

Leto stared ahead. After a series of switchbacks which were visible from here only as a twisting shadow, the high road crossed the river on a faery bridge, climbed to a buffer ridge and then sloped down to the city which presented a vista of glittering spires at this distance.

"The Duncan acts subdued," Leto said. "Have you had your long conversation with him?"

"Precisely as you required, Lord."

"Well, it's only been four days," Leto said. "They often take longer to recover."

"He has been busy with your Guard, Lord. They were out until late again last night."

"The Duncans do not like to walk in the open. They think about the things which could be used to attack us."

"I know, Lord."

Leto turned and looked squarely at Moneo. The major-domo wore a green cloak over his white uniform. He stood beside the open bubble cover, exactly in the place where duty required that he station himself on these excursions.

"You are very dutiful, Moneo," Leto said.

"Thank you, Lord."

Guards and courtiers kept themselves at a respectful distance well behind the cart. Most of them were trying to avoid even the appearance of eavesdropping on Leto and Moneo. Not so Idaho. He had positioned some of the Fish Speaker guards at both sides of the Royal Road, spreading them out. Now, he stood staring at the cart. Idaho wore a black uniform with white piping, a gift of the Fish Speakers, Moneo had said.

"They like this one very much. He is good at what he does."

"What does he do, Moneo?"

"Why, guard your person, Lord."

The women of the Guard all wore skintight green uniforms, each with a red Atreides hawk at the left breast.

"They watch him very closely," Leto said.

"Yes. He is teaching them hand signals. He says it's the Atreides way."

"That is certainly correct. I wonder why the previous one didn't do that?"

"Lord, if you don't know . . ."

"I jest, Moneo. The previous Duncan did not feel

110

threatened until it was too late. Has this one accepted our explanations?"

"So I'm told, Lord. He is well started in your service."

"Why is he carrying only that knife in the belt sheath?"

"The women have convinced him that only the specially trained among them should have lasguns."

"Your caution is groundless, Moneo. Tell the women that it's much too early for us to begin fearing this one."

"As my Lord commands."

It was obvious to Leto that his new Guard Commander did not enjoy the presence of the courtiers. He stood well away from them. Most of the courtiers, he had been told, were civil functionaries. They were decked out in their brightest and finest for this day when they could parade themselves in their full power and in the presence of the God Emperor. Leto could see how foolish the courtiers must appear to Idaho. But Leto could remember far more foolish finery and he thought that this day's display might be an improvement.

"Have you introduced him to Siona?" Leto asked.

At the mention of Siona, Moneo's brows congealed into a scowl.

"Calm yourself," Leto said. "Even when she spied on me I cherished her."

"I sense danger in her, Lord. I think sometimes she sees into my most secret thoughts."

"The wise child knows her father."

"I do not joke, Lord."

"Yes, I can see that. Have you noticed that the Duncan grows impatient?"

"They scouted the road almost to the bridge," Moneo said.

"What did they find?"

"The same thing I found—a few Museum Fremen."

"Another petition?"

"Do not be angry, Lord."

Once more, Leto peered ahead. This necessary exposure to the open air, the long and stately journey with all of its

111

ritual requirements to reassure the Fish Speakers, all of it troubled Leto. And now, another petition!

Idaho strode forward to stop directly behind Moneo.

There was a sense of menace about Idaho's movements. *Surely not this soon*, Leto thought.

"Why are we stopping, m'Lord?" Idaho asked.

"I often stop here," Leto said.

It was true. He turned and looked beyond the faery bridge. The way twisted downward out of the canyon heights into the Forbidden Forest and thence through fields beside the river. Leto had often stopped here to watch the sunrise. There was something about this morning, though, the sun striking across the familiar vista . . . something which stirred old memories.

The fields of the Royal Plantations reached outward beyond the forest and, when the sun lifted over the far curve of land, it beamed glowing gold across grain rippling in the fields. The grain reminded Leto of sand, of sweeping dunes which once had marched across this very ground.

And will march once more.

The grain was not quite the bright silica amber of his remembered desert. Leto looked back at the cliff-enclosed distances of his Sareer, his sanctuary of the past. The colours were distinctly different. All the same, when he looked once more toward Festival City, he felt an ache where his many hearts once more were reforming in their slow transformation toward something profoundly alien.

What is it about this morning that makes me think about my lost humanity? Leto wondered.

Of all the Royal party looking at that familiar scene of grain fields and forest, Leto knew that only he still thought of the lush landscape as the *bahr bela ma*, the ocean without water.

"Duncan," Leto said. "You see that out there toward the city? That was the Tanzerouft."

"The Land of Terror?" Idaho revealed his surprise in the quick look toward Onn and the sudden return of his gaze to Leto.

"The *bahr bela ma*," Leto said. "It has been concealed under a carpet of plants for more than three thousand years. Of all who live on Arrakis today, only the two of us ever saw the desert original."

Idaho looked toward Onn. "Where is the Shield Wall?" he asked.

"Muad'Dib's Gap is right there, right where we built the city."

"That line of little hills, that was the Shield Wall? What happened to it?"

"You are standing on it."

Idaho looked up at Leto, then down to the roadway and all around.

"Lord, shall we proceed?" Moneo asked.

Moneo, with that clock ticking in his breast, is the goad to duty, Leto thought. There were important visitors to see and other vital matters. Time pressed him. And he did not like it when his God Emperor talked about old times with the Duncans.

Leto was suddenly aware that he had paused here far longer than ever before. The courtiers and guards were cold after their run in the morning air. Some had chosen their clothing more for show than protection.

Then again, Leto thought, *perhaps show is a form of protection*.

"There were dunes," Idaho said.

"Stretching for thousands of kilometres," Leto agreed.

Moneo's thoughts churned. He was familiar with the God Emperor's reflective mood, but there was a sense of sadness in it this day. Perhaps the recent death of a Duncan. Leto sometimes let important information drop when he was sad. You never questioned the God Emperor's moods or his whims, but sometimes they could be employed.

Siona will have to be warned, Moneo thought. *If the young fool will listen to me!*

She was far more of a rebel than he had been. Far more. Leto had tamed his Moneo, sensitized him to the Golden

113

Path and the rightful duties for which he had been bred, but methods used on a Moneo would not work with Siona. In his observation of this, Moneo had learned things about his own training which he had never before suspected.

"I don't see any identifiable landmarks," Idaho was saying.

"Right over there," Leto said, pointing. "Where the forest ends. That was the way to Splintered Rock."

Moneo shut out their voices. *It was ultimate fascination with the God Emperor which finally brought me to heel.* Leto never ceased to surprise and amaze. He could not be reliably predicted. Moneo glanced at the God Emperor's profile. *What has he become?*

As part of his early duties, Moneo had studied the Citadel's private records, the historical accounts of Leto's transformation. But symbiosis with sandtrout remained a mystery which even Leto's own words could not dispel. If the accounts were to be believed, the sandtrout skin made his body almost invulnerable to time and violence. The great body's ribbed core could even absorb lasgun bursts!

First the sandtrout, then the worm—all part of the great cycle which had produced melange. That cycle lay within the God Emperor . . . marking time.

"Let us proceed," Leto said.

Moneo realized that he had missed something. He came out of his reverie and looked at a smiling Duncan Idaho.

"We used to call that woolgathering," Leto said.

"I'm sorry, Lord," Moneo said. "I was . . ."

"You were woolgathering, but it's all right."

His mood's improved, Moneo thought. *I can thank the Duncan for that, I think.*

Leto adjusted his position on the cart, closed part of the bubble cover and left only his head free. The cart crunched over small rocks on the roadbed as Leto activated it.

Idaho took up position at Moneo's shoulder and trotted along beside him.

"There are floater bulbs under that cart but he uses the wheels," Idaho said. "Why is that?"

"It pleases the Lord Leto to use wheels instead of anti-gravity."

"What makes the thing go? How does he steer it?"

"Have you asked him?"

"I haven't had the opportunity."

"The Royal Cart is of Ixian manufacture."

"What does that mean?"

"It is said that the Lord Leto activates his cart and steers it just by thinking in a particular way."

"Don't you know?"

"Questions such as this do not please him."

Even to his intimates, Moneo thought, *the God Emperor remains a mystery*.

"Moneo!" Leto called.

"You had better return to your guards," Moneo said, gesturing to Idaho to fall back.

"I'd rather be out in front with them," Idaho said.

"The Lord Leto does not want that! Now go back."

Moneo hurried to place himself close beside Leto's face, noting that Idaho was falling back through the courtiers to the rear ring of guards.

Leto looked down at Moneo. "I thought you handled that very well, Moneo."

"Thank you, Lord."

"Do you know why the Duncan wants to be out in front?"

"Certainly, Lord. It's where your guard should be."

"And this one senses danger."

"I don't understand you, Lord. I cannot understand why you do these things."

"That's true, Moneo."

*The female sense of sharing originated as familial sharing—
care of the young, the gathering and preparation of food,
sharing joys, love and sorrows. Funeral lamentation
originated with women. Religion began as a female monopoly, wrested from them only after its social power became
too dominant. Women were the first medical researchers and
practitioners. There has never been any clear balance
between the sexes because power goes with certain roles as it
certainly goes with knowledge.*

—The Stolen Journals

For the Reverend Mother Tertius Eileen Anteac this had
been a disastrous morning. She had arrived on Arrakis with
her fellow Truthsayer, Marcus Claire Luyseyal, both of
them coming down with their official party less than three
hours ago aboard the first shuttle from the Guild Heighliner hanging in stationary orbit. First, they had been
assigned rooms at the absolute edge of the Festival City's
Embassy Quarter. The rooms were small and not quite
clean.

"Any farther out and we'd be camping in the slums,"
Luyseyal had said.

Next they had been denied communications facilities.
All of the screens remained blank no matter how many
switches were toggled and palm-dials turned.

Anteac had addressed herself sharply to the heavyset
officer commanding the Fish Speaker escort, a glowering
woman with low brows and the muscles of a manual
labourer.

"I wish to complain to your commander!"

"No complaints allowed at Festival Time," the amazon
had rasped.

Anteac had glared at the officer, a look which in Anteac's
old and seamed face had been known to make even her
fellow Reverend Mothers hesitate.

The amazon had merely smiled and said: "I have a
message. I am to tell you that your audience with the God

116

Emperor has been moved to the last position."

Most of the Bene Gesserit party had heard this and even the lowliest attendant-postulate had recognized the significance. All of the spice allotments would be fixed or *(The Gods protect us!)* even gone by that time.

"We were to have been third," Anteac had said, her voice remarkably mild in the circumstances.

"It is the God Emperor's command!"

Anteac knew that tone in a Fish Speaker. To defy it risked violence.

A morning of disasters and now this!

Anteac occupied a low stool against one wall of a tiny, almost empty room near the centre of their inadequate quarters. Beside her there was a low pallet, no more than you would assign to an acolyte! The walls were a pale, scabrous green and there was but one aging glowglobe so defective it could not be tuned out of the yellow. The room gave signs of having been a storage chamber. It smelled musty. Dents and scratches marred the black plastic of the floor.

Smoothing her black aba robe across her knees, Anteac leaned close to the postulant messenger who knelt, head bowed, directly in front of the Reverend Mother. The messenger was a doe-eyed blonde creature with the perspiration of fear and excitement on her face and neck. She wore a dusty tan robe with the dirt of the streets along its hem.

"You are certain, absolutely certain?" Anteac spoke softly to soothe the poor girl, who still trembled with the gravity of her message.

"Yes, Reverend Mother." She kept her gaze lowered.

"Go through it once more," Anteac said, and she thought: *I'm sparring for time. I heard her correctly.*

The messenger lifted her gaze to Anteac and looked directly into the totally blue eyes as all the postulants and acolytes were taught to do.

"As I was commanded, I made contact with the Ixians at their Embassy and presented your greetings. I then

117

inquired if they had any messages for me to bring back."

"Yes, yes, girl! I know. Get to the heart of it."

The messenger gulped. "The spokesman identified himself as Othwi Yake, temporary superior in the Embassy and assistant to the former Ambassador."

"You're sure he was not a Face Dancer substitute?"

"None of the signs were there, Reverend Mother."

"Very well. We know this Yake. You may continue."

"Yake said they were awaiting the arrival of the new . . ."

"Hwi Noree, the new Ambassador, yes. She's due here today."

The messenger wet her lips with her tongue.

Anteac made a mental note to return this poor creature to a more elementary training schedule. Messengers should have better self-control, although some allowance had to be made for the seriousness of this message.

"He then asked me to wait," the messenger said. "He left the room and returned shortly with a Tleilaxu, a Face Dancer, I'm sure of it. There were the certain signs of the . . ."

"I'm sure you're correct, girl," Anteac said. "Now, get to the . . ." Anteac broke off as Luyseyal entered.

"What's this I hear about messages from the Ixians and Tleilaxu?" Luyseyal asked.

"The girl's repeating it now," Anteac said.

"Why wasn't I summoned?" Anteac looked up at her fellow Truthsayer, thinking that Luyseyal might be one of the finest practitioners of the *art* but she remained too conscious of rank. Luyseyal was young, however, with the sensuous oval features of the Jessica-type, and those genes tended to carry a headstrong nature.

Anteac spoke softly: "Your acolyte said you were meditating."

Luyseyal nodded, sat down on the pallet and spoke to the messenger. "Continue."

"The Face Dancer said he had a message for the

Reverend Mothers. He used the plural," the messenger said.

"He knew there were two of us this time," Anteac said.

"Everyone knows it," Luyseyal said.

Anteac returned her full attention to the messenger. "Would you enter memory-trance now, girl, and give us the Face Dancer's words verbatim."

The messenger nodded, sat back on to her heels and clasped her hands in her lap. She took three deep breaths, closed her eyes and let her shoulders sag. When she spoke, her voice had a high-pitched, nasal twang.

"Tell the Reverend Mothers that by tonight the Empire will be rid of its God Emperor. We will strike him today before he reaches Onn. We cannot fail."

A deep breath shook the messenger. Her eyes opened and she looked up at Anteac.

"The Ixian, Yake, told me to hurry back with this message. He then touched the back of my left hand in that particular way, further convincing me that he was not . . ."

"Yake is one of ours," Anteac said. "Tell Luyseyal the message of the fingers."

The messenger looked at Luyseyal. "We have been invaded by Face Dancers and cannot move."

As Luyseyal started and began to rise from the pallet, Anteac said: "I already have taken the appropriate steps to guard our doors." Anteac looked at the messenger. "You may go now, girl. You have been adequate to your task."

"Yes, Reverend Mother." The messenger lifted her lithe body with a certain amount of grace, but there was no doubt in her movements that she knew the import of Anteac's words. *Adequate* was not *well done*.

When the messenger had gone, Luyseyal said: "She should've made some excuse to study the Embassy and find out how many of the Ixians have been replaced."

"I think not," Anteac said. "In that respect, she performed well. No, but it would have been better had she found a way to get a more detailed report from Yake. I fear we have lost him."

"The reason the Tleilaxu sent us that message is obvious, of course," Luyseyal said.

"They are really going to attack him," Anteac said.

"Naturally. It's what the *fools* would do. But I address myself to why they sent the message to us."

Anteac nodded. "They think we now have no choice except to join them."

"And if we try to warn the Lord Leto, the Tleilaxu will learn our messengers and their contacts."

"What if the Tleilaxu succeed?" Anteac asked.

"Not likely."

"We do not know their actual plan, only its general timing."

"What if this girl, this Siona, has a part in it?" Luyseyal asked.

"I have asked myself that same question. Have you heard the full report from the Guild?"

"Only the summary. Is that enough?"

"Yes, with high probability."

"You should be careful with terms such as *high probability*," Luyseyal said. "We don't want anyone thinking you're a mentat."

Anteac's tone was dry. "I presume you will not give me away."

"Do you think the Guild is right about this Siona?" Luyseyal asked.

"I do not have enough information. If they are right, she is something extraordinary."

"As the Lord Leto's father was extraordinary?"

"A Guild Navigator could conceal himself from the oracular eye of the Lord Leto's father."

"But not from the Lord Leto."

"I have read the full Guild report with care. She does not so much conceal herself and the actions around her as, well . . ."

"She fades, they said. She fades from their *sight*."

"She alone," Anteac said.

"And from the *sight* of the Lord Leto as well?"

"They do not know."

"Do we dare make contact with her?"

"Do we dare not?" Anteac asked.

"This all may be moot if the Tleilaxu . . . Anteac, we should at least make the attempt to warn him."

"We have no communications devices and there now are Fish Speaker guards at the door. They permit our people to enter, but not to leave."

"Should we speak to one of them?"

"I have thought about that. We can always say we feared they were Face Dancer substitutes."

"Guards at the door," Luyseyal muttered. "Is it possible that he knows?"

"Anything is possible."

"With the Lord Leto that's the only thing you can say for sure," Luyseyal said.

Anteac permitted herself a small sigh as she lifted herself from the stool. "How I long for the old days when we had all of the spice we could ever need."

"*Ever* was just another illusion," Luyseyal said. "I hope we have learned our lesson well, no matter how the Tleilaxu make out today."

"They will do it clumsily whatever the outcome," Anteac grumbled. "Gods! There are no good assassins to be found anymore."

"There are always the ghola Idahos," Luyseyal said.

"What did you say?" Anteac stared at her companion.

"There are always . . ."

"Yes!"

"The gholas are too slow in the body," Luyseyal said.

"But not in the head."

"What're you thinking?"

"Is it possible that the Tleilaxu . . . No, not even they could be that . . ."

"An Idaho Face Dancer?" Luyseyal whispered.

Anteac nodded mutely.

"Put it out of your mind," Luyseyal said. "They could not be that stupid."

"That's a dangerous judgment to make about Tleilaxu," Anteac said. "We must prepare ourselves for the worst. Get one of those Fish Speaker guards in here!"

> *Unceasing warfare gives rise to its own social conditions which have been similar in all epochs. People enter a permanent state of alertness to ward off attacks. You see the absolute rule of the autocrat. All new things become dangerous frontier districts—new planets, new economic areas to exploit, new ideas or new devices, visitors—everything suspect. Feudalism takes firm hold, sometimes disguised as a politbureau or similar structure, but always present. Hereditary succession follows the lines of power. The blood of the powerful dominates. The vice-regents of heaven or their equivalent apportion the wealth. And they know they must control inheritance or slowly let the power melt away. Now, do you understand Leto's Peace?*
>
> —**The Stolen Journals**

"Have the Bene Gesserit been informed of the new schedule?" Leto asked.

His entourage had entered the first shallow cut which would wind into switchbacks at the approach to the bridge across the Idaho River. The sun stood at the morning's first quarter and a few courtiers were shedding cloaks. Idaho walked with a small troop of Fish Speakers at the left flank, his uniform beginning to show traces of dust and perspiration. Walking and trotting at the speed of a Royal peregrination was hard work.

Moneo stumbled and caught himself. "They have been informed, Lord." The change of schedule had not been easy, but Moneo had learned to expect erratic shifts of direction at Festival time. He kept contingency plans at the ready.

"Are they still petitioning for a permanent Embassy on Arrakis?" Leto asked.

"Yes, Lord. I gave them the usual answer."

"A simple *'no'* should suffice," Leto said. "They no longer need to be reminded that I abhor their religious pretensions."

"Yes, Lord." Moneo held himself to just within the prescribed distance beside Leto's cart. The Worm was very much present this morning—the bodily signs quite apparent to Moneo's eyes. No doubt it was the moisture in the air. That always seemed to bring out the Worm.

"Religion always leads to rhetorical despotism," Leto said. "Before the Bene Gesserit, the Jesuits were the best at it."

"Jesuits, Lord?"

"Surely you've met them in your histories?"

"I'm not certain, Lord. When were they?"

"No matter. You learn enough about rhetorical despotism from a study of the Bene Gesserit. Of course, they do not begin by deluding themselves with it."

The Reverend Mothers are in for a bad time, Moneo told himself. *He's going to preach at them. They detest that. This could cause serious trouble.*

"What was their reaction?" Leto asked.

"I'm told they were disappointed but did not press the matter."

And Moneo thought: *I'd best prepare them for more disappointment. And they'll have to be kept away from the delegations of Ix and Tleilax.*

Moneo shook his head. This could lead to some very nasty plotting. The Duncan had better be warned.

"It leads to self-fulfilling prophecy and justifications for all manner of obscenities," Leto said.

"This . . . rhetorical despotism, Lord?"

"Yes! It shields evil behind walls of self-righteousness which are proof against all arguments against the evil."

Moneo kept a wary eye on Leto's body, noting the way the hands twisted, almost a random movement, the twitching of the great ribbed segments. *What will I do if the Worm comes out of him here?* Perspiration broke out on Moneo's forehead.

"It feeds on deliberately twisted meanings to discredit opposition," Leto said.

"All of that, Lord?"

"The Jesuits called that 'securing your power base'. It leads directly to hypocrisy which is always betrayed by the gap between actions and explanations. They never agree."

"I must study this more carefully, Lord."

"Ultimately, it rules by guilt because hypocrisy brings on the witch hunt and the demand for scapegoats."

"Shocking, Lord."

The cortège rounded a corner where the rock had been opened for a glimpse of the bridge in the distance.

"Moneo, are you paying close attention to me?"

"Yes, Lord. Indeed."

"I'm describing a tool of the religious power base."

"I recognize that, Lord."

"Then why are you so afraid?"

"Talk of religious power always makes me uneasy, Lord."

"Because you and the Fish Speakers wield it in my name?"

"Of course, Lord."

"Power bases are very dangerous because they attract people who are truly insane, people who seek power only for the sake of power. Do you understand?"

"Yes, Lord. That is why you so seldom grant petitions for appointments in your government."

"Excellent, Moneo!"

"Thank you, Lord."

"In the shadow of every religion lurks a Torquemada," Leto said. "You have never encountered that name. I know because I caused it to be expunged from all the records."

"Why was that, Lord?"

"He was an obscenity. He made living torches out of people who disagreed with him."

Moneo pitched his voice low. "Like the historians who angered you, Lord?"

"Do you question my actions, Moneo?"

"No, Lord!"

"Good. The historians died peacefully. Not a one felt the flames. Torquemada, however, delighted in commending to his god the agonized screams of his burning victims."

"How horrible, Lord."

The cortège turned another corner with a view of the bridge. The span appeared to be no closer.

Once more, Moneo studied his God Emperor. The Worm appeared no closer. Still too close, though. Moneo could feel the menace of that unpredictable presence, the Holy Presence which could kill without warning.

Moneo shuddered.

What had been the meaning of that strange . . . sermon? Moneo knew that few had ever heard the God Emperor speak thus. It was a privilege and a burden. It was part of the price paid for Leto's Peace. Generation after generation marched in their ordered way under the dictates of that peace. Only the Citadel's inner circle knew all of the infrequent breaks in that peace—the *incidents* when Fish Speakers were sent out in anticipation of violence.

Anticipation!

Moneo glanced at the now-silent Leto. The God Emperor's eyes were closed and a look of brooding had come over his face. That was another of the Worm signs—a bad one. Moneo trembled.

Did Leto anticipate even his own moments of wild violence? It was the anticipation of violence which sent tremors of awe and fear throughout the Empire. Leto knew where guards must be posted to put down a transitory uprising. He knew it before the event.

Even thinking about such matters dried Moneo's mouth. There were times, Moneo believed, when the God Emperor could read any mind. Oh, Leto employed spies. An occasional shrouded figure passed by the Fish Speakers for the climb to Leto's tower aerie or descended to the crypt. Spies, no doubt of it, but Moneo suspected they were used merely to confirm what Leto already knew.

As though to confirm the fears in Moneo's mind, Leto said: "Do not try to force an understanding of my ways, Moneo. Let understanding come of itself."

"I will try, Lord."

"No, do *not* try. Tell me, instead, if you have announced yet that there will be no changes in the spice allotments?"

"Not yet, Lord."

"Delay the announcement. I am changing my mind. You know, of course, that there will be new offers of bribes."

Moneo sighed. The amounts offered him in bribes had reached ridiculous heights. Leto, however, had appeared amused by the escalation.

"Draw them out," he had said earlier. "See how high they will go. Make it appear that you can be bribed at last."

Now, as they turned another corner with a view of the bridge, Leto asked: "Has House Corrino offered you a bribe?"

"Yes, Lord."

"Do you know the myth which says that someday House Corrino will be restored to its ancient powers?"

"I have heard it, Lord."

"Have the Corrino killed. It is a task for the Duncan. We will test him."

"So soon, Lord?"

"It is still known that melange can extend human life. Let it also be known that the spice can shorten life."

"As you command, Lord."

Moneo knew this response in himself. It was the way he spoke when he could not voice a deep objection which he felt. He also knew that the Lord Leto understood this and was amused by it. The amusement rankled.

"Try not to be impatient with me, Moneo," Leto said.

Moneo suppressed his feeling of bitterness. Bitterness brought peril. Rebels were bitter. The Duncans grew bitter before they died.

"Time has a different meaning for you than it has for me, Lord," Moneo said. "I wish I could know that meaning."

"You could but you will not."

Moneo heard rebuke in the words and fell silent, turning his thoughts instead to the melange problems. It was not often that the Lord Leto spoke of the spice, and then it usually was to set allotments or withdraw them, to apportion rewards or send the Fish Speakers after some newly revealed hoard. The greatest remaining store of spice, Moneo knew, lay in some place known only to the God Emperor. In his first days of Royal Service, Moneo had been covered in a hood and led by the Lord Leto himself to that secret place along twisting passages which Moneo had sensed were underground.

When I removed the hood we were underground.

The place had filled Moneo with awe. Great bins of melange lay all around in a gigantic room cut from native rock and illuminated by glowglobes of an ancient design with arabesques of metal scrollwork upon them. The spice had glowed radiant blue in the dim silver light. And the smell—bitter cinnamon, unmistakable. There had been water dripping nearby. Their voices had echoed against the stone.

"One day all of this will be gone," the Lord Leto had said.

Shocked, Moneo had asked: "What will Guild and Bene Gesserit do then?"

"What they are doing now, but more violently."

Staring around the gigantic room with its enormous store of melange, Moneo could only think of things he knew were happening in the Empire at that moment—bloody assassinations, piratical raids, spying and intrigue. The God Emperor kept a lid on the worst of it, but what remained was bad enough.

"The temptation," Moneo whispered.

"The temptation, indeed."

"Will there be no more melange, ever, Lord?"

"Someday, I will go back into the sand. I will be the source of spice then."

"You, Lord?"

"And I will produce something just as wonderful—more

127

sandtrout—a hybrid and a prolific breeder."

Trembling at this revelation, Moneo stared at the shadowy figure of the God Emperor who spoke of such marvels.

"The sandtrout," Lord Leto said, "will link themselves into large living bubbles to enclose this planet's water deep underground. Just as it was in the Dune times."

"All of the water, Lord?"

"Most of it. Within three hundred years, the sandworm once more will reign here. It will be a new kind of sandworm, I promise you."

"How is that, Lord?"

"It will have animal awareness and a new cunning. The spice will be more dangerous to seek and far more perilous to keep."

Moneo had looked up at the cavern's rocky ceiling, his imagination probing through the rock to the surface.

"Everything desert again, Lord?"

"Watercourses will fill with sand. Crops will be choked and killed. Trees will be covered by great moving dunes. The sand-death will spread until . . . until a subtle signal is heard in the barren lands."

"What signal, Lord?"

"The signal for the next cycle, the coming of the Maker, the coming of Shai-Hulud."

"Will that be you, Lord?"

"Yes! The great sandworm of Dune will rise once more from the deeps. This land will be again the domain of spice and worm."

"But what of the people, Lord? All of the people?"

"Many will die. Food plants and the abundant growth of this land will be parched. Without nourishment, meat animals will die."

"Will everyone go hungry, Lord?"

"Undernourishment and the old diseases will stalk the land while only the hardiest survive . . . the hardiest and most brutal."

"Must that be, Lord?"

"The alternatives are worse."

"Teach me about those alternatives, Lord."

"In time, you will know them."

As he marched beside the God Emperor in the morning light of their peregrination to Onn, Moneo could only admit that he had, indeed, learned of alternative evils.

To most of the Empire's docile citizens, Moneo knew, the firm knowledge which he held in his own head lay concealed in the Oral History, in the myths and wild stories told by infrequent mad prophets who cropped up on one planet or another to gather a short-lived following.

But I know what the Fish Speakers do.

And he knew also about evil men who sat at table, gorging themselves on rare delicacies while they watched the torture of fellow humans.

Until the Fish Speakers came, and gore erased such scenes.

"I enjoyed the way your daughter watched me," Leto said. "She was so unaware that I knew."

"Lord, I fear for her! She is my blood, my . . ."

"Mine, too, Moneo. Am I not Atreides? You would be better employed fearing for yourself."

Moneo cast a fearful glance along the God Emperor's body. The signs of the Worm remained too near. Moneo glanced at the cortège following, then along the road ahead. They now were into the steep descent, the switchbacks short and cut into high walls in the man-piled rocks of the cliff barrier which girdled the Sareer.

"Siona does not offend me, Moneo."

"But she . . ."

"Moneo! Here, in its mysterious capsule, is one of life's great secrets. To be *surprised*, to have a new thing occur, *that* is what I desire most."

"Lord, I . . ."

"New! Isn't that a radiant, a *wonderful* word?"

"If you say it, Lord."

Leto was forced to remind himself then: *Moneo is my creature. I created him.*

129

"Your child is worth almost any price to me, Moneo. You decry her companions, but there may be one among them that she will love."

Moneo cast an involuntary glance back at Duncan Idaho marching with the guards. Idaho was glaring ahead as though trying to probe each turn in the road before they reached it. He did not like this place with its high walls all around from which attack might come. Idaho had sent scouts up there in the night and Moneo knew that some of them still lurked on the heights, but there also were ravines ahead before the marchers reached the river. And there had not been enough guards to station them everywhere.

"We will depend upon the Fremen," Moneo had reassured him.

"Fremen?" Idaho did not like what he heard about the Museum Fremen.

"At least they can sound an alarm against intruders," Moneo had said.

"You saw them and asked them to do that?"

"Of course."

Moneo had not dared to broach the subject of Siona to Idaho. Time enough for that later, but now the God Emperor had said a disturbing thing. Had there been a change in plans?

Moneo returned his attention to the God Emperor and lowered his voice.

"Love a companion, Lord? But you said the Duncan . . ."

"I said *love*, not *breed with!*"

Moneo trembled, thinking of how his own mating had been arranged, the wrenching away from . . .

No! Best not follow those memories!

There had been affection, even a real love . . . later, but in the first days . . .

"You are woolgathering again, Moneo."

"Forgive me, Lord, but when you speak of love . . ."

"You think I have no tender thoughts?"

"It's not that, Lord, but . . ."

130

"You think I have no memories of love and breeding, then?" The cart swerved toward Moneo, forcing him to dodge away, frightened by the glowering look on the Lord Leto's face.

"Lord, I beg your . . ."

"This *body* may never have known such tenderness, but *all* of the memories are mine!"

Moneo could see the signs of the Worm growing more dominant in the God Emperor's body and there was no escaping recognition of this mood.

I am in grave danger. We all are.

Moneo grew aware of every sound around him, the creaking of the Royal Cart, the coughs and low conversation from the entourage, the feet on the roadway. There was an exhalation of cinnamon from the God Emperor. The air here between the enclosing rock walls still held its morning chill and there was dampness from the river.

Was it the moisture bringing out the Worm?

"Listen to me, Moneo, as though your life depended on it."

"Yes, Lord," Moneo whispered, and he knew his life did depend on the care he took now, not only in listening but in observing.

"Part of me dwells forever underground without thought," Leto said. "That part reacts. It does things without a care for knowing or logic."

Moneo nodded, his attention glued on the God Emperor's face. Were the eyes about to glaze?

"I am forced to stand off and watch such things, nothing more," Leto said. "Such a reaction could cause your death. The choice is not mine. Do you hear?"

"I hear you, Lord," Moneo whispered.

"There is no such thing as *choice* in such an event! You accept it, merely accept it. You will never understand it or know it. What do you say to that?"

"I fear the unknown, Lord."

"But I don't fear it. Tell me why!"

131

Moneo had been expecting a crisis such as this and, now that it had come, he almost welcomed it. He knew that his life depended on his answer. He stared at his God Emperor, mind racing.

"It is because of all your memories, Lord."

"Yes?"

An incomplete answer, then. Moneo grasped at words. "You see everything that we know . . . all of it as it once was—unknown! A surprise to you . . . a surprise must be merely something new for you to know?" As he spoke, Moneo realized he had put a defensive question mark on something that should have been a bold statement, but the God Emperor only smiled.

"For such wisdom I grant you a boon, Moneo. What is your wish?"

Sudden relief only opened a path for other fears to emerge. "Could I bring Siona back to the Citadel?"

"That will cause me to test her sooner."

"She must be separated from her companions, Lord."

"Very well."

"My Lord is gracious."

"I am selfish."

The God Emperor turned away from Moneo then and fell silent.

Looking along the segmented body, Moneo observed that the Worm's signs had subsided somewhat. This had turned out well after all. He thought then of the Fremen with their petition and fear returned.

That was a mistake. They will only arouse Him again. Why did I say they could present their petition?

The Fremen would be waiting up ahead, marshalled on this side of the river with their foolish papers waving in their hands.

Moneo marched in silence, his apprehension increasing with each step.

132

Over here sand blows; over there sand blows.
Over there a rich man waits; over here I wait.

—The Voice of Shai-Hulud,
from the Oral History

Sister Chenoeh's account, found among her papers after her death:

I obey both my tenets as a Bene Gesserit and the commands of the God Emperor by withholding these words from my report while secreting them that they may be found when I am gone. For the Lord Leto said to me: "You will return to your Superiors with my message, but these words keep secret for now. I will visit my rage upon your Sisterhood if you fail."

As the Reverend Mother Syaksa warned me before I left: "You must do nothing which will bring down his wrath upon us."

While I ran beside the Lord Leto on that short peregrination of which I have spoken, I thought to ask him about his likeness to a Reverend Mother. I said:

"Lord, I know how it is that a Reverend Mother acquires the memories of her ancestors and of others. How was it with you?"

"It was a design of our genetic history and the working of the spice. My twin sister, Ghanima, and I were awakened in the womb, aroused before birth into the presence of our ancestral memories."

"Lord . . . my Sisterhood calls that Abomination."

"And rightly so," the Lord Leto said. "The ancestral numbers can be overwhelming. And who knows before the event which force will command such a horde—good or evil?"

"Lord, how did you overcome such a force?"

"I did not overcome it," the Lord Leto said. "But the

133

persistence of the pharaonic model saved both Ghani and me. Do you know that model, Sister Chenoeh?"

"We of the Sisterhood are well coached in history, Lord."

"Yes, but you do not think of this as I do," the Lord Leto said. "I speak of a disease of government which was caught by the Greeks who spread it to the Romans who distributed it so far and wide that it never has completely died out."

"Does my Lord speak riddles?"

"No riddles. I hate this thing but it saved us. Ghani and I formed powerful internal alliances with ancestors who followed the pharaonic model. They helped us form a mingled identity within that long-dormant mob."

"I find this disturbing, Lord."

"And well you should."

"Why are you telling me this now, Lord? You have never answered one of us before in this manner, not that I know of."

"Because you listen well, Sister Chenoeh; because you will obey me and because I will never see you again."

The Lord Leto spoke those strange words to me and then he asked:

"Why have you not inquired about what your Sisterhood calls my *insane tyranny*?"

Emboldened by his manner, I ventured to say: "Lord, we know about some of your bloody executions. They trouble us."

The Lord Leto then did a strange thing. He closed his eyes as we went, and he said:

"Because I know you have been trained to record accurately whatever words you hear, I will speak to you now, Sister Chenoeh, as though you were a page in one of my journals. Preserve these words well for I do not want them lost."

I assure my Sisterhood now that what follows, exactly as he spoke them, are the words uttered then by the Lord Leto:

"To my certain knowledge, when I am no longer consciously present here among you, when I am here only as a fearsome creature of the desert, many people will look back upon me as a tyrant.

"Fair enough. I have been tyrannical.

"A tyrant—not fully human, not insane, merely a tyrant. But even ordinary tyrants have motives and feelings beyond those usually assigned them by facile historians, and they will think of me as a *great* tyrant. Thus, my feelings and motives are a legacy I would preserve lest history distort them too much. History has a way of magnifying some characteristics while it discards others.

"People will try to understand me and to frame me in their words. They will seek truth. But the truth always carries the ambiguity of the words used to express it.

"You will not understand me. The harder you try the more remote I will become until finally I vanish into eternal myth—a Living God at last!

"That's it, you see. I am not a leader nor even a guide. A god. Remember that. I am quite different from leaders and guides. Gods need take no responsibility for anything except genesis. Gods accept everything and thus accept nothing. Gods must be identifiable yet remain anonymous. Gods do not need a spirit world. My spirits dwell within me, answerable to my slightest summons. I share with you, because it pleases me to do so, what I have learned about them and through them. They are *my* truth.

"Beware of *the* truth, gentle sister. Although much sought after, truth can be dangerous to the seeker. Myths and reassuring lies are much easier to find and believe. If you find a truth, even a temporary one, it can demand that you make painful changes. Conceal your truths within words. Natural ambiguity will protect you then. Words are much easier to absorb than are the sharp delphic stabs of wordless portent. With words, you can cry out in the chorus:

"'Why didn't someone warn me?'

"But I did warn you. I warned you by example, not with words.

135

"There are inevitably more than enough words. You record them in your marvellous memory even now. And someday, my journals will be discovered—more words. I warn you that you read my words at your peril. The wordless movement of terrible events lies just below their surface. Be deaf! You do not need to hear or, hearing, you do not need to remember. How soothing it is to forget. And how dangerous!

"Words such as mine have long been recognized for their mysterious power. There is a secret knowledge here which can be used to rule the forgetful. My truths are the substance of myths and lies which tyrants have always counted on to manoeuvre the masses for selfish design.

"You see? I share it all with you, even the greatest mystery of all time, the mystery by which I compose my life. I reveal it to you in words:

"The only past which endures lies wordlessly within you."

The God Emperor fell silent then. I dared to ask: "Are those all of the words that my Lord wishes me to preserve?"

"Those are the words," the God Emperor said, and I thought he sounded tired, discouraged. He had the sound of someone uttering a last testament. I recalled that he had said he would never see me again, and I was fearful but I praise my teachers because the fear did not emerge in my voice.

"Lord Leto," I said, "these journals of which you speak, for whom are they written?"

"For posterity after the span of millennia. I personalize those distant readers, Sister Chenoeh. I think of them as distant cousins filled with family curiosities. They are intent on unravelling the dramas which only I can recount. They want to make the personal connections to their own lives. They want the meanings, the *truth*!"

"But you warn us against truth, Lord," I said.

"Indeed! All of history is a malleable instrument in my hands. Ohhh, I have accumulated all of these pasts and I possess every *fact*—yet the facts are mine to use as I will

136

and, even using them truthfully, I change them. What am I speaking to you now? What is a diary, a journal? Words."

Again, the Lord Leto fell silent. I weighed the portent of what he had said, weighed it against the admonition of Reverend Mother Syaksa, and against the things that the God Emperor had uttered to me earlier. He said I was his messenger and thus I felt that I was under his protection and might dare more than any other. Thus it was that I said:

"Lord Leto, you have said that you will not see me again. Does that mean you are about to die?"

I swear it here in my record of this event, the Lord Leto laughed! Then he said:

"No, gentle sister, it is you who will die. You will not live to be a Reverend Mother. Do not be saddened by this for by your presence here today, by carrying my message back to the Sisterhood, by preserving my secret words as well, you will achieve a far greater status. You become here an integral part of my myth. Our distant cousins will pray to you for intercession with me!"

Again, the Lord Leto laughed, but it was gentle laughter and he smiled upon me warmly. I find it difficult to record here with that accuracy which I am enjoined to employ in every accounting such as this one, yet in the moment that the Lord Leto spoke these terrible words to me, I felt a profound bond of friendship with him, as though some physical thing had leaped between us, tying us together in a way that words cannot fully describe. It was not until the instant of this experience that I understood what he had meant by the *wordless truth*. It happened, yet I cannot describe it.

ARCHIVIST'S NOTE: Because of intervening events, the discovery of this private record is now little more than a footnote to history, interesting because it contains one of the earliest references to the God Emperor's secret journals. For those wishing to explore further into this account, reference may be made to Archive Records, sub-headings: *Chenoeh, Holy Sister Quintinius Violet; Chenoeh*

Report, The, and *Melange Rejection, Medical Aspects of.*
    (Footnote: Sister Quintinius Violet Chenoeh died in the fifty-third year of her Sisterhood, the cause being ascribed to melange incompatibility during her attempt to achieve the status of Reverend Mother.)

> Our ancestor, Assur-nasir-apli, who was known as the cruellest of the cruel, seized the throne by slaying his own father and starting the reign of the sword. His conquests included the Urumia Lake region which led him to Commagene and Khabur. His son received tribute from the Shuites, from Tyre, Sidon, Gebel and even from Jehu, son of Omri, whose very name struck terror into thousands. The conquests which began with Assur-nasir-apli carried arms into Media and later into Israel, Damascus, Edom, Arpad, Babylon and Umlias. Does anyone remember these names and places now? I have given you enough clues: try to name the planet.

> **—The Stolen Journals**

The air was stagnant deep within the carved cut of the Royal Roadway leading down to the flat approach to the bridge across the Idaho River. The road turned to the right out of the man-made immensity of rock and earth. Moneo, walking beside the Royal Cart, saw the paved ribbon leading across a narrow ridgetop to the lacery of plasteel which was the bridge almost a kilometre distant.

The river, still deep in a chasm, turned inward toward him on the right and then ran straight through multistage cascades toward the far side of the Forbidden Forest where the confining walls dropped down almost to the level of the water. There at the outskirts of Onn lay the orchards and gardens which helped to feed the city.

Moneo, looking at the distant stretch of river visible from where he walked, saw that the canyon top was bathed in light while the water still flowed in shadows broken only by

138

the faint silvery shimmering of the cascades.

Straight ahead of him, the road to the bridge was brilliant in sunlight, the dark shadows of erosion gullies on both sides set off like arrows to indicate the correct path. The rising sun already had made the roadway hot. The air trembled above it, a warning of the day to come.

We'll be safely into the city before the worst of the heat, Moneo thought.

He trotted along in the weary patience which always overcame him at this point, his gaze fixed forward in expectation of the petitioning Museum Fremen. They would come up out of one of the erosion gullies, he knew. Somewhere on this side of the bridge. That was the agreement he had made with them. No way to stop them now. And the God Emperor still showed signs of the Worm.

Leto heard the Fremen before any of his party either saw or heard them.

"Listen!" he called.

Moneo came to full alert.

Leto rolled his body on the cart, arched the front upward out of the bubble shield and peered ahead.

Moneo knew this kind of thing well. The God Emperor's senses, so much more acute than any of those around him, had detected a disturbance ahead. The Fremen were beginning to move up to the road. Moneo let himself fall back one pace and moved out to the limit of his dutiful position. He heard it himself then.

There was the sound of gravel spilling.

The first Fremen appeared, coming up out of gullies on both sides of the road no more than a hundred metres ahead of the Royal party.

Duncan Idaho dashed forward and slowed himself to a trot beside Moneo.

"Are those the Fremen?" Idaho asked.

"Yes." Moneo spoke with his attention on the God Emperor, who had lowered his bulk back on to the cart.

The Museum Fremen assembled on the road, dropped their outer robes to reveal inner robes of red and purple.

139

Moneo gasped. The Fremen were togged out as pilgrims with some kind of black garment under the colourful robes. The ones in the foreground waved rolls of paper as the entire group began singing and dancing toward the royal entourage.

"A petition, Lord," the leaders cried. "Hear our petition!"

"Duncan!" Leto cried. "Clear them out!"

Fish Speakers surged forward through the courtiers as their Lord shouted. Idaho waved them forward and began running toward the approaching mob. The guards formed a phalanx, Idaho at the apex.

Leto slammed closed the bubble cover of his cart, increased its speed and called out in an amplified roar: "Clear away! Clear away!"

The Museum Fremen, seeing the guards run forward, the cart picking up speed as Leto shouted, made as though to open a path up the centre of the road. Moneo, forced to run to keep up with the cart, his attention momentarily on the running footsteps of the courtiers behind him, saw the first unexpected change of programme by the Fremen.

As one person, the chanting throng threw off the pilgrim cloaks to reveal black uniforms identical to those worn by Idaho.

What are they doing? Moneo wondered.

Even while he was asking himself this question, Moneo saw the flesh of the approaching faces melt away in Face Dancer mockery, every face resolving into a likeness of Duncan Idaho.

"Face Dancers!" someone screamed.

Leto, too, had been distracted by the confusion of events, the sounds of many feet running on the road, the barked orders as Fish Speakers formed their phalanx. He had applied more speed to his cart, closing the distance between himself and the guards, beginning then to ring a warning bell and sound the cart's distortion klaxon. White noise blared across the scene, disorienting even some of the Fish Speakers who were conditioned to it.

140

At that instant, the petitioners discarded their pilgrim cloaks and began the transformation manoeuvre, their faces flickering into likenesses of Duncan Idaho. Leto heard the scream: "Face Dancers!" He identified its source, a consort clerk in Royal Accounting.

Leto's initial reaction was amusement.

Guards and Face Dancers collided. Screams and shouts replaced the petitioners' chanting. Leto recognized Tleilaxu battle commands. A thick knot of Fish Speakers formed around the black-clad figure of his Duncan. The guards were obeying Leto's oft-repeated instruction to protect their ghola-commander.

But how will they tell him from the others?

Leto brought his cart almost to a stop. He could see Fish Speakers on the left swinging their stunclubs. Sunlight flashed from knives. Then came the buzzing hum of lasguns, a sound Leto's grandmother had once described as "the most terrible in our universe". More hoarse shouts and screams erupted from the vanguard.

Leto reacted with the first sound of lasguns. He swerved the Royal Cart off the road to his right, shifted from wheels to suspensors and drove the vehicle back like a battering ram into a clot of Face Dancers trying to enter the fray from his side. Turning in a tight arc, he hit more of them on the other side, feeling the crushing impact of flesh against plasteel, a red spray of blood, then he was down off the road into an erosion gully. The brown serrated sides of the gully flashed past him. He swept upward and swooped across the river canyon to a high, rock-girt viewpoint beside the Royal Road. There, he stopped and turned, well beyond the range of hand-held lasguns.

What a surprise!

Laughter shook his great body with grunting, trembling convulsions. Slowly, the amusement subsided.

From his vantage, Leto could see the bridge and the area of the attack. Bodies lay in tangled disarray all across the scene and into the flanking gullies. He recognized courtier finery, Fish Speaker uniforms, the bloodied black of the

141

Face Dancer disguises. Surviving courtiers huddled in the background while Fish Speakers sped among the fallen making sure the attackers were dead with a swift knife stroke into each body.

Leto swept his gaze across the scene searching for the black uniform of his Duncan. There was not one such uniform standing. Not one! Leto put down a surge of frustration, then saw a clutch of Fish Speaker guards among the courtiers and . . . and a naked figure there.

Naked!

It was his Duncan! *Naked! Of course!* The Duncan Idaho *without* a uniform was not a Face Dancer.

Again, laughter shook him. Surprises on both sides. What a shock that must have been to the attackers. Obviously, they had not prepared themselves for such a response.

Leto eased his cart out on to the roadway, dropped the wheels into position and rolled down to the bridge. He crossed the bridge with a sense of *déjà vu*, aware of the countless bridges in his memories, the crossings to view the aftermaths of battles. As he cleared the bridge, Idaho broke from the knot of guards and ran toward him, skipping and dodging the bodies. Leto stopped his cart and stared at the naked runner. The Duncan was like a Greek warrior-messenger dashing toward his commander to report the outcome of battle. The condensation of history stunned Leto's memories.

Idaho skidded to a stop beside the cart. Leto opened the bubble cover.

"Face Dancers, every damned one!" Idaho panted.

Not trying to conceal his amusement, Leto asked: "Whose idea was it to strip off your uniform?"

"Mine! But they wouldn't let me fight!"

Moneo came running up then with a group of guards. One of the Fish Speakers tossed a guard's blue cloak to Idaho, calling out: "We're trying to salvage a complete uniform from the bodies."

"I ripped mine off," Idaho explained.

"Did any of the Face Dancers escape?" Moneo asked.

"Not a one," Idaho said. "I admit your women are good fighters, but why wouldn't they let me get into . . ."

"Because they have instructions to protect you," Leto said. "They always protect the most valuable . . ."

"Four of them died getting me out of there!" Idaho said.

"We lost more than thirty people all together, Lord," Moneo said. "We're still counting."

"How many Face Dancers?" Leto asked.

"It looks like there were an even fifty of them, Lord," Moneo said. He spoke softly, a stricken look on his face.

Leto began to chuckle.

"Why are you laughing?" Idaho demanded. "More than thirty of our people . . ."

"But the Tleilaxu were so inept," Leto said. "Do you not realize that only about five hundred years ago they would've been far more efficient, far more dangerous. Imagine them daring that foolish masquerade! And not anticipating your brilliant response!"

"They had lasguns," Idaho said.

Leto twisted his bulky forward segments around and pointed at a hole burned in his canopy almost at the cart's midpoint. A melted and fused starburst surrounded the hole.

"They hit several other places underneath," Leto said. "Fortunately, they did not damage any suspensors or wheels."

Idaho stared at the hole in the canopy, noted that it lined up with Leto's body.

"Didn't it hit you?" he asked.

"Oh, yes," Leto said.

"Are you injured?"

"I am immune to lasguns," Leto lied. "When we get time, I will demonstrate."

"Well, I'm not immune," Idaho said. "And neither are your guards. Every one of us should have a shield belt."

"Shields are banned throughout the Empire," Leto said. "It is a capital offence to have a shield."

"The question of shields," Moneo ventured.

Idaho thought Moneo was asking for an explanation of shields and said: "The belts develop a force field which will repel any object trying to enter at a dangerous speed. They have one major drawback. If you intersect the force field with a lasgun beam, the resultant explosion rivals that of a very large fusion bomb. Attacker and attacked go together."

Moneo only stared at Idaho, who nodded.

"I see why they were banned," Idaho said. "I presume the Great Convention against atomics is still in force and working well?"

"Working even better since we searched out all of the Family atomics and removed them to a safe place," Leto said. "But we do not have time to discuss such matters here."

"We can discuss one thing," Idaho said. "Walking out here in the open is too dangerous. We should . . ."

"It is the tradition and we will continue it," Leto said.

Moneo leaned close to Idaho's ear. "You are disturbing the Lord Leto," he said.

"But . . ."

"Have you not considered how much easier it is to control a *walking* population?" Moneo asked.

Idaho jerked around to stare into Moneo's eyes with sudden comprehension.

Leto took the opportunity to begin issuing orders. "Moneo, see that there is no sign of the attack left here, not one spot of blood or a torn rag of clothing—nothing."

"Yes, Lord."

Idaho turned at the sound of people pressing close around them, saw that all of the survivors, even the wounded wearing emergency bandages, had come up to listen.

"All of you," Leto said, addressing the throng around the cart. "Not a word of this. Let the Tleilaxu worry." He looked at Idaho.

"Duncan, how did those Face Dancers get into a region

where only my Museum Fremen should roam free?"

Idaho glanced involuntarily at Moneo.

"Lord, it is my fault," Moneo said. "I was the one who arranged for the Fremen to present their petition here. I even reassured Duncan Idaho about them."

"I recall your mentioning the petition," Leto said.

"I thought it might amuse you, Lord."

"Petitions do not amuse me, they annoy me. I am especially annoyed by petitions from people whose one purpose in my scheme of things is to preserve the ancient forms."

"Lord, it was just that you have spoken so many times about the boredom of these peregrinations into . . ."

"But I am not here to ease the boredom of others!"

"Lord?"

"The Museum Fremen understand nothing about the old ways. They are only good at going through the motions. This naturally bores them and their petitions always seek to introduce changes. *That's* what annoys me. I will not permit changes. Now, where did you learn of the supposed petition?"

"From the Fremen themselves," Moneo said. "A dele . . ." He broke off, scowling.

"Were the members of the delegation known to you?"

"Of course, Lord. Otherwise I'd . . ."

"They're dead," Idaho said.

Moneo looked at him, uncomprehending.

"The people you knew were killed and replaced by Face Dancer mimics," Idaho said.

"I have been remiss," Leto said. "I should've taught all of you how to detect Face Dancers. It will be corrected now that they grow foolishly bold."

"Why are they so bold?" Idaho asked.

"Perhaps to distract us from something else," Moneo said.

Leto smiled at Moneo. Under the stress of personal threat, the majordomo's mind worked well. He had failed his Lord by mistaking Face Dancer mimics for known Fremen. Now, Moneo felt that his continued service might

145

depend upon those abilities for which the God Emperor had originally chosen him.

"And now we have time to prepare ourselves," Leto said.

"Distract us from what?" Idaho demanded.

"From another plot in which they participate," Leto said. "They think I will punish them severely for this, but the Tleilaxu core remains safe because of you, Duncan."

"They didn't intend to fail here," Idaho said.

"But it was a contingency for which they were prepared," Moneo said.

"They believe I will not destroy them because they hold the original cells of my Duncan Idaho," Leto said. "Do you understand, Duncan?"

"Are they right?" Idaho demanded.

"They approach being wrong," Leto said. He returned his attention to Moneo. "No signs of this event must go with us to Onn. Fresh uniforms, new guards to replace the dead and wounded . . . everything just as it was."

"There are dead among your courtiers, Lord," Moneo said.

"Replace them!"

Moneo bowed. "Yes, Lord."

"And send for a new canopy to my cart!"

"As my Lord commands."

Leto backed his cart a few paces away, turned it and headed for the bridge, calling back to Idaho. "Duncan, you will accompany me."

Slowly at first, reluctance heavy in every movement, Idaho left Moneo and the others, then increasing his pace, came up beside the cart's open bubble and walked there while staring in at Leto.

"What troubles you, Duncan?" Leto asked.

"Do you really think of me as *your* Duncan?"

"Of course, just as you think of me as *your* Leto."

"Why didn't you *know* this attack was coming?"

"Through my vaunted prescience?"

"Yes!"

"The Face Dancers have not attracted my attention for a long time," Leto said.

"I presume that is changed now?"

"Not to any great degree."

"Why not?"

"Because Moneo was correct. I will not let myself be distracted."

"Could they really have killed you there?"

"A distinct possibility. You know, Duncan, few understand what a disaster my end will be."

"What're the Tleilaxu plotting?"

"A snare, I think. A lovely snare. They have sent me a signal, Duncan."

"What signal?"

"There is a new escalation in the desperate motives which drive some of my subjects."

They left the bridge and began the climb to Leto's viewpoint. Idaho walked in a fermenting silence.

At the top, Leto lifted his gaze over the far cliffs and looked at the barrens of the Sareer.

The lamentations of those in his entourage who had lost loved ones continued at the attack scene beyond the bridge. With his acute hearing, Leto could separate Moneo's voice warning them that the time of mourning was necessarily short. They had other loved ones at the Citadel and they well knew the God Emperor's wrath.

Their tears will be gone and smiles will be pasted on their faces by the time we reach Onn, Leto thought. *They think I spurn them! What does that really matter? This is a flickering nuisance among the short-lived and the short-thoughted.*

The view of the desert soothed him. He could not see the river in its canyon from this point without turning completely around and looking toward the Festival City. The Duncan remained mercifully silent beside the cart. Turning his gaze slightly to the left, Leto could see an edge of the Forbidden Forest. Against that glimpse of verdant landscape, his memory suddenly compressed the Sareer into a tiny, weak remnant of the planet-wide desert which once

147

had been so mighty that all men feared it, even the wild Fremen who had roamed it.

It is the river, Leto thought. *If I turn, I will see the thing that I have done.*

The man-made chasm through which the Idaho River tumbled was only an extension of the gap which Paul-Muad'Dib had blasted through the towering Shield Wall for the passage of his worm-mounted legions. Where water flowed now, Muad'Dib had led his Fremen out of a coriolis storm's dust into history . . . *and into this.*

Leto heard Moneo's familiar footsteps, the sounds of the majordomo labouring up to the viewpoint. Moneo came up to stand beside Idaho and paused a moment to catch his breath.

"How long until we can go on?" Idaho asked.

Moneo waved him to silence and addressed Leto. "Lord, we have had a message from Onn. The Bene Gesserit send word that the Tleilaxu will attack before you reach the bridge."

Idaho snorted. "Aren't they a little late?"

"It is not their fault," Moneo said. "The captain of the Fish Speaker guard would not believe them."

Other members of Leto's entourage began trickling on to the viewpoint level. Some of them appeared drugged, still in shock. The Fish Speakers moved briskly among them, commanding a show of good spirits.

"Remove the guard from the Bene Gesserit Embassy," Leto said. "Send them a message. Tell them that their audience will still be the last one, but they are not to fear this. Tell them that the last will be first. They will know the allusion."

"What about the Tleilaxu?" Idaho asked.

Leto kept his attention on Moneo. "Yes, the Tleilaxu. We will send them a signal."

"Yes, Lord?"

"When I order it, and not until then, you will have the Tleilaxu Ambassador publicly flogged and expelled."

"Lord!"

"You disagree?"

"If we are to keep this secret . . ." Moneo glanced over his shoulder, ". . . how will you explain the flogging?"

"We will not explain."

"We will give no reason at all?"

"No reason."

"But, Lord, the rumours and the stories that will . . ."

"I am reacting, Moneo! Let them sense the underground part of me which does things without my knowing because it has not the wherewithal of knowing."

"This will cause great fear, Lord."

A gruff burst of laughter escaped Idaho. He stepped between Moneo and the cart. "He does a kindness to this Ambassador! There've been rulers who would've killed the fool over a slow fire."

Moneo tried to speak to Leto around Idaho's shoulder. "But, Lord, this action will confirm for the Tleilaxu that you were attacked."

"They already know that," Leto said. "But they will not talk about it."

"And when none of the attackers return . . ." Idaho said.

"Do you understand, Moneo?" Leto asked. "When we march into Onn apparently unscathed, the Tleilaxu will believe they have suffered utter failure."

Moneo glanced around at the Fish Speakers and courtiers listening spellbound to this conversation. Seldom had any of them heard such a revealing exchange between the God Emperor and his most immediate aides.

"When will my Lord signal punishment of the Ambassador?" Moneo asked.

"During the audience."

Leto heard 'thopters coming, saw the glint of sunlight on their wings and rotors and, when he focused intently, made out the fresh canopy for his cart slung beneath one of them.

"Have this damaged canopy returned to the Citadel and restored," Leto said, still peering at the approaching 'thopters. "If questions are asked, tell the artisans to say that it's just routine, another canopy scratched by blown sand."

Moneo sighed. "Yes, Lord. It will be done as you say."

"Come, Moneo, cheer up," Leto said. "Walk beside me as we continue." Turning to Idaho, Leto said, "Take some of the guards and scout ahead."

"Do you think there'll be another attack?" Idaho asked.

"No, but it'll give the guards something to do. And get a fresh uniform. I don't want you wearing something that has been contaminated by the dirty Tleilaxu."

Idaho moved off in obedience.

Leto signalled Moneo to come closer, closer. When Moneo was bending into the cart, face less than a metre from Leto's, Leto pitched his voice low and said:

"There is a special lesson here for you, Moneo."

"Lord, I know I should have suspected the Face . . ."

"Not the Face Dancers! It is a lesson for your daughter."

"Siona? What could she . . ."

"Tell her this: In a fragile way, she is like that force within me which acts without knowing. Because of her, I remember what it was to be human . . . and to love."

Moneo stared at Leto without comprehension.

"Simply give her the message," Leto said. "You needn't try to understand it. Merely tell her my words."

Moneo withdrew. "As my Lord commands."

Leto closed the bubble canopy, making a single unit of the entire cover for the approaching crews on the 'thopters to replace.

Moneo turned and glanced around at the people waiting on the flat area of the viewpoint. He noted then a thing he had not observed earlier, a thing revealed by the disarray which some of the people had not yet repaired. Some of the courtiers had fitted themselves with delicate devices to assist their hearing. They had been eavesdropping. And such devices could only come from Ix.

I will warn the Duncan and the guard, Moneo thought.

Somehow, he thought of this discovery as a symptom of rot. How could they prohibit such things when most of the courtiers and the Fish Speakers either knew or suspected that the God Emperor traded with Ix for forbidden machines?

> *I am beginning to hate water. The sandtrout skin which impels my metamorphosis has learned the sensitivities of the worm. Moneo and many of my guards know my aversion. Only Moneo suspects the truth, that this marks an important waypoint. I can feel my ending in it, not soon as Moneo measures time, but soon enough as I endure it. Sandtrout swarmed to water in the Dune days, a problem during the early stages of our symbiosis. The enforcement of my willpower controlled the urge then, and until we reached a time of balance. Now, I must avoid water because there are no other sandtrout, only the half-dormant creatures of my skin. Without sandtrout to bring this world back to desert, Shai-Hulud will not emerge; the sandworm cannot evolve until the land is parched. I am their only hope.*

> **—The Stolen Journals**

It was mid-afternoon before the Royal Entourage came down the final slope into the precincts of the Festival City. Throngs lined the streets to greet them, held back by tight lines of ursine Fish Speakers in uniforms of Atreides green, their stunclubs crossed and linked.

As the Royal party approached, a bedlam of shouts erupted from the crowd. Then the Fish Speaker guardians began to chant:

"Siaynoq! Siaynoq! Siaynoq!"

As it echoed back and forth between the high buildings, the chanted word had a strange effect on the crowd which was not initiated into the meanings of it. A wave of silence swept up the thronged avenues while the guardians continued to chant. People stared in awe at the women armed

151

with stunclubs who guarded the royal passage, the women who chanted while they fixed their gaze on the face of their passing Lord.

Idaho, marching with the Fish Speaker guards behind the Royal Cart, heard the chant for the first time and felt the hair on the back of his neck rise.

Moneo marched beside the cart, not looking left or right. He had once asked Leto the meaning of the word.

"I give the Fish Speakers only one ritual," Leto had said. They had been in the God Emperor's audience chamber beneath Onn's central plaza at the time, with Moneo fatigued after a long day of directing the flow of dignitaries who crowded the city for Decennial festivities.

"What has the chanting of that word to do with it, Lord?"

"The ritual is called Siaynoq—the Feast of Leto. It is the adoration of my person in my presence."

"An ancient ritual, Lord?"

"It was with the Fremen before they were Fremen. But the keys to the Festival secrets died with the old ones. Only I remember them now. I recreate the Festival in my own likeness and for my own ends."

"Then the Museum Fremen do not use this ritual?"

"Never. It is mine and mine alone. I claim eternal right to it because I *am* that ritual."

"It is a strange word, Lord. I have never heard its like."

"It had many meanings, Moneo. If I tell them to you, will you hold them secret?"

"My Lord commands!"

"Never share this with another nor reveal to the Fish Speakers what I tell you now."

"I swear it, Lord."

"Very well. Siaynoq means giving honour to one who speaks with sincerity. It signifies the remembrance of things which are spoken with sincerity."

"But, Lord, doesn't sincerity really mean that the speaker *believes* . . . has faith in what is said?"

"Yes, but Siaynoq also contains the idea of light as that

152

which reveals reality. You continue to shine light on what you see."

"Reality . . . that is a very ambiguous word, Lord."

"Indeed! But Siaynoq also stands for fermentation because reality—or the belief that you know a reality, which is the same thing—always sets up a ferment in the universe."

"All of that in a single word, Lord?"

"And more! Siaynoq also contains the summoning to prayer *and* the name of the Recording Angel, Sihaya, who interrogates the newly dead."

"A great burden for one word, Lord."

"Words can carry any burden we wish. All that's required is agreement and a tradition upon which to build."

"Why do I not speak of this to the Fish Speakers, Lord?"

"Because this is a word reserved for them. They resent my sharing it with a male."

Moneo's lips pressed into a thin line of remembrance as he marched beside the Royal Cart into the Festival City. He had heard the Fish Speakers chant the God Emperor into their presence many times since that first explanation and had even added his own meanings to the strange word.

It means mystery and prestige. It means power. It invokes a licence to act in the name of God.

"Siaynoq! Siaynoq! Siaynoq!"

The word had a sour sound in Moneo's ears.

They were well into the city, almost to the central plaza. Afternoon sunlight came down the Royal Road behind the procession to illuminate the way. It gave brilliance to the citizenry's colourful costumes. It shone on the upturned faces of the Fish Speakers lining the way.

Marching beside the cart with the guards, Idaho put down a first alarm as the chant continued. He asked one of the Fish Speakers beside him about it.

"It is not a word for men," she said. "But sometimes the Lord shares Siaynoq with a Duncan."

A *Duncan*! He had asked Leto about it earlier and disliked the mysterious evasions.

153

"You will learn about it soon enough."

Idaho relegated the chant to the background while he looked around him with a tourist's curiosity. In preparation for his duties as Guard Commander, Idaho had inquired after the history of Onn, finding that he shared Leto's wry amusement in the fact that it was the Idaho River flowing nearby.

They had been in one of the large open rooms of the Citadel at the time, an airy place full of morning light and with wide tables upon which Fish Speaker archivists had spread charts of the Sareer and of Onn. Leto had wheeled his cart on to a ramp which allowed him to look down on the charts. Idaho stood across a chart-littered table from him studying the plan of the Festival City.

"Peculiar design for a city," Idaho mused.

"It has one primary purpose—public viewing of the God Emperor."

Idaho looked up at the segmented body on the cart, brought his gaze to the cowled face. He wondered if he would ever find it easy to look on that bizarre figure.

"But that's only once every ten years," Idaho said.

"At the Great Sharing, yes."

"And you just close it down between times?"

"The Embassies are there, the offices of the trading factors, the Fish Speaker schools, the service and maintenance cadres, the museums and libraries."

"What space do they take?" Idaho rapped the chart with his knuckles. "A tenth of the city at most?"

"Less than that."

Idaho let his gaze wander pensively over the chart.

"Are there other purposes in this design, m'Lord?"

"It is dominated by the need for public viewing of my person."

"There must be clerks, government workers, even common labourers. Where do they live?"

"Mostly in the suburbs."

Idaho pointed at the chart. "These tiers of apartments?"

"Note the balconies, Duncan."

"All around the plaza." He leaned close to peer down at the chart. "That plaza is two kilometres across!"

"Note how the balconies are set back in steps right up to the ring of spires. The elite are lodged in the spires."

"And they can all look down on you in the plaza?"

"You do not like that?"

"There's not even an energy barrier to protect you!"

"What an inviting target I make."

"Why do you do it?"

"There is a delightful myth about the design of Onn. I foster and promote the myth. It is said that once there lived a people whose ruler was required to walk among them once a year in total darkness, without weapons or armour. The mythical ruler wore a luminescent suit while he made his walk through the night-shrouded throng of his subjects. And his subjects—they wore black for the occasion and were never searched for weapons."

"What's that have to do with Onn . . . and you?"

"Well, obviously, if the ruler survived his walk he was a good ruler."

"You don't search for weapons?"

"Not openly."

"You think people see you in this myth." It was not a question.

"Many do."

Idaho stared up at Leto's face deep in its grey cowl. The blue on blue eyes stared back at him without expression.

Melange eyes, Idaho thought. But Leto said he no longer consumed any spice. His body supplied what spice his addiction demanded.

"You don't like my holy obscenity, my enforced tranquillity," Leto said.

"I don't like you playing god!"

"But a god can conduct the Empire as a musical conductor guides a symphony through its movements. My performance is limited only by my restriction to Arrakis. I must direct the symphony from here."

Idaho shook his head and looked once more at the city

plan. "What're these apartments behind the spires?"

"Lesser accommodation for our visitors."

"They can't see the plaza."

"But they can. Ixian devices project my image into those rooms."

"And the inner ring looks directly down on you. How do you enter the plaza?"

"A presentation stage rises from the centre to display me to my people."

"Do they cheer?" Idaho looked directly into Leto's eyes.

"They are permitted to cheer."

"You Atreides always did see yourselves as part of history."

"How astute of you to understand a cheer's meaning."

Idaho returned his attention to the city map. "And the Fish Speaker schools are here?"

"Under your left hand, yes. That's the academy where Siona was sent to be educated. She was ten at the time."

"Siona . . . I must learn more about her," Idaho mused.

"I assure you that nothing will get in the way of your desire."

As he marched along in the Royal peregrination, Idaho was lifted from his reverie by awareness that the Fish Speaker chant was diminishing. Ahead of him, the Royal Cart had begun its descent into the chambers beneath the plaza, rolling down a long ramp. Idaho, still in sunlight, looked up and around at the glistening spires—this reality for which the charts had not prepared him. People crowded the balconies of the great tiered ring around the plaza, silent people who stared down at the procession.

No cheering from the privileged, Idaho thought. The silence of the people on the balconies filled Idaho with foreboding.

He entered the ramp-tunnel and its lip hid the plaza. The Fish Speaker chant faded away as he descended into the depths. The sound of marching feet all around him was curiously amplified.

Curiosity replaced the sense of oppressive foreboding.

156

Idaho stared around him. The flat-floored tube was artificially illuminated and wide, very wide. Idaho estimated that seventy people could march abreast into the bowels of the plaza. There were no mobs of greeters here, only a widely-spaced line of Fish Speakers who did not chant, contenting themselves to stare at the passage of their God.

Memory of the charts told Idaho the layout of this gigantic complex beneath the plaza—a private city within the City, a place where only the God Emperor, the courtiers and the Fish Speakers could go without escort. But the charts had told nothing of the thick pillars, the sense of massive, guarded spaces, the eerie quiet broken by the tramping of feet and the creaking of Leto's cart.

Idaho looked suddenly at the Fish Speakers lining the way and realized that their mouths were moving in unison, a silent word on their lips. He recognized the word:

"Siaynoq."

> *"Another Festival so soon?" the Lord Leto asked.*
> *"It has been ten years," the majordomo said.*
> *Do you think by this exchange that the Lord Leto betrays an ignorance of time's passage?*

> **—The Oral History**

During the private audience period preceding the Festival proper, many commented that the God Emperor spent more than the allotted time with the new Ixian Ambassador, a young woman named Hwi Noree.

She was brought down at mid-morning by two Fish Speakers who were still full of first-day excitement. The private audience chamber beneath the plaza was brilliantly illuminated. The light revealed a room about fifty metres long by thirty-five wide. Antique Fremen rugs decorated the walls, their bright patterns worked in jewels and precious metals, all combined in weavings of priceless

157

spice-fibres. The dull reds of which the old Fremen had been so fond predominated. The chamber's floor was mostly transparent, a setting for exotic fishes worked in radiant crystal. Beneath the floor flowed a stream of clear blue water, all of its moisture sealed away from the audience chamber, but excitingly near Leto, who rested on a padded elevation at the end of the room opposite the door.

His first view of Hwi Noree revealed a remarkable likeness to her Uncle Malky, but her grave movements and the calmness of her stride were equally remarkable in their difference from Malky. She did have that dark skin, though, the oval face with its regular features. Placid brown eyes stared back at Leto. And where Malky's hair had been grey, hers was a luminous brown.

Hwi Noree radiated an inner peace which Leto sensed spreading its influence around her as she approached. She stopped six paces away below him. There was a classical balance about her, something not accidental.

With growing excitement, Leto realized a betrayal of Ixian machinations in the new Ambassador. They were well along in their own programme to breed selected types for specific functions. Hwi Noree's function was distressingly obvious—to charm the God Emperor, to find a chink in his armour.

Despite this, as the meeting progressed, Leto found himself truly enjoying her company. Hwi Noree stood in a puddle of daylight which was guided into the chamber by a system of Ixian prisms. The light filled Leto's end of the chamber with glowing gold which centred on the Ambassador, dimming behind the God Emperor where stood a short line of Fish Speaker guards—twelve women chosen for their inability to hear or speak.

Hwi Noree wore a simple gown of purple ambiel decorated only by a silver necklace pendant stamped with the symbol of Ix. Soft sandals the colour of her gown peeked from beneath her hem.

"Are you aware," Leto asked her, "that I killed one of your ancestors?"

158

She smiled softly. "My Uncle Malky included that information in my early training, Lord."

As she spoke, Leto realized that part of her education had been conducted by the Bene Gesserit. She had their way of controlling her responses, of sensing the undertones in a conversation. He could see, however, that the Bene Gesserit overlay had been a delicate thing, never penetrating the basic sweetness of her nature.

"You were told that I would introduce this subject," he said.

"Yes, Lord. I know that my ancestor had the temerity to bring a weapon here in the attempt to harm you."

"As did your immediate predecessor. Were you told that, as well?"

"I did not learn it until my arrival, Lord. They were fools! Why did you spare my predecessor?"

"When I did not spare your ancestor?"

"Yes, Lord."

"Kobat, your predecessor, was more valuable to me as a messenger."

"Then they told me the truth," she said. Again, she smiled. "One cannot always depend on hearing truth from one's associates and superiors."

The response was so utterly open that Leto could not suppress a chuckle. Even as he laughed, he realized that this young woman still possessed the Mind of First Awakening, the elemental mind which came in the first shock of birth-awareness. She was alive!

"Then you do not hold it against me that I killed your ancestor?" he asked.

"He tried to assassinate you! I am told you crushed him, Lord, with your own body."

"True."

"And next you turned his weapon against your own Holy Self to demonstrate that the weapon was ineffectual . . . and it was the best lasgun we Ixians could make."

"The witnesses reported correctly," Leto said.

And he thought: *Which shows how much you can depend*

on witnesses! As a matter of historical accuracy, he knew that he had turned the lasgun only against his ribbed body, not against his hands, face or flippers. The pre-worm body possessed a remarkable capacity for absorbing heat. The chemical factory within him converted heat to oxygen.

"I never doubted the story," she said.

"Why has Ix repeated this foolish gesture?" Leto asked.

"They have not told me, Lord. Perhaps Kobat took it on himself to behave this way."

"I think not. It has occurred to me that your people desired only the death of their chosen assassin."

"The death of Kobat?"

"No, the death of the one they chose to use the weapon."

"Who was that, Lord? I've not been told."

"It's unimportant. Do you recall what I said at the time of your ancestor's foolishness?"

"You threatened terrible punishment should such violence ever again enter our thoughts." She lowered her gaze, but not before Leto glimpsed a deep determination in her eyes. She would use the best of her abilities to blunt his wrath.

"I promised that none of you would escape my anger," Leto said.

She jerked her attention up to his face. "Yes, Lord." And now her manner revealed personal fear.

"None can escape me, not even the futile colony you've recently planted at . . ." And Leto reeled off for her the standard chart coordinates of a new colony the Ixians had planted secretly far beyond what they thought were the reaches of his Empire.

She betrayed no surprise. "Lord, I think it was because I warned them you would know of this that I was chosen as Ambassador."

Leto studied her more carefully. *What have we here?* he wondered. Her observation had been subtle and penetrating. The Ixians, he knew, had thought distance and enormously magnified transportation costs would insulate the

160

new colony. Hwi Noree thought not and had said so. But she believed her masters had chosen her as Ambassador because of this—a comment on the Ixian caution. They thought they had a friend at court here, but one who also would be seen as Leto's friend. He nodded as the pattern took shape. Quite early in his ascendancy he had revealed to the Ixians the exact location of the supposedly secret Ixian Core, the heartland of the technological federation which they governed. It had been a secret the Ixians thought safe because they paid gigantic bribes for it to the Spacing Guild. Leto had winkled them out by prescient observation and deduction—and by consulting his memories where there were more than a few Ixians.

At the time, Leto had warned the Ixians that he would punish them if they acted against him. They had responded with consternation and accused the Guild of betraying them. This had amused Leto and he had responded with such a burst of laughter that the Ixians were abashed. He had then informed them in a cold and accusatory tone that he had no need of spies or traitors or other ordinary trappings of government.

Did they not believe he was a God?

For a time thereafter, the Ixians were responsive to his requests. Leto had not abused the relationship. His demands were modest—a machine for this, a device for that. He would state his needs and presently the Ixians would deliver the required technological toy. Only once had they tried to deliver a violent instrument inside one of his machines. He had slain the entire Ixian delegation before they could even unwrap the thing.

Hwi Noree waited patiently while Leto mused. Not the slightest sign of impatience surfaced.

Beautiful, he thought.

In view of his long association with the Ixians, this new stance sent the juices coursing through Leto's body. Ordinarily, the passions, crises and necessities which had produced and impelled him burned low. He often felt that he had outlived his times. But the presence of a Hwi Noree

161

said he was needed. This pleased him. Leto felt that it might even be possible that the Ixians had achieved a partial success with their machine to amplify the linear prescience of a Guild Navigator. A small *blip* in the flow of great events might have escaped him. Could they really make such a machine? What a marvel that would be! Purposefully, he refused to use his powers for even the smallest search through this possibility.

I wish to be surprised!

Leto smiled benignly at Hwi. "How have they prepared you to woo me?" he asked.

She did not blink. "I was provided with a set of memorized responses for particular exigencies," she said. "I learned them as I was required but I do not intend to use them."

Which is exactly what they want, Leto thought.

"Tell your masters," he said, "that you are precisely the right kind of bait to dangle in front of me."

She bowed her head. "If it pleases my Lord."

"Yes, you do."

He indulged himself then in a small temporal probe to examine Hwi's immediate future, tracing the threads of her past through this. Hwi appeared in a fluid future, a current whose movements were susceptible to many deflections. She would know Siona in only a casual way unless . . . Questions flowed through Leto's mind. A Guild Steersman was advising the Ixians and he obviously had detected Siona's disturbance in the temporal fabric. Did the Steersman really believe he could prove security against the God Emperor's detection?

The temporal probe took several minutes, but Hwi did not fidget. Leto looked at her carefully. She seemed timeless—*outside* of time in a deeply peaceful way. He had never before encountered a common mortal able to wait thus in front of him without some nervousness.

"Where were you born, Hwi?" he asked.

"On Ix itself, Lord."

"I mean specifically—the building, its location, your

parents, the people around you, friends and family, your schooling—all of it."

"I never knew my parents, Lord. I was told they died while I was still an infant."

"Did you believe this?"

"At first . . . of course. Later, I built fantasies. I even imagined that Malky was my father . . . but . . ." She shook her head.

"You did not like your Uncle Malky?"

"No, I didn't. Oh, I admired him."

"My reaction precisely," Leto said. "But what of your friends and your schooling?"

"My teachers were specialists, even some Bene Gesserits were brought in to train me in emotional control and observation. Malky said I was being prepared for great things."

"And your friends?"

"I don't think I ever had any real friends—only people who were brought in contact with me for specific purposes in my education."

"And these great things for which you were trained, did anyone ever speak of those?"

"Malky said I was being prepared to charm you, Lord."

"How old are you, Hwi?"

"I don't know my exact age. I guess I'm about twenty-six. I've never celebrated a birthday. I only learned about birthdays by accident, one of my teachers giving an excuse for her absence. I never saw that teacher again."

Leto found himself fascinated by this response. His observations provided him with certainty that there had been no Tleilaxu interventions into her Ixian flesh. She had not come from a Tleilaxu axlotl tank. Why the secrecy, then?

"Does your Uncle Malky know your age?"

"Perhaps. But I haven't seen him for many years."

"Didn't *anyone* ever tell you how old you were?"

"No."

"Why do you suppose that is?"

"Maybe they thought I'd ask if I were interested."

"Were you interested?"

"Yes."

"Then why didn't you ask?"

"I thought at first there might be a record somewhere. I looked. There was nothing. I reasoned then that they would not answer my question."

"For what it tells me about you, Hwi, that answer pleases me *very* much. I, too, am ignorant of your background, but I can make an enlightened guess at your birthplace."

Her eyes focused on his face with a charged intensity which had no pretence in it.

"You were born within this machine your masters are trying to perfect for the Guild," Leto said. "You were conceived there, as well. It may even be that Malky was your father. That is not important. Do you know about this machine, Hwi?"

"I'm not supposed to know about it, Lord, but . . ."

"Another indiscretion by one of your teachers?"

"By my uncle himself."

A burst of laughter erupted from Leto. "What a rogue!" he said. "What a charming rogue!"

"Lord?"

"This is his revenge on your masters. He did not like being removed from my court. He told me at the time that his replacement was less than a fool."

Hwi shrugged. "A complex man, my uncle."

"Listen to me carefully, Hwi. Some of your associations here on Arrakis could be dangerous to you. I will protect you as I can. Do you understand?"

"I think so, Lord." She stared up at him solemnly.

"Now, a message for your masters. It is clear to me that they have been listening to a Guild Steersman *and* they have joined themselves to the Tleilaxu in a perilous fashion. Tell them for me that their purposes are quite transparent."

"Lord, I have no knowledge of . . ."

164

"I am aware of how they use you, Hwi. For this reason you may tell your masters also that you are to be the permanent Ambassador to my court. I will not welcome another Ixian. And should your masters ignore my warnings, trying further interference with my wishes, I shall crush them."

Tears welled from her eyes and ran down her cheeks, but Leto was grateful that she did not indulge in any other display such as falling to her knees.

"I already have warned them," she said. "Truly I did. I told them they must obey you."

Leto could see that this was true.

What a marvellous creature, this Hwi Noree, he thought. She appeared the epitome of goodness, obviously bred and conditioned for this quality by her Ixian masters with their careful calculation of the effect this would have on the God Emperor.

Out of his thronging ancestral memories, Leto could see her as an idealized nun, kindly and self-sacrificing, all sincerity. It was her most basic nature, the place where she lived. She found it easiest to be truthful and open, capable of shading this only to prevent pain for others. He saw this latter trait as the deepest change the Bene Gesserit had been able to effect in her. Hwi's real manner remained outgoing, sensitive and naturally sweet. Leto could find little sense of manipulative calculation in her. She appeared immediately responsive and wholesome, excellent at listening (another Bene Gesserit attribute). There was nothing openly seductive about her, yet this very fact made her profoundly seductive to Leto.

As he had remarked to one of the earlier Duncans on a similar occasion: "You must understand this about me, a thing which some obviously suspect—sometimes it's unavoidable that I have delusionary sensations, the feeling that somewhere inside this changeling form of mine there exists an adult human body with all of the necessary functions."

"*All* of them, Lord?" the Duncan had asked.

"All! I feel the vanished parts of myself. I can feel my legs, quite unremarkable and so real to my senses. I can feel the pumping of my human glands, some of which no longer exist. I can even feel genitalia which I know, intellectually, vanished centuries ago."

"But surely if you know . . ."

"Knowledge does not suppress such feelings. The vanished parts of myself are still there in my personal memories and in the multiple identity of all my ancestors."

As Leto looked at Hwi standing in front of him, it helped not one whit to know he had no skull and that what once had been his brain was now a massive web of ganglia spread through his pre-worm flesh. Nothing helped. He could still feel his *brain* aching where it once had reposed; he could still feel his *skull* throbbing.

By just standing there in front of him, Hwi cried out to his lost humanity. It was too much for him and he moaned in despair:

"Why do your masters torture me?"

"Lord?"

"By sending you!"

"I would not hurt you, Lord."

"Just by existing you hurt me!"

"I did not know." Tears fell unrestrained from her eyes. "They never told me what they were really doing."

He calmed himself and spoke softly: "Leave me now, Hwi. Go about your business, but return quickly if I summon you!"

She left quietly, but Leto could see that Hwi, too, was tortured. There was no mistaking the deep sadness in her for the humanity Leto had sacrificed. She knew what Leto knew: they would have been friends, lovers, companions in an ultimate sharing between the sexes. Her masters had planned for her to know.

The Ixians are cruel! he thought. *They knew what our pain would be.*

Hwi's departure ignited memories of her Uncle Malky. Malky was cruel, but Leto had rather enjoyed his company.

Malky had possessed all of the industrious virtues of his people and enough of their vices to make him thoroughly human. Malky had revelled in the company of Leto's Fish Speakers. "Your houris," he had called them, and Leto could seldom think of the Fish Speakers thereafter without recalling Malky's label.

Why do I think of Malky now? It's not just because of Hwi. I shall ask her what charge her masters gave her when they sent her to me.

Leto hesitated on the verge of calling her back.

She'll tell me if I ask.

Ixian ambassadors had always been told to find out why the God Emperor tolerated Ix. They knew they could not hide from him. This stupid attempt to plant a colony beyond his vision! Were they testing his limits? The Ixians suspected that Leto did not really need their industries.

I've never concealed my opinion of them. I said it to Malky:

"Technological innovators? No! You are the criminals of science in my Empire!"

Malky had laughed.

Irritated, Leto had accused: "Why try to hide secret laboratories and factories beyond the Empire's rim? You cannot escape me."

"Yes, Lord." Laughing.

"I know your intent: leak a bit of this and some of that back into my Imperial domains. Disrupt! Cause doubts and questioning!"

"Lord, you yourself are one of our best customers!"

"That's not what I mean and you know it, you terrible man!"

"You like me *because* I'm a terrible man. I tell you stories about what we do out there."

"I know it without your stories!"

"But some stories are believed and some are doubted. I dispel your doubts."

"I have no doubts!"

Which had only ignited more of Malky's laughter.

167

And I must continue tolerating them, Leto thought. The Ixians operated in the terra incognita of creative invention which had been outlawed by the Butlerian Jihad. They made their devices in the image of the mind—the very thing which had ignited the Jihad's destruction and slaughter. That was what they did on Ix and Leto could only let them continue.

I buy from them! I could not even write my journals without their dictatels to respond to my unspoken thought. Without Ix, I could not have hidden my journals and the printers.

But they must be reminded of the dangers in what they do!

And the Guild could not be allowed to forget. That was easier. Even while Guildsmen cooperated with Ix, they distrusted the Ixians mightily.

If this new Ixian machine works, the Guild has lost its monopoly on space travel!

> *From that welter of memories which I can tap at will, patterns emerge. They are like another language which I see so clearly. The social-alarm signals which put societies into the postures of defence/attack are like shouted words to me. As a people, you react against threats to innocence and the peril of the helpless young. Unexplained sounds, visions and smells raise the hackles you have forgotten you possess. When alarmed, you cling to your native language because all the other patterned sounds are strange. You demand acceptable dress because a strange costume is threatening. This is system-feedback at its most primitive level. Your cells remember.*

> —The Stolen Journals

The acolyte Fish Speakers who served as pages at the portal of Leto's audience chamber brought in Duro Nunepi, the Tleilaxu Ambassador. It was early for an audience and Nunepi was being taken out of his announced order, but he moved calmly with only the faintest hint of resigned acceptance.

Leto waited silently stretched out along his cart on the raised platform at the end of the chamber. As he watched Nunepi approach, Leto's memories produced a comparison: the swimming-cobra of a periscope brushing its almost invisible wake upon water. The memory brought a smile to Leto's lips. That was Nunepi—a proud, flinty-faced man who had come up through the ranks of Tleilaxu management. Not a Face Dancer himself, he considered the Dancers his personal servants; they were the *water* through which he moved. One had to be truly adept to see his wake. Nunepi was a nasty piece of business who had left his traces in the attack along the Royal Road.

Despite the early hour, the man wore his full ambassadorial regalia—billowing black trousers and black sandals trimmed in gold, a flowery red jacket open at the breast to reveal a bushy chest behind his Tleilaxu crest worked in gold and jewels.

At the required ten paces distance, Nunepi stopped and swept his gaze along the rank of armed Fish Speaker guards in an arc around and behind Leto. Nunepi's grey eyes were bright with some secret amusement when he brought his attention to his Emperor and bowed slightly.

Duncan Idaho entered then, a lasgun holstered at his hip, and took up his position beside the God Emperor's cowled face.

Idaho's appearance required a careful study by Nunepi, a study which did not please the Ambassador.

"I find Shape Changers particularly obnoxious," Leto said.

"I am not a Shape Changer, Lord," Nunepi said. His voice was low and cultured with only a trace of hesitancy in it.

"But you represent them and that makes you an item of annoyance," Leto said.

Nunepi had expected an open statement of hostility, but this was not the language of diplomacy, and it shocked him into a bald reference to what he believed to be Tleilaxu strength.

"Lord, by preserving the flesh of the original Duncan Idaho and providing you with restored gholas in his image and identity, we have always assumed . . ."

"Duncan!" Leto glanced at Idaho. "If I command it, Duncan, will you lead an expedition to exterminate the Tleilaxu?"

"With pleasure, m'Lord."

"Even if it means the loss of your *original cells* and all of the axlotl tanks?"

"I do not find the tanks a pleasant memory, m'Lord, and those cells are not me."

"Lord, how have we offended you?" Nunepi asked.

Leto scowled. Did this inept fool really expect the God Emperor to speak openly of the recent Face Dancer attack?

"It has come to my attention," Leto said, "that you and your people have been spreading lies about what you call my 'disgusting sexual habits'."

Nunepi gaped. The accusation was a bold lie, completely unexpected. But Nunepi realized that if he denied it, no one would believe him. The God Emperor had said it. This was an attack of unknown dimensions. Nunepi started to speak while looking at Idaho.

"Lord, if we . . ."

"Look at me!" Leto commanded.

Nunepi jerked his gaze up to Leto's face.

"I will inform you only this once," Leto said. "I have no sexual habits whatsoever. None."

Perspiration rolled off Nunepi's face. He stared at Leto with the fixed intensity of a trapped animal. When Nunepi found his voice, it no longer was the low, controlled instrument of a diplomat, but a trembling and fearful thing.

"Lord, I . . . there must be a mistake of . . ."

"Be still, you Tleilaxu sneak!" Leto roared. Then: "I am a metamorphic vector of the holy sandworm—Shai-Hulud! I am your God!"

"Forgive us, Lord," Nunepi whispered.

"Forgive you?" Leto's voice was full of sweet reason. "Of course I forgive you. That is your God's function. Your crime is forgiven. However, your stupidity requires a response."

"Lord, if I could but . . ."

"Be still! The spice allotment passes over the Tleilaxu for this decade. You get nothing. As for you personally, my Fish Speakers will now take you into the plaza."

Two burly guardswomen moved in and held Nunepi's arms. They looked up to Leto for instructions.

"In the plaza," Leto said, "his clothing is to be stripped from him. He is to be publicly flogged—fifty lashes."

Nunepi struggled against the grip of his guards, consternation on his face mingled with rage.

"Lord, I remind you that I am the Ambassador of . . ."

"You are a common criminal and will be treated as such." Leto nodded to the guards who began dragging Nunepi away.

"I wish they'd killed you!" Nunepi raged. "I wish . . ."

"Who?" Leto called. "You wish who had killed me? Don't you know I cannot be killed?"

The guards dragged Nunepi out of the chamber as he still raged: "I am innocent! I am innocent!" The protest faded away.

Idaho leaned close to Leto.

"Yes, Duncan?" Leto asked.

"M'Lord, all the envoys will feel fear at this."

"Yes. I teach a lesson in responsibility."

"M'Lord?"

"Membership in a conspiracy, as in an army, frees people from the sense of personal responsibility."

"But this will cause trouble, m'Lord. I'd best post extra guards."

"Not one additional guard!"

"But you invite . . ."

"I invite a bit of military nonsense."

"That's what I . . ."

171

"Duncan, I am a teacher. Remember that. By repetition, I impress the lesson."

"What lesson?"

"The ultimately suicidal nature of military foolishness."

"M'Lord, I don't . . ."

"Duncan, consider the inept Nunepi. He is the essence of this lesson."

"Forgive my denseness, m'Lord, but I do not understand this thing about military . . ."

"They believe that by risking death they pay the price of any violent behaviour against enemies of their own choosing. They have the invader mentality. Nunepi does not believe himself responsible for anything done against *aliens*."

Idaho looked at the portal where the guards had taken Nunepi. "He tried and he lost, m'Lord."

"But he cut himself loose from the restraints of the past and he objects to paying the price."

"To his people he's a patriot."

"And how does he see himself, Duncan? As an instrument of history."

Idaho lowered his voice and leaned closer to Leto.

"How are you different, m'Lord?"

Leto chuckled. "Ahhh, Duncan, how I love your perceptiveness. You have observed that I am the ultimate alien. Do you not wonder if I also can be a loser?"

"The thought has crossed my mind."

"Even losers can shroud themselves in the proud mantle of 'the past', old friend."

"Are you and Nunepi alike in that?"

"Militant missionary religions can share this illusion of the 'proud past', but few understand the ultimate peril to humankind—that false sense of freedom from responsibility for your own actions."

"These are strange words, m'Lord. How do I take their meaning?"

"Their meaning is whatever speaks to you. Are you incapable of listening?"

172

"I have ears, m'Lord!"

"Do you now? I cannot see them."

"Here, m'Lord. Here and here!" Idaho pointed at his own ears as he spoke.

"But they do not hear. Therefore you have no ears, neither here nor hear."

"You make a joke of me, m'Lord?"

"To hear is to hear. That which exists cannot be made into itself for it already exists. To be is to be."

"Your strange words . . ."

"Are but words. I spoke them. They are gone. No one heard them, therefore they no longer exist. If they no longer exist, perhaps they can be made to exist again and then perhaps someone will hear them."

"Why do you poke fun at me, m'Lord?"

"I poke nothing at you except words. I do it without fear of offending because I have learned that you have no ears."

"I don't understand you, m'Lord."

"That is the beginning of knowledge—the discovery of something we do not understand."

Before Idaho could respond, Leto gave a hand signal to a nearby guard who waved a hand in front of a crystalline control panel on the wall behind the God Emperor's dais. A three-dimensional view of Nunepi's punishment appeared in the centre of the chamber.

Idaho stepped down to the floor of the chamber and peered closely at the scene. It was shown from a slight elevation looking down on the plaza, and was complete with sounds of the swelling throng who had run to the scene at the first signs of excitement.

Nunepi was bound to two legs of a tripod, his feet spread wide, his arms tied together above him almost at the apex of the tripod. His clothing had been ripped from his body and lay around him in rags. A bulky, masked Fish Speaker stood nearby holding an improvised whip fashioned of elacca rope which had been frayed at the end into wirelike fine strands. Idaho though he recognized the masked woman as the *Friend* of his first interview.

173

At a signal from a Guard officer, the masked Fish Speaker stepped forward and brought the elacca whip down in a slashing arc on to Nunepi's exposed back.

Idaho winced. The crowd gasped.

Welts appeared where the whip had struck, but Nunepi remained silent.

Again, the whip descended. Blood betrayed the lines of this second stroke.

Once more, the whip flayed Nunepi's back. More blood appeared.

Leto felt remote sadness. *Nayla is too ardent,* he thought. *She will kill him and that will cause problems.*

"Duncan!" Leto called.

Idaho turned from his fascinated examination of the projected scene just as a shout lifted from the crowd—response to a particularly bloody stroke.

"Send someone to stop the flogging after twenty lashes," Leto said. "Have it announced that the magnanimity of the God Emperor has reduced the punishment."

Idaho raised a hand to one of the guards who nodded and ran from the chamber.

"Come here, Duncan," Leto said.

Still smarting under what he believed was Leto's poking fun at him, Idaho returned to Leto's side.

"Whatever I do," Leto said, "it is to teach a lesson."

Idaho rigidly willed himself not to look back at the scene of Nunepi's punishment. Was that the sound of Nunepi groaning? The shouts of the crowd pierced Idaho. He stared up into Leto's eyes.

"There is a question in your mind," Leto said.

"Many questions, m'Lord."

"Speak them."

"What is the lesson in that fool's punishment? What do we say when asked?"

"We say that no one is permitted to blaspheme against the God Emperor."

"A *bloody* lesson, m'Lord."

"Not as bloody as some I've taught."

174

Idaho shook his head from side to side in obvious dismay. "Nothing good's going to come of this!"

"Precisely!"

> Safaris through ancestral memories teach me many things. The patterns, ahhh, the patterns. Liberal bigots are the ones who trouble me most. I distrust the extremes. Scratch a conservative and you find someone who prefers the past over any future. Scratch a liberal and find a closet aristocrat. It's true! Liberal governments always develop into aristocracies. The bureaucracies betray the true intent of people who form such governments. Right from the first, the little people who formed the governments which promised to equalize the social burdens found themselves suddenly in the hands of bureaucratic aristocracies. Of course, all bureaucracies follow this pattern, but what a hypocrisy to find this even under a communized banner. Ahhh, well, if patterns teach me anything it's that patterns are repeated. My oppressions, by and large, are no worse than any of the others and, at least, I teach a new lesson.

> —The Stolen Journals

It was well into the darkness of Audience Day before Leto could meet with the Bene Gesserit delegation. Moneo had prepared the Reverend Mothers for the delay, repeating the God Emperor's reassurances.

Reporting back to his Emperor, Moneo had said: "They expect a rich reward."

"We shall see," Leto had said. "We shall see. Now, tell me what it was the Duncan demanded of you as you entered."

"He wished to know if you had ever before had someone flogged."

"And you replied?"

"That there was no record of, nor had I ever before witnessed, such a punishment."

"His response?"

175

"This is not Atreides."

"Does he think I'm insane?"

"He did not say that."

"There was more to your encounter. What else troubles our new Duncan?"

"He has met the Ixian Ambassador, Lord. He finds Hwi Noree attractive. He inquired of . . ."

"That must be prevented, Moneo! I trust you to raise barriers against any liaison between the Duncan and Hwi."

"My Lord commands."

"Indeed I do! Go now and prepare for our meeting with the women of the Bene Gesserit. I will receive them at False Sietch."

"Lord, is there significance in this choice of a meeting place?"

"A whim. On your way out, tell the Duncan he may take out a troop of guards and scour the City for trouble."

Waiting for the Bene Gesserit delegation at False Sietch, Leto reviewed this exchange, finding some amusement in it. He could imagine the reactions through the Festival City at the approach of a disturbed Duncan Idaho in command of a Fish Speaker troop.

Like the quick silence of frogs when a predator comes.

Now that he was in False Sietch, Leto found himself pleased by the choice. A free-form building of irregular domes at the edge of Onn, False Sietch was almost a kilometre across. It had been the first abode of the Museum Fremen and now was their school, its corridors and chambers patrolled by alert Fish Speakers.

The reception hall where Leto waited, an oval about two hundred metres in its long dimension, was illuminated by giant glowglobes which floated in blue-green isolation some thirty metres above the floor. The light muted the dull browns and tans of the imitation stone from which the entire structure had been fashioned. Leto waited on a low ledge at one end of the chamber, looking outward through a half-circle window longer than his body. The opening, four stories above the ground, framed a view which included a remnant of the ancient Shield Wall preserved for its cliffside caves where Atreides troops had once been slaughtered by Harkonnen attackers. The frosty light of First Moon silvered the cliff's outlines. Fires dotted the cliffside, the flames exposed where no Fremen would have dared betray his presence. The fires winked at Leto as people passed in front of them—Museum Fremen exercising their right to occupy the sacred precincts.

Museum Fremen! Leto thought.

They were such narrow thinkers with near horizons.

But why should I object? They are what I made them.

Leto heard the Bene Gesserit delegation then. They chanted as they approached, a heavy sound all a-jostle with vowels.

Moneo preceded them with a guard detail which took up position on Leto's ledge. Moneo stood on the chamber floor just below Leto's face, glanced at Leto, turned to the open hall.

The women entered in a double file, ten of them led by two Reverend Mothers in traditional black robes.

"That is Anteac on the left, Luyseyal on the right," Moneo said.

The names recalled for Leto the earlier words about the Reverend Mothers brought in by Moneo, agitated and distrustful. Moneo did not like the *witches*.

"They're both Truthsayers," Moneo had said. "Anteac is much older than Luyseyal, but the latter is reputed to be the best Truthsayer the Bene Gesserit have. You may note that Anteac has a scar on her forehead whose origin we have been unable to discover. Luyseyal has red hair and appears remarkably young for one of her reputation."

As he watched the Reverend Mothers approach with their entourage, Leto felt the quick surge of his memories. The women wore their hoods forward, shrouding their faces. The attendants and acolytes walked at a respectful distance behind . . . it was all of a piece. Some patterns did not change. These women might have been entering a real sietch with real Fremen here to honour them.

177

Their heads know what their bodies deny, he thought.

Leto's penetrating vision saw the subservient caution in their eyes, but they strode up the long chamber like people confident of their religious power.

It pleased Leto to think that the Bene Gesserit possessed only such powers as he permitted. The reason for this indulgence was clear to him. Of all the people in his Empire, Reverend Mothers were most like him—limited to the memories of only their female ancestors and the collateral female identities of their inheritance ritual—still, each of them did exist as somewhat of an integrated mob.

The Reverend Mothers came to a stop at the required ten paces from Leto's ledge. The entourage spread out on each side.

It amused Leto to greet such delegations in the voice and persona of his grandmother, Jessica. The Bene Gesserit had come to expect this and he did not disappoint them.

"Welcome, Sisters," he said. The voice was a smooth contralto, definitely Jessica's controlled feminine tones with just a hint of mockery—a voice recorded and often studied in the Sisterhood's Chapter House.

As he spoke, Leto sensed menace. Reverend Mothers were never pleased when he greeted them this way, but the reaction here carried different undertones. Moneo, too, sensed it. He raised a finger and the guards moved closer to Leto.

Anteac spoke first: "Lord, we watched that display in the plaza this morning. What do you gain by such antics?"

So that's the tone we wish to set, he thought.

Speaking in his own voice, he said: "You are temporarily in my good graces. Would you change that?"

"Lord," Anteac said, "we are shocked that you could thus punish an Ambassador. We do not understand what you gain by this."

"I gain nothing. I am diminished."

Luyseyal spoke up: "This could only reinforce thoughts of oppression."

"I wonder why so few ever thought of the Bene Gesserit as oppressors?" Leto asked.

Anteac spoke to her companion: "If it pleases the God Emperor to inform us, he will do so. Let us get to the purposes of our Embassy."

Leto smiled. "The two of you can come closer. Leave your attendants and approach."

Moneo stepped two paces to his right as the Reverend Mothers moved in characteristic silent gliding to within three paces of the ledge.

"It's almost as though they had no feet!" Moneo had once complained.

Recalling this, Leto observed how carefully Moneo watched the two women. They were menacing, but Moneo dared not object to their nearness. The God Emperor had ordered it; thus it would be.

Leto lifted his attention to the attendants waiting where the Bene Gesserit entourage had first stopped. The acolytes wore hoodless black gowns. He saw tiny clues to forbidden rituals about them—an amulet, a small trinket, a colourful corner of a kerchief so arranged that more colour might be flashed carefully. Leto knew that the Reverend Mothers allowed this because they no longer could share the spice as once they had.

Ritual substitutes.

There were significant changes across the past ten years. A new parsimony had entered the Sisterhood's thinking.

They are coming out, Leto told himself. *The old, old mysteries are still here.*

The ancient patterns had lain dormant in the Bene Gesserit memories for all of those millennia.

Now, they emerge. I must warn my Fish Speakers.

He returned his attention to the Reverend Mothers.

"You have requests?"

"What is it like to be you?" Luyseyal asked.

Leto blinked. That was an interesting attack. They had not tried it in more than a generation. Well . . . why not?

"Sometimes my dreams are blocked off and redirected

179

into strange places," he said. "If my cosmic memories are a web, as you two certainly know, then think about the dimensions of *my* web and where such memories and dreams might lead."

"You speak of our certain knowledge," Anteac said. "Why can't we join forces at last? We are more alike than we are different."

"I would sooner link myself to those degenerate Great Houses bewailing their lost spice riches!"

Anteac held herself still, but Luyseyal pointed a finger at Leto. "We offer community!"

"And I insist on conflict?"

Anteac stirred, then: "It is said that there is a principle of conflict which originated with the single cell and has never deteriorated."

"Some things remain incompatible," Leto agreed.

"Then how does our Sisterhood maintain its community?" Luyseyal demanded.

Leto hardened his voice. "As you well know, the secret of community lies in suppression of the incompatible."

"There can be enormous value in cooperation," Anteac said.

"To you, not to me."

Anteac contrived a sigh. "Then, Lord, will you tell us about the physical changes in your person?"

"Someone besides yourself should know about and record such things," Luyseyal said.

"In case something dreadful should happen to me?" Leto asked.

"Lord!" Anteac protested. "We do not . . ."

"You dissect me with words when you would prefer sharper instruments," Leto said. "Hypocrisy offends me."

"We protest, Lord," Anteac said.

"Indeed you do. I hear you."

Luyseyal crept a few millimetres closer to the ledge, bringing a sharp stare from Moneo, who glanced up at Leto then. Moneo's expression demanded action, but Leto ignored him, curious now about Luyseyal's intentions. The sense of menace was centred in the red-haired one.

What is she? Leto wondered. *Could she be a Face Dancer, after all?*

No. None of the telltale signs were there. No. Luyseyal presented an elaborately relaxed appearance, not even a little twist of her features to test the God Emperor's powers of observation.

"Will you now tell us about your physical changes, Lord?" Anteac asked.

Diversion! Leto thought.

"My brain grows enormous," he said. "Most of the human skull has dissolved away. There are no severe limits to the growth of my cortex and its attendant nervous system."

Moneo darted a startled glance at Leto. Why was the God Emperor giving away such vital information? These two would trade it.

But both women were obviously fascinated by this revelation, hesitating in whatever plan they had evolved.

"Does your brain have a centre?" Luyseyal asked.

"I am the centre," Leto said.

"A location?" Anteac asked. She gestured vaguely at him. Luyseyal glided a few millimetres closer to the ledge.

"What value do you place on the things I reveal to you?" Leto asked.

The two women betrayed no change of expression, which was betrayal enough by itself. A smile flitted across Leto's lips.

"The marketplace has captured you," he said. "Even the Bene Gesserit has been infected by the *suk* mentality."

"We do not deserve that accusation," Anteac said.

"But you do. The *suk* mentality dominates my Empire. The uses of the market have only been sharpened and amplified by the demands of our times. We have all become traders."

"Even you, Lord?" Luyseyal asked.

"You tempt my wrath," he said. "You're a specialist in that, aren't you?"

"Lord?" Luyseyal's voice was calm, but overly controlled.

"Specialists are not to be trusted," Leto said. "Specialists are masters of exclusion, experts in the narrow."

"We hope to be architects of a better future," Anteac said.

"Better than what?" Leto asked.

Luyseyal eased herself a fractional pace closer to Leto.

"We hope to set our standards by your judgment, Lord," Anteac said.

"But you would be architects. Would you build higher walls? Never forget, Sisters, that I know you. You are efficient purveyors of blinders."

"Life continues, Lord," Anteac said.

"Indeed! And so does the universe."

Luyseyal eased herself a bit closer, ignoring the fixity of Moneo's attention.

Leto smelled it then and almost laughed aloud.

Spice essence!

They had brought some spice essence. They knew the old stories about sandworms and spice essence, of course. Luyseyal carried it. She thought of it as a specific poison for sandworms. That was obvious. Bene Gesserit records and the Oral History agreed on this. The essence shattered the worm, precipitating its dissolution and resulting (eventually) in sandtrout which would produce more sandworms— etcetera, etcetera, etcetera . . .

"There is another change in me that you should know about," Leto said. "I am not yet sandworm, not fully. Think of me as something closer to a colony creature with sensory alterations."

Luyseyal's left hand moved almost imperceptibly toward a fold in her gown. Moneo saw it and looked to Leto for instructions, but Leto only returned the hooded glare of Luyseyal's eyes.

"There have been fads in smells," Leto said.

Luyseyal's hand hesitated.

"Perfumes and essences," he said. "I remember them all, even the cults of the non-smells are mine. People have used underarm sprays and crotch sprays to mask their natural odours. Did you know that? Of course you knew it!"

Anteac's gaze moved toward Luyseyal.

Neither woman dared speak.

"People knew instinctively that their pheromones betrayed them," Leto said.

The women stood immobile. They heard him. Of all his people, Reverend Mothers were best equipped to understand his hidden message.

"You'd like to mine me for my riches of memory," Leto said, his voice accusing.

"We are jealous, Lord," Luyseyal confessed.

"You have misread the history of spice essence," Leto said. "Sandtrout sense it only as water."

"It was a test, Lord," Anteac said. "That is all."

"You would test me?"

"Blame our curiosity, Lord," Anteac said.

"I, too, am curious. Put your spice essence on the ledge beside Moneo. I will keep it."

Slowly, demonstrating by the steadiness of her movements that she intended no attack, Luyseyal reached beneath her gown and removed a small vial which glistened with an inner blue radiance. She placed the vial gently on the ledge. Not by any sign did she indicate that she might try something desperate.

"Truthsayer, indeed," Leto said.

She favoured him with a faint grimace which might have been a smile, then withdrew to Anteac's side.

"Where did you get the spice essence?" Leto asked.

"We bought it from smugglers," Anteac said.

"There've been no smugglers for almost twenty-five hundred years."

"Waste not, want not," Anteac said.

"I see. And now you must re-evaluate what you think of as your own patience, is that not so?"

183

"We have been watching the evolution of your body, Lord," Anteac said. "We thought . . ." She permitted herself a small shrug, the level of gesture warranted for use with a Sister and not given lightly.

Leto pursed his lips in response. "I cannot shrug," he said.

"Will you punish us?" Luyseyal asked.

"For amusing me?"

Luyseyal glanced at the vial on the ledge.

"I swore to reward you," Leto said. "I shall."

"We would prefer to protect you in our community, Lord," Anteac said.

"Do not seek too great a reward," he said.

Anteac nodded. "You deal with the Ixians, Lord. We have reason to believe they may venture against you."

"I fear them no more than I fear you."

"Surely you've heard what the Ixians are doing," Luyseyal said.

"Moneo brings me an occasional copy of a message between persons or groups in my Empire. I hear many stories."

"We speak of a new Abomination, Lord!" Anteac said.

"You think the Ixians can produce an artificial intelligence?" he asked. "Conscious the way you are conscious?"

"We fear it, Lord," Anteac said.

"You would have me believe that the Butlerian Jihad survives among the Sisterhood?"

"We do not trust the unknown which can arise from imaginative technology," Anteac said.

Luyseyal leaned toward him. "The Ixians boast that their machine will transcend time in the way that you do it, Lord."

"And the Guild says there's Time-chaos around the Ixians," Leto mocked. "Are we to fear all creation, then?"

Anteac drew herself up stiffly.

"I speak truth with you two," Leto said. "I recognize your abilities. Will you not recognize mine?"

Luyseyal gave him a curt nod. "Tleilax and Ix make

184

alliance with the Guild and seek our full cooperation."

"And you fear Ix the most?"

"We fear anything we do not control," Anteac said.

"And you do not control me."

"Without you, people would need us!" Anteac said.

"Truth at last!" Leto said. "You come to me as your Oracle and you ask me to put your fears to rest."

Anteac's voice was frigidly controlled. "Will Ix make a mechanical brain?"

"A brain? Of course not!"

Luyseyal appeared to relax, but Anteac remained unmoving. She was not satisfied with the Oracle.

Why is it that foolishness repeats itself with such monotonous precision? Leto wondered. His memories offered up countless scenes to match this one—caverns, priests and priestesses caught up in holy ecstasy, portentous voices delivering dangerous prophecies through the smoke of holy narcotics.

He glanced down at the iridescent vial on the ledge beside Moneo. What was the current value of that thing? Enormous. It was the *essence*. Concentrated wealth concentrated.

"You have already paid the Oracle," he said. "It amuses me to give you full value."

How alert the women became!

"Hear me!" he said. "What you fear is not what you fear."

Leto liked the sound of that. Sufficiently portentous for any Oracle. Anteac and Luyseyal stared up at him, dutiful supplicants. Behind them, an acolyte cleared her throat.

That one will be identified and reprimanded later, Leto thought.

Anteac had now had sufficient time to ruminate on Leto's words. She said: "An obscure truth is not the truth."

"But I have directed your attention correctly," Leto said.

"Are you telling us not to fear the machine?" Luyseyal asked.

185

"You have the power of reason," he said. "Why come begging to me?"

"But we do not have *your* powers," Anteac said.

"You complain then that you do not sense the gossamer waves of Time. You do not sense my continuum. And you fear a mere machine!"

"Then you will not answer us," Anteac said.

"Do not make the mistake of thinking me ignorant about your Sisterhood's ways," he said. "You are alive. Your senses are exquisitely tuned. I do not stop this, nor should you."

"But the Ixians play with automation!" Anteac protested.

"Discrete pieces, finite bits linked one to another," he agreed. "Once set in motion, what is to stop it?"

Luyseyal discarded all pretence of Bene Gesserit self-control, a fine comment on her recognition of Leto's powers. Her voice almost screeched: "Do you know what the Ixians boast? That their machine will predict *your* actions!"

"Why should I fear that? The closer they come to me, the more they must be my allies. They cannot conquer me, but I can conquer them."

Anteac made to speak but stopped when Luyseyal touched her arm.

"Are you already allied with Ix?" Luyseyal asked. "We hear that you conferred overlong with their new Ambassador, this Hwi Noree."

"I have no allies," he said. "Only servants, students and enemies."

"And you do not fear the Ixians' machine?" Anteac insisted.

"Is automation synonymous with conscious intelligence?" he asked.

Anteac's eyes went wide and filmy as she withdrew into her memories. Leto found himself caught by fascination with what she must be encountering there within her own internal mob.

186

We share some of those memories, he thought.

Leto felt then the seductive attraction of community with Reverend Mothers. It would be so familiar, so supportive . . . and so deadly. Anteac was trying to lure him once more.

She spoke: "The machine cannot anticipate every problem of importance to humans. It is the difference between serial bits and an unbroken continuum. We have the one; machines are confined to the other."

"You still have the power of reason," he said.

"Share!" Luyseyal said. It was a command to Anteac and it revealed with sharp abruptness who really dominated this pair—the younger over the older.

Exquisite, Leto thought.

"Intelligence adapts," Anteac said.

Parsimonious with her words, too, Leto thought, hiding his amusement.

"Intelligence creates," Leto said. "That means you must deal with responses never before imagined. You must confront the *new*."

"Such as the possibility of the Ixian Machine," Anteac said. It was not a question.

"Isn't it interesting," Leto asked, "that being a superb Reverend Mother is not enough?"

His acute senses detected the sudden fearful tightening in both of the women. Truthsayers, indeed!

"You are right to fear me," he said. Raising his voice, he demanded: "How do you know you're even alive?"

As Moneo had done so many times, they heard in his voice the deadly consequences of failure to answer him correctly. It fascinated Leto that both women glanced at Moneo before either responded.

"I am the mirror of myself," Luyseyal said, a pat Bene Gesserit answer which Leto found offensive.

"I don't need pre-set tools to deal with my human problems," Anteac said. "Your question is sophomoric!"

"Hah, hah!" Leto laughed. "How would you like to quit the Bene Gesserit and join me?"

187

He could see her consider and then reject the invitation, but she did not hide her amusement.

Leto looked at the puzzled Luyseyal. "If it falls outside your yardsticks, then you are engaged with intelligence, not with automation," he said. And he thought: *That Luyseyal will never again dominate old Anteac.*

Luyseyal was angry now and not bothering to conceal it. She said: "The Ixians are rumoured to have provided you with machines that simulate human thinking. If you have such a low opinion of them, why . . ."

"She should not be let out of the Chapter House without a guardian," Leto said, addressing Anteac. "Is she afraid to address her own memories?"

Luyseyal paled, but remained silent.

Leto studied her coldly. "Our ancestors' long unconscious relationship with machines has taught us something, don't you think?"

Luyseyal merely glared at him, not ready yet to risk death through open defiance of the God Emperor.

"Would you say we at least know the attraction of machines?" Leto asked.

Luyseyal nodded.

"A well maintained machine can be more reliable than a human servant," Leto said. "We can trust machines not to indulge in emotional distractions."

Luyseyal found her voice. "Does this mean you intend to remove the Butlerian prohibition against abominable machines?"

"I swear to you," Leto said, speaking in his icy voice of disdain, "that if you display further such stupidity I will have you publicly executed. I am *not* your Oracle!"

Luyseyal opened her mouth and closed it without speaking.

Anteac touched her companion's arm, sending a quick tremor through Luyseyal's body. Anteac spoke softly in an exquisite demonstration of Voice: "Our God Emperor will never openly defy the proscriptions of the Butlerian Jihad."

Leto smiled at her, a gentle commendation. It was such a pleasure to see a professional performing at her best.

"That should be obvious to any conscious intelligence," he said. "There are limits of my own choosing, places where I will not interfere."

He could see both women absorbing the multi-pronged thrust of his words, weighing the possible meanings and intents. Was the God Emperor distracting them, focusing their attention on the Ixians while he manoeuvred elsewhere? Was he telling the Bene Gesserit that the time had come to choose sides against the Ixians? Was it possible his words had no more than their surface motivations? Whatever his reasons, they could not be ignored. He was undoubtedly the most devious creature the universe had ever spawned.

Leto scowled at Luyseyal, knowing he could only add to their confusion. "I point out to you, Marcus Claire Luyseyal, a lesson from past over-machined societies which you appear *not* to have learned. The devices themselves condition the users to employ each other the way they employ machines."

He turned his attention to Moneo. "Moneo?"

"I see him, Lord."

Moneo craned his neck to peer over the Bene Gesserit entourage. Duncan Idaho had entered the far portal, and strode across the open floor of the chamber toward Leto. Moneo did not relax his wariness, his distrust of the Bene Gesserit, but he recognized the nature of Leto's lecture. *He is testing, always testing.*

Anteac cleared her throat. "Lord, what of our reward?"

"You are brave," Leto said. "No doubt that's why you were chosen for this Embassy. Very well, for the next decade I will continue your spice allotment at its present level. As for the rest, I will ignore what you really intended with the spice essence. Am I not generous?"

"Most generous, Lord," Anteac said, and there was not the slightest hint of bitterness in her voice.

Duncan Idaho brushed past the women then and stopped

beside Moneo to peer up at Leto. "M'Lord, there's . . ." He broke off and glanced at the two Reverend Mothers.

"Speak openly," Leto commanded.

"Yes, m'Lord." There was reluctance in him, but he obeyed. "We were attacked at the southeast edge of the city, a distraction I believe because there now are reports of more violence in the city and in the Forbidden Forest—many scattered raiding parties."

"They are hunting my wolves," Leto said. "In the forest and in the city, they are hunting my wolves."

Idaho's brows contracted into a puzzled frown. "Wolves in the city, m'Lord?"

"Predators," Leto said. "Wolves—to me there is no essential difference."

Moneo gasped.

Leto smiled at him, thinking how beautiful it was to observe a moment of realization—a veil pulled away from the eyes, the mind opened.

"I have brought a large force of guards to protect this place," Idaho said. "They are posted through the . . ."

"I knew you would," Leto said. "Now pay close attention while I tell you where to send the rest of your forces."

As the Reverend Mothers watched in awe, Leto laid out for Idaho the exact points for ambushes, detailing the size of each force and even some of the specific personnel, the timing, the necessary weapons, the precise deployments at each place. Idaho's capacious memory catalogued each instruction. He was too caught up in the recital to question it until Leto fell silent, but a look of puzzled fear came over Idaho then.

For Leto, it was as though he peered directly into Idaho's most essential awareness to read the thoughts there. *I was a trusted soldier of the original Lord Leto*, Idaho was thinking. *That Leto, the father of this one, saved me and took me into his household like a son. But even though that Leto still has some kind of existence in this one . . . this is not him.*

"M'Lord, why do you need *me*?" Idaho asked.

"For your strength and loyalty."

Idaho shook his head. "But . . ."

"You obey," Leto said, and he noted the way these words were being absorbed by the Reverend Mothers. *Truth, only truth for they are Truthsayers.*

"Because I owe a debt to the Atreides," Idaho said.

"That is where we place our trust," Leto said. "And Duncan?"

"M'Lord?" Idaho's voice said he had found ground where he could stand.

"Leave at least one survivor at each place," Leto said. "Otherwise, our efforts are wasted."

Idaho nodded once, curtly, and left, striding back across the hall the way he had come. And Leto thought it would take an extremely sensitive eye indeed to see that it was a different Idaho leaving, far different from the one who had entered.

Anteac said: "This comes of flogging that Ambassador."

"Exactly," Leto agreed. "Recount this carefully to your Superior, the admirable Reverend Mother Syaksa. Tell her for me that I prefer the company of predators above that of the prey." He glanced at Moneo, who drew himself to attention. "Moneo, the wolves are gone from my forest. They must be replaced by human wolves. See to it."

> *The trance-state of prophecy is like no other visionary experience. It is not a retreat from the raw exposure of the senses (as are many trance-states) but an immersion in a multitude of new movements. Things move. It is an ultimate pragmatism in the midst of infinity, a demanding consciousness where you come at last into the unbroken awareness that the universe moves of itself, that it changes, that its rules change, that nothing remains permanent or absolute throughout all such movement, that mechanical explanations for anything can work only within precise confinements and, once the walls are broken down, the old explanations shatter and dissolve, blown away by new movements. The things you see in this trance are sobering, often shattering. They demand your utmost effort to remain whole and, even so, you emerge from that state profoundly changed.*
> —The Stolen Journals

That night of Audience Day, while others slept and fought and dreamed and died, Leto took his repose in the isolation of his audience chamber, only a few trusted Fish Speaker guards at the portals.

He did not sleep. His mind whirled with necessities and disappointments.

Hwi! Hwi!

He knew why Hwi Noree had been sent to him now. How well he knew!

My most secret secret is exposed.

They had discovered his secret. Hwi was the evidence of it.

He thought desperate thoughts. Could this terrible meta-morphosis be reversed? Could he return to a human state?

Not possible.

Even if it were possible, the process would take him just as long as it had taken to reach this point. Where would Hwi be in more than three thousand years? Dry dust and bones in the crypt.

I could breed something like her and prepare that one for me . . . but that would not be my gentle Hwi.

And what of the Golden Path while he indulged in such selfish goals?

To hell with the Golden Path! Have these folly-bound idiots ever thought once of me? Not once!

But that was not true. Hwi thought of him. She shared his torture.

These were thoughts of madness and he tried to put them away while his senses reported the soft movement of the guards and the flow of water beneath his chamber.

When I made this choice, what were my expectations?

How the mob within laughed at that question! Did he not have a task to complete? Was that not the very essence of the agreement which kept the mob in check?

"You have a task to complete," they said. "You have but one purpose."

Single purpose is the mark of the fanatic and I am not a fanatic!

"You must be cynical and cruel. You cannot break the trust."

Why not?

"Who took that oath? You did. You chose this course."

Expectations!

"The expectations which history creates for one generation are often shattered in the next generation. Who knows that better than you?"

Yes . . . and shattered expectations can alienate whole populations. I alone am a whole population!

"Remember your oath!"

Indeed. I am the disruptive force unleashed across the centuries. I limit expectations . . . including my own. I dampen the pendulum.

"And then release it. Never forget that."

I am tired. Oh, how tired I am. If only I could sleep . . . really sleep.

"You're full of self-pity, too."

Why not? What am I? The ultimate loner forced to look at what might have been. Every day I look at it . . . and now, Hwi!

"Your original unselfish choice fills you now with selfishness."

There is danger all around. I must wear my selfishness like a suit of armour.

"There's danger for everyone who touches you. Isn't that your very nature?"

Danger even for Hwi. Dear, delectable, dear Hwi.

"Did you build high walls around you only to sit within them and indulge in self-pity?"

The walls were built because great forces have been unleashed in my Empire.

"You unleashed them. Will you now compromise with them?"

It's Hwi's doing. These feelings have never before been this powerful in me. It's the damnable Ixians!

"How interesting that they should assault you with flesh rather than with a machine."

193

Because they have discovered my secret.

"You know the antidote."

Leto's great body trembled through its entire length at this thought. He well knew the antidote which had always worked before: lose himself for a time in his own past. Not even the Bene Gesserit Sisters could take such safaris, striking inward along the axis of memories—back, back to the very limits of cellular awareness, or stopping by a wayside to revel in a sophisticated sensory delight. Once, after the death of a particularly superb Duncan, he had toured great musical performances preserved in his memories. Mozart had tired him quickly. *Pretentious! But Bach . . . ahhh, Bach.*

Leto remembered the joy of it.

I sat at the organ and let the music drench me.

Only three times in all memory had there been an equal to Bach. But even Licallo was not better; as good, but not better.

Would female intellectuals be the proper choice for this night? Grandmother Jessica had been one of the best. Experience told him that someone as close to him as Jessica would not be the proper antidote for his present tensions. The search would have to venture much farther.

He imagined then describing such a safari to some awe-struck visitor, a totally imaginary visitor because none would dare question him about such a *holy* matter.

"I course backward down the flight of ancestors, hunting along the tributaries, darting into nooks and crannies. You would not recognize many of their names. Who has ever heard of Norma Cenva? I have lived her!"

"Lived her?" his imaginary visitor asked.

"Of course. Why else would one keep one's ancestors around? You think a man designed the first Guild ship? Your history books told you it was Aurelius Venport? They lied. It was his mistress, Norma. She gave him the design along with five children. He thought his ego would take no less. In the end, the knowledge that he had not really fulfilled his own image, that was what destroyed him."

194

"You have lived him, too?"

"Naturally. And I have traversed the far wanderings of the Fremen. Through my father's line and the others, I have gone right back to the House of Atreus."

"Such an illustrious line!"

"With its fair share of fools."

Distraction is what I need, he thought.

Would it be a tour through sexual dalliances and exploits, then?

"You have no idea what internal orgies are available to me! I am the ultimate voyeur—participant(s) and observer(s). Ignorance and misunderstandings about sexuality have caused so much distress. How abysmally narrow we have been—how miserly."

Leto knew he could not make that choice, not this night, not with Hwi out there in his city.

Would he choose a review of warfare then?

"Which Napoleon was the greater coward?" he asked his imaginary visitor. "I will not reveal it, but I know. Oh, yes, I know."

Where can I go? With all of the past open to me, where can I go?

The brothels, the atrocities, the tyrants, the acrobats, nudists, surgeons, male whores, musicians, magicians, ungenciers, priests, artisans, priestesses . . .

"Are you aware," he asked his imaginary visitor, "that the hula preserves an ancient sign language which once belonged only to males? You've never heard of the hula? Of course. Who dances it anymore? Dancers have preserved many things, though. The translations have been lost, but I know them.

"One whole night I was a series of caliphs moving eastward and westward with Islam—a traverse of centuries. I will not bore you with the details. Be gone now, visitor!"

How seductive it is, he thought, *this call of the siren which would have me live only in the past.*

And how useless that past now, thanks to the damnable Ixians. How boring the past when Hwi is here. She would come to me right now if I summoned her. But I cannot call for her . . . not now . . . not tonight.

The past continued to beckon.

I could make a pilgrimage into my past. It does not have to be a safari. I could go alone. Pilgrimage purifies. Safaris make me into a tourist. That's the difference. I could go alone into my inner world.

And never return.

Leto felt the inevitability of it, that the dreamstate would eventually trap him.

I create a special dreamstate throughout my Empire. Within this dream, new myths form, new directions appear and new movements. New . . . new . . . new . . . The things emerge from my own dreams, out of my myths. Who more susceptible to them than I? The hunter is caught in his own net.

Leto knew then that he had encountered a condition for which no antidote existed—past, present or future. His great body trembled and shivered in the gloom of his audience chamber.

At the portal, one Fish Speaker guard whispered to another: "Is God troubled?"

And her companion replied: "The sins of this universe would trouble anyone."

Leto heard them and wept silently.

> *When I set out to lead humankind along my Golden Path, I promised them a lesson their bones would remember. I know a profound pattern which humans deny with their words even while their actions affirm it. They say they seek security and quiet, the condition they call peace. Even as they speak they create the seeds of turmoil and violence. If they find their quiet security they squirm in it. How boring they find it. Look at them now. Look at what they do while I record these words. Hah! I give them enduring eons of enforced tranquillity which plods on and on despite their every effort to escape into chaos. Believe me, the memory of Leto's Peace shall abide with them forever. They will seek their quiet security thereafter only with extreme caution and steadfast preparation.*
>
> —The Stolen Journals

Much against his will, Idaho found himself at dawn with Siona beside him being taken to "a safe place" in an Imperial ornithopter. It raced eastward toward the golden arc of sunlight which lifted over a landscape carved into rectangular green plantations.

The 'thopter was a big one, large enough to carry a small squad of Fish Speakers with their two *guests*. The pilot captain of the squad, a brawny woman with a face Idaho could believe had never smiled, had given her name as Inmeir. She sat in the pilot's seat directly ahead of Idaho, two muscular Fish Speaker guards on either side of her. Five more guards sat behind Idaho and Siona.

"God has ordered me to take you away from the city," Inmeir had said, coming up to him in the command post beneath the central plaza. "It is for your own safety. We will return by tomorrow morning for Siaynoq."

Idaho, fatigued by a night of alarms, had sensed the futility of arguing against the orders of "God Himself". Inmeir appeared quite capable of trundling him off under one of her thick arms. She had led him from the command post into a chilly night canopied with stars like stone-edged facets of shattered brilliants. It was only when they reached the 'thopter and Idaho recognized Siona waiting there that he had begun to question the purpose of this outing.

During the night, Idaho had come to realize that not all of the violence in Onn had originated with the organized rebels. When he had inquired after Siona, Moneo had sent word that "my daughter is safely out of the way", adding at the end of the message: "I commend her to your care".

In the 'thopter, Siona had not responded to Idaho's questions. Even now, she sat in sullen silence beside him. She reminded him of himself in those first bitter days when he had vowed vengeance against the Harkonnens. He wondered at her bitterness. What drove her?

Without knowing why, Idaho found himself comparing Siona with Hwi Noree. It had not been easy to encounter Hwi, but he had managed it, in spite of the importunate

197

demands of Fish Speakers that he attend to duties elsewhere.

Gentle, that was the word for Hwi. She acted from a core of unchanging gentleness which was, in its own way, a thing of enormous power. He found this intensely attractive.

I must see more of her.

For now, though, he had to contend with the sullen silence of Siona seated beside him. Well . . . silence could be met with silence.

Idaho peered down at the passing landscape. Here and there he could see the clustered lights of villages winking out as the sunlight approached. The desert of the Sareer lay far behind and this was land that, by its appearance, might never have been parched.

Some things do not change very much, he thought. *They are merely taken from one place and reformed in another place.*

This landscape reminded him of Caladan's lush gardens and made him wonder what had become of the verdant planet where the Atreides had lived for so many generations before coming to Dune. He could identify narrow roads, market roads with a scattered traffic of vehicles drawn by six-legged animals which he guessed were horses. Moneo had said that horses tailored to the needs of such a landscape were the main work beasts not only here but throughout the Empire.

"A population which walks is easier to control."

Moneo's words rang in Idaho's memory as he peered downwards. Pastureland appeared ahead of the 'thopter, softly rolling green hills cut into irregular patterns by black stone walls. Idaho recognized sheep and several kinds of large cattle. The 'thopter passed over a narrow valley still in gloom and with only a hint of the water coursing down its depths. A single light and a blue plume of smoke lifting out of the valley's shadows spoke of human occupation.

Siona suddenly stirred and tapped their pilot on the shoulder, pointing off to the right ahead of them.

"Isn't that Goygoa over there?" Siona asked.

"Yes." Inmeir spoke without turning, her voice clipped and touched by some emotion which Idaho could not identify.

"Is that not a safe place?" Siona asked.

"It is safe."

Siona looked at Idaho. "Order her to take us to Goygoa."

Without knowing why he complied, Idaho said: "Take us to that place."

Inmeir turned then and her features, which Idaho had thought a square block of non-emotion during the night, revealed the clear evidence of some deep feeling. Her mouth was drawn down into a scowl. A nerve twitched at the corner of her right eye.

"Not Goygoa, Commander," Inmeir said. "There are better . . ."

"Did the God Emperor tell you to take us to a specific place?" Siona demanded.

Inmeir glared her anger at this interruption, but did not look directly at Siona. "No, but He . . ."

"Then take us to this Goygoa," Idaho said.

Inmeir jerked her attention back to the 'thopter's controls and Idaho was thrown against Siona as the craft banked sharply and flew toward a round pocket nestled in the green hills.

Idaho peered over Inmeir's shoulder to look at their destination. At the very centre of the pocket lay a village built of the same black stones as the surrounding fences. Idaho saw orchards on some of the slopes above the village, terraced gardens rising in steps toward a small saddle where hawks could be seen gliding on the day's first updrafts.

Looking at Siona, Idaho asked: "What is this Goygoa?"

"You will see."

Inmeir set the 'thopter into a shallow glide which brought them to a gentle landing on a flat stretch of grass at the edge of the village. One of the Fish Speakers opened the door on the village side. Idaho's nostrils were immediately assaulted by a heady mixture of aromas—crushed grass, animal droppings, the acridity of cooking fires. He slipped out of the 'thopter and looked up a village street where people were emerging from their houses to stare at the visitors. Idaho saw an older woman in a long green dress bend over and whisper something to a child who immediately turned and went dashing away up the street.

"Do you like this place?" Siona asked. She dropped down beside him.

"It appears pleasant."

Siona looked at Inmeir as the pilot and the other Fish Speakers joined them on the grass. "When do we go back to Onn?"

"You do not go back," Inmeir said. "My orders are to take you to the Citadel. The Commander goes back."

"I see." Siona nodded. "When will we leave?"

"At dawn tomorrow. I will see the village leader about quarters." Inmeir strode off into the village.

"Goygoa," Idaho said. "That's a strange name. I wonder what this place was in the Dune days?"

"I happen to know," Siona said. "It is on the old charts as Shuloch, which means 'haunted place'. The Oral History says great crimes were committed here before all of the inhabitants were wiped out."

"Jacurutu," Idaho whispered, recalling the old legends of the water stealers. He glanced around, looking for the evidence of dunes and ridges; there was nothing—only two older men with placid faces returning with Inmeir. The men wore faded blue trousers and ragged shirts. Their feet were bare.

"Did you know this place?" Siona asked.

"Only as a name in a legend."

"Some say there are ghosts," she said, "but I do not believe it."

Inmeir stopped in front of Idaho and motioned the two barefooted men to wait behind her. "The quarters are poor but adequate," she said, "unless you would care to stay in one of the private residences." She turned and looked at Siona as she said this.

"We will decide later," Siona said. She took Idaho's arm. "The Commander and I wish to stroll through Goygoa and admire the sights."

Inmeir shaped her mouth to speak, but remained silent.

Idaho allowed Siona to lead him past the peering faces of the two local men.

"I will send two guards with you," Inmeir called out.

Siona stopped and turned. "Is it not safe in Goygoa?"

"It is very peaceful here," one of the men said.

"Then we will not need guards," Siona said. "Have them guard the 'thopter."

Again, she led Idaho toward the village.

"All right," Idaho said, disengaging his arm from Siona's grasp. "What is this place?"

"It is very likely that you will find this a very restful place," Siona said. "It is not like the old Shuloch at all. Very peaceful."

"You're up to something," Idaho said, striding beside her. "What is it?"

"I've always heard that gholas were full of questions," Siona said. "I, too, have questions."

"Oh?"

"What was he like in your day, the man Leto?"

"Which one?"

"Yes, I forget there were two—the grandfather and our Leto. I mean our Leto, of course."

"He was just a child, that's all I know."

"The Oral History says one of his early brides came from this village."

"Brides? I thought . . ."

"When he still had a manly shape. It was after the death of his sister but before he began to change into the worm. The Oral History says the brides of Leto vanished into the maze of the Imperial Citadel, never to be seen again except as faces and voices transmitted by holo. He has not had a bride for thousands of years."

201

They had arrived at a small square at the centre of the village, a space about fifty metres on a side and with a low-walled pool of clear water in its centre. Siona crossed to the pool's wall and sat on the rock ledge, patting beside her for Idaho to join her there. Idaho looked around at the village first, noting how people peered out at him from behind curtained windows, how the children pointed and whispered. He turned and stood looking down at Siona.

"What is this place?"

"I've told you. Tell me what Muad'Dib was like."

"He was the best friend a man could ever have."

"So the Oral History is true, but it calls the caliphate of his heirs *The Desposyni*, and that has an evil sound."

She's baiting me, Idaho thought.

He allowed himself a tight smile, wondering at Siona's motives. She appeared to be waiting for some important event, anxious . . . even dreading . . . but with an undertone of something like elation. It was all there. Nothing she said now could be accounted as more than small talk, a way of occupying the moments until . . . until what?

The light sound of running feet intruded on his reverie. Idaho turned and saw a child of perhaps eight years racing toward him out of a side-street. The child's bare feet kicked up little dust geysers as he ran and there was the sound of a woman shouting, a despairing sound somewhere up the street. The runner stopped about ten paces away and stared up at Idaho with a hungering look, an intensity which Idaho found disturbing. The child appeared vaguely familiar—a boy, a stalwart figure with dark curly hair, an unfinished face but with hints of the man to be—rather high cheekbones, a flat line across the brows. He wore a faded blue singlesuit which betrayed the effects of much laundering but obviously had begun as a garment of excellent material. It had the look of punji cotton woven in a cordlock that did not permit even the frayed edges to unravel.

"You're not my father," the child said. Whirling away, he raced back up the street and vanished around a corner.

Idaho turned and scowled at Siona, almost afraid to ask

the question: *Was that a child of my predecessor?* He knew the answer without asking—that familiar face, the geno-type carried true. *Myself as a child.* Realization left him with an empty feeling, a sense of frustration. *What is my responsibility?*

Siona put both hands over her face and hunched her shoulders. It had not happened at all the way she had imagined it might. She felt betrayed by her own desires for revenge. Idaho was not simply a *ghola*, something alien and unworthy of consideration. She had felt him thrown against her in the 'thopter, had seen the obvious emotions on his face. And that child . . . .

"What happened to my predecessor?" Idaho asked. His voice came out flat and accusatory.

She lowered her hands. There was suppressed rage in his face.

"We are not certain," she said, "but he entered the Citadel one day and never emerged."

"That was his child?"

She nodded.

"You're sure you did not kill my predecessor?"

"I . . ." She shook her head, shocked by the doubts, the latent accusation in him.

"That child, that is the reason we came here?"

She swallowed. "Yes."

"What am I supposed to do about him?"

She shrugged, feeling soiled and guilty because of her own actions.

"What about his mother?" Idaho asked.

"She and the others live up that street." Siona nodded in the direction the boy had gone.

"Others?"

"There is an older son . . . a daughter. Will you . . . I mean, I could arrange . . ."

"No! The boy was right. I'm not his father."

"I'm sorry," Siona whispered. "I should not have done this."

"Why did *he* choose this place?" Idaho asked.

"The father . . . your . . ."

"My *predecessor!*"

"Because this was Irti's home and she would not leave. That is what people said."

"Irti . . . the mother?"

"Wife, by the old rite, the one from the Oral History."

Idaho looked around at the stone fronts of the buildings which enclosed the square, the curtained windows, the narrow doors. "So he lived here?"

"When he could."

"How did he die, Siona?"

"Truly, I do not know . . . but the Worm has killed others. We know that for sure!"

"How do you know it?" He centred a probing stare on her face. The intensity of it forced her to look away.

"I do not doubt the stories of my ancestors," she said. "They are told in bits and pieces, a note here, a whispered account there, but I believe them. My father believes them, too!"

"Moneo has said nothing to me of this."

"One thing you can say about the Atreides," she said. "We're loyal and that's a fact. We keep our word."

Idaho opened his mouth to speak, closed it without making a sound. *Of course! Siona, too, was Atreides*. The thought shook him. He had known it, but he had not accepted it. Siona was some kind of a rebel, a rebel whose actions were almost sanctioned by Leto. The limits of his permission were unclear, but Idaho sensed them.

"You must not harm her," Leto had said. "She is to be tested."

Idaho turned his back on Siona.

"You don't know anything for sure," he said. "Bits and pieces, rumours!"

Siona did not respond.

"He's an Atreides!" Idaho said.

"He's the Worm!" Siona said and the venom in her voice was almost palpable.

"Your damned Oral History is nothing but a bunch of

204

ancient gossip!" Idaho accused. "Only a fool would believe it."

"You still trust him," she said. "That will change."

Idaho whirled and glared at her.

"You've never talked to him!"

"I have. When I was a child."

"You're still a child. He's all of the Atreides who were, all of them. It's a terrible thing, but I knew those people. They were my friends."

Siona only shook her head.

Again, Idaho turned away. He felt that he had been wrung dry of emotion. He was spiritually boneless. Without willing it, he began walking across the square and up the street where the boy had gone. Siona came running after him and fell into step, but he ignored her.

The street was narrow, enclosed by the one-storey stone walls, the doors set back within arched frames, all of the doors closed. The windows were small versions of the doors. Curtains twitched as he passed.

At the first cross-street, Idaho stopped and looked to the right where the boy had gone. Two grey-haired women in long black skirts and dark green blouses stood a few paces away down the street, gossiping with their heads close together. They fell silent when they saw Idaho and stared at him with open curiosity. He returned their stare, then looked down the side-street. It was empty.

Idaho turned toward the women, passed them within a pace. They drew closer together and turned to watch him. They looked only once at Siona, then returned their attention to Idaho. Siona moved quietly beside him, an odd expression on her face.

Sadness? he wondered. *Regret? Curiosity?*

It was difficult to say. He was more curious about the doorways and windows they were passing.

"Have you ever been to Goygoa before?" Idaho asked.

"No." Siona spoke in a subdued voice, as though afraid of it.

Why am I walking down this street? Idaho wondered.

205

Even as he asked himself the question, he knew the answer. *This woman, this Irti: What kind of a woman would bring me to Goygoa?*

The corner of a curtain on his right lifted and Idaho saw a face—the boy from the square. The curtain dropped then was flung aside to reveal a woman standing there. Idaho stared speechlessly at her face, stopped in a completed step. It was the face of a woman known only to his deepest fantasies—a soft oval with penetrating dark eyes, a full and sensuous mouth . . .

"Jessica," he whispered.

"What did you say?" Siona asked.

Idaho could not answer. It was the face of Jessica resurrected out of a past he had believed gone forever, a genetic prank—Muad'Dib's mother recreated in new flesh.

The woman closed the curtain, leaving the memory of her features in Idaho's mind, an after-image which he knew he could never remove. She had been older than the Jessica who had shared their dangers on Dune—age lines beside the mouth and eyes, the body a bit more full . . .

More motherly, Idaho told himself. Then: *Did I ever tell her . . . who she resembled?*

Siona tugged at his sleeve. "Do you wish to go in, to meet her?"

"No. This was a mistake."

Idaho started to turn back the way they had come, but the door of Irti's house was flung open. A young man emerged and closed the door behind him, turning then to confront Idaho.

Idaho guessed the youth's age at sixteen and there was no denying the parentage—that karakul hair, the strong features.

"You are the new one," the youth said. His voice had already deepened into manhood.

"Yes." Idaho found it difficult to speak.

"Why have you come?" the youth asked.

"It was not my idea," Idaho said. He found this easier to say, the words driven by resentment against Siona.

The youth looked at Siona. "We have had word that my father is dead."

Siona nodded.

The youth returned his attention to Idaho. "Please go away and do not return. You cause pain for my mother."

"Of course," Idaho said. "Please apologize to the Lady Irti for this intrusion. I was brought here against my will."

"Who brought you?"

"The Fish Speakers," Idaho said.

The youth nodded once, a curt movement of the head. He looked once more at Siona. "I always thought that you Fish Speakers were taught to treat your own more kindly." With that, he turned and re-entered the house, closing the door firmly behind him.

Idaho turned back the way they had come, grabbing Siona's arm as he strode away. She stumbled, then fell into step, disengaging his grasp.

"He thought I was a Fish Speaker," she said.

"Of course. You have the look." He glanced at her. "Why didn't you tell me that Irti was a Fish Speaker?"

"It didn't seem important."

"Oh."

"That's how they met."

They came to the intersection with the street from the square. Idaho turned away from the square, striding briskly up to the end where the village merged into gardens and orchards. He felt insulated by shock, his awareness recoiling from too much that could not be assimilated.

A low wall blocked his path. He climbed over it, heard Siona follow. Trees around them were in bloom, white flowers with orange centres where dark brown insects worked. The air was full of insect buzzing and a floral scent which reminded Idaho of jungle flowers from Caladan.

He stopped when he reached the crest of a hill where he could turn and look back down at Goygoa's rectangular neatness. The roofs were flat and black.

Siona sat down on the thick grass of the hilltop and embraced her knees.

"That was not what you intended, was it?" Idaho asked.

She shook her head and he saw that she was close to tears.

"Why do you hate him so much?" he asked.

"We have no lives of our own!"

Idaho looked down at the village. "Are there many villages like this one?"

"This is the shape of the Worm's Empire!"

"What's wrong with it?"

"Nothing—if that's all you want."

"You're saying that this is all he allows?"

"This, a few market cities . . . Onn. I'm told that even planetary capitals are just big villages."

"And I repeat: What's wrong with that?"

"It's a prison!"

"Then leave it."

"Where? How? You think we can just get on a Guild ship and go anywhere else, anywhere we want?" She pointed down toward Goygoa where the 'thopter could be seen off to one side, the Fish Speakers seated on the grass nearby. "Our jailers won't let us leave!"

"They leave," Idaho said. "They go anywhere they want."

"Anywhere the Worm sends them!"

She pressed her face against her knees and spoke, her voice muffled. "What was it like in the old days?"

"It was different, often very dangerous." He looked around at the walls which set off pastureland, gardens and orchards. "Here on Dune, there were no imaginary lines to show the limits of ownership on the land. It was all the Dukedom of the Atreides."

"Except for the Fremen."

"Yes. But they knew where they belonged—on this side of a particular escarpment . . . or beyond where the pan turns white against the sand."

"They could go wherever they wanted!"

"With some limits."

"Some of us long for the desert," she said.

"You have the Sareer."

She lifted her head to glare at him. "That little thing!"

"Fifteen hundred kilometres by five hundred—not so little."

Siona got to her feet. "Have you asked the Worm why he confines us this way?"

"Leto's Peace, the Golden Path to insure our survival. That's what he *says*."

"Do you know what he told my father? I spied on them when I was a child. I heard him."

"What did he say?"

"He said he denies us most crises, to limit our forming forces. He said: 'People can be sustained by affliction, but I am the affliction now. Gods can become afflictions.' Those were his words, Duncan. The Worm is a sickness!"

Idaho did not doubt the accuracy of her recital, but the words failed to stir him. He thought instead of the Corrino he had been ordered to kill. *Affliction*. The Corrino, descendant of a Family which once had ruled this Empire, had been revealed as a softly fat middle-aged man who hungered after power and conspired for spice. Idaho had ordered a Fish Speaker to kill him, an act which had aroused Moneo to a fit of intense questioning.

"Why didn't you kill him yourself?"

"I wanted to see how the Fish Speakers performed."

"And your judgment of their performance?"

"Efficient."

But the death of the Corrino had inflicted Idaho with a sense of unreality. A fat little man lying in a pool of his own blood, an undistinguished shadow among the night shadows of a plastone street. It was unreal. Idaho could remember Muad'Dib saying: *"The mind imposes this framework which it calls 'reality'. That arbitrary framework has a tendency to be quite independent of what your senses report."* What *reality* moved the Lord Leto?

Idaho looked at Siona standing against the orchard background and the green hills of Goygoa. "Let's go down to the village and find our quarters. I'd like to be alone."

"The Fish Speakers will put us in the same quarters."

"With them?"

"No, just the two of us together. The reason's simple enough. The Worm wants me to breed with the great Duncan Idaho."

"I pick my own partners," Idaho growled.

"I'm sure one of our Fish Speakers would be delighted," Siona said. She whirled away from him and set off down the hill.

Idaho watched her for a moment, the lithe young body swaying like the limbs of the orchard trees in the wind.

"I'm not his stud," Idaho muttered. "That's one thing he'll have to understand."

As each day passes, you become increasingly unreal, more alien and remote from what I find myself to be on that new day. I am the only reality and, as you differ from me, you lose reality. The more curious I become the less curious are those who worship me. Religion suppresses curiosity. What I do subtracts from the worshipper. Thus it is that eventually I will do nothing, giving it all back to frightened people who will find themselves on that day alone and forced to act for themselves.

—The Stolen Journals

It was a sound like no other, the sound of a waiting mob, and it came down the long tunnel to where Idaho marched ahead of the Royal Cart—nervous whispers magnified into an ultimate whisper, the shuffling of one gigantic foot, the stirring of an enormous garment. And the smell—sweet perspiration mixed with the milky breath of sexual excitement.

Inmeir and the others of his Fish Speaker escort had brought Idaho here in the first hour after dawn, coming down to the plaza of Onn while it lay in cold green shadows. They had lifted off immediately after turning him over to other Fish Speakers, Inmeir obviously unhappy because she was required to take Siona to the Citadel and thus would miss the ritual of Siaynoq.

The new escort, vibrant with repressed emotion, had taken him into a region deep beneath the plaza, a place not on any of the city charts Idaho had studied. It was a maze—first one direction and then another through corridors wide enough and high enough to accommodate the Royal Cart. Idaho lost track of directions and fell to reflecting on the preceding night.

The sleeping quarters in Goygoa, although spartan and small, had been comfortable—two cots to a room, each room a box with whitewashed walls, a single window and a single door. The rooms were strung along a corridor in a building designated as Goygoa's "Guest House".

And Siona had been right. Without asking if it suited him, Idaho had been quartered with her, Inmeir acting as though this were an accepted thing.

When the door closed on them, Siona said: "If you touch me I will try to kill you."

It was uttered with such dry sincerity that Idaho almost laughed. "I would prefer privacy," he said. "Consider yourself alone."

He had slept with a light wariness, remembering dangerous nights in the Atreides service, the readiness for combat. The room was seldom truly dark—moonlight coming through the curtained window, even starlight reflecting from the chalk-white walls. He had found himself nervously sensitive to Siona, to the smell of her, the stirrings, her breathing. Several times he had come fully awake to listen, aware on two of those occasions that she, too, was listening.

Morning and the flight to Onn had come as a relief. They had broken their fast with a drink of cold fruit juice, Idaho glad to enter the pre-dawn darkness for a brisk walk to the 'thopter. He did not speak directly to Siona and he found himself resenting the curious glances of the Fish Speakers.

Siona spoke to him only once, leaning out of the 'thopter as he left it in the plaza.

"It would not offend me to be your friend," she said.

Such a curious way of putting it. He had felt vaguely embarrassed. "Yes . . . well, certainly."

The new escort had led him away then, coming at last to a terminal in the maze. Leto awaited him there on the Royal Cart. The meeting place was a wide spot in a corridor which stretched off into the converging distance on Idaho's right. The walls were dark brown streaked with golden lines which glittered in the yellow light of glowglobes. The escort took up positions behind the cart, moving smartly and leaving Idaho to stand confronting Leto's cowled face.

"Duncan, you will precede me when we go to Siaynoq," Leto said.

Idaho stared into the dark blue wells of the God Emperor's eyes, angered by the mystery and secrecy, the obvious air of private excitement in this place. He felt that everything he had been told about Siaynoq only deepened the mystery.

"Am I truly the Commander of your Guard, m'Lord?" Idaho asked, resentment heavy in his voice.

"Indeed! And I bestow a signal honour upon you now. Few adult males ever share Siaynoq."

"What happened in the city last night?"

"Bloody violence in some places. It is quite calm this morning, however."

"Casualties?"

"Not worth mentioning."

Idaho nodded. Leto's prescient powers had warned of some peril to *his Duncan*. Thus, the flight into the rural safety of Goygoa.

"You have been to Goygoa," Leto said. "Were you tempted to stay?"

"No!"

"Do not be angry with me," Leto said. "I did not send you to Goygoa."

212

Idaho sighed. "What was the danger which required that you send me away?"

"It was not to you," Leto said. "But you excite my guards to excessive displays of their abilities. Last night's activities did not require this."

"Oh?" This thought shocked Idaho. He had never thought of himself as one to inspire particular heroism unless he personally demanded it. One *whipped up* the troops. Leaders such as the original Leto, this one's grandfather, had inspired by their presence.

"You are extremely precious to me, Duncan," Leto said.

"Yes . . . well, I'm still not your stud!"

"Your wishes will be honoured, of course. We will discuss it another time."

Idaho glanced at the Fish Speaker escort, all of them wide-eyed and attentive.

"Is there always violence when you come to Onn?" Idaho asked.

"It goes in cycles. The malcontents are quite subdued now. It will be more peaceful for a time."

Idaho looked back at Leto's inscrutable face. "What happened to my predecessor?"

"Haven't my Fish Speakers told you?"

"They say he died in defence of his God."

"And you have heard a contrary rumour."

"What happened?"

"He died because he was too close to me. I did not remove him to a safe place in time."

"A place like Goygoa."

"I would have preferred him to live out his days there in peace, but you well know, Duncan, that you are not a seeker after peace."

Idaho swallowed, encountering an odd lump in his throat. "I would still like the particulars of his death. He has a family . . ."

"You will get the particulars and do not fear for his family. They are my wards. I will keep them safely at a distance. You know how violence seeks me out. That is one

213

of my functions. It is unfortunate that those I admire and love must suffer because of this."

Idaho pursed his lips, not satisfied with what he heard.

"Set your mind at ease, Duncan," Leto said. "Your predecessor died because he was too close to me."

The Fish Speaker escort stirred restively. Idaho glanced at them, then looked to the right up the tunnel.

"Yes, it is time," Leto said. "We must not keep the women waiting. March close ahead of me, Duncan, and I will answer your questions about Siaynoq."

Obedient because he could think of no suitable alternative, Idaho turned on his heel and led off the procession. He heard the cart creak into motion behind him, the faint footsteps of the escort following.

The cart fell silent with an abruptness which jerked Idaho's attention around. The reason was immediately apparent.

"You're on the suspensors," he said, returning his attention to the front.

"I have retracted the wheels because the women will press close around me," Leto said. "We can't crush their feet."

"What is Siaynoq? What is it really?" Idaho asked.

"I have told you. It is the Great Sharing."

"Do I smell spice?"

"Your nostrils are sensitive. There is a small amount of melange in the wafers."

Idaho shook his head.

Trying to understand this event, Idaho had asked Leto directly at the first opportunity after their arrival in Onn. "What is the Feast of Siaynoq?"

"We share a wafer, no more. Even I partake."

"Is it like the Orange Catholic ritual?"

"Oh, no! It is not my flesh. It is the Sharing. They are reminded that they are only female, as you are only male, but I am *all*. They share with the *all*."

Idaho had not liked the tone of this. "*Only* male?"

214

"Do you know who they lampoon at the Feast, Duncan?"

"Who?"

"Men who have offended them. Listen to them when they talk softly among themselves."

Idaho had taken this as a warning: *Don't offend the Fish Speakers. You incur their wrath at your mortal peril!*

Now, as he marched ahead of Leto in the tunnel, Idaho felt that he had heard the words correctly but learned nothing from them. He spoke over his shoulder.

"I don't understand the Sharing."

"We are together in the ritual. You will see it. You will feel it. My Fish Speakers are the repository of a special knowledge, an unbroken line which only they share. Now, you will partake of it and they will love you for it. Listen to them carefully. They are open to ideas of affinity. Their terms of endearment for each other have no reservations."

More words, Idaho thought. *More mystery.*

He could discern a gradual widening in the tunnel; the ceiling sloped higher. There were more glowglobes, tuned now into the deep orange. He could see the high arch of an opening about three hundred metres away, rich red light there in which he could make out glistening faces which swayed gently left and right. Their bodies below the faces presented a dark wall of clothing. The perspiration of excitement was thick here.

As he neared the waiting women, Idaho saw a passage through them and a ramp slanting up to a low ledge on his right. A great arched ceiling curved away above the women, a gigantic space illuminated by glowglobes tuned high into the red.

"Go up the ramp on your right," Leto said. "Stop just beyond the centre of the ledge and turn to face the women."

Idaho lifted his right hand in acknowledgment. He was emerging into the open space now and the dimensions of this enclosed place awed him. He set his trained eyes the task of estimating the dimensions as he mounted to the ledge and guessed the hall to be at least eleven hundred metres on a side—a square with rounded corners. It was packed with women, and Idaho reminded himself that these were only the chosen representatives of the far scattered Fish Speaker regiments—three women from each planet. They stood now, their bodies pressed so closely together that Idaho doubted one of them could fall. They had left only a space about fifty metres wide along the ledge where Idaho now stopped and surveyed the scene. The faces looked up at him—faces, faces.

Leto stopped his cart just behind Idaho and lifted one of his silver-skinned arms.

Immediately, a roaring cry of "Siaynoq! Siaynoq!" filled the great hall.

Idaho was deafened by it. *Surely that sound must be heard throughout the city,* he thought. *Unless we are too far underground.*

"My brides," Leto said. "I welcome you to Siaynoq."

Idaho glanced up at Leto, saw the dark eyes glistening, the radiant expression. Leto had said: "This cursed holiness!" But he basked in it.

Has Moneo ever seen this gathering? Idaho wondered. It was an odd thought, but Idaho knew its origin. There had to be some other mortal human with whom this could be discussed. The escort had said Moneo was dispatched on "affairs of state" whose details they did not know. Hearing this, Idaho had felt himself sense another element in Leto's government. The lines of power extended directly from Leto out into the populace, but the lines did not often cross. That required many things, including trusted servants who would accept responsibility for carrying out orders without question.

"Few see the God Emperor do hurtful things," Siona had said. "Is that like the Atreides you knew?"

Idaho looked out over the massed Fish Speakers as these thoughts flitted through his mind. The adulation in their eyes! The awe! How had Leto done this? Why?

"My beloveds," Leto said. His voice boomed out over

216

the upturned faces, carried to the farthest corners by subtle Ixian amplifiers concealed in the Royal Cart.

The steaming images of the women's faces filled Idaho with memory of Leto's warning. *Incur their wrath at your mortal peril!*

It was easy to believe that warning in this place. One word from Leto and these women would tear an offender to pieces. They would not question. They would act. Idaho began to feel a new appreciation of these women as an army. Personal peril would not stop them. They served God!

The Royal Cart creaked slightly as Leto arched his front segments upward, lifting his head.

"You are the keepers of the faith!" Leto said.

They replied as one voice: "Lord, we obey!"

"In me you live without end!" Leto said.

"We are the infinite!" they shouted.

"I love you as I love no others!" Leto said.

"Love!" they screamed.

Idaho shuddered.

"I give you my beloved Duncan!" Leto said.

"Love!" they screamed.

Idaho felt his whole body trembling. He felt that he might collapse from the weight of this adulation. He wanted to run away and he wanted to stay and accept this. There was power in this room. Power!

In a lower voice, Leto said: "Change the Guard."

The women bowed their heads, a single movement, un-hesitating. From off to Idaho's right a line of women in white gowns appeared. They marched into the open space below the ledge and Idaho noted that some of them carried babies and small children, none more than a year or two old.

From the outline explanation provided for him earlier, Idaho recognized these women as the ones leaving the immediate service of the Fish Speakers. Some would become priestesses and some would spend full time as mothers . . . but none would truly leave Leto's service.

217

As he looked down on the children, Idaho thought how the buried memory of this experience must be impressed on any of the male children. They would carry the mystery of it throughout their lives, a memory lost to consciousness but always present, shading responses from this moment onward.

The last of the newcomers came to a stop below Leto and looked up at him. The other women in the hall now lifted their faces and focused on Leto.

Idaho glanced left and right. The whiteclad women filled the space below the ledge for at least five hundred metres in both directions. Some of them lifted their children toward Leto. The awe and submission was something absolute. If Leto ordered it, Idaho sensed, these women would smash their babies to death against the ledge. They would do anything!

Leto lowered his front segments on to the cart, a gentle rippling motion. He peered down benignly and his voice came as a soft caress. "I give you the reward which your faith and service have earned. Ask and it shall be given."

The entire hall reverberated to the response: "It shall be given!"

"What is mine is thine," Leto said.

"What is mine is thine," the women shouted.

"Share with me now," Leto said, "the silent prayer for my intercession in all things—that humankind may never end."

As one, every head in the hall bowed. The whiteclad women cradled their children close, looking down at them. Idaho felt the silent unity, a force which sought to enter him and take him over. He opened his mouth wide and breathed deeply, fighting against something which he sensed as a physical invasion. His mind searched frantically for something to which he could cling, something to shield him.

These women were an army whose force and union Idaho had not suspected. He knew he did not understand

218

this force. He could only observe it, recognize that it existed.

This was what Leto had created.

Leto's words from a meeting at the Citadel came back to Idaho: "Loyalty in a male army fastens on to the army itself rather than on to the civilization which fosters the army. Loyalty in a female army fastens on to the leader."

Idaho stared out across the visible evidence of Leto's creation, seeing the penetrating accuracy of those words, fearing that accuracy.

He offers me a share in this, Idaho thought.

His own response to Leto's words struck Idaho now as puerile.

"I don't see the reason," Idaho had said.

"Most people are not creatures of reason."

"No army, male or female, guarantees peace! Your Empire isn't peaceful! You only . . ."

"My Fish Speakers have provided you with our histories?"

"Yes, but I've also walked about in your city and I've watched your people. Your people are aggressive!"

"You see, Duncan? Peace encourages aggression."

"And you say that your Golden Path . . ."

"Is not precisely peace. It is tranquillity, a fertile ground for the growth of rigid classes and many other forms of aggression."

"You talk riddles!"

"I talk accumulated observations which tell me that the peaceful posture is the posture of the defeated. It is the posture of the victim. Victims invite aggression."

"Your damned enforced tranquillity! What good does it do?"

"If there is no enemy, one must be invented. The military force which is denied an external target always turns against its own people."

"What's your game?"

"I modify the human desire for war."

"People don't want war!"

219

"They want chaos. War is the most readily available form of chaos."

"I don't believe any of this! You're playing some dangerous game of your own."

"Very dangerous. I address ancient wellsprings of human behaviour to redirect them. The danger is that I could suppress the forces of human survival. But I assure you that my Golden Path endures."

"You haven't suppressed antagonism!"

"I dissipate energies in one place and point them toward another place. What you cannot control, you harness."

"What's to keep your female army from taking over?"

"I am their leader."

As he looked out over the massed women in the great hall, Idaho could not deny the focus of leadership. He saw also that part of this adulation was directed at his own person. The temptation in this held him fixated—anything he wanted from them . . . anything! The latent power in this great hall was explosive. This realisation forced him into a deeper questioning of Leto's earlier words.

Leto had said something about exploding violence. Even as he watched the women at their silent prayer, Idaho recalled what Leto had said: "Men are susceptible to class fixations. They create layered societies. The layered society is an ultimate invitation to violence. It does not fall apart. It explodes."

"Women never do this?"

"Not unless they are almost completely male dominated or locked into a male role model."

"The sexes can't be that different!"

"But they are. Women make common cause based on their sex, a cause which transcends class and caste. That is why I let my women hold the reins."

Idaho was forced to admit that these praying women held the reins.

What part of that power would he pass into my hands?

The temptation was monstrous! Idaho found himself trembling with it. With chilling abruptness, he realized that this must be Leto's intention—*to tempt me!*

On the floor of the great hall, the women finished their prayer and lifted their gaze to Leto. Idaho felt that he had never before seen such rapture in human faces—not in the ecstasy of sex, not in glorious victory-at-arms—nowhere had he seen anything to approach this intense adulation.

"Duncan Idaho stands beside me today," Leto said. "Duncan is here to declare his loyalty that all may hear it. Duncan?"

Idaho felt a physical chill shoot through his intestines. Leto gave him a simple choice: *Declare your loyalty to the God Emperor or die!*

If I sneer, vacillate or object in any way, the women will kill me with their own hands.

A deep anger suffused Idaho. He swallowed, cleared his throat, then: "Let no one question my loyalty. I am loyal to the Atreides."

He heard his own voice booming out over the room, amplified by Leto's Ixian device.

The effect startled Idaho.

"We share!" the women screamed. "We share! We share!"

"We share," Leto said.

Young Fish Speaker trainees, identifiable by their short green robes, swarmed into the hall from all sides, little knots of movement which eddied throughout the pattern of the adoring faces. Each trainee carried a tray piled high with tiny brown wafers. As the trays moved through the throng, hands reached out in waves of graceful grasping, an undulant dancing of the arms. Each hand took a wafer and held it aloft. When a tray bearer came to the ledge and lifted her burden toward Idaho, Leto said:

"Take two and pass one into my hand."

Idaho knelt and took two wafers. The things felt crisp and fragile. He stood and passed one gently to Leto.

In a stentorian voice, Leto asked: "Has the new Guard been chosen?"

"Yes, Lord!" the women shouted.

221

"Do you keep my faith?"

"Yes, Lord!"

"Do you walk the Golden Path?"

"Yes, Lord!"

The vibration of the women's shouts sent shock waves through Idaho, stunning him.

"Do we share?" Leto asked.

"Yes, Lord!"

As the women responded, Leto popped his wafer into his mouth. Each mother below the ledge took a bite from her wafer and offered the rest to her child. The massed Fish Speakers behind the whiteclad women lowered their arms and ate their wafers.

"Duncan, eat your wafer," Leto said.

Idaho slipped the thing into his mouth. His ghola body had not been conditioned to the spice but memory spoke to his senses. The wafer tasted faintly bitter with a soft under-tone of melange. The taste swept old memories through Idaho's awareness—meals in sietch, banquets at the Atreides Residency . . . the way spice flavours permeated everything in the old days.

As he swallowed the wafer, Idaho grew conscious of the stillness in the hall, a breath-held quiet into which came a loud *click* from Leto's cart. Idaho turned and sought the source of the sound. Leto had opened a compartment in the bed of his cart and was removing a crystal box from it. The box glowed with a blue-grey inner light. Leto placed the box on the bed of his cart, opened the glowing lid and removed a crysknife. Idaho recognized the blade im-mediately—the hawk engraved on the handle's butt, the green jewels at the hilt.

The crysknife of Paul-Muad'Dib!

Idaho found himself deeply moved at the sight of this blade. He stared at it as though the image in his eyes might reproduce the original owner.

Leto lifted the blade and held it high, revealing the elegant curve and milky iridescence.

"The talisman of our lives," Leto said.

The women remained silent, raptly attentive.

"The knife of Muad'Dib," Leto said. "The tooth of Shai-Hulud. Will Shai-Hulud come again?"

The response was a subdued murmur made deeply powerful by contrast with the previous shouting.

"Yes, Lord."

Idaho returned his attention to the enraptured faces of the Fish Speakers.

"Who is Shai-Hulud?" Leto asked.

Again, that deep murmur: "You, Lord."

Idaho nodded to himself. Here was undeniable evidence that Leto had tapped into a monstrous reservoir of power never before unleashed in quite this way. Leto had said it but the words were a meaningless noise compared to the thing seen and felt in this great hall. Leto's words came back to Idaho, though, as if they had waited for this moment to cloak themselves in their true meaning. Idaho recalled that they had been in the crypt, that dank and shadowy place which Leto seemed to find so attractive but which Idaho found so repellent—the dust of centuries there and the odours of ancient decay.

"I have been forming this human society, shaping it for more than three thousand years, opening a door out of adolescence for the entire species," Leto had said.

"Nothing you say explains a female army!" Idaho had protested.

"Rape is foreign to women, Duncan. You ask for a sex-rooted behavioural difference? There's one."

"Stop changing the subject!"

"I do not change it. Rape was always the pay-off in male military conquest. Males did not have to abandon any of their adolescent fantasies while engaging in rape."

Idaho recalled the glowering anger which had come over him at this thrust.

"My houris tame the males," Leto said. "It is domestication, a thing that females know from eons of necessity."

Idaho stared wordlessly at Leto's cowled face.

"To tame," Leto said. "To fit into some orderly survival

223

pattern. Women learned it at the hands of men; now men learn it at the hands of women."

"But you said . . ."

"My houris often submit to a form of rape at first only to convert this into a deep and binding mutual dependence."

"Dammit! You're . . ."

"Binding, Duncan! Binding."

"I don't feel bound to . . ."

"Education takes time. You are the ancient norm against which the new can be measured."

Leto's words momentarily flushed Idaho of all emotion except a deep sense of loss.

"My houris teach maturation," Leto said. "They know that they must supervise the maturation of males. Through this they find their own maturation. Eventually, houris merge into wives and mothers and we wean the violent drives away from their adolescent fixations."

"I'll have to see it to believe it!"

"You will see it at the Great Sharing."

As he stood beside Leto in the hall of Siaynoq, Idaho admitted to himself that he had seen something of enormous power, something which *might* create the kind of human universe Leto's words projected.

Leto was restoring the crysknife to its box, returning the box to its compartment in the bed of the Royal Cart. The women watched in silence, even the small children quiet—everyone subdued by the force which could be felt in this great hall.

Idaho looked down at the children, knowing from Leto's explanation that these children would be rewarded with positions of power—male or female, each in a puissant niche. The male children would be female dominated throughout their lives, making (in Leto's words) "an easy transition from adolescence into breeding males".

Fish Speakers and their progeny lived lives "possessed of a certain excitement not available to most others".

What will happen to Irti's children? Idaho wondered. *Did*

224

my predecessor stand here and watch his whiteclad wife share in Leto's ritual?

What does Leto offer me here?

With that female army, an ambitious commander could take over Leto's Empire. Or could he? No . . . not while Leto lived. Leto said the women were not militarily aggressive "by nature".

He said: "I do not foster that in them. They know a cyclical pattern with a Royal Festival every ten years, a changing of the Guard, a blessing for the new generation, a silent thought for fallen sisters and loved ones gone forever. Siaynoq after Siaynoq marches onward in predictable measure. The change itself becomes non-change."

Idaho lifted his gaze from the women in white and their children. He looked across the mass of silent faces, telling himself that this was only a small core of that enormous female force which spread its feminine web across the Empire. He could believe Leto's words:

"The power does not weaken. It grows stronger every decade."

To what end? Idaho asked himself.

He glanced at Leto who was lifting his hands in benediction over the hall of his houris.

"We will move among you now," Leto said.

The women below the ledge opened a path, pressing backward. The path opened deeper into the throng like a fissure spreading through the earth after some tremendous natural upheaval.

"Duncan, you will precede me," Leto said.

Idaho swallowed in a dry throat. He put a palm on the lip of the ledge and dropped down into the open space, moving out into the *fissure* because he knew only that could end this trial.

A quick glance backward showed him Leto's cart drifting majestically down on its suspensors.

Idaho turned and quickened his pace.

The women narrowed the path through their ranks. It was done in an odd stillness, with fixity of attention—first

225

on Idaho and then on that gross pre-worm body riding behind Idaho on the Ixian cart.

As Idaho marched stoically ahead, women reached from all sides to touch him, to touch Leto, or merely to touch the Royal Cart. Idaho felt the restrained passion in their touch and knew the deepest fear in his experience.

> *The problem of leadership is inevitably: Who will play God?*
>
> **—Muad'Dib (from the Oral History)**

Hwi Noree followed a young Fish Speaker guide down a wide ramp which spiralled into the depths of Onn. The summons from the Lord Leto had come in late evening of the Festival's third day, interrupting a development which had taxed her ability to maintain emotional balance.

Her first assistant, Othwi Yake, was not a pleasant man—a sandy-haired creature with a long, narrow face and eyes which never looked long at anything and never *ever* looked directly into the eyes of someone he addressed. Yake had presented her with a single sheet of memerase paper containing what he described as "a summation of recently reported violence in the Festival City".

Standing close to the desk at which she was seated, he had stared down somewhere to her left and said: "Fish Speakers are slaughtering Face Dancers throughout the City". He did not appear particularly moved by this.

"Why?" she demanded.

"It is said that the Bene Tleilax made an attempt on the God Emperor's life."

A thrill of fear shot through her. She sat back and glanced around the ambassadorial office—a round room with a single half-circle desk which concealed the controls for many Ixian devices beneath its highly polished surface. The room was a darkly important appearing place with brown wood panels covering instruments which shielded it from spying. There were no windows.

Trying not to show her upset, Hwi looked up at Yake. "And the Lord Leto is . . ."

"The attempt on his life appears to have been totally without effect. But it might explain that flogging."

"Then you think there *was* such an attempt?"

"Yes."

The Fish Speaker from the Lord Leto entered at that moment, hard on the announcement of her presence in the outer office. She was followed by a Bene Gesserit crone, a person she introduced as "The Reverend Mother Anteac". Anteac stared intently at Yake while the Fish Speaker, a young woman with smooth, almost childlike features, delivered her message:

"He told me to remind you: 'Return quickly if I summon you'. He summons you."

Yake began fidgeting as the Fish Speaker spoke. He darted his attention all around the room as though looking for something which was not there. Hwi paused only to pull a dark blue robe over her gown, instructing Yake to remain in the office until she returned.

In orange evening light outside the Embassy, on a street oddly empty of other traffic, Anteac looked at the Fish Speaker and said simply: "Yes". Anteac left them then and the Fish Speaker had brought Hwi through empty streets to a tall, windowless building whose depths contained this down-plunging spiral ramp.

The tight curves of the ramp made Hwi dizzy. Brilliant tiny white glowglobes drifted in the central well, illuminating a purple-green vine with elephantine leaves. The vine was suspended on shimmering golden wires.

The soft black surface of the ramp swallowed the sounds of their feet, making Hwi extremely conscious of the faint abrasive swishing caused by the movements of her robe.

"Where are you taking me?" Hwi asked.

"To the Lord Leto."

"I know, but where is he?"

"In his private room."

"It's awfully far down."

"Yes, the Lord often prefers the depths."

"It makes me dizzy walking around and around like this."

"It helps if you do not look at the vine."

"What is that plant?"

"It is called a Tunyon Vine and is supposed to have absolutely no smell."

"I've never heard of it. Where does it come from?"

"Only the Lord Leto knows."

They walked on in silence, Hwi trying to understand her own feelings. The God Emperor filled her with sadness. She could sense the man in him, the man who might have been. Why had such a man chosen this course for his life? Did anyone know? Did Moneo know?

Perhaps Duncan Idaho knew.

Her thoughts gravitated to Idaho—such a physically attractive man. So intense! She could feel herself drawn to him. If only Leto had the body and appearance of Idaho. She knew then that she could not discuss Leto's change with Idaho. Moneo, though—that was another matter. She looked at the back of her Fish Speaker escort.

"Can you tell me about Moneo?" Hwi asked.

The Fish Speaker glanced back over her shoulder, an odd expression in her pale blue eyes—apprehension or some bizarre form of awe.

"Is something wrong?" Hwi asked.

The Fish Speaker returned her attention to the downward spiral of the ramp.

"The Lord said you would ask about Moneo," she said.

"Then tell me about him."

"What is there to say? He is the Lord's closest confidant."

"Closer even than Duncan Idaho?"

"Oh, yes. Moneo is an Atreides."

"Moneo came to me yesterday," Hwi said. "He said I should know something about the God Emperor. Moneo said the God Emperor is capable of doing *anything*, anything at all if it is thought to be instructive."

"Many believe this," the Fish Speaker said.

"You do not believe it?"

Hwi asked the question as the ramp rounded a final turn and opened into a small anteroom with an arched entrance only a few steps away.

"The Lord Leto will receive you immediately," the Fish Speaker said. She turned back up the ramp then, without speaking of her own belief.

Hwi stepped through the arch and found herself in a low-ceilinged room. It was much smaller than the audience chamber. The air felt crisp and dry. Pale yellow light came from a concealed source at the upper corners. She allowed her eyes to adjust to the lowered illumination, noting carpets and soft cushions scattered around a low mound of . . . She put a hand to her mouth as the mound moved, realizing then that it was the Lord Leto on his cart, but the cart lay in a sunken area. She knew immediately why the room provided this feature. It made him less imposing to human guests, less overpowering by his physical elevation. Nothing could be done, however, about his length and the inescapable mass of his body except to keep them in shadows, throwing most of the light on to his face and hands.

"Come in and sit down," Leto said. He spoke in a low voice, pleasantly conversational.

Hwi crossed to a red cushion only a few metres in front of Leto's face and sat on it.

Leto watched her movements with obvious pleasure. She wore a dark golden gown and her hair was tied back in braids which made her face appear fresh and innocent.

"I have sent your message to Ix," she said. "And I have told them that you wish to know my age."

"Perhaps they will answer," he said. "Their answer may even be truthful."

"I would like to know when I was born, all of the circumstances," she said, "but I don't know why this interests you."

"Everything about you interests me."

"They will not like it that you make me the permanent Ambassador."

"Your masters are a curious mixture of punctilio and laxity," he said. "I do not suffer fools gladly."

"You think me a fool, Lord?"

"Malky was not a fool; neither are you, my dear."

"I have not heard from my uncle in years. Sometimes I wonder if he still lives."

"Perhaps we will learn that as well. Did Malky ever discuss with you my practice of *Taquiyya*?"

She thought about this a moment, then: "It was called *Ketman* among the ancient Fremen?"

"Yes. It is the practice of concealing the identity when revealing it might be harmful."

"I recall it now. He told me you wrote pseudonymous histories, some of them quite famous."

"That was the occasion when we discussed *Taquiyya*."

"Why do you speak of this, Lord?"

"To avoid other subjects. Did you know that I wrote the books of Noah Arkwright?"

She could not suppress a chuckle. "How amusing, Lord. I was required to read about his *life*."

"I wrote that account, too. What secrets were you asked to wrest from me?"

She did not even blink at his strategic change of subject.

"They are curious about the inner workings of the religion of the Lord Leto."

"Are they now?"

"They wish to know how you took religious control away from the Bene Gesserit."

"No doubt hoping to repeat my performance for themselves?"

"I'm sure that's in their minds, Lord."

"Hwi, you are a terrible representative of the Ixians."

"I am your servant, Lord."

"Have you no curiosities of your own?"

"I fear that my curiosities might disturb you," she said.

He stared at her a moment, then: "I see. Yes, you are

230

right. We should avoid more intimate conversation for now. Would you like me to talk about the Sisterhood?"

"Yes, that would be good. Do you know that I met one of the Bene Gesserit delegation today?"

"That would be Anteac."

"I found her frightening," she said.

"You have nothing to fear from Anteac. She went to your Embassy at my command. Were you aware that you had been invaded by Face Dancers?"

Hwi gasped, then held herself still while a cold sensation filled her breast. "Othwi Yake?" she asked.

"You suspected?"

"It's just that I did not like him, and I had been told that . . ." She shrugged, then, as realization swept over her: "What has happened to him?"

"The original? He is dead. That's the usual Face Dancer practice in such circumstances. My Fish Speakers have explicit orders to leave no Face Dancer alive in your Embassy."

Hwi remained silent, but tears trickled down her cheeks. *This explained the empty streets, Anteac's enigmatic "Yes". It explained many things.*

"I will provide Fish Speaker assistants for you until you can make other arrangements," Leto said. "My Fish Speakers will guard you well."

Hwi shook the tears from her face. The Inquisitors of Ix would react with rage against Tleilax. Would Ix believe her report? Everyone in her Embassy taken over by Face Dancers! It was difficult to believe.

"Everyone?" she asked.

"The Face Dancers had no reason to leave any of your original people alive. You would have been next."

She shuddered.

"They delayed," he said, "because they knew they would have to copy you with a precision to defy my senses. They are not sure about my abilities."

"Then Anteac . . ."

"The Sisterhood and I share an ability to detect Face

231

Dancers. And Anteac . . . well, she is very good at what she does."

"No one trusts the Tleilaxu," she said. "Why haven't they been wiped out long ago?"

"Specialists have their uses as well as their limitations. You surprise me, Hwi. I had not suspected you could be that bloody-minded."

"The Tleilaxu . . . they are too cruel to be human. They aren't human!"

"I assure you that humans can be just as cruel. I myself have been cruel on occasion."

"I know, Lord."

"With provocation," he said. "But the only people I have considered eliminating are the Bene Gesserit."

Her shock was too great for words.

"They are so close to what they should be and yet so far," he said.

She found her voice. "But the Oral History says . . ."

"The Religion of the Reverend Mothers, yes. Once they designed specific religions for specific societies. They called it *engineering*. How does that strike you?"

"Callous."

"Indeed. The results fit the mistake. Even after all the grand attempts at ecumenism there were countless gods, minor deities and would-be prophets throughout the Empire."

"You changed that, Lord."

"Somewhat. But gods die hard, Hwi. My monotheism dominates, but the original pantheon remains; it has gone underground in various disguises."

"Lord, I sense in your words . . . a . . ." She shook her head.

"Am I as coldly calculating as the Sisterhood?"

She nodded.

"It was the Fremen who deified my father, the great Muad'Dib. Although he doesn't really care to be called great."

"But were the Fremen . . ."

232

"Were they right? My dearest Hwi, they were sensitive to the uses of power and they were greedy to maintain their ascendancy."

"I find this . . . disturbing, Lord."

"I can see that. You don't like the idea that becoming a god could be that simple, as though anyone could do it."

"It sounds much too casual, Lord." Her voice had a remote and testing quality.

"I assure you that *anyone* could *not* do it."

"But you imply that you inherited your godhood from . . ."

"Never suggest that to a Fish Speaker," he said. "They react violently against heresy."

She tried to swallow in a dry throat.

"I say this only to protect you," he said.

Her voice was faint: "Thank you, Lord."

"My godhood began when I told my Fremen I no longer could give the death water to the tribes. You know about the death water?"

"In the Dune days, the water recovered from the bodies of the dead," she said.

"Ahhh, you have read Noah Arkwright."

She managed a faint smile.

"I told my Fremen the water would be consecrated to a supreme deity, left nameless. Fremen were still allowed to control this water through my largesse."

"Water must have been very precious in those days."

"Very! And I, as delegate of this nameless deity, held loose control of that precious water for almost three hundred years."

She chewed at her lower lip.

"It still sounds calculating?" he asked.

She nodded.

"It was. When it came time to consecrate my sister's water, I performed a miracle. The voices of all the Atreides spoke from Ghani's urn. Thus, my Fremen discovered that I was their Supreme Deity."

Hwi spoke fearfully, her voice full of puzzled uncertainties at this revelation. "Lord, are you telling me that you are not really a god?"

"I am telling you that I do not play hide-and-seek with death."

She stared at him for several minutes before responding in a way which assured him that she understood his deeper meaning. It was a reaction which only intensified her endearment to him.

"Your death will not be like other deaths," she said.

"Precious Hwi," he murmured.

"I wonder that you do not fear the judgment of a true Supreme Deity," she said.

"Do you judge me, Hwi?"

"No, but I fear for you."

"Think on the price I pay," he said. "Every descendant part of me will carry some of my awareness locked away within it, lost and helpless."

She put both hands over her mouth and stared at him.

"This is the horror which my father could not face and which he tried to prevent: the infinite division and sub-division of a blind identity."

She lowered her hands and whispered: "You will be conscious?"

"In a way . . . but mute. A little pearl of my awareness will go with every sandworm and every sandtrout—knowing yet unable to move a single cell, aware in an endless dream."

She shuddered.

Leto watched her try to understand such an existence. Could she imagine the final *clamour* when the subdivided bits of his identity grappled for a fading control of the Ixian machine which recorded his journals? Could she sense the wrenching silence which would follow that awful frag-mentation?

"Lord, they would use this knowledge against you were I to reveal it."

"Will you tell?"

"Of course not!" She shook her head slowly from side to

234

side. Why had he accepted this terrible transformation? Was there no escape?

Presently, she said: "The machine which writes your thoughts, could it not be attuned to . . ."

"To a million of me? To a billion? To more? My dear Hwi, none of those knowing-pearls will be truly me."

Her eyes filmed with tears. She blinked and inhaled a deep breath. Leto recognized the Bene Gesserit training in this, the way she accepted a flow of calmness.

"Lord, you have made me terribly afraid."

"And you do not understand why I have done this."

"Is it possible for me to understand?"

"Oh, yes. Many could understand it. What people do with understanding is another matter."

"Will you teach me what to do?"

"You already know."

She absorbed this silently, then: "It has something to do with your religion. I can feel it."

Leto smiled. "I can forgive your Ixian masters almost anything for the precious gift of you. Ask and you shall receive."

She leaned toward him, rocking forward on her pillow. "Tell me about the inner workings of your religion."

"You will know all of me soon enough, Hwi. I promise it. Just remember that sun worship among our primitive ancestors was not far off the mark."

"Sun . . . worship?" She rocked backward.

"That sun which controls all of the movement but which cannot be touched—that sun is death."

"Your . . . death?"

"Any religion circles like a planet around a sun which it must use for its energy, upon which it depends for its very existence."

Her voice came barely above a whisper: "What do you see in *your* sun, Lord?"

"A universe of many windows through which I may peer. Whatever the window frames, that is what I see."

"The future?"

235

"The universe is timeless as its roots and contains therefore all times and all futures."

"It's true then," she said. "You saw a thing which this . . ." she gestured at his long, ribbed body, ". . . prevents."

"Do you find it in you to believe that this may be, in some small way, holy?" he asked.

She could only nod her head.

"If you share it all with me," he said, "I warn you that it will be a terrible burden."

"Will it make your burden lighter, Lord?"

"Not lighter, but easier to accept."

"Then I will share. Tell me, Lord."

"Not yet, Hwi. You must be patient a while longer."

She swallowed her disappointment, sighing.

"It's only that my Duncan Idaho grows impatient," Leto said. "I must deal with him."

She glanced backward, but the small room remained empty.

"Do you wish me to leave now?"

"I wish you would never leave me."

She stared at him, noting the intensity of his regard, a hungry emptiness in his expression which filled her with sadness. "Lord, why do you tell *me* your secrets?"

"I would not ask you to be the bride of a god."

Her eyes went wide with shock.

"Do not answer," he said.

Barely moving her head, she sent her gaze along the shadowy length of his body.

"Do not search for parts of me which no longer exist," he said. "Some forms of physical intimacy are no longer possible for me."

She returned her attention to his cowled face, noting the pink skin of his cheeks, the intensely human effect of his features in that alien frame.

"If you require children," he said, "I would ask only that you let me choose the father. But I have not yet asked you anything."

Her voice was faint. "Lord, I do not know what to . . ."

"I will return to the Citadel soon," he said. "You will come to me there and we will talk. I will tell you then about the thing which I prevent."

"I am frightened, Lord, more frightened than I ever imagined I could be."

"Do not fear me. I can be nothing but gentle with my gentle Hwi. As for other dangers, my Fish Speakers will shield you with their own bodies. They dare not let harm come to you!"

Hwi lifted herself to her feet and stood trembling.

Leto saw how deeply his words had affected her and he felt the pain of it. Hwi's eyes glistened with tears. She clasped her hands tightly to still the trembling. He knew she would come to him willingly at the Citadel. No matter what he asked, her response would be the response of his Fish Speakers:

"Yes, Lord."

It came to Leto that if she could change places with him, take up his burden, she would offer herself. The fact that she could not do this added to her pain. She was intelligence built on profound sensitivity, without any of Malky's hedonistic weaknesses. She was frightening in her perfection. Everything about her reaffirmed his awareness that she was *precisely* the kind of woman who, if he had grown to normal manhood, he would have wanted (*No! Demanded!*) as his mate.

And the Ixians knew it.

"Leave me now," he whispered.

I am both father and mother to my people. I have known the ecstasy of birth and the ecstasy of death and I know the patterns that you must learn. Have I not wandered intoxicated through the universe of shapes? Yes! I have seen you outlined in light. That universe which you say you see and feel, that universe is my dream. My energies focus upon it and I am in any realm and every realm. Thus, you are born.

—The Stolen Journals

"My Fish Speakers tell me that you went to the Citadel immediately after Siaynoq," Leto said.

He stared accusingly at Idaho, who stood near where Hwi had sat only an hour ago. Such a small passage of time—yet Leto felt the emptiness as centuries.

"I needed time to think," Idaho said. He looked into the shadowy pit where Leto's cart rested.

"And to talk to Siona?"

"Yes." Idaho lifted his gaze to Leto's face.

"But you asked for Moneo," Leto said.

"Do they report on every movement I make?" Idaho demanded.

"Not *every* movement."

"Sometimes people need to be alone."

"Of course. But do not blame the Fish Speakers for being concerned about you."

"Siona says she is to be tested!"

"Was that why you asked for Moneo?"

"What is this test?"

"Moneo knows. I presumed that was why you wanted to see him."

"You presume nothing! You *know*."

"Siaynoq has upset you, Duncan. I am sorry."

"Do you have any idea what it's like to be me . . . here?"

"The ghola's lot is not easy," Leto said. "Some lives are harder than others."

"I don't need any juvenile philosophy!"

"What do you need, Duncan?"

"I need to know some things."

"Such as?"

"I don't understand *any* of these people around you! Without showing any surprise about it, Moneo tells me that Siona was part of a rebellion against you. His own daughter!"

"In his day, Moneo too was a rebel."

"See what I mean? Did you test him, too?"

"Yes."

"Will you test me?"

238

"I am testing you."

Idaho glared at him, then: "I don't understand your government, your Empire, anything. The more I find out, the more I realize that I don't know what's going on."

"How fortunate that you have discovered the way to wisdom," Leto said.

"What?" Idaho's baffled outrage raised his voice to a battlefield roar which filled the small room.

Leto smiled. "Duncan, have I not told you that when you think you know something, that is a most perfect barrier against learning?"

"Then tell me what's going on."

"My friend Duncan Idaho is acquiring a new habit. He is learning always to look beyond what he thinks he knows."

"All right, all right." Idaho nodded his head slowly in time to the words. "Then what's *beyond* letting me take part in that Siaynoq thing?"

"I am binding the Fish Speakers to the Commander of my Guard."

"And I have to fight them off! The escort that took me out to the Citadel wanted to stop for an orgy. And the ones who brought me back here when you . . ."

"They know how much it pleases me to see children of Duncan Idaho."

"Damn you! I'm not your stud!"

"No need to shout, Duncan."

Idaho took several deep breaths, then: "When I tell them *no* they act hurt at first and then they treat me like some damned . . ." he shook his head, ". . . holy man or something."

"Don't they obey you?"

"They don't question anything . . . unless it's contrary to your orders. I didn't want to come back here."

"Yet they brought you."

"You know damned well they won't disobey *you!*"

"I'm glad you came, Duncan."

"Oh, I can see that!"

"The Fish Speakers know how special you are, how fond

I am of you, how much I owe you. It's never a question of obedience and disobedience where you and I are concerned."

"Then what is it a question of?"

"Loyalty."

Idaho fell into pensive silence.

"You felt the power of Siaynoq?" Leto asked.

"Mumbo jumbo."

"Then why are you disturbed by it?"

"Your Fish Speakers aren't an army, they're a police force."

"By my name, I assure you that's not so. Police are inevitably corrupted."

"You tempted me with power," Idaho accused.

"That's the test, Duncan."

"You don't trust me?"

"I trust your loyalty to the Atreides implicitly, without question."

"Then what's this talk of corruption and testing?"

"You were the one who accused me of having a police force. Police always observe that criminals prosper. It takes a pretty dull policeman to miss the fact that the position of authority is the most prosperous criminal position available."

Idaho wet his lips with his tongue and stared at Leto with obvious puzzlement. "But the moral training of . . . I mean, the legal . . . the prisons to . . ."

"What good are laws and prisons when the breaking of a law is not a sin?"

Idaho cocked his head slightly to the right. "Are you trying to tell me that your damned religion is . . ."

"Punishment of sins can be quite extravagant."

Idaho hooked a thumb over his shoulder toward the world outside the door. "All this talk about death penalties . . . that flogging and . . ."

"I try to dispense with casual laws and prisons wherever possible."

"You have to have *some* prisons!"

"Do I? Prisons are needed only to provide the illusion that courts and police are effective. They're a kind of job insurance."

Idaho turned slightly and thrust a pointing finger toward the door through which he had entered the small room. "You've got whole planets that are nothing but prisons!"

"I guess you could think of anywhere as a prison if that's the way your illusions go."

"Illusions!" Idaho dropped his hand to his side and stood dumbfounded.

"Yes. You talk of prisons and police and legalities, the perfect illusions behind which a prosperous power structure can operate while observing, quite accurately, that it is above its own laws."

"And you think crimes can be dealt with by . . ."

"Not crimes, Duncan, sins."

"So you think your religion can . . ."

"Have you noted the primary sins?"

"What?"

"Attempting to corrupt a member of my government, and corruption by a member of my government."

"And what is this corruption?"

"Essentially, it's the failure to observe and worship the holiness of the God Leto."

"You?"

"Me."

"But you told me right at the beginning that . . ."

"You think I don't believe in my own godhead? Be careful, Duncan."

Idaho's voice came with angry flatness. "You told me that one of my jobs was to help keep your secret, that you . . ."

"You don't know my secret."

"That you're a tyrant? That's no . . ."

"Gods have more power than tyrants, Duncan."

"I don't like what I'm hearing."

"When has an Atreides ever asked you to *like* your job?"

"You ask me to command your Fish Speakers who are judge, jury and executioner and . . ." Idaho broke off.

"And what?"

Idaho remained silent.

Leto stared across the chill distance between them, so short a space yet so far.

It's like playing a fish on a line, Leto thought. *You must calculate the breaking point of every element in the contest.*

The problem with Idaho was that bringing him to the net always hastened his end. And it was happening too rapidly this time. Leto felt sadness.

"I won't worship you," Idaho said.

"The Fish Speakers recognize that you have a special dispensation," Leto said.

"Like Moneo and Siona?"

"Much different."

"So rebels are a special case."

Leto grinned. "All of my most trusted administrators were rebels at one time."

"I wasn't a . . ."

"You were a brilliant rebel! You helped the Atreides wrest an empire from a reigning monarch."

Idaho's eyes went out of focus with introspection. "So I did." He shook his head sharply as though tossing something out of his hair. "And look what you've done with that empire!"

"I have set up a pattern in it, a pattern of patterns."

"So you say."

"Information is frozen in patterns, Duncan. We can use one pattern to solve another pattern. Flow patterns are the hardest to recognize and understand."

"More mumbo jumbo."

"You made that mistake once before."

"Why do you let the Tleilaxu keep bringing me back to life—one ghola after another? Where's the *pattern* in that?"

242

"Because of the qualities which you possess in abundance. I will let my father say it."

Idaho's mouth drew into a grim line.

Leto spoke in Muad'Dib's voice, and even the cowled face fell into a semblance of the paternal features. "You were my truest friend, Duncan, better even than Gurney Halleck. But I am the past."

Idaho swallowed hard. "The things you're doing!"

"They cut against the Atreides grain?"

"You're damned right!"

Leto resumed his ordinary tones. "Yet I'm still Atreides."

"Are you really?"

"What else could I be?"

"I wish I knew!"

"You think I play tricks with words and voices?"

"What in all the seven hells are you really doing?"

"I preserve life while setting the stage for the next cycle."

"You preserve it by killing?"

"Death has often been useful to life."

"That's not Atreides!"

"But it is. We often saw the value of death. The Ixians, however, have never seen that value."

"What've the Ixians got to do with . . ."

"Everything. They would make a machine to conceal their other machinations."

Idaho spoke in a musing tone. "Is that why the Ixian Ambassador was here?"

"You've seen Hwi Noree," Leto said.

Idaho pointed upward. "She was leaving as I arrived."

"You spoke to her?"

"I asked her what she was doing here. She said she was choosing sides."

A burst of laughter erupted from Leto. "Oh, my," he said. "She is so good. Did she reveal her choice?"

"She said she serves the God Emperor now. I didn't believe her, of course."

"But you should believe her."

"Why?"

"Ahhh, yes; I forgot that you once doubted even my grandmother, the Lady Jessica."

"I had good reason!"

"Do you also doubt Siona?"

"I'm beginning to doubt everyone!"

"And you say you don't know your value to me," Leto accused.

"What about Siona?" Idaho demanded. "She says you want us . . . I mean, dammit . . ."

"The thing you must always trust about Siona is her creativity. She can create the new and beautiful. One always trusts the truly creative."

"Even the machinations of the Ixians?"

"That is not creative. You always know the creative because it is revealed openly. Concealment betrays the existence of another force entirely."

"Then you don't trust this Hwi Noree but you . . ."

"I *do* trust her, and precisely for the reasons I have just given you."

Idaho scowled, then relaxed and sighed. "I had better cultivate her acquaintance. If she is someone you . . ."

"No! You will stay away from Hwi Noree. I have something special in mind for her."

I have isolated the city-experience within me and have examined it closely. The idea of a city fascinates me. The formation of a biological community without a functioning, supportive social community leads to havoc. Whole worlds have become single biological communities without an inter-related social structure and this has always led to ruin. It becomes dramatically instructive under overcrowded conditions. The ghetto is lethal. Psychic stresses of overcrowding create pressures which will erupt. The city is an attempt to manage these forces. The social forms by which cities make the attempt are worth study. Remember that there exists a certain malevolence about the formation of any social order. It is the struggle for existence by an artificial entity. Despotism and slavery hover at the edges. Many injuries occur and, thus, the need for laws. The law develops its own power structure, creating more wounds and new injustices. Such trauma can be healed by cooperation, not by confrontation. The summons to cooperate identifies the healer.

—The Stolen Journals

Moneo entered Leto's small chamber with evident agitation. He actually preferred this meeting place because the God Emperor's cart lay in a depression from which a deadly attack by the worm would be more difficult, and there was the undeniable fact that Leto allowed his major-domo to descend in an Ixian tube-lift rather than via that interminable ramp. But Moneo felt that the news he brought this morning was guaranteed to arouse The Worm Who Is God.

How to present it?

Dawn lay only an hour past, the fourth Festival Day, a fact Moneo could greet with equanimity only because it brought him that much nearer the end of these tribulations.

Leto stirred as Moneo entered the small chamber. Illumination came on at his signal, focusing only on his face.

"Good morning, Moneo," he said. "My guard tells me you insisted on entering immediately. Why?"

The danger, Moneo knew from experience, lay in the temptation to reveal too much too soon.

"I have spent some time with the Reverend Mother Anteac," he said. "Although she keeps it well hidden, I'm sure she is a mentat."

"Yes. The Bene Gesserit were bound to disobey me sometime. This form of disobedience amuses me."

"Then you will not punish them?"

"Moneo, I am ultimately the only parent my people have. A parent must be generous as well as severe."

He's in a good mood, Moneo thought. A small sigh escaped Moneo, at which Leto smiled.

"Anteac objected when I told her you had ordered an amnesty for a selected few Face Dancers among our captives."

"I have a Festive use for them," Leto said.

"Lord?"

"I will tell you later. Let's get to the news which brings you bursting in upon me at this hour."

"I . . . ahhhh . . ." Moneo chewed at his upper lip. "The Tleilaxu have been quite garrulous in the attempt to ingratiate themselves with me."

"Of course they have. And what have they revealed?"

"They . . . ahhh, provided the Ixians with sufficient advice and equipment to make a . . . uhhhh, not exactly a ghola, and not even a clone. Perhaps we should use the Tleilaxu term: *a cellular re-structuring*. The . . . ahhh, *experiment* was conducted within some sort of shielding device which the Guildsmen assured them your powers could not penetrate."

"And the result?" Leto felt that he was asking the question in a cold vacuum.

"They are not certain. Tleilaxu were not permitted to witness. However, they did observe that Malky entered this . . . ahhh, chamber and that he emerged later with an infant."

"Yes! I know!"

"You do?" Moneo was puzzled.

246

"By inference. And all of this happened some twenty-six years ago?"

"That is correct, Lord."

"They identify the infant as Hwi Noree?"

"They are not certain, Lord, but . . ." Moneo shrugged.

"Of course. And what do you deduce from this, Moneo?"

"There is a deep purpose built into the new Ixian Ambassador."

"Certainly there is. Moneo, has it not struck you as odd how much Hwi, the gentle Hwi, represents a mirror of the redoubtable Malky? His opposite in everything, including sex."

"I had not thought of that, Lord."

"I have."

"I will have her sent back to Ix immediately," Moneo said.

"You will do nothing of the kind!"

"But, Lord, if they . . ."

"Moneo, I have observed that you seldom turn your back on danger. Others often do, but you—seldom. Why would you have me engage in such an obvious stupidity?"

Moneo swallowed.

"Good. I like it when you recognize the error of your ways," Leto said.

"Thank you, Lord."

"I also like it when you express your gratitude sincerely, as you have just done. Now, Anteac was with you when you heard these revelations?"

"As you ordered, Lord."

"Excellent. That will stir things up a bit. You will leave now and go to the Lady Hwi. You will tell her that I desire to see her immediately. This will disturb her. She is thinking that we will not meet again until I summon her to the Citadel. I want you to quiet her fears."

"In what way, Lord?"

Leto spoke sadly: "Moneo, why do you ask advice on something at which you are an expert? Calm her and bring

247

her here reassured of my kindly intentions toward her."

"Yes, Lord." Moneo bowed and backed away a step.

"One moment, Moneo!"

Moneo stiffened, his gaze fixed on Leto's face.

"You are puzzled, Moneo," Leto said. "Sometimes you do not know what to think of me. Am I all-powerful and all-prescient? You bring me these little dibs and dabs and you wonder: *Does he already know this? If he does, why do I bother?* But I have ordered you to report such things, Moneo. Is your obedience not instructive?"

Moneo started to shrug and thought better of it. His lips trembled.

"Time can also be a place, Moneo," Leto said. "Everything depends upon where you are standing, on where you look or what you hear. The measure of it is found in consciousness itself."

After a long silence, Moneo ventured: "Is that all, Lord?"

"No, it is *not* all. Siona will receive today a package delivered to her by a Guild courier. Nothing is to interfere with delivery of that package. Do you understand?"

"What is . . . what is in the package, Lord?"

"Some translations, reading matter which I wish her to see. You will do nothing to interfere. There is no melange in the package."

"How . . . how did you know what I feared was in the . . ."

"Because you fear the spice. It could extend your life, but you avoid it."

"I fear its *other* effects, Lord."

"A bountiful nature has decreed that melange will unveil for some of us unexpected depths of the psyche, yet you fear this?"

"I am *Atreides*, Lord!"

"Ahhh, yes, and for the Atreides, melange may roll the mystery of Time through a peculiar process of internal revelation."

"I have only to remember the way you tested me, Lord."

248

"Do you not see the necessity for you to sense the Golden Path?"

"That is not what I fear, Lord."

"You fear the other astonishment, the thing which made me make *my* choice."

"I have only to look at you, Lord, and know that fear. We Atreides . . ." He broke off, his mouth dry.

"You do not want all of these memories of ancestors and the others who flock within me!"

"Sometimes . . . sometimes, Lord, I think the spice is the Atreides curse!"

"Do you wish that *I* had never occurred?"

Moneo remained silent.

"But melange has its values, Moneo. The Guild Navigators need it. And without it, the Bene Gesserit would degenerate into a helpless band of whining females!"

"We must live with it or without it, Lord. I know that."

"Very perceptive, Moneo. But you choose to live without it."

"Do I not have that choice, Lord?"

"For now."

"Lord, what do you . . ."

"There are twenty-eight different words for melange in common Galach. They describe it by its intended use, by its dilution, by its age, by whether it came through honest purchase, through theft or conquest, whether it was the dower gift for a male or for a female, and in many other ways is it named. What do you make of this, Moneo?"

"We are offered many choices, Lord."

"Only where the spice is concerned?"

Moneo's brows wrinkled in thought, then: "No."

"You so seldom say *no* in my presence," Leto said. "I enjoy watching your lips form around the word."

Moneo's mouth twitched in an attempted smile.

Leto spoke briskly: "Well! You must go now to the Lady Hwi. I will give you one parting piece of advice which may help."

249

Moneo paid studious attention to Leto's face.

"Drug knowledge originated mostly with males because they tend to be more venturesome—an outgrowth of male aggression. You've read your Orange Catholic Bible, thus you know the story of Eve and the apple. Here's an interesting fact about that story: Eve was not the first to pluck and sample the apple. Adam was first and he learned by this to put the blame on Eve. My story tells you something about how our societies find a structural necessity for subgroups."

Moneo tipped his head slightly to the left. "Lord, how does this help me?"

"It will help you with the Lady Hwi!"

The singular multiplicity of this universe draws my deepest attention. It is a thing of ultimate beauty.

—The Stolen Journals

Leto heard Moneo in the antechamber just before Hwi entered the small audience room. She wore voluminous pale green pantaloons tightly tied at the ankles with darker green bows to match her sandals. A loose blouse of the same dark green could be seen under her black cloak.

She appeared calm as she approached Leto and sat without being invited, choosing a golden cushion rather than the red one she had occupied earlier. It had taken less than an hour for Moneo to bring her. Leto's acute hearing detected Moneo fidgeting in the anteroom and Leto sent a signal which sealed the arched doorway there.

"Something had disturbed Moneo," Hwi said. "He tried very hard not to reveal this to me, but the more he tried to soothe me the more he aroused my curiosity."

"He did not frighten you?"

"Oh, no. He did say something very interesting, though.

He said that I must remember it at all times, that the God Leto is a different person to each of us."

"How is this interesting?" Leto asked.

"The interesting thing is the question for which this was the preface. He said he often wonders what part we play in creating that difference in you?"

"That *is* interesting."

"I think it is a truthful insight," Hwi said. "Why have you summoned me?"

"At one time, your masters on Ix . . ."

"They are no longer my masters, Lord."

"Forgive me. I will refer to them hereafter as the Ixians."

She nodded gravely, prompting: "At one time . . ."

"The Ixians contemplated making a weapon—a type of hunter-seeker, self-propelled death with a machine mind. It was to be designed as a self-improving thing which would seek out life and reduce that life to its inorganic matter."

"I have not heard of this thing, Lord."

"I know that. The Ixians do not recognize that machine-makers always run the risk of becoming totally machine. This is ultimate sterility. Machines always fail . . . given time. And when these machines failed there would be nothing left, no life at all."

"Sometimes I think they are mad," she said.

"Anteac's opinion. That is the immediate problem. The Ixians are now engaged in an endeavour which they are concealing."

"Even from you?"

"Even from me. I am sending the Reverend Mother Anteac to investigate for me. To help her, I want you to tell her everything you can about the place where you spent your childhood. Omit no detail, no matter how small. Anteac will help you remember. We want every sound, every smell, the shapes and names of visitors, the colours and even the tinglings of your skin. The slightest thing may be vital."

"You think it is the place of concealment?"

"I know it is."

"And you think they are making this weapon in . . ."

"No, but this will be our excuse for investigating the place where you were born."

She opened her mouth and gradually formed a smile, then: "My Lord is devious. I will speak to the Reverend Mother immediately." Hwi started to rise, but he stopped her with a gesture.

"We must not give the appearance of haste," he said.

She sank back on to the cushion.

"Each of us is different in the way of Moneo's observation," he said. "Genesis does not stop. Your god continues creating you."

"What will Anteac find? You know, don't you?"

"Let us say that I have a strong conviction. Now, you have not once mentioned the subject which I broached earlier. Have you no questions?"

"You will provide the answers as I require them." It was a statement full of such trust that it stopped Leto's voice. He could only look at her, realizing how extraordinary was this accomplishment of the Ixians—this *human*. Hwi remained precisely true to the dictates of her personally-chosen morality. She was comely, warm and honest and possessed of an empathic sense which forced her to share every anguish in those with whom she identified. He could imagine the dismay of her Bene Gesserit teachers when confronted by this immovable core of self-honesty. The teachers obviously had been reduced to adding a touch here, an ability there, everything strengthening that power which prevented her from becoming a Bene Gesserit. How that must have rankled!

"Lord," she said, "I would know the motives which forced you to choose your life."

"First, you must understand what it is like to see our future."

"With your help, I will try."

"Nothing is ever separated from its source," he said. "Seeing futures is a vision of a *continuum* in which all things take shape like bubbles forming beneath a waterfall. You see them and then they vanish into the stream. If the *stream* ends, it is as though the bubbles never were. That stream is my Golden Path and I saw it end."

"Your choice . . ." she gestured at his body, ". . . changed that?"

"It is changing. The change comes not only from the manner of my life but from the manner of my death."

"You know how you will die?"

"Not *how*. I know only the Golden Path in which it will occur."

"Lord, I do not . . ."

"It is difficult to understand, I know. I will die four deaths—the death of the flesh, the death of the soul, the death of the myth and the death of reason. And all of these deaths contain the seed of resurrection."

"You will return from . . ."

"The seeds will return."

"When you are gone, what will happen to your religion?"

"All religions are a single communion. The spectrum remains unbroken within the Golden Path. It is only that humans see first one part and then another. Delusions can be called accidents of the senses."

"People will still worship you," she said.

"Yes."

"But when *forever* ends there will be anger," she said. "There will be denial. Some will say you were just an ordinary tyrant."

"Delusion," he agreed.

A lump in her throat prevented her from speaking for a moment, then: "How does your life and your death change the . . ." She shook her head.

"Life will continue."

"I believe that, Lord, but how?"

"Each cycle is a reaction to the preceding cycle. If you think about the shape of my Empire, then you know the shape of the next cycle."

She looked away from him. "Everything I learned about

253

your family told me that you would do this . . ." she gestured blindly in his direction without looking at him, ". . . only with a selfless motive. I do not think I truly know the *shape* of your Empire, though."

"Leto's Golden Peace?"

"There is less peace than some would have us believe," she said, looking back at him.

The honesty of her! he thought. *Nothing deterred it.*

"This is the time of the stomach," he said. "This is the time when we expand as a single cell expands."

"But something is missing," she said.

She is like the Duncans, he thought. *Something is missing and they sense it immediately.*

"The flesh grows but the psyche does not grow," he said.

"The psyche?"

"That reflexive awareness which tells us how *very* alive we can become. You know it well, Hwi. It is that sense which tells you how to be true to yourself."

"Your religion is not enough," she said.

"No religion can ever be enough. It is a matter of choice—a single, lonely choice. Do you understand now why your friendship and your company mean so much to me?"

She blinked back tears, nodding, then: "Why don't people know this?"

"Because the conditions don't permit it."

"The conditions which you dictate?"

"Precisely. Look throughout my Empire. Do you see the shape?"

She closed her eyes, thinking.

"One wishes to sit by a river and fish every day?" he asked. "Excellent. That is this life. You desire to sail a small boat across an inland sea and visit strangers? Superb! What else is there to do?"

"Travel in space?" she asked and there was a defiant note in her voice. She opened her eyes.

"You have observed that the Guild and I do not allow this."

254

"*You* do not allow it."

"True. If the Guild disobeys me it gets no spice."

"And holding people planetbound keeps them out of mischief."

"It does something more important than that. It fills them with a longing to travel. It creates a *need* to make far voyages and see strange things. Eventually, travel comes to mean freedom."

"But the spice dwindles," she said.

"And freedom becomes more precious every day."

"This can only lead to desperation and violence," she said.

"A wise man in my ancestry—I was actually that person, you know? Do you understand that there are no strangers in my past?"

She nodded, awed.

"This wise man observed that wealth is a tool of freedom. But the pursuit of wealth is the way to slavery."

"The Guild and the Sisterhood enslave themselves!"

"And the Ixians and the Tleilaxu and all the others. Oh, they ferret out a bit of hidden melange from time to time and that keeps the attention fixed. A very interesting game, don't you think?"

"But when the violence comes . . ."

"There will be famines and hard thoughts."

"Here on Arrakis, too?"

"Here, there, everywhere. People will look back on my tyranny as *the good old days*. I will be the mirror of their future."

"But it will be terrible!" she objected.

She could have no other reaction, he thought.

He said: "As the land refuses to support the people, the survivors will crowd into smaller and smaller refuges. A terrible selection process will be repeated on many worlds—explosive birthrates and dwindling food."

"But couldn't the Guild . . ."

"The Guild will be largely helpless without sufficient melange to operate available transports."

"Won't the rich escape?"

"Some of them."

"Then you haven't really changed anything. We will just go on struggling and dying."

"Until the sandworm reigns once more on Arrakis. We will have tested ourselves by then with a profound experience shared by all. We will have learned that a thing which can happen on one planet can happen on any planet."

"So much pain and death," she whispered.

"Don't you understand about death?" he asked. "You must understand. The species must understand. All life must understand."

"Help me, Lord," she whispered.

"It is the most profound experience of any creature," he said. "Short of death come the things which risk and mirror it—life-threatening diseases, injuries and accidents . . . childbirth for a woman . . . and once it was combat for the males."

"But your Fish Speakers are . . ."

"They teach about survival," he said.

Her eyes went wide with understanding. "The survivors. Of course!"

"How precious you are," he said. "How rare and precious. Bless the Ixians!"

"And curse them?"

"That, too."

"I did not think I could ever understand about your Fish Speakers," she said.

"Not even Moneo sees it," he said. "And I despair of the Duncans."

"You have to appreciate life before you want to preserve it," she said.

"And it's the survivors who maintain the most light and poignant hold upon the beauties of living. Women know this more often than men because birth is the reflection of death."

"My Uncle Malky always said you had good reasons for

denying combat and casual violence to men. What a bitter lesson!"

"Without readily available violence, men have few ways of testing how they will meet that final experience," he said. "Something is missing. The psyche does not grow. What is it people say about Leto's Peace?"

"That you make us wallow in pointless decadence like pigs in our own filth."

"Always recognize the accuracy of folk wisdom," he said. "Decadence."

"Most men have no principles," she said. "The women of Ix complain about it constantly."

"When I need to identify rebels, I look for men with principles," he said.

She stared at him silently, and he thought how that simple reaction spoke so deeply of her intelligence.

"Where do you think I find my best administrators?" he asked.

A small gasp escaped her.

"Principles," he said, "are what you fight for. Most men go through a lifetime unchallenged except at the final moment. They have so few unfriendly arenas in which to test themselves."

"They have you," she said.

"But I am so powerful," he said. "I am the equivalent of suicide. Who would seek certain death?"

"Madmen . . . or desperate ones. Rebels?"

"I am their equivalent of war," he said. "The ultimate predator. I am the cohesive force which shatters them."

"I've never thought of myself as a rebel," she said.

"You are something far better."

"And you would use me in some way?"

"I would."

"Not as an administrator," she said.

"I already have good administrators—uncorruptible, sagacious, philosophical and open about their errors, quick to see decisions."

257

"They were rebels?"

"Most of them."

"How are they chosen?"

"I could say they choose themselves."

"By surviving?"

"That, too. But there's more. The difference between a good administrator and a bad one is about five heartbeats. Good administrators make immediate choices."

"Acceptable choices?"

"They usually can be made to work. A bad administrator, on the other hand, hesitates, diddles around, asks for committees, for research and reports. Eventually, he acts in ways which create serious problems."

"But don't they sometimes need more information to make . . ."

"A bad administrator is more concerned with reports than with decisions. He wants the hard record which he can display as an excuse for his errors."

"And good administrators?"

"Oh, they depend on verbal orders. They never lie about what they've done if their verbal orders cause problems, and they surround themselves with people able to act wisely on the basis of verbal orders. Often, the most important piece of information is that something has gone wrong. Bad administrators hide their mistakes until it's too late to make corrections."

Leto watched her as she thought about the people who served him—especially about Moneo.

"Men of decision," she said.

"One of the hardest things for a tyrant to find," he said, "is people who actually make decisions."

"Doesn't your intimate knowledge of the past give you some . . ."

"It gives me some amusement. Most bureaucracies before mine sought out and promoted people who avoided decisions."

"I see. How would you use me, Lord?"

"Will you wed me?"

258

A faint smile touched her lips. "Women, too, can make decisions. I will wed you."

"Then go and instruct the Reverend Mother. Make sure she knows what she's looking for."

"For my genesis," she said. "You and I already know my purpose."

"Which is not separated from its source," he said.

She arose, then: "Lord, could you be wrong about your Golden Path? Does the possibility of failure . . ."

"Anything and anyone can fail," he said, "but brave good friends help."

> Groups tend to condition their surroundings for group survival. When they deviate from this it may be taken as a sign of group sickness. There are many telltale symptoms. I watch the sharing of food. This is a form of communication, an inescapable sign of mutual aid which also contains a deadly signal of dependency. It is interesting that men are the ones who usually tend the landscape today. They are husband-men. Once, that was the sole province of women.

> —The Stolen Journals

"You must forgive the inadequacies of this report," the Reverend Mother Anteac wrote. "Ascribe it to the necessity for haste. I leave on the morrow for Ix, my purpose being the same one I reported in greater detail earlier. The God Emperor's intense and sincere interest in Ix cannot be denied, but what I must recount here is the strange visit I have just had from the Ixian Ambassador, Hwi Noree."

Anteac sat back on the inadequate stool which was the best she could manage in these spartan quarters. She sat alone in her tiny bedchamber, the space within a space which the Lord Leto had refused to change even after the Bene Gesserit warning of Tleilaxu treachery.

On Anteac's lap lay a small square of inky black about ten millimetres on a side and no more than three millimetres thick. She wrote upon this square with a glittering needle—one word upon another, all of them absorbed into the square. The completed message would be impressed upon the nerve receptors of an acolyte-messenger's eyes, latent there until they could be replayed at the Chapter House.

Hwi Noree posed such a dilemma!

Anteac knew the accounts of Bene Gesserit teachers sent to instruct Hwi on Ix. But those accounts left out more than they told. They raised greater questions.

What adventures have you experienced, child?

What were the hardships of your youth?

Anteac sniffed and glanced down at the waiting square of black. Such thoughts reminded her of the Fremen belief that the land of your birth made you what you were.

"Are there strange animals on your planet?" the Fremen would ask.

Hwi had come with an impressive Fish Speaker escort, more than a hundred brawny women, all of them heavily armed. Anteac had seldom seen such a display of weapons—lasguns, long knives, sliver-blades, stun-grenades . . .

It had been at mid-morning. Hwi had swept in, leaving the Fish Speakers to invest the Bene Gesserit quarters, all except this spartan inner room.

Anteac swept her gaze around her quarters. The Lord Leto was telling her something by keeping her here.

"This is how you measure your worth to the God Emperor!"

Except . . . now he sent a Reverend Mother to Ix and the avowed purpose of this journey suggested many things about the Lord Leto. Perhaps times were about to change, new honours and more melange for the Sisterhood.

Everything depends upon how well I perform.

Hwi had entered this room alone and had sat demurely on Anteac's pallet, her head lower than that of the Reverend Mother's. A nice touch, and no accident. The Fish Speakers obviously could have placed the two of them anywhere in any relationship Hwi commanded. Hwi's shocking first words left little doubt of that.

"You must know at the outset that I will wed the Lord Leto."

It had required the deep control to keep from gaping. Anteac's truthsense told her the sincerity of Hwi's words, but the full portent could not be assessed.

"The Lord Leto commands that you say nothing of this to anyone," Hwi added.

Such a dilemma! Anteac thought. *Can I even report this to my Sisters at the Chapter House?*

"Everyone will know in time," Hwi said. "This is not the time. I tell you because it helps impress upon you the gravity of the Lord Leto's trust."

"His trust in you?"

"In both of us."

This had sent a barely-concealed shuddering thrill through Anteac. The power inherent in such trust!

"Do you know why Ix chose you as Ambassador?" Anteac asked.

"Yes. They intended me to beguile him."

"You appear to have succeeded. Does this mean that the Ixians believe those Tleilaxu stories about the Lord Leto's gross habits?"

"Even the Tleilaxu don't believe them."

"I take it that you confirm the falsehood of such stories?"

Hwi had spoken in an odd flatness which even Anteac's truthsense and abilities as a mentat found hard to decipher.

"You have talked to him and observed him. Answer that question for yourself."

Anteac put down a small surge of irritation. Despite her youth, this Hwi was not an acolyte . . . and would never make a good Bene Gesserit. Such a pity!

"Have you reported this to your government on Ix?" Anteac asked.

"No."

"Why?"

"They will learn soon enough. Premature revelation

could harm the Lord Leto."

She is truthful, Anteac reminded herself.

"Isn't your first loyalty to Ix?" Anteac asked.

"Truth is my first loyalty." She smiled then. "Ix contrived better than it thought."

"Does Ix think of you as a threat to the God Emperor?"

"I think their primary concern is knowledge. I discussed this with Ampre before leaving."

"The Director of Ix's Outfederation Affairs? That Ampre?"

"Yes. Ampre is convinced that the Lord Leto permits threats to his person only up to certain limits."

"Ampre said that?"

"Ampre does not believe the future can be hidden from the Lord Leto."

"But my mission to Ix has about it the suggestion that . . ." Anteac broke off and shook her head, then: "Why does Ix provide the Lord with machines and weapons?"

"Ampre believes that Ix has no choice. Overwhelming force destroys people who pose too great a threat."

"And if Ix refused, that would pass the Lord Leto's limits. No middle point. Have you thought about the consequences of wedding the Lord Leto?"

"You mean the doubts such an act will raise about his godhead?"

"Some will believe the Tleilaxu stories."

Hwi only smiled.

Damnation! Anteac thought. *How did we lose this girl?*

"He is changing the design of his religion," Anteac accused. "That's it, of course."

"Do not make the mistake of judging all others by yourselves," Hwi said. And, as Anteac started to bridle, Hwi added: "But I did not come here to argue with you about the Lord."

"No. Of course not."

"The Lord Leto has commanded me," Hwi said, "to tell you every detail in my memory about the place where I was born and raised."

As she reflected on Hwi's words, Anteac stared down at the cryptic square of black in her lap. Hwi had proceeded to recount the details which her Lord (and now bridegroom!) had commanded, details which would have been boring at times were it not for Anteac's mentat abilities at data absorption.

Anteac shook her head as she considered what must be reported to her Sisters at the Chapter House. They already would be studying the import of her previous message. A machine which could shield itself and contents from the penetrating prescience of even the God Emperor? Was that possible? Or was this a different kind of test, a test of Bene Gesserit candour with their Lord Leto? But now! If he did *not* already know the genesis of this enigmatic Hwi Noree . . .

This new development reinforced Anteac's mentat summation of why she had been chosen for the mission to Ix. The God Emperor did not trust this knowledge to his Fish Speakers. He did not want Fish Speakers suspecting a weakness in their Lord!

Or was that as obvious as it appeared? Wheels within wheels—that was the way of the Lord Leto.

Again, Anteac shook her head. She bent then and resumed her account for the Chapter House, leaving out the revelation that the God Emperor had chosen a bride.

They would learn it soon enough. Meanwhile, Anteac herself would consider the implications.

If you know all of your ancestors, you were a personal witness to the events which created the myths and religions of our past. Recognizing this, you must think of me as a myth-maker.

—The Stolen Journals

The first explosion came just as darkness enfolded the City of Onn. The blast caught a few venturesome revellers outside the Ixian Embassy, passing on their way to a party where (it was promised) Face Dancers would perform an ancient drama about a king who slew his children. After the violent events of the first four Festival Days, it had taken some courage for the revellers to emerge from the relative safety of their quarters. Stories of death and injury to innocent bystanders circulated all through the City—and here it was again—more fuel for the cautious.

None of the victims and survivors would have appreciated Leto's observation that innocent bystanders were in relatively short supply.

Leto's acute senses detected the explosion and located it. With an instant fury which he was later to regret, he shouted for his Fish Speakers and commanded them to "wipe out the Face Dancers", even the ones he had spared earlier.

On immediate reflection, the sensation of fury itself fascinated Leto. It had been so long since he had felt even mild anger. Frustration, irritation—these had been his limits. But now, at a threat to Hwi Noree, fury!

Reflection caused him to modify his initial command, but not before some Fish Speakers had raced from the Royal Presence, their most violent desires released by what they had seen in their Lord.

"God is furious!" some of them shouted.

The second blast caught some of the Fish Speakers emerging into the plaza, limiting the spread of Leto's modified command and igniting more violence. The third explosion, located near the first one, sent Leto himself into action. He propelled his cart like a berserk juggernaut out of his resting chamber into the Ixian lift and surged to the surface.

Leto emerged at the edge of the plaza to find a scene of chaos lighted by thousands of free-floating glowglobes released by his Fish Speakers. The central stage of the plaza had been shattered, leaving only the plasteel base intact beneath the paved surface. Broken pieces of masonry lay all around, mixed with dead and wounded.

In the direction of the Ixian Embassy directly across the plaza from him there was a wild surging of combat.

"Where is my Duncan?" Leto bellowed.

A guard bashar came racing across the plaza to his side where she reported through panting breaths: "We have taken him to the Citadel, Lord!"

"What is happening over there?" Leto demanded, pointing at the battle outside the Ixian Embassy.

"The rebels and the Tleilaxu are attacking the Ixian Embassy, Lord. They have explosives."

Even as she spoke, another blast erupted in front of the Embassy's shattered façade. He saw bodies twisting in the air, arching outward and falling at the perimeter of a bright flash which left an orange afterimage studded with black dots.

With no thought of consequences, Leto shifted his cart on to suspensors and sent it bulleting across the plaza—a hurtling behemoth which sucked glowglobes into its wake. At the battle's edge, he arched over his own defenders and lunged into the attackers' flank, aware only then of lasguns which sent livid blue arcs leaping toward him. He felt his cart thudding into flesh, scattering bodies all around.

The cart spilled him directly in front of the Embassy, rolling him off on to a hard surface as it struck the rubble there. He felt lasgun beams tickle his ribbed body, then the inner surge of heat followed by a venting belch of oxygen at his tail. Instinct tucked his face deep into its cowl and folded his arms into the protective depths of his front segment. The worm body took over, arching and flailing, rolling like an insane wheel, lashing out on all sides.

Blood lubricated the street. Blood was buffered water to his body, but death released the water. His flailing body slipped and slithered in it, the water igniting blue smoke from every flexion place where it slipped through the sandtrout skin. This filled him with water-agony which ignited more violence in the great flailing body.

At Leto's first lashing out, the Fish Speaker perimeter fell back. An alert bashar saw the opportunity now presented. She shouted above the battle noise:

"Pick off the stragglers!"

The ranks of guardian women rushed forward.

It was bloody play among the Fish Speakers for a few minutes, blades thrusting in the merciless light of the glowglobes, the dancing of lasgun arcs, even hands chopping and toes digging into vulnerable flesh. The Fish Speakers left no survivors.

Leto rolled beyond the bloody mush in front of the Embassy, barely able to think through the waves of water-agony. The air was heavy with oxygen all around him and this helped his human senses. He summoned his cart and it drifted toward him, tipping perilously on damaged suspensors. Slowly, he wriggled on to the tipping cart and gave it the mental command to return to his quarters beneath the plaza.

Long ago, he had prepared himself against water damage—a room where blasts of superheated dry air would cleanse and restore him. Sand would serve but there was no place in the confines of Onn for the necessary expanse of sand in which he might heat and rasp his surface to its normal purity.

In the lift, he thought of Hwi and sent a message to have her brought down to him immediately.

If she survived.

He had no time now to make a prescient search; he could only hope while his body, both pre-worm and human, longed for the cleansing heat.

Once into the cleansing room, he thought to reaffirm his modified command—"Save some of the Face Dancers!" But by then the maddened Fish Speakers were spreading out through the City and he had not the strength to make a prescient sweep which would send his messengers to the proper meeting points.

A Guard captain brought him word as he was emerging from the cleansing room that Hwi Noree, although slightly wounded, was safe and would be brought to him as soon as the local commander thought it prudent.

Leto promoted the Guard captain to sub-bashar on the spot. She was a heavyset Nayla-type but without Nayla's square face—features more rounded and closer to the older norms. She trembled in the warmth of her Lord's approval and, when he told her to return and "make doubly certain" no more harm came to Hwi, she whirled and dashed from his presence.

I didn't even ask her name, Leto thought, as he rolled himself on to a new cart in the depression of his small audience room. It took a few moments of reflection to recall the new sub-bashar's name—Kieuemo. The promotion would have to be reaffirmed. He lodged a mental reminder to do this personally. The Fish Speakers, all of them, would have to learn immediately how much he valued Hwi Noree. Not that there could be much doubt after tonight.

He made his prescient scan then and dispatched messengers to his rampaging Fish Speakers. By then the damage had been done—corpses all over Onn, some Face Dancers and some only suspected Face Dancers.

And many have seen me kill, he thought.

While he waited for Hwi's arrival, he reviewed what had just happened. This had not been a typical Tleilaxu attack, but the previous attack on the road to Onn fitted into a new pattern, all of it pointing at a single mind with lethal purpose.

I could have died out there, he thought.

That began to explain why he had not anticipated this attack, but there was a deeper reason. Leto could see that reason rising into his awareness, a summation of all the clues. What human knew the God Emperor best? What human possessed a secret place from which to conspire?

Malky!

Leto summoned a guard and told her to ask if the Reverend Mother Anteac had yet left Arrakis. The guard returned in a moment to report.

"Anteac is still in her quarters. The commander of the Fish Speaker guard there says they have not come under attack."

"Send word to Anteac," Leto said. "Ask if she now understands why I put her delegation in quarters at a distance from me? Then tell her that while she is on Ix she must locate Malky. She is to report that location to our local garrison on Ix."

"Malky, the former Ixian Ambassador?"

"The same. He is not to remain alive and free. You will inform our garrison commander on Ix that she is to make close liaison with Anteac, providing every necessary assistance. Malky is to be brought here to me or executed, whichever our commander finds necessary."

The guard-messenger nodded, shadows lurching across her features where she stood in the ring of light around Leto's face. She did not ask for a repetition of the orders. Each of his close guards had been trained as a human-recorder. They could repeat Leto's words exactly, even the intonations, and would never forget what they had heard him say.

When the messenger had gone, Leto sent a private signal of inquiry and, within seconds, had a response from Nayla. The Ixian device within his cart reproduced a non-identifiable version of her voice, a flatly metallic recital for his ears alone.

Yes, Siona was at the Citadel. No, Siona had not contacted her rebel companions. *"No, she does not yet know that I am here observing her."* The attack on the Embassy? That had been by a splinter group called "The Tleilaxu-Contact Element."

Leto allowed himself a mental sigh. Rebels always gave their groups such pretentious labels.

"Any survivors?" he asked.

"No known survivors."

Leto found it amusing that, while the metallic voice provided no emotional tones, his memory supplied them.

"You will make contact with Siona," he said. "Reveal

268

that you are a Fish Speaker. Tell her you did not reveal this earlier because you knew she would not trust you and because you feared exposure since you are quite alone among Fish Speakers in your allegiance to Siona. Reaffirm your oath to her. Tell her that you swear *by all that you hold holy* to obey Siona in anything. If she commands it, you will do it. All of this is truth as you well know."

"Yes, Lord."

Memory supplied the fanatic emphasis in Nayla's response. She would obey.

"If possible, provide opportunities for Siona and Duncan Idaho to be alone together," he said.

"Yes, Lord."

Let propinquity take its usual course, he thought.

He broke contact with Nayla, thought for a moment, then sent for the commander of his plaza forces. The bashar arrived presently, her dark uniform stained and dusty, evidence of gore still on her boots. She was a tall, bone-thin woman with age lines which gave her aquiline features an air of powerful dignity. Leto recalled her troop-name, Iylyo, which meant *Dependable* in Old Fremen. He called her, however, by her matronymic, Nyshae, *Daughter of Shae,* which set a tone of subtle intimacy for this meeting.

"Rest yourself on a cushion, Nyshae," he said. "You have been working hard."

"Thank you, Lord."

She sank on to the red cushion which Hwi had used. Leto noted the fatigue lines around Nyshae's mouth, but her eyes remained alert. She stared up at him, eager to hear his words.

"Matters are once more tranquil in my city." He made it not quite a question, leaving the interpretation to Nyshae.

"Tranquil but not good, Lord."

He glanced at the gore on her boots.

"The street in front of the Ixian Embassy?"

"It is being cleansed, Lord. Repairs already are underway."

"The plaza?"

"By morning, it will appear as it has always appeared."

Her gaze remained steady on his face. Both of them knew he had not yet reached the nubbin of this interview. But Leto now identified a thing lurking within Nyshae's expression.

Pride in her Lord!

For the first time, she had seen the God Emperor kill. The seeds of a terrible dependency had been planted. *If disaster threatens, my Lord will come.* That was how it appeared in her eyes. She would no longer act with complete independence, taking her power from the God Emperor and being personally responsible for the use of that power. There was something possessive in her expression. A terrible death-machine waited in the wings, available at her summons.

Leto did not like what he saw, but the damage had been done. Any remedies would require slow and subtle pressures.

"Where did the attackers get lasguns?" he asked.

"From our own stores, Lord. The Arsenal Guard has been replaced."

Replaced. It was a euphemism with a certain nicety. Errant Fish Speakers were isolated and reserved until Leto found a problem which required Death Commandos. They would die gladly, of course, believing that thus they expiated their sin. And even the rumour that such berserkers had been dispatched could quiet a trouble spot.

"The Arsenal was breached by explosives?" he asked.

"*Stealth* and explosives, Lord. The Arsenal Guard was careless."

"The source of the explosives?"

Some of Nyshae's fatigue was visible in her shrug.

Leto could only agree. He knew he could search out and identify those sources, but it would serve little purpose. Resourceful people could always find the ingredients for home-made explosives—common things such as sugar and bleaches, quite ordinary oils and innocent fertilizers, plastics and solvents and extracts from the dirt beneath a

270

manure pile. The list was virtually endless, growing with each addition to human experience and knowledge. Even a society such as the one he had created, one which tried to limit the admixture of technology and new ideas, had no real hope of totally eliminating dangerously violent small weapons. The whole idea of controlling such things was a chimera, a dangerous and distracting myth. The key was to limit the *desire* for violence. In that respect, this night had been a disaster.

So much new injustice, he thought.

As though she read his thoughts, Nyshae sighed.

Of course. Fish Speakers were trained from childhood to avoid injustice wherever possible.

"We must see to the survivors in the populace," he said. "See to it that their needs are met. They must be brought to the realization that the Tleilaxu were to blame."

Nyshae nodded. She had not reached bashar rank while remaining ignorant of the drill. By now, she believed it. Merely by hearing Leto say it, she believed in the Tleilaxu guilt. And there was a certain practicality in her understanding. She knew why they did not slay *all* of the Tleilaxu.

You do not eliminate every scapegoat.

"And we must provide a distraction," Leto said. "Luckily, there may be one ready at hand. I will send word to you after conferring with the Lady Hwi Noree."

"The Ixian Ambassador, Lord? Is she not implicated in . . ."

"She is entirely guiltless," he said.

He saw belief settle into Nyshae's features, a readymade plastic underlayment which could lock her jaw and glaze her eyes. *Even Nyshae.* He knew the reasons because he had created those reasons, but sometimes he felt a bit awed by his creation.

"I hear the Lady Hwi arriving in my anteroom," he said. "Send her in as you leave. And, Nyshae . . ."

She already was on her feet, but she stood expectantly silent.

"Tonight, I have elevated Kieuemo to sub-bashar," he

271

said. " See that it is made official. As for yourself, I am pleased. Ask and you shall receive."

He saw the formula send a wave of pleasure through Nyshae, but she tempered it immediately, proving once more her worth to him.

"I shall test Kieuemo, Lord," she said. "If she suits, I may take a holiday. I have not seen my family on Salusa Secundus for many years."

"At a time of your own choosing," he said.

And he thought: *Salusa Secundus. Of course!*

That one reference to her origins reminded him of whom she resembled: *Harq al-Ada. She has Corrino blood. We are closer relatives than I had thought.*

"My Lord is generous," she said.

She left him then, a new spring in her stride. He heard her voice in the anteroom: "Lady Hwi, our Lord will see you now."

Hwi entered, backlighted and framed in the archway for a moment, hesitancy in her step until her eyes adjusted to the inner chamber. She came like a moth to the brightness around Leto's face, looking away only to seek along his shadowy length for signs of injury. He knew that no such sign was visible, but there were still aches and interior tremblings.

His eyes detected a slight limp, Hwi favouring her right leg, but a long gown of jade green concealed the injury. She stopped at the edge of the declivity which held his cart, looking directly into his eyes.

"They said you were wounded, Hwi. Are you in pain?"

"A cut on my leg below the knee, Lord. A small piece of masonry from the explosion. Your Fish Speakers treated it with a salve which removed the pain. Lord, I feared for you."

"And I feared for you, gentle Hwi."

"Except for that first explosion, I was not in danger, Lord. They rushed me into a room deep beneath the Embassy."

So she did not see my performance, he thought. *I can be thankful for that.*

"I sent for you to ask your forgiveness," he said.

She sank on to a golden cushion. "What is there to forgive, Lord? You are not the reason for . . ."

"I am being tested, Hwi."

"You?"

"There are those who wish to know the depths of my concern for the safety of Hwi Noree."

She pointed upward. "That . . . was because of me?"

"Because of us."

"Oh. But who . . ."

"You have agreed to wed me, Hwi, and I . . ." He raised a hand to silence her as she started to speak. "Anteac has told us what you revealed to her, but this did not originate with Anteac."

"Then who is . . ."

"The *who* is not important. It is important that you reconsider. I must give you this opportunity to change your mind."

She lowered her gaze.

How sweet her features are, he thought.

It was possible for him to create only in his imagination an entire *human* lifetime with Hwi. Enough examples lay in the welter of his memories upon which to build a fantasy of wedded life. It gathered nuances in his fancy—small details of mutual experience, a touch, a kiss, all of the sweet sharings upon which arose something of painful beauty. He ached with it, a pain far deeper than the physical reminders of his violence at the Embassy.

Hwi lifted her chin and looked into his eyes. He saw there a compassionate longing to help him.

"But how else may I serve you, Lord?"

He reminded himself that she was a primate, while he no longer was fully primate. The differences grew deeper by the minute.

The ache remained within him.

Hwi was an inescapable reality, something so basic that

273

no word could ever fully express it. The ache within him was almost more than he could bear.

"I love you, Hwi. I love you as a man loves a woman . . . but it cannot be. That will never be."

Tears flowed from her eyes. "Should I leave? Should I return to Ix?"

"They would only hurt you trying to find out what went wrong with their plan."

She has seen my pain, he thought. *She knows the futility and frustration. What will she do? She will not lie. She will not say she returns my love as a woman to a man. She recognizes the futility. And she knows her own feelings for me—compassion, awe, a questioning which ignores fear.*

"Then I will stay," she said. "We will take such pleasure as we can from being together. I think it is best that we do this. If it means we should wed, so be it."

"Then I must share knowledge with you which I have shared with no other person," he said. "It will give you a power over me which . . ."

"Do not do this, Lord! What if someone forced me to . . ."

"You will never again leave my household. My quarters here, the Citadel, the safe places of the Sareer—these will be your home."

"As you will."

How gentle and open her quiet acceptance, he thought.

The aching pulse within him had to be calmed. In itself, it was a danger to him and to the Golden Path.

Those clever Ixians!

Malky had seen how the all-powerful were forced to contend with a constant siren song—the will to self-delight.

Constant awareness of the power in your slightest whim.

Hwi took his silence to be uncertainty. "Will we wed, Lord?"

"Yes."

"Should anything be done about the Tleilaxu stories which . . ."

"Nothing."

She stared at him, remembering their earlier conversation. *The seeds of dissolution were being planted.*

"It is my fear, Lord, that I will weaken you," she said.

"Then you must find ways to strengthen me."

"Can it strengthen you if we diminish belief in the God Leto?"

He heard a hint of Malky in her voice, that measured weighing which had made him so revoltingly charming. *We never completely escape the teachers of our childhood.*

"Your question begs the answer," he said. "Many will continue to worship according to my design. Others will believe the lies."

"Lord . . . would you ask *me* to lie for you?"

"Of course not. But I will ask you to remain silent when you might wish to speak."

"But if they revile . . ."

"You will not protest."

Once more, tears flowed down her cheeks. Leto longed to touch them, but they were water . . . painful water.

"It must be done this way," he said.

"Will you explain it to me, Lord?"

"When I am gone, they must call me Shaitan, the Emperor of Gehenna. The wheel must turn and turn and turn along the Golden Path."

"Lord, could the anger not be directed at me alone. I would not . . ."

"No! The Ixians made you much more perfectly than they thought. I truly love you. I cannot help it."

"I do not wish to cause you pain!" The words were wrenched from her.

"What's done is done. Do not mourn it."

"Help me to understand."

"The hate which will blossom after I am gone, that, too, will fade into the inevitable past. A long time will pass. Then, on a far-distant day, my journals will be found."

"Journals?" She was shaken by the seeming shift of subject.

"My chronicle of my time. My arguments, the apologia.

275

Copies exist and scattered fragments will survive, some in distorted form, but the original journals will wait and wait and wait. I have hidden them well."

"And when they are discovered?"

"People will learn that I was something quite different from what they supposed."

Her voice came in a trembling hush: "I already know what they will learn."

"Yes, my darling Hwi, I think you do."

"You are neither devil nor god, but something never seen before and never to be seen again because your presence removes the need."

She brushed tears from her cheeks.

"Hwi, do you realize how dangerous you are?"

Alarm showed in her expression, the tensing of her arms.

"You have the makings of a saint," he said. "Do you understand how painful it can be to find a saint in the wrong place at the wrong time?"

She shook her head.

"People have to be prepared for saints," he said. "Otherwise, they simply become followers, supplicants, beggars and weakened sycophants forever in the shadow of the saint. People are destroyed by this because it nurtures only weakness."

After a moment of thought, she nodded, then: "Will there be saints when you are gone?"

"That's the purpose of my Golden Path."

"Moneo's daughter, Siona, will she . . . ."

"For now she is only a rebel. As to sainthood, we will let her decide. Perhaps she will only do what she was bred to do."

"What is that, Lord?"

"Stop calling me *Lord*," he said. "We will be Worm and wife. Call me Leto if you wish. *Lord* interferes."

"Yes, L . . . Leto. But what is . . ."

"Siona was bred to rule. There is danger in such breeding. When you rule you gain knowledge of power. This can lead into impetuous irresponsibility, into painful excesses and that can lead to the terrible destroyer—wild hedonism."

"Siona would . . ."

"All we know about Siona is that she can remain dedicated to a particular performance, to the pattern which fills her senses. She is necessarily an aristocrat, but aristocracy looks mostly to the past. That's a failure. You don't see much of any path unless you are Janus, looking simultaneously backward and forward."

"Janus? Oh, yes, the god with the two opposed faces." She wet her lips with her tongue. "Are you Janus, Leto?"

"I am Janus magnified a billionfold. And I am also something less. I have been, for example, what my administrators admire most—the decision maker whose every decision can be made to work."

"But if you fail them . . ."

"They will turn against me, yes."

"Will Siona replace you if . . ."

"Ahhh, what an enormous if! You observe that Siona threatens my person. However, she does not threaten the Golden Path. There is also the fact that my Fish Speakers have a certain *attachment* to the Duncan."

"Siona seems . . . so young."

"And I am her favourite poseur, the sham who holds power under false pretences, never consulting the needs of his people."

"Could I not talk to her and . . ."

"No! You must never try to persuade Siona of anything. Promise me, Hwi."

"If you ask it, of course, but I . . ."

"All gods have this problem, Hwi. In the perception of deeper needs, I must often ignore immediate ones. Not addressing immediate needs is an offence to the young."

"Could you not reason with her and . . ."

"Never attempt to reason with people who know they are right!"

"But when you know they are wrong . . ."

"Do you believe in me?"

"Yes."

"And if someone tried to convince you that I am the greatest evil of all time . . ."

"I would become very angry. I would . . ." She broke off.

"Reason is valuable," he said, "only when it performs against the wordless physical background of the universe."

Her brows drew together in thought. It fascinated Leto to sense the arousal of her awareness. "Ahhhhh." She breathed the word.

"No reasoning creature will ever again be able to deny the Leto experience," he said. "I see your understanding begin. Beginnings! They are what life is all about!"

She nodded.

No arguments, he thought. *When she sees the tracks she follows them to find where they will lead.*

"As long as there is life, every ending is a beginning," he said. "And I would save humankind, even from itself."

Again, she nodded. The tracks still led onward.

"This is why no death in the perpetuation of humankind can be a complete failure," he said. "This is why a birth touches us so deeply. This is why the most tragic death is the death of a youth."

"Does Ix still threaten your Golden Path? I've always known they conspired in something evil."

They *conspire. Hwi does not hear the inner message of her own words. She has no need to hear it.*

He stared at her, full of the marvel that was Hwi. She possessed a form of honesty which some would call naive, but which Leto recognized as merely not-self-conscious. The honesty was not her core, it was Hwi herself.

"Then I will arrange a performance in the plaza tomorrow," Leto said. "It will be a performance of the surviving Face Dancers. Afterward, our betrothal will be announced."

*Let there be no doubt that I am the assemblage of our
ancestors, the arena in which they exercise my moments.
They are my cells and I am their body. This is the favrashi of
which I speak, the soul, the collective unconscious, the source
of archetypes, the repository of all trauma and joy. I am the
choice of their awakening. My samhadi is their samhadi.
Their experiences are mine! Their knowledge distilled is my
inheritance. Those billions are my one.*

—**The Stolen Journals**

The Face Dancer performance occupied almost two hours
of the morning and afterward came the announcement
which sent shock waves through the Festival City.

"It has been centuries since he took a bride!"

"More than a thousand years, my dear."

The trooping of the Fish Speakers had been brief. They
cheered him loudly, but they were disturbed.

"You are my only brides," he had said. Was that not the
meaning of Siaynoq?

Leto thought the Face Dancers performed well despite
their obvious terror. Garments had been found in the
depths of a Fremen museum—hooded black robes with
white cord belts, spread-winged green hawks appliquéd
across the shoulders at the back—uniforms of Muad'Dib's
itinerant priests. The Face Dancers had put on dark,
seamed faces with these robes and performed a dance
which told how Muad'Dib's legions had spread *their*
religion through the Empire.

Hwi, wearing a brilliant silver dress with a green jade
necklace, sat beside Leto on the Royal Cart throughout the
ritual. Once, she leaned close to his face and asked: "Is that
not a parody?"

"To me, perhaps."

"Do the Face Dancers know?"

"They suspect."

"Then they are not as frightened as they appear."

"Oh, yes, they are frightened. It's just that they are

279

braver than most people expect them to be."

"Bravery can be so foolish," she whispered.

"And vice-versa."

She had favoured him with a measuring stare before returning her attention to the performance. Almost two hundred Face Dancers had survived unscathed. All of them had been pressed into the dance. The intricate weavings and posturings could fascinate the eye. It was possible to watch them and, for a time, forget the bloody preliminaries to this day.

Leto remembered this as he lay alone in his small reception room shortly before noon when Moneo arrived. Moneo had seen the Reverend Mother Anteac on to a Guild lighter, had conferred with the Fish Speaker Command about the previous night's violence, had made a quick flight to the Citadel and back to make sure Siona was under a secure watch and that she had not been implicated in the Embassy attack. He had returned to Onn just after the betrothal announcement, having had no previous warning.

Moneo was furious. Leto had never seen him this angry. He stormed into the room and stopped only two metres from Leto's face.

"Now the Tleilaxu lies will be believed!" he said.

Leto responded in a reasoned tone. "How persistent it is, this demand that our gods be perfect. The Greeks were much more reasonable about such things."

"Where is she?" Moneo demanded. "Where is this . . ."

"Hwi is resting. It was a difficult night and a long morning. I want her well rested when we return to the Citadel this evening."

"How did she work this?" Moneo demanded.

"Really, Moneo! Have you lost all sense of caution?"

"I am concerned about you! Have you any idea what they're saying in the City?"

"I'm fully aware of the stories."

"What *are* you doing?"

"You know, Moneo, I think that only the old pantheists

280

had the right idea about deities: mortal foibles in immortal guise."

Moneo raised both arms to the heavens. "I saw the looks on their faces!" He lowered his arms. "It'll be all over the Empire within two weeks."

"Surely it'll take longer than that."

"If your enemies needed one thing to bring them all together . . ."

"The defiling of the god is an ancient human tradition, Moneo. Why should I be an exception?"

Moneo tried to speak, found he could not utter a word. He stamped down along the edge of the pit which held Leto's cart, stamped back and resumed his former position glaring into Leto's face.

"If I am to help you, I need an explanation," Moneo said. "Why are you doing this?"

"Emotions."

Moneo's mouth formed the word without speaking it.

"They have come over me just when I thought them gone forever," Leto said. "How sweet these last few sips of humanity are."

"With Hwi? But you surely cannot . . ."

"Memories of emotions are never enough, Moneo."

"Are you telling me that you are indulging yourself in a . . ."

"Indulgence? Certainly not! But the tripod upon which eternity swings is composed of flesh and thought and emotion. I felt that I had been reduced to flesh and thought."

"She has worked some kind of witchery," Moneo accused.

"Of course she has. And how grateful I am for it. If we deny the need for thought, Moneo, as some do, we lose the powers of reflection; we cannot define what our senses report. If we deny the flesh, we unwheel the vehicle which bears us. But if we deny emotion, we lose all touch with our internal universe. It was emotions which I missed the most."

"I insist, Lord, that you . . ."

"You are making me angry, Moneo. That *is* an emotion."

Leto saw Moneo's frustrated fury cool, quenched like a hot iron plunged into icy water. There was still some steam in him, though.

"I care not for myself, Lord. My concern is mostly for you, and you know this."

Leto spoke softly. "It is your *emotion*, Moneo, and I hold it dear."

Moneo inhaled a deep, trembling breath. He had never before seen the God Emperor in this mood, reflecting this *emotion*. Leto appeared both elated and resigned, if Moneo were reading it correctly. One could not be certain.

"That which makes life sweet for the living," Leto said, "that which makes life warm and filled with beauty, that is what I would preserve even though it were denied to me."

"Then this Hwi Noree . . ."

"She makes me recall the Butlerian Jihad in a poignant way. She is the antithesis of all that's mechanical and non-human. How odd it is, Moneo, that the Ixians, of all people, should produce this one person who so perfectly embodies those qualities which I hold most dear."

"I do not understand your reference to the Butlerian Jihad, Lord. Machines that think have no place in . . ."

"The target of the Jihad was a machine-attitude as much as the machines," Leto said. "Humans had set those machines to usurp our sense of beauty, our necessary self-dom out of which we make living judgments. Naturally the machines were destroyed."

"Lord, I still resent the fact that you welcome this . . ."

"Moneo! Hwi reassures me merely by her presence. For the first time in centuries, I am not lonely unless she is away from my side. If I had no other proof of the emotion, this would serve."

Moneo fell silent, obviously touched by Leto's evocation of loneliness. Surely, Moneo could understand the absence of the intimate sharing in love. His expression betrayed as much.

For the first time in a long while, Leto noted how much Moneo had aged.

It happens so suddenly to them, Leto thought.

It made Leto deeply aware of how much he cared for Moneo.

I should not let attachments happen to me, but I cannot help it . . . especially now that Hwi is here.

"They will laugh at you and make obscene jests," Moneo said.

"That is a good thing."

"How can it be good?"

"This is something new. Our task has always been to bring the new into balance and, with it, modify behaviour while not suppressing survival."

"Even so, how can you welcome this?"

"The making of obscenities?" Leto asked. "What is the opposite of obscenity?"

Moneo's eyes went wide with a sudden questioning awareness. He had seen the action of many polarities—the thing made known by its opposite.

The thing stands out against a background which defines it, Leto thought. *Surely Moneo will see this.*

"It's too dangerous," Moneo said.

The ultimate verdict of conservatism!

Moneo was not convinced. A deep sigh wracked him.

I must remember not to take away their doubts, Leto thought. *That's how I failed my Fish Speakers in the plaza. The Ixians are holding on to the ragged end of human doubts. Hwi is the evidence of that.*

A disturbance sounded in the anteroom. Leto sealed the portal against impetuous intrusions.

"My Duncan has come," he said.

"He's probably heard about your wedding plans!"

"Probably."

Leto watched Moneo wrestle with doubts, his thoughts utterly transparent. In that moment, Moneo fitted so precisely into his human niche that Leto wanted to hug him.

He has the full spectrum: doubt-to-trust, love-to-hate . . . everything! All of those dear qualities which come to fruition in the warmth of emotion, in the willingness to spend yourself on Life.

"Why is Hwi accepting this?" Moneo asked.

Leto smiled. *Moneo cannot doubt me; he must doubt others.*

"I admit it is not a conventional union. She is a primate and I no longer am fully primate."

Again, Moneo wrestled with things he could only feel and not express.

Watching Moneo, Leto felt the flow of an observational-awareness, a thought process which occurred so rarely but with such vivid amplification when it did occur, that Leto did not stir lest he cause a ripple in the flow.

The primate thinks and, by thinking, survives. Beneath his thinking is a thing which came with his cells. It is the current of human concerns for the species. Sometimes, they cover it up, wall it off and hide it behind thick barriers, but I have deliberately sensitized Moneo to these workings of his innermost self. He follows me because he believes I hold the best course for human survival. He knows there is a cellular awareness. It is what I find when I scan the Golden Path. This is humanity and both of us agree: it must endure!

"Where, when and how will the wedding ceremony be conducted?" Moneo asked.

Not why? Leto noted. Moneo no longer sought to understand the *why*. He had returned to safe ground. He was the majordomo, the director of the God Emperor's Household, the First Minister.

He has names and verbs and modifiers with which he can perform. The words will work for him in their usual ways. Moneo may never glimpse the transcendental potential of his words, but he well understands their everyday, mundane uses.

"What of my question?" Moneo pressed.

Leto blinked at him, thinking: *I, on the other hand, feel*

that words are mostly useful if they open for me a glimpse of
attractive and undiscovered places. But the use of words is
so little understood by a civilization which still believes
unquestioningly in a mechanical universe of absolute cause
and effect—obviously reducible to one single root-cause and
one primary seminal-effect.

"How like a limpet the Ixian-Tleilaxu fallacy clings to human affairs," Leto said.

"Lord, it disturbs me deeply when you don't pay attention."

"But I do pay attention, Moneo."

"Not to me."

"Even to you."

"Your attention wanders, Lord. You do not have to conceal that from me. I would betray myself before I would betray you."

"You think I'm woolgathering?"

"What gathering, Lord?" Moneo had never questioned this word earlier, but now . . .

Leto explained the allusion, thinking: *How ancient!* The looms and shuttles clicked in Leto's memory. *Animal fur to human garments . . . huntsman to herdsman . . . the long steps up the ladder of awareness . . . and now they must make another long step, longer even than the ancient ones.*

"You indulge in idle thoughts," Moneo accused.

"I have time for idle thoughts. That's one of the most interesting things about my existence as a singular multitude."

"But, Lord, there are matters which demand our . . ."

"You'd be surprised what comes of idle thinking, Moneo. I've never minded spending an entire day on things a human would not bother with for one minute. Why not? With my life expectancy of some four thousand years, what's one day more or less? How much time does one human life count? A million minutes? I've already experienced almost that many days."

Moneo stood frozen in silence, diminished by this comparison. He felt his own lifetime reduced to a mote in

Leto's eye. The source of the allusion did not escape him.

Words . . . words . . . words, Moneo thought.

"Words are often almost useless in sentient affairs," Leto said.

Moneo held his breathing to a shallow minimum. *The Lord can read thoughts!*

"Throughout our history," Leto said, "the most potent use of words has been to round out some transcendental event, giving that event a place in the accepted chronicles, *explaining* the event in such a way that ever afterward we can use those words and say: "'This is what it meant.'"

Moneo felt beaten down by these words, terrified by unspoken things they might make him think.

"That's how events get lost in history," Leto said.

After a long silence, Moneo ventured: "You have not answered my question, Lord. The wedding?"

How tired he sounds, Leto thought. *How utterly defeated.*

Leto spoke briskly: "I have never needed your good offices more. The wedding must be arranged with utmost care. It must have the precision of which only you are capable."

"Where, Lord?"

A bit more life in his voice.

"At Tabur Village in the Sareer."

"When?"

"I leave the date to you. Announce it when all things are arranged."

"And the ceremony itself?"

"I will conduct it."

"Will you need assistants, Lord? Artifacts of any kind?"

"The trappings of ritual?"

"Any particular thing which I may not . . ."

"We will not need much for our little charade."

"Lord! I beg of you! Please . . ."

"You will stand beside the bride and give her in marriage," Leto said. "We will use the old Fremen ritual."

"We will need water rings then," Moneo said.

286

"Yes! I will use Ghani's water rings."

"And who will attend, Lord?"

"Only a Fish Speaker guard and the aristocracy."

Moneo stared at Leto's face. "What . . . what does my Lord mean by aristocracy?"

"You, your family, the household entourage, the courtiers of the Citadel."

"My fam . . ." Moneo swallowed. "Do you include Siona?"

"If she survives the test."

"But . . ."

"Is she not family?"

"Of course, Lord, she is Atreides and . . ."

"Then by all means include Siona!"

Moneo brought a tiny memocorder from his pocket, a dull black Ixian artifact whose existence crowded the proscriptions of the Butlerian Jihad. A soft smile touched Leto's lips. Moneo knew his duties and would now perform them.

The clamour of Duncan Idaho outside the portal grew more strident, but Moneo ignored the sound.

Moneo knows the price of his privileges, Leto thought. *It is another kind of marriage—the marriage of privilege and duty. It is the aristocrat's explanation and his excuse.*

Moneo finished his note-taking.

"A few details, Lord," Moneo said. "Will there be some special garb for Hwi?"

"The stillsuit and robe of a Fremen bride, real ones."

"Jewelry or other baubles?"

Leto's gaze locked on Moneo's fingers scrabbling over the tiny recorder, seeing there a dissolution.

Leadership, courage, a sense of knowledge and order— Moneo has these in abundance. They surround him like a holy aura, but they conceal from all eyes except mine the rot which eats from within. It is inevitable. Were I gone, it would be visible to everyone.

"Lord?" Moneo pressed. "Are you woolgathering?"

Ahhh! He likes that new word!

"That is all," Leto said. "Only the robe, the stillsuit and the water rings."

Moneo bowed and turned away.

He is looking ahead now, Leto thought, *but even this new thing will pass. He will turn toward the past once more. And I had such high hopes for him once. Well . . . perhaps Siona . . .*

> *"Make no heroes,"* my father said.
>
> —The Voice of Ghanima
> from the Oral History

Just by the way Idaho strode across the small chamber, his loud demands for audience now gratified, Leto could see an important transformation in the ghola. It was a thing repeated so many times that it had become deeply familiar to Leto. The Duncan had not even exchanged words of greeting with the departing Moneo. It all fitted into the pattern. How boring that pattern had become!

Leto had a name for this transformation of the Duncans. He called it "The Since Syndrome".

The gholas often nurtured suspicions about the *secret things* which might have been developed across the centuries of oblivion *since* they last knew awareness. What had people been doing all that time? Why could they possibly want me, this relic from their past? No ego could overcome such doubts forever—especially in a doubting man.

One of the gholas had accused Leto: "You've put things in my body, things I know nothing about! These things in my body tell you everything I'm doing! You spy on me everywhere!"

Another had charged him with possessing a "manipulative machine which makes us want to do whatever you want".

Once it started, the Since Syndrome could never be entirely eliminated. It could be checked, even diverted, but the dormant seed might sprout at the slightest provocation.

Idaho stopped where Moneo had stood and there was a veiled look of non-specific suspicions in his eyes, in the set of his shoulders. Leto allowed the situation to simmer, bringing the condition to a head. Idaho locked gazes with him, then broke away to dart his glances around the room. Leto recognized the manner behind that gaze.

The Duncans never forget!

As he studied the room, using the sightful ways he had been taught centuries before by the Lady Jessica and the mentat Thufir Hawat, Idaho began to feel a giddy sense of dislocation. He thought the room rejected him, each thing—the soft cushions: big bulbous things in gold, green and a red that was almost purple; the Fremen rugs, each a museum piece, lapping over each other in thick piles around Leto's pit; the false sunlight of Ixian glowglobes, light which enveloped the emperor's face in dry warmth, making the shadows around it deeper and more mysterious; the smell of spice tea somewhere nearby and that rich melange odour which radiated from the worm body.

Idaho felt that too much had happened to him too fast since the Tleilaxu had abandoned him to the mercies of Luli and Friend in that featureless prison-cell room.

Too much . . . too much . . .

Am I really here? he wondered. *Is this me? What are these thoughts that I think?*

He stared at Leto's quiescent body, the shadowy and enormous mass which lay so silently there on its cart within the pit. The very quietness of that fleshy mass only suggested mysterious energies, terrible energies which might be unleashed in ways nobody could anticipate.

Idaho had heard the stories about the fight at the Ixian Embassy, but the Fish Speaker accounts had an aura of *miraculous visitation* about them which obscured the physical data.

"He flew down from above them and executed a terrible slaughter among the sinners."

"How did he do that?" Idaho had asked.

"He was an *angry* God," his informant had said.

Angry, Idaho thought. *Was it because of the threat to Hwi?* The stories he had heard! None were believable. Hwi wedded to this gross . . . It was not possible! Not the lovely Hwi, the Hwi of gentle delicacy. *He is playing some terrible game, testing us . . . testing us . . .* There was no honest reality in these times, no peace except in the presence of Hwi. All else was insanity.

As he returned his attention to Leto's face—that silently waiting Atreides face—the sense of dislocation grew stronger in Idaho. He began to wonder if, by a slight increase in mental effort along some strange new pathway, he might break through ghostly barriers to remember all of the experiences of the other ghola Idahos.

What did they think when they entered this room? Did they feel this dislocation, this rejection?

Just a little extra effort.

He felt dizzy and wondered if he were going to faint.

"Is something wrong, Duncan?" It was Leto's most reasonable and calming tone.

"It's not real," Idaho said. "I don't belong here."

Leto chose to misunderstand. "But my guard tells me you came here of your own accord, that you flew back from the Citadel and demanded an immediate audience."

"I mean *here*, now! In this time!"

"But I need you."

"For what?"

"Look around you, Duncan. The ways you can help me are so numerous that you could not do them all."

"But your women won't let me fight! Every time I want to go where . . ."

"Do you question that you're more valuable alive than dead?" Leto made a clucking sound, then: "Use your wits, Duncan! That's what I value."

"And my sperm. You value that."

"Your sperm is your own to put where you wish."

"I will not leave a widow and orphans behind me the way . . ."

"Duncan! I've said the choice is yours."

Idaho swallowed, then: "You've committed a crime against us, Leto, against all of us—the gholas you resurrect without ever asking us if that's what we want."

This was a new turn in Duncan-thinking. Leto peered at Idaho with renewed interest.

"What crime?"

"Oh, I've heard you spouting your deep thoughts," Idaho accused. He hooked a thumb over his shoulder, pointing at the room's entrance. "Did you know you can be heard out there in the anteroom?"

"When I wish to be heard, yes." *But only my Journals hear it all!* "I would like to know the nature of my crime, though."

"There's a time, Leto, a time when you're alive. A time when you're supposed to be alive. It can have a magic, that time, while you're living it. You know you're never going to see a time like that again."

Leto blinked, touched by the Duncan's distress. The words were evocative.

Idaho raised both hands, palms up, to chest height, a beggar asking for something he knew he could not receive.

"Then . . . one day you wake up and you remember dying . . . and you remember the axlotl tank . . . and the Tleilaxu nastiness which awakened you . . . and it's supposed to start all over again. But it doesn't. It never does, Leto. That's a crime!"

"I have taken away the magic?"

"Yes!"

Idaho dropped his hands to his sides and clenched them into fists. He felt that he stood alone in the path of a millrace tide which would overwhelm him at his slightest relaxation.

And what of my time? Leto thought. *This, too, will never happen again. But the Duncan would not understand the difference.*

"What brought you rushing back from the Citadel?" Leto asked.

Idaho took a deep breath, then: "Is it true? You're to be married?"

"That's correct."

"To this Hwi Noree, the Ixian Ambassador?"

"True."

Idaho darted a quick glance along Leto's supine length.

They always look for genitalia, Leto thought. *Perhaps I should have something made, a gross protuberance to shock them.* He choked back the small burst of amusement which threatened to erupt from his throat. *Another emotion amplified. Thank you, Hwi. Thank you, Ixians.*

Idaho shook his head. "But you . . ."

"There are strong elements to a marriage other than sex," Leto said. "Will we have children of our flesh? No. But the effects of this union will be profound."

"I listened while you were talking to Moneo," Idaho said. "I thought it must be some kind of joke, a . . ."

"Careful, Duncan!"

"Do you *love* her?"

"More deeply than any man ever loved a woman."

"Well, what about her? Does she . . ."

"She feels . . . a compelling compassion, a need to share with me, to give whatever she can give. It is her nature."

Idaho suppressed a feeling of revulsion.

"Moneo's right. They'll believe the Tleilaxu stories."

"That is one of the profound effects."

"And you still want me to . . . to mate with Siona!"

"You know my wishes. I leave the choice to you."

"Who's that Nayla woman?"

"You've met Nayla! Good."

"She and Siona act like sisters. That big hunk! What's going on there, Leto?"

"What would you want to go on? And what does it matter?"

"I've never met such a brute! She reminds me of Beast Rabban. You'd never know she was female if she didn't . . ."

"You have met her before," Leto said. "You knew her as Friend."

Idaho stared at him in quick silence, the silence of a burrowing creature who senses the hawk.

"Then you trust her," Idaho said.

"Trust? What is trust?"

The moment arrives, Leto thought. He could see it shaping in Idaho's thoughts.

"Trust is what goes with a pledge of loyalty," Idaho said.

"Such as the trust between you and me?" Leto asked.

A bitter smile touched Idaho's lips. "So that's what you're doing with Hwi Noree. A marriage, a pledge . . ."

"Hwi and I already have trust for each other."

"Do you trust me, Leto?"

"If I cannot trust Duncan Idaho, I cannot trust anyone."

"And if I can't trust you?"

"Then I pity you."

Idaho took this as almost a physical shock. His eyes were wide with unspoken demands. He *wanted* to trust. He *wanted* the magic which would never come again.

Idaho indicated his thoughts were taking off in an odd tangent then.

"Can they hear us out in the anteroom?" he asked.

"No." *But my Journals hear!*

"Moneo was furious. Anyone could see it. But he went away like a docile lamb."

"Moneo is an aristocrat. He is married to duty, to responsibilities. When he is reminded of these things, his anger vanishes."

"So that's how you control him," Idaho said.

"He controls himself," Leto said, remembering how Moneo had glanced up from the note-taking, not for reassurances, but to prompt his sense of duty.

"No," Idaho said, "he doesn't control himself. You do it."

"Moneo has locked *himself* into his past. I did not do that."

"But he's an aristocrat . . . an Atreides."

293

Leto recalled Moneo's aging features, thinking how inevitable it was that the aristocrat would refuse his final duty—which was to step aside and vanish into history. He would have to be driven aside. And he would be. No aristocrat had ever overcome the demands of change.

Idaho was not through. "Are you an aristocrat, Leto?"

Leto smiled. "The ultimate aristocrat dies within me." And he thought: *Privilege becomes arrogance. Arrogance promotes injustice. The seeds of ruin blossom.*

"Maybe I will not attend your wedding," Idaho said. "I never thought of myself as an aristocrat."

"But you were. You were *the* aristocrat of the sword."

"Paul was better," Idaho said.

Leto spoke in the voice of Muad'Dib: "Because you taught me!" He resumed his normal tones: "The aristocrat's unspoken duty—to teach, and sometimes by horrible example."

And he thought: *Pride of birth trails out into penury and the weaknesses of interbreeding. The way is opened for pride of wealth and accomplishment. Enter the* nouveau riche, *riding to power as the Harkonnens did, on the backs of the* ancien régime.

The cycle repeated itself with such persistence that Leto felt anyone should have seen how it must be built into long forgotten survival patterns which the species had outgrown, but never lost.

But no, we still carry the detritus which I must weed out.

"Is there some frontier?" Idaho asked. "Is there some frontier where I could go and never again be a part of this?"

"If there is to be any frontier, you must help me create it," Leto said. "There is now no place to go where others of us cannot follow and find you."

"Then you won't let me go."

"Go if you wish. Others of you have tried it. I tell you there is no frontier, no place to hide. Right now, as it has been for a long, long time, humankind is like a single-celled creature, bound together by a dangerous glue."

"No new planets? No strange . . ."

"Oh, we grow, but we do not separate."

"Because *you* hold us together!" he accused.

"I do not know if you can understand this, Duncan, but if there is a frontier, any kind of frontier, then what lies behind you cannot be more important than what lies ahead."

"You're the past!"

"No, Moneo is the past. He is quick to raise the traditional aristocratic barriers against all frontiers. You must understand the power of those barriers. They not only enclose planets and land on those planets, they enclose ideas. They repress change."

"*You* repress change!"

He will not deviate, Leto thought. *One more try.*

"The surest sign that an aristocracy exists is the discovery of barriers against change, curtains of iron or steel or stone or of any substance which excludes the new, the different."

"I know there must be a frontier somewhere," Idaho said. "You're hiding it."

"I hide nothing of frontiers. I want frontiers! I want surprises!"

They come right up against it, Leto thought. *Then they refuse to enter.*

True to this prediction, Idaho's thoughts darted off on a new track. "Did you really have Face Dancers perform at your betrothal?"

Leto felt a surge of anger followed immediately by a wry enjoyment of the fact that he could experience the emotion in such depth. He wanted to let it shout at Duncan . . . but that would solve nothing.

"The Face Dancers performed," he said.

"Why?"

"I want everyone to share in my happiness."

Idaho stared at him as though just discovering a repellent insect in his drink. In a flat voice, Idaho said: "That is the most cynical thing I have ever heard an Atreides say."

"But an Atreides said it."

"You're deliberately trying to put me off! You're avoiding my question."

Once more into the fray, Leto thought. He said: "The Face Dancers of the Bene Tleilax are a colony organism. Individually, they are mules. This is a choice they made for and *by* themselves."

Leto waited, thinking: *I must be patient. They have to discover it for themselves. If I say it, they will not believe. Think, Duncan. Think!*

After a long silence, Idaho said: "I have given you my oath. That is important to me. It is still important. I don't know what you're doing or why. I can only say I don't like what's happening. There! I've said it."

"Is that why you returned from the Citadel?"

"Yes!"

"Will you go back to the Citadel now?"

"What other *frontier* is there?"

"*Very* good, Duncan! Your anger knows even when your reason does not. Hwi goes to the Citadel tonight. I will join her there tomorrow."

"I want to know her better," Idaho said.

"You will avoid her," Leto said. "That is an order. Hwi is not for you."

"I've always known there were witches," Idaho said. "Your grandmother was one."

He turned on his heel and, not asking leave, strode back the way he had come.

How like a little boy he is, Leto thought, watching the stiffness in Idaho's back. *The oldest man in our universe and the youngest—both in one flesh.*

The prophet is not diverted by illusions of past, present and future. The fixity of language determines such linear distinctions. Prophets hold a key to the lock in a language. The mechanical image remains only an image to them. This is not a mechanical universe. The linear progression of events is imposed by the observer. Cause and effect? That's not it at all. The prophet utters fateful words. You glimpse a thing "destined to occur". But the prophetic instant releases something of infinite portent and power. The universe undergoes a ghostly shift. Thus, the wise prophet conceals actuality behind shimmering labels. The uninitiated then believe the prophetic language is ambiguous. The listener distrusts the prophetic messenger. Instinct tells you how the utterance blunts the power of such words. The best prophets lead you up to the curtain and let you peer through for yourself.

—**The Stolen Journals**

Leto addressed Moneo in the coldest voice he had ever used: "The Duncan disobeys me."

They were in the airy room of golden stone atop the Citadel's south tower, Leto's third full day back from the Decennial Festival in Onn. An open portal beside him looked out over the harsh noonday of the Sareer. The wind made a deep humming sound through the opening. It stirred up dust and sand which made Moneo squint. Leto seemed not to notice the irritation. He stared out across the Sareer where the air was alive with heat movements. The distant flow of dunes suggested a mobility in the landscape which only his eyes observed.

Moneo stood immersed in the sour odours of his own fear, knowing that the wind conveyed the message of these odours to Leto's senses. The arrangements for the wedding, the upset among the Fish Speakers—everything was paradox. It reminded Moneo of something the God Emperor had said in the first days of their association.

"Paradox is a pointer telling you to look beyond it. If paradoxes bother you, that betrays your deep desire for

absolutes. The relativist treats a paradox merely as inter-esting, perhaps amusing or even, dreadful thought, educational."

"You do not respond," Leto said. He turned from his examination of the Sareer and focused the weight of his attention on Moneo.

Moneo could only shrug. *How near is the Worm?* he wondered. Moneo had noticed that the return to the Citadel from Onn sometimes aroused the Worm. No sign of that awful shift in the God Emperor's presence had yet betrayed itself, but Moneo sensed it. Could the Worm come without warning?

"Accelerate arrangements for the wedding," Leto said. "Make it as soon as possible."

"Before you test Siona?"

Leto was silent for a moment, then: "No. What will you do about the Duncan?"

"What would you have me do, Lord?"

"I told him not to see Noree, to avoid her. I told him it was an order."

"She has sympathy for him, Lord. Nothing more."

"Why should she have sympathy for him?"

"He is a ghola. He has no connection to our times, no roots."

"He has roots as deep as mine!"

"But he does not know this, Lord."

"Are you arguing with me, Moneo?"

Moneo backed away a half-step, knowing that this did not remove him from danger. "Oh, no, Lord. But I always try to tell you truly what I believe is happening."

"I will tell *you* what is happening. He is courting her."

"But she initiates their meetings, Lord."

"Then you knew about this!"

"I did not know you had absolutely prohibited it, Lord."

Leto spoke in a musing voice: "He is clever with women, Moneo, exceedingly clever. He sees into their souls and makes them do what he wants. It has always been that way with the Duncans."

"I did not know you had prohibited all meetings between them, Lord!" Moneo's voice was almost strident.

"He is more dangerous than any of the others," Leto said. "It is the fault of our times."

"Lord, the Tleilaxu do not have a successor for him ready to deliver."

"And we need this one?"

"You said it yourself, Lord. It is a paradox which I do not understand, but you did say it."

"How long until there could be a replacement?"

"At least a year, Lord. Shall I inquire as to a specific date?"

"Do it today."

"He may hear about it, Lord. The previous one did."

"I do not want it to happen this way, Moneo!"

"I know, Lord."

"And I dare not speak of this to Noree," Leto said. "The Duncan is not for her. Yet, I cannot hurt her!" This last was almost a wail.

Moneo stood in awed silence.

"Can't you see this?" Leto demanded. "Moneo, help me!"

"I see that it is different with Noree," Moneo said. "But I do not know what to do."

"What is different?" Leto's voice had a penetrating quality which cut right through Moneo.

"I mean your attitude toward her, Lord. It is different from anything I have ever seen in you."

Moneo noted then the first signs—twitching in the God Emperor's hands, the beginning glaze in the eyes. *Gods! The Worm is coming!* Moneo felt totally exposed. A simple flick of the great body would crush Moneo against a wall. *I must appeal to the human in him.*

"Lord," Moneo said, "I have read the accounts and heard your own words about your marriage to your sister, Ghanima."

"If only she were with me now," Leto said.

"She was never your mate, Lord."

"What're you suggesting?" Leto demanded.

299

The twitching of Leto's hands had become a spasmodic vibration.

"She was . . . I mean, Lord, that Ghanima was Harq al-Ada's mate."

"Of course she was! All of you Atreides are descended from them!"

"Is there something you have not told me, Lord? Is it possible . . . that is, with Hwi Noree . . . could you mate?"

Leto's hands shook so strongly Moneo wondered that their owner did not know it. The glazing of the great blue eyes deepened.

Moneo backed another step toward the door to the stairs leading down from this deadly place.

"Do not question me about possibilities," Leto said, and his voice was hideously distant, gone somewhere into the layers of his past.

"Never again, Lord," Moneo said. He bowed himself back to only a single pace from the door. "I will speak to Noree, Lord . . . and to the Duncan."

"Do what you can." Leto's voice was far away in those interior chambers which only he could enter.

Softly, Moneo let himself out of the door. He closed it behind him and placed his back against it, trembling. *Ahhh, that was the closest ever.*

And the paradox remained. Where did it point? What was the meaning of the God Emperor's odd and painful decisions? What had brought *The Worm Who Is God?*

A thumping sounded from within Leto's aerie, a heavy beating against stone. Moneo dared not open the door to investigate. He pushed himself away from the surface which reflected that dreadful thumping and went down the stairs, moving cautiously, not drawing an easy breath until he reached ground level and the Fish Speaker guard there.

"Is he disturbed?" she asked, looking up the stairs.

Moneo nodded. They both could hear the thumping quite plainly.

"What disturbs him?" the guard asked.

"He is God and we are mortal," Moneo said. This was an

300

answer which usually satisfied Fish Speakers, but new forces were at work now.

She looked directly at him and Moneo saw the killer training close to the surface of her soft features. She was a relatively young woman with auburn hair and a face usually dominated by a turned-up nose and full lips, but now her eyes were hard and demanding. Only a fool would turn his back on those eyes.

"I did not disturb him," Moneo said.

"Of course not," she agreed. Her look softened slightly. "But I would like to know *who* or what did."

"I think he is impatient for his marriage," Moneo said. "I think that's all it is."

"Then hurry the day!" she said.

"That's what I'm about," Moneo said. He turned and hurried away down the long hall to his own area of the Citadel. Gods! The Fish Speakers were becoming as dangerous as the God Emperor.

That stupid Duncan! He puts us all in peril! And Hwi Noree! What's to be done about her?

> *The pattern of monarchies and similar systems has a message of value for all political forms. My memories assure me that governments of any kind could profit from this message. Goevernments can be useful to the governed only so long as inherent tendencies toward tyranny are restrained. Monarchies have some good features beyond their star qualities. They can reduce the size and parasitic nature of the management bureaucracy. They can make speedy decisions when necessary. They fit an ancient human demand for a parental (tribal/feudal) hierarchy where every person knows his place. It is valuable to know your place, even if that place is temporary. It is galling to be held in place against your will. This is why I teach about tyranny in the best possible way—by example. Even though you read these words after a passage of eons, my tyranny will not be forgotten. My Golden Path assures this. Knowing my message, I expect you to be exceedingly careful about the powers you delegate to any government.*

> **—The Stolen Journals**

Leto prepared with patient care for his first private meeting with Siona since her childhood banishment to the Fish Speaker schools in the Festival City. He told Moneo that he would see her at the Little Citadel, a vantage tower he had built in the central Sareer. The site had been chosen to provide views of old and new and places between. There were no roads to the Little Citadel. Visitors arrived by 'thopter. Leto went there as though by magic.

With his own hands, in the early days of his ascendancy, Leto had used an Ixian machine to dig a secret tunnel under the Sareer to his tower, doing all of the work himself. In those days, a few wild sandworms still roamed the desert. He had lined his tunnel with massive walls of fused silica and had imbedded countless bubbles of worm-repelling water in the outer layers. The tunnel anticipated his maximum growth and the requirements of a Royal Cart which, at that time, had been only a figment of his visions.

In the early pre-dawn hours of the day assigned to Siona Leto descended to the crypt and gave orders to his guard that he was not to be disturbed by anyone. His cart sped him down one of the crypt's dark spokes where he opened a hidden portal, emerging in less than an hour at the Little Citadel.

One of his delights was to go out alone on to the sand. No cart. Only his pre-worm body to carry him. The sand felt luxuriously sensuous against him. The heat of his passage through the dunes in the day's first light sent up a wake of steam which required him to keep moving. He brought himself to a stop only when he found a relatively dry pocket about five kilometres out. He lay there at the centre of an uncomfortable dampness from the trace dew, his body just outside the long shadow of the tower which stretched eastward across the dunes.

From a distance, the three thousand metres of the tower could be seen as an impossible needle stabbing the sky. Only the inspired blend of Leto's commands and Ixian imagination made the structure conceivable. One hundred and fifty metres in diameter, the tower sat on a foundation which plunged as deeply under the sand as it climbed above. The magic of plasteel and superlight alloys kept it supple in the wind and resistant to sandblast abrasions.

Leto enjoyed the place so much that he rationed his visits, making up a long list of personal rules which had to be met. The rules added up to "Great Necessity".

For a few moments while he lay there he could shed the loads of the Golden Path. Moneo, good and reliable Moneo, would see that Siona arrived promptly just at nightfall. Leto had a full day in which to relax and think, to play and pretend that he possessed no cares, to drink up the raw sustenance of the earth in a feeding frenzy which he could never indulge in at Onn or at the Citadel. In those places, he was required to confine himself to furtive burrowings through narrow passages where only prescient caution kept him from encountering water pockets. Here, though, he could race through the sand and across it, feed and grow strong.

Sand crunched beneath him as he rolled, flexing his body in pure animal enjoyment. He could feel his worm-self being restored, an electric sensation which sent messages of health all through him.

The sun was well above the horizon now, painting a golden line up the side of the tower. There was the smell of bitter dust in the air and an odour of distant spiny plants which had responded to the morning's trace dew. Gently at first, then more rapidly, he moved out in a wide circle around the tower, thinking about Siona as he went.

There could be no more delays. She had to be tested. Moneo knew this as well as Leto did.

Just that morning, Moneo had said: "Lord, there is terrible violence in her."

"She has the beginnings of adrenalin addiction," Leto had said. "It's cold-turkey time."

"Cold what, Lord?"

"It's an ancient expression. It means she must be subjected to a complete withdrawal. She must go through a necessity-shock."

303

"Oh . . . I see."

For once, Leto realized, Moneo did *see*. Moneo had gone through his own cold-turkey time.

"The young generally are incapable of making hard decisions unless those decisions are associated with immediate violence and the consequent sharp flow of adrenalin," Leto had explained.

Moneo had held himself in reflective silence, remembering, then: "It is a great peril."

"That's the violence you see in Siona. Even old people can cling to it, but the young wallow in it."

As he circled his tower in the growing light of the day, enjoying the feel of the sand even more as it dried, Leto thought about that conversation. He slowed his passage over the sand. A wind from behind him carried the vented oxygen and a burnt-flint smell over his human nostrils. He inhaled deeply, lifting his magnified awareness to a new level.

This preliminary day contained a multiple purpose. He thought of the coming encounter much as an ancient bullfighter had thought about the first examination of a horned adversary. Siona possessed her own version of horns, although Moneo would make certain that she brought no physical weapons to this encounter. Leto had to be sure, though, that he knew Siona's every strength and every weakness. And he would have to create special susceptibilities in her wherever possible. She had to be prepared for the test, her psychic muscles blunted by well-planted barbs.

Shortly after noon, his worm-self satiated, Leto returned to the tower, crawled back on to his cart and lifted on suspensors to the very tip and a portal there which opened only at his command. Throughout the rest of the day he lay in the aerie, thinking, plotting.

The fluttering wings of an ornithopter whispered on the air just at nightfall to signal Moneo's arrival.

Faithful Moneo.

Leto caused a landing-lip to extrude from his aerie. The

'thopter glided in, its wings cupped. It settled gently on to the lip. Leto stared out through the gathering darkness. Siona emerged and darted in toward him, fearful of the unprotected height. She wore a white robe over a black uniform suit without insignia. She stole one look backward when she stopped just inside the tower, then she turned her attention to Leto's bulk waiting on the cart almost at the centre of the aerie. The 'thopter lifted away and jetted off into the darkness. Leto left the lip extruded, the portal open.

"There is a balcony on the other side of the tower," he said. "We will go there."

"Why?"

Siona's voice carried almost pure suspicion.

"I'm told it's a cool place," Leto said. "And there is indeed a faint sensation of cold on my cheeks when I expose them to the breeze there."

Curiosity brought her closer to him.

Leto closed the portal behind her.

"The night view from the balcony is magnificent," Leto said.

"Why are we here?"

"Because here we will not be overheard."

Leto turned his cart and moved it silently out to the balcony. The faintest of hidden illumination within the aerie showed her his movement. He heard her follow.

The balcony was a half-ring on the southeast arc of the tower, a lacy railing at chest height around the perimeter. Siona moved to the rail and swept her gaze around the open land.

Leto sensed the waiting receptivity. Something was to be spoken here for her ears alone. Whatever it was, she would listen and respond from the well of her own motives. Leto looked across her toward the edge of the Sareer where the man-made boundary wall was a low flat line just barely visible in the light of First Moon lifting above the horizon. His amplified vision identified the distant movement of a convoy from Onn, a dull glow of lights from the beast-

305

drawn vehicles pacing along the high road toward Tabur Village.

He could call up a memory image of the village nestled among the plants which grew in the moist area along the inner base of the wall. His Museum Fremen tended date palms, tall grasses and even market gardens there. It was not like the old days when any inhabited place, even a tiny basin with a few low plants fed by a single cistern and windtrap, could appear lush by comparison with the open sand. Tabur Village was a water-rich paradise when compared with Sietch Tabr. Everyone in today's village knew that just beyond the Sareer's boundary wall the Idaho river slid southward in a long straight line which would be silver now in the moonlight. Museum Fremen could not climb the wall's sheer inner face, but they knew the water was there. The earth knew, too. If a Tabur inhabitant put an ear against the ground, the earth spoke with the sound of distant rapids.

There would be nightbirds along the embankment now, Leto thought, creatures which would live in sunlight on another world. Dune had worked its evolutionary magic on them and they still lived at the mercies of the Sareer. Leto had seen the birds draw dumb shadows across the water and, when they dipped to drink, there were ripples which the river took away.

Even at this distance, Leto sensed a power in that far-away water, something forceful out of his past which moved away from him like the current slipping southward into the reaches of farm and forest. The water searched through rolling hills, along the margins of an abundant plantlife which had replaced all of Dune's desert except for this one last place, this Sareer, this sanctuary of the past.

Leto recalled the growling thrust of Ixian machines which had inflicted that watercourse upon the landscape. It seemed such a short time ago, little more than three thousand years.

Siona stirred and looked back at him, but Leto remained silent, his attention fixed beyond her. A pale amber light shone above the horizon, reflection of a town on far away clouds. From its direction and distance, Leto knew it to be the town of Wallport, transplanted far into a warmer clime of the south from its once austere location in the cold, low-slanted light of the north. The glow of the town was like a window into his past. He felt the beam of it striking through to his breast, straight through the thick and scaled membrane which had replaced his human skin.

I am vulnerable, he thought.

Yet, he knew himself to be the master of this place. And the planet was the master of him.

I am part of it.

He devoured the soil directly, rejecting only the water. His human mouth and lungs had been relegated to breathing just enough to sustain a remnant humanity . . . and talking.

Leto spoke to Siona's back: "I like to talk and I dread the day when I no longer will be able to engage in conversations."

With a certain diffidence, she turned and stared at him in the moonlight, quite obvious distaste in her expression.

"I agree that I am a monster in many human eyes," he said.

"Why am I here?"

Directly to the point! She would not deviate. Most of the Atreides had been that way, he thought. It was a characteristic which he hoped to maintain in the breeding of them. It spoke of a strong inner sense of identity.

"I need to find out what time has done to you," he said.

"Why do you need that?"

A little fear in her voice there, he thought. *She thinks I will probe after her puny rebellion and the names of her surviving associates.*

When he remained silent, she said: "Do you intend to kill me the way you killed my friends?"

So she has heard about the fight at the Embassy. And she assumes I know all about her past rebellious activities. Moneo has been lecturing her, damn him! Well . . . I might

307

have done the same in his circumstances.

"Are you really a god?" she demanded. "I don't understand why my father believes that."

She has some doubts, he thought. *I still have room to manoeuvre.*

"Definitions vary," he said. "To Moneo I am a god . . . and that is a truth."

"You were human once."

He began to enjoy the leaps of her intellect. She had that sure, hunting curiosity which was the hallmark of the Atreides.

"You are curious about me," he said. "It is the same with me. I am curious about you."

"What makes you think I'm curious?"

"You used to watch me very carefully when you were a child. I see that same look in your eyes tonight."

"Yes, I have wondered what it's like to be you."

He studied her for a moment. The moonlight drew shadows under her eyes, concealing them. He could let himself imagine that her eyes were the total blue of his own eyes, the blue of spice addiction. With that imaginative addition, Siona bore a curious resemblance to his long-dead Ghani. It was in the outline of her face and the placement of the eyes. He almost told Siona this, then thought better of it.

"Do you eat human food?" Siona asked.

"For a long time after I put on the sandtrout skin I felt stomach hunger," he said. "Occasionally, I would attempt food. My stomach mostly rejected it. The cilia of the sandtrout spread almost everywhere in my human flesh. Eating became a bothersome thing. These days, I only ingest dry substances which sometimes contain a bit of the spice."

"You . . . eat melange?"

"Sometimes."

"But you no longer have human hungers?"

"I didn't say that."

She stared at him, waiting.

Leto admired the way she let unspoken questions work

for her. She was bright and she had learned much during her short life.

"The stomach hunger was a black feeling, a pain I could not relieve," he said. "I would run then, run like an insane creature across the dunes."

"You . . . ran?"

"My legs were longer in proportion to my body in those days. I could move myself about quite easily. But the hungry pain has never left me. I think it's hunger for my lost humanity."

He saw the beginnings of reluctant sympathy in her, the questioning.

"You still have this . . . pain?"

"It's only a soft burning now. That's one of the signs of my final metamorphosis. In a few hundred years I'll be back under the sand."

He saw her clench her fists at her sides. "Why?" she demanded. "Why did you do this?"

"This change isn't all bad. Today, for example, has been very pleasant. I feel quite mellow."

"There are changes we cannot see," she said. "I know there must be." She relaxed her hands.

"My sight and hearing have become extremely acute, but not my sense of touch. Except for my face, I don't feel things the way I could once. I miss that."

Again, he noted the reluctant sympathy, the striving toward an empathic understanding. She wanted to *know*!

"When you live so long," she said, "how does the passage of time feel? Does it move more rapidly as the years go by?"

"That's a strange thing, Siona. Sometimes, time rushes by me; sometimes, it creeps."

Gradually, as they spoke, Leto had been dimming the concealed lights of his aerie, moving his cart closer and closer to Siona. Now, he shut off the lights, leaving only the moon. The front of his cart protruded on to the balcony, his face only about two metres from Siona.

"My father tells me," she said, "that the older you get

309

the slower your time goes. Is that what you told him?"

Testing my veracity, he thought. *She's not a Truthsayer, then.*

"All the things are relative, but compared to the human timesense, this is true."

"Why?"

"It is involved in what I will become. At the end, time will stop for me and I will be frozen like a pearl caught in ice. My new bodies will scatter, each with a pearl hidden within it."

She turned and looked away from him, peering out at the desert, speaking without looking at him.

"When I talk to you like this here in the darkness I can almost forget what you are."

"That's why I chose this hour for our meeting."

"But why this place?"

"Because it is the last place where I can feel at home."

Siona turned against the rail, leaning on it and looking at him. "I want to see you."

He turned on all of the aerie's lights, including the harsh white globes along the roof of the balcony's outer edge. As the light came on, an Ixian-made transparent mask slid out of wall recesses and sealed off the balcony behind Siona. She felt it move behind her and was startled, but nodded as though she understood. She thought it was a defence against attack. It was not. The wall merely kept out the damp insects of the night.

Siona stared at Leto, sweeping her gaze along his body, pausing at the stubs which once had been his legs, bringing her attention then to his arms and hands, then to his face.

"Your approved histories tell us that all Atreides are descended from you and your sister, Ghanima," she said. "The Oral History disagrees."

"The Oral History is correct. Your ancestor was Harq al-Ada. Ghani and I were married only in name, a move to consolidate the power."

"Like your marriage to this Ixian woman?"

"That is different."

"You will have children?"

"I have never been capable of having children. I chose the metamorphosis before that was possible."

"You were a child and then you were . . ." she pointed, ". . . this?"

"Nothing between."

"How does a child know what to choose?"

"I was one of the oldest children this universe has ever seen. Ghani was the other."

"That story about your ancestral memories!"

"A true story. We're all here. Doesn't the Oral History agree?"

She whirled away and held her back stiffly presented to him. Once more, Leto found himself fascinated by this *human* gesture: rejection coupled to vulnerability. Presently, she turned around and concentrated on his features within the hooded folds.

"You have the Atreides look," she said.

"I come by it just as honestly as you do."

"You're so old . . . why aren't you wrinkled?"

"Nothing about the human part of me ages in a normal way."

"Is that why you did this to yourself?"

"To enjoy long life? No."

"I don't see how anyone could make such a choice," she muttered. Then louder: "Never to know love . . ."

"You're playing the fool!" he said. "You don't mean love, you mean sex."

She shrugged.

"You think the most terrible thing I gave up was sex? No, the greatest loss was something far different."

"What?" She asked it reluctantly, betraying how deeply he touched her.

"I cannot walk among my fellows without their special notice. I am no longer one of you. I am alone. Love? Many people love me, but my shape keeps us apart. We are separated, Siona, by a gulf that no other human dares to bridge."

311

"Not even your Ixian woman?"

"Yes, she would if she could, but she cannot. She's not an Atreides."

"You mean that I . . . could?" She touched her breast with a finger.

"If there were enough sandtrout around. Unfortunately, all of them enclose my flesh. However, if I were to die . . ."

She shook her head in dumb horror at the thought. "The Oral History tells it accurately," he said. "And we must never forget that you believe the Oral History."

She continued to shake her head from side to side.

"There's no secret about it," he said. "The first moments of the transformation are the critical ones. Your awareness must drive inward and outward simultaneously, one with infinity. I could provide you with enough melange to accomplish this. Given enough spice, you can live through those first awful moments . . . and all the other moments."

She shuddered uncontrollably, her gaze fixed on his eyes.

"You know I'm telling you the truth, don't you?"

She nodded, inhaled a deep trembling breath, then: "Why did you do it?"

"The alternative was far more horrible."

"What alternative?"

"In time, you may understand it. Moneo did."

"Your damned Golden Path!"

"Not damned at all. Quite holy."

"You think I'm a fool who can't . . ."

"I think you're inexperienced, but possessed of great capability whose potential you do not even suspect."

She took three deep breaths and regained some of her composure, then: "If you can't mate with the Ixian, what . . ."

"Child, why do you persist in misunderstanding? It's not sex. Before Hwi I could not *pair*. I had no other like me. In all of the cosmic void, I was the only one."

"She's like . . . you?"

"Deliberately so. The Ixians made her that way."

"Made her . . ."

"Don't be a complete fool!" he snapped. "She is the essential god-trap. Even the victim cannot reject her."

"Why do you tell me these things?" she whispered.

"You stole two copies of my journals," he said. "You've read the Guild translations and you already know what could catch me."

"You knew?"

He saw boldness return to her stance, a sense of her own power. "Of course you knew," she said, answering her own question.

"It *was* my secret," he said. "You cannot imagine how many times I have loved a companion and seen that companion slip away . . . as your father is slipping away now."

"You love . . . him?"

"And I loved your mother. Sometimes they go quickly; sometimes with agonizing slowness. Each time I am racked. I can play at being callous and I can make the necessary decisions, even decisions which kill, but I cannot escape the suffering. For a long, long time—those journals you stole tell it truly—that was the only emotion I knew."

He saw the moistness in her eyes, but the line of her jaw still spoke of angry resolution.

"None of this gives you the right to govern," she said.

Leto suppressed a smile. At least they were down to the root of Siona's rebellion.

By what right? Where is justice in my rule? By imposing my rules upon them with the weight of Fish Speaker arms, am I being fair to the evolutionary thrust of humankind? I know all of the revolutionary cant, the catch-prattle and the resounding phrases.

"Nowhere do you see your own rebellious hand in the power I wield," he said.

Her youth still demanded its moment.

"I never chose you to govern," she said.

"But you strengthen me."

"How?"

313

"By opposing me. I sharpen my claws on the likes of you."

She shot a sudden glance at his hands.

"A figure of speech," he said.

"So I've offended you at last," she said, hearing only the cutting anger in his words and tone.

"You've not offended me. We're related and can speak bluntly to each other within the family. The fact is, I have much more to fear from you than you from me."

This took her aback, but only momentarily. He saw belief stiffen her shoulders, then doubt. Her chin lowered and she peered upward at him.

"What could the great God Leto fear from me?"

"Your ignorant violence."

"Are you saying that you're *physically* vulnerable?"

"I will not warn you again, Siona. There are limits to the word games I will play. You and the Ixians both know that it's the ones I love who are physically vulnerable.

"Soon, most of the Empire will know it. This is the kind of information which travels fast."

"And they'll *all* ask what right you have to rule?"

There was glee in her voice. It aroused an abrupt anger in Leto. He found it difficult to suppress. This was a side of human emotions he detested. *Gloating!* It was some time before he dared answer, then he chose to slash through her defences at the vulnerability he already had seen.

"I rule by the right of loneliness, Siona. My loneliness is part freedom and part slavery. It says I cannot be bought by any human group. My slavery to you says that I will serve all of you to the best of my lordly abilities."

"But the Ixians have caught you!" she said.

"No. They have given me a gift which strengthens me."

"It weakens you!"

"That, too," he admitted. "But very powerful forces still obey me."

"Ohhhh, yes." She nodded. "I understand *that*."

"You don't understand it."

"Then I'm sure you'll explain it to me," she taunted.

314

He spoke so softly that she had to lean toward him to hear: "There are no others of any kind anywhere who can call upon me for anything—not for sharing, not for compromise, not even for the slightest beginning of another government. I am the only one."

"Not even this Ixian woman can . . ."

"She is so much like me that she would not weaken me in that way."

"But when the Ixian Embassy was attacked . . ."

"I can still be irritated by stupidity," he said.

She scowled at him.

Leto thought it a pretty gesture in that light, quite unconscious. He knew he had made her think. He was sure she had never before considered that any rights might adhere to uniqueness.

He addressed her silent scowl: "There has never before been a government exactly like mine. Not in all of our history. I am responsible only to myself, exacting payment in full for what I have sacrificed."

"Sacrificed!" she sneered, but he heard the doubts. "Every despot says something like that. You're responsible only to yourself!"

"Which makes every living thing my responsibility. I watch over you through these times."

"Through what times?"

"The times that might have been and then no more."

He saw the indecision in her. She did not trust her *instincts*, her untrained abilities at prediction. She might leap occasionally as she had done when she took his journals, but the motivation for the leap was lost in the revelation which followed.

"My father says you can be very tricky with words," she said.

"And he ought to know. But there is knowledge you can only gain by participating in it. There's no way to learn it by standing off and looking and talking."

"That's the kind of thing he means," she said.

"You're quite right," he agreed. "It's not logical. But it

315

is a light, an eye which can see, but does not see itself."

"I'm tired of talking," she said.

"As am I." And he thought: *I have seen enough, done enough. She is wide open to her doubts. How vulnerable they are in their ignorance!*

"You haven't convinced me of anything," she said.

"That was not the purpose of this meeting."

"What was the purpose?"

"To see if you are ready to be tested."

"Test . . ." She tipped her head a bit to the right and stared at him.

"Don't play the innocent with me," he said. "Moneo has told you. And I tell you that you are ready!"

She tried to swallow, then: "What are . . ."

"I have sent for Moneo to return you to the Citadel," he said. "When we meet again, we will really learn what you are made of."

> *You know the myth of the Great Spice Hoard? Yes, I know about that story, too. A majordomo brought it to me one day to amuse me. The story says there is a hoard of melange, a gigantic hoard, big as a great mountain. The hoard is concealed in the depths of a distant planet. It is not Arrakis, that planet. It is not Dune. The spice was hidden there long ago, even before the First Empire and the Spacing Guild. The story says Paul-Muad'Dib went there and lives yet beside the hoard, kept alive by it, waiting. The majordomo did not understand why the story disturbed me.*

—**The Stolen Journals**

Idaho trembled with anger as he strode along the grey plastone halls toward his quarters in the Citadel. At each guard post he passed, the woman there snapped to attention. He did not respond. Idaho knew he was causing disturbance among them. Nobody could mistake the Commander's mood. But he did not abate his purposeful stride.

316

The heavy thumping of his boots echoed along the walls.

He could still taste the noon meal—oddly familiar Atreides chopstick-fare of mixed grains herb-seasoned and baked around a pungent morsel of pseudomeat, all of it washed down with a drink of clear cidrit juice. Moneo had found him at table in the Guard Mess, alone in a corner with a regional operations schedule propped up beside his plate.

Without invitation, Moneo had seated himself opposite Idaho and had pushed aside the operations schedule.

"I bring a message from the God Emperor," Moneo said.

The tightly controlled tone warned Idaho that this was no casual encounter. Others sensed it. Listening silence settled over the women at nearby tables, spreading out through the room.

Idaho put down his chopsticks. "Yes?"

"These were the words of the God Emperor," Moneo said. "It is my bad luck that Duncan Idaho should become enamoured of Hwi Noree. This mischance must not continue."

Anger thinned Idaho's lips, but he remained silent.

"Such foolishness endangers us all," Moneo said. "Noree is the God Emperor's intended."

Idaho tried to control his anger, but the words were a betrayal: "He can't marry her!"

"Why not?"

"What game is he playing, Moneo?"

"I am a messenger with a single message, no more," Moneo said.

Idaho's voice was low and threatening. "But he confides in you."

"The God Emperor sympathizes with you," Moneo lied.

"Sympathizes!" Idaho shouted the word, creating a new depth to the room's silence.

"Noree is a woman of obvious attractions," Moneo said. "But she is not for you."

317

"The God Emperor has spoken," Idaho sneered, "and there is no appeal."

"I see that you understand the message," Moneo said.

Idaho started to push himself away from the table.

"Where are you going?" Moneo demanded.

"I'm going to have this out with him right now!"

"That is certain suicide," Moneo said.

Idaho glared at him, aware suddenly of the listening intensity in the women at the tables around them. An expression which Muad'Dib would have recognized immediately came over Idaho's face: *"Playing to the Devil's Gallery"*, Muad'Dib had called it.

"D'you know what the original Atreides Dukes always said?" Idaho asked. There was a mocking tone in his voice.

"Is it pertinent?"

"They said your liberties all vanish when you look up to any absolute ruler."

Rigid with fear, Moneo leaned toward Idaho. Moneo's lips barely moved. His voice was little more than a whisper. "Don't say such things."

"Because one of these women will report it?"

Moneo shook his head in disbelief. "You are more reckless than any of the others."

"Really?"

"Please! It is perilous in the extreme to take this attitude."

Idaho heard the nervous stirring that swept through the room.

"He can only kill us," Idaho said.

Moneo spoke in a tight whisper: "You fool! The Worm can dominate him at the slightest provocation!"

"The Worm, you say?" Idaho's voice was unnecessarily loud.

"You must trust him," Moneo said.

Idaho glanced left and right. "Yes, I think they heard that."

"He is billions upon billions of people united in that one body," Moneo said.

318

"So I've been told."

"He is God and we are mortal," Moneo said.

"How is it a god can do evil things?" Idaho asked.

Moneo thrust his chair backward and leaped to his feet. "I wash my hands of you!" Whirling away, he dashed from the room.

Idaho looked out into the room, finding himself the centre of attention for all of the guards' faces.

"Moneo doesn't judge but I do," Idaho said.

It surprised him then to glimpse a few wry smiles among the women. They all returned to their eating.

As he strode down the hall of the Citadel, Idaho replayed the conversation, seeking out the oddities in Moneo's behaviour. The terror could be recognized and even understood, but it had seemed far more than fear of death . . . far, far more.

The Worm can dominate him.

Idaho felt that this had slipped out of Moneo, an inadvertent betrayal. What could it mean?

More reckless than any of the others.

It galled Idaho that he should have to bear comparison to himself-as-an-unknown. How careful had *the others* been?

Idaho came to his own door, put a hand on the palm lock and hesitated. He felt like a hunted animal retreating to his den. The guards in the mess surely would have reported that conversation to Leto by now. What would the *God* Emperor do? Idaho's hand moved across the lock. The door swung inward. He entered the anteroom of his apartment and sealed the door, looking at it.

Will he send his Fish Speakers for me?

Idaho glanced around the entry area. It was a conventional space—racks for clothing and shoes, a full length mirror, a weapons cupboard. He looked at the closed door of the cupboard. Not one of the weapons behind that door offered any real threat to the God Emperor. There wasn't even a lasgun . . . although even lasguns were ineffectual against *the worm*, according to all the accounts.

He knows I will defy him.

Idaho sighed and looked toward the arched portal which led into the sitting area. Moneo had replaced the soft furniture with heavier, stiffer pieces, some of them recognizably Fremen—culled from the coffers of the Museum Fremen.

Museum Fremen!

Idaho spat and strode through the portal. Two steps into the room he stopped, shocked. The soft light from the north windows revealed Hwi Noree seated on the low sling-divan. She wore a shimmering blue gown which draped itself revealingly around her figure. Hwi looked up at his entrance.

"Thank the gods you've not been harmed," she said.

Idaho glanced back at his entry, at the palm-locked door. He returned a speculative look to Hwi. No one but a few selected guards should be able to open that door.

She smiled at his confusion. "We Ixians manufactured those locks," she said.

He found himself filled with fear for her. "What are you doing here?"

"We must talk."

"About what?"

"Duncan . . ." She shook her head. "About us."

"They warned you," he said.

"I've been told to reject you."

"Moneo sent you!"

"Two guardswomen who overheard you in the mess— they brought me. They think you are in terrible danger."

"Is that why you're here?"

She stood, one graceful motion which reminded him of the way Leto's grandmother, Jessica, had moved—the same fluid control of muscles, every movement beautiful.

Realization came as a shock. "You're Bene Gesserit . . ."

"No! They were among my teachers, but I am not Bene Gesserit."

Suspicions clouded his mind. What allegiances were

really at work in Leto's Empire? What does a ghola know about such things?

The changes since last I lived . . .

"I suppose you're still just a simple Ixian," he said.

"Please don't sneer at me, Duncan."

"What are you?"

"I am the intended bride of the God Emperor."

"And you'll serve him faithfully!"

"I will."

"Then there's nothing for us to talk about."

"Except this thing between us."

He cleared his throat. "What thing?"

"This attraction." She raised a hand as he started to speak. "I want to hurl myself into your arms, to find the love and shelter I know is there. You want it, too."

He held himself rigid. "The God Emperor forbids!"

"But I am here." She took two steps toward him, the gown rippling across her body.

"Hwi . . ." He tried to swallow in a dry throat. "It's best you leave."

"Prudent, but not best," she said.

"If he finds that you've been here . . ."

"It is not my way to leave you like this." Again, she stopped his response with a lifted hand. "I was bred and trained for just one purpose."

Her words filled him with icy caution. "What purpose?"

"To woo the God Emperor. Oh, he knows this. He would not change a thing about me."

"Nor would I."

She moved a step closer. He smelled the milky warmth of her breath.

"They made me too well," she said. "I was designed to please an Atreides. Leto says his Duncan is more an Atreides than many born to the name."

"Leto?"

"How else should I address the one I'll wed?"

Even as she spoke, Hwi leaned toward Idaho. As though a magnet had found its point of critical attraction, they

321

moved together. Hwi pressed her cheek against his tunic, her arms around him feeling the hard muscles. Idaho rested his chin in her hair, the musk filling his senses.

"This is insane," he whispered.

"Yes."

He lifted her chin and kissed her.

She pressed herself against him.

Neither of them doubted where this must lead. She did not resist when he lifted her off her feet and carried her into the bedroom.

Only once did Idaho speak. "You're not a virgin."

"Nor are you, love."

"Love," he whispered. "Love, love, love . . ."

"Yes . . . yes!"

In the post-coital peace, Hwi put both hands behind her head and stretched, twisting on the rumpled bed. Idaho sat with his back to her looking out of the window.

"Who were your other lovers?" he asked.

She lifted herself on one elbow. "I've had no other lovers."

"But . . ." He turned and looked down at her.

"In my teens," she said, "there was a young man who needed me very much." She smiled. "Afterward, I was very ashamed. How trusting I was! I thought I had failed the people who depended on me. But they found out and they were elated. You know, I think I was being tested."

Idaho scowled. "Is that how it was with me? I needed you?"

"No, Duncan." Her features were grave. "We gave joy to each other because that's how it is with love."

"Love!" he said, and it was a bitter sound.

She said: "My Uncle Malky used to say that love was a bad bargain because you get no guarantees."

"Your Uncle Malky was a wise man."

"He was stupid! Love *needs* no guarantees."

A smile twitched at the corners of Idaho's mouth.

She grinned up at him. "You know it's love when you want to give joy and damn the consequences."

322

He nodded. "I think only of the danger to you."

"We are what we are," she said.

"What will we do?"

"We'll cherish this for as long as we live."

"You sound . . . so final."

"I am."

"But we'll see each other every . . ."

"Never again like this."

"Hwi!" He hurled himself across the bed and buried his face in her breast.

She stroked his hair.

His voice muffled against her, he said: "What if I've impreg . . ."

"Shush! If there's to be a child, there will be a child."

Idaho lifted his head and looked at her. "But he'll know for sure!"

"He'll know anyway."

"You think he really knows everything?"

"Not everything, but he'll know this."

"How?"

"I will tell him."

Idaho pushed himself away from her and sat up on the bed. Anger warred with confusion in his expression.

"I must," she said.

"If he turns against you . . . Hwi, there are stories. You could be in terrible danger!"

"No. I have needs, too. He knows this. He will not harm either of us."

"But he . . ."

"He will not destroy *me*. He will know that if he harms you that would destroy me."

"How can you marry him?"

"Dear Duncan, have you not seen that he needs me more than you do?"

"But he cannot . . . I mean, you can't possibly . . ."

"The joy that you and I have in each other, I'll not have that with Leto. It's impossible for him. He has confessed this to me."

"Then why can't . . . If he loves you . . ."

"He has larger plans and larger needs." She reached out and took Idaho's right hand in both of hers. "I've known that since I first began to study about him. Needs larger than either of us have."

"What plans? What needs?"

"Ask him."

"Do *you* know?"

"Yes."

"You mean you believe those stories about . . ."

"There is honesty and goodness in him. I know it by my own responses to him. What my Ixian masters made in me was, I think, a reagent which reveals more than they wanted me to know."

"Then you believe him!" Idaho accused. He tried to pull his hand away from her.

"If you go to him, Duncan, and . . ."

"He'll never see me again!"

"He will."

She pushed his hand to her mouth and kissed his fingers.

"I'm a hostage," he said. "You've made me fearful . . . the two of you together . . ."

"I never thought it would be easy to serve God," she said. "I just didn't think it would be this hard."

Memory has a curious meaning to me, a meaning I have hoped others might share. It continually astonishes me how people hide from their ancestral memories, shielding themselves behind a thick barrier of mythos. Ohhh, I do not expect them to seek the terrible immediacy of every living moment which I must experience. I can understand that they might not want to be submerged in a mush of petty ancestral details. You have reason to fear that your living moments might be taken over by others. Yet, the meaning is there within those memories. We carry all of our ancestry forward like a living wave, all of the hopes and joys and griefs, the agonies and the exultations of our past. Nothing within those memories remains completely without meaning or influence, not as long as there is a humankind somewhere. We have that bright infinity all around us, that Golden Path of forever to which we can continually pledge our puny but inspired allegiance.

—**The Stolen Journals**

"I have summoned you, Moneo, because of what my guards tell me," Leto said.

They stood in the darkness of the crypt where, Moneo reminded himself, some of the God Emperor's most painful decisions originated. Moneo, too, had heard reports. He had been expecting the summons all afternoon and, when it came shortly after the evening meal, a moment of terror had engulfed him.

"Is it about . . . about the Duncan, Lord?"

"Of course it's about the Duncan!"

"I'm told, Lord . . . his behaviour . . ."

"Terminal behaviour, Moneo?"

Moneo bowed his head. "If you say it, Lord."

"How long until the Tleilaxu could supply us with another one?"

"They say they have had problems, Lord. It might be as much as two years."

"Do you know what my guards tell me, Moneo?"

Moneo held his breath. If the God Emperor had learned

325

about this latest . . . No! Even the Fish Speakers were terrified by the affront. Had it been anyone but a Duncan the women would have taken it upon themselves to eliminate him.

"Well, Moneo?"

"I am told, Lord, that he called out a levy of guards and questioned them about their origins. On what worlds were they born? What of their parentage, their childhood?"

"And the answers did not please him."

"He frightened them, Lord. He kept insisting."

"As though repetition could elicit the truth, yes."

Moneo allowed himself to hope that this might be the whole of his Lord's concern. "Why do the Duncans always do this, Lord?"

"It was their early training, the Atreides training."

"But how did that differ from . . ."

"The Atreides lived in the service of the people they governed. The measure of their government was found in the lives of the governed. Thus, the Duncans always want to know how the people live."

"He has spent a night in one village, Lord. He has been to some of the towns. He has seen . . ."

"It's all in how you interpret the results, Moneo. Evidence is nothing without judgments."

"I have observed that he judges, Lord."

"We all do, but the Duncans tend to believe that this universe is hostage to my will. And they know that you cannot do wrong in the name of right."

"Is that what he says you . . ."

"It is what *I* say, what all of the Atreides in me say. This universe will not permit it. The things you attempt will not endure if you . . ."

"But, Lord! You do no wrong!"

"Poor Moneo. You cannot see that I have created a vehicle of injustice."

Moneo could not speak. He realized that he had been diverted by a seeming return to mildness in the God Emperor. But now, Moneo sensed changes moving in that

326

great body, and at this proximity . . . Moneo glanced around the crypt's central chamber, reminding himself of the many deaths which had occurred here and which were enshrined here.

Is it my time?

Leto spoke in a musing tone. "You cannot succeed by taking hostages. That is a form of enslavement. One kind of human cannot own another kind of human. This universe will not permit it."

The words lay there, simmering in Moneo's awareness, a terrifying contrast to the rumblings of transformation which he sensed in his Lord.

The Worm comes!

Again, Moneo glanced around the crypt chamber. This place was far worse than the aerie! Sanctuary was too remote.

"Well, Moneo, do you have any response?" Leto asked.

Moneo ventured a whisper: "The Lord's words enlighten me."

"Enlighten? You are not enlightened!"

Moneo spoke out of desperation. "But I serve my Lord!"

"You claim service to God?"

"Yes, Lord."

"Who created your religion, Moneo?"

"You did, Lord."

"That's a sensible answer."

"Thank you, Lord."

"Don't thank me! Tell me what religious institutions perpetuate!"

Moneo backed away four steps.

"Stand where you are!" Leto ordered.

Trembling all through his body, Moneo shook his head dumbly. At last, he had encountered the question without answer. Failure to answer would precipitate his death. He waited for it, head bowed.

"Then I will tell you, poor servant," Leto said.

Moneo dared to hope. He lifted his gaze to the God Emperor's face, noting that the eyes were not glazed . . .

and the hands were not trembling. Perhaps the Worm did not come.

"Religious institutions perpetuate a mortal master-servant relationship," Leto said. "They create an arena which attracts prideful human power-seekers with all of their near-sighted prejudices!"

Moneo could only nod. Was that a trembling in the God Emperor's hands? Was the terrible face withdrawing slightly into its cowl?

"The secret revelations of infamy, that is what the Duncans ask after," Leto said. "The Duncans have too much compassion for their fellows and too sharp a limit on fellowship."

Moneo had studied holos of Dune's ancient sandworms, the gigantic mouths full of crysknife teeth around consuming fire. He noted the tumescence of the latent rings on Leto's tubular surface. Were they more prominent? Would a new mouth open below that cowled face?

"The Duncans know in their hearts," Leto said, "that I have deliberately ignored the admonition of Mohammed and Moses. Even you know it, Moneo!"

It was an accusation. Moneo started to nod, then shook his head from side to side. He wondered if he dared renew his retreat. Moneo knew from experience that lectures in this tenor did not long continue without the coming of the Worm.

"What might that admonition be?" Leto asked. There was a mocking lightness in his voice.

Moneo allowed himself a faint shrug.

Abruptly, Leto's voice filled the chamber with a rumbling baritone, an ancient voice which spoke across the centuries: "You are servants unto *God*, not servants unto servants!"

Moneo wrung his hands and cried out: "I *serve* you, Lord!"

"Moneo, Moneo," Leto said, his voice low and resonant, "a million wrongs cannot give rise to one right. The right is known because it endures."

328

Moneo could only stand in trembling silence.

"I had intended Hwi to mate with *you*, Moneo," Leto said. "Now, it is too late."

The words took a moment penetrating Moneo's consciousness. He felt that their meaning was out of any known context. *Hwi? Who was Hwi? Oh, yes—the God Emperor's Ixian bride-to-be. Mate . . . with me?*

Moneo shook his head.

Leto spoke with infinite sadness: "You, too, shall pass away. Will all your works be as dust forgotten?"

Without any warning, even as he spoke, Leto's body convulsed in a thrashing roll which heaved him from the cart. The speed of it, the monstrous violence, threw him within centimetres of Moneo, who screamed and fled across the crypt.

"Moneo!"

Leto's call stopped the majordomo at the entrance to the lift.

"The test, Moneo! I will test Siona tomorrow!"

The realization of what I am occurs in the timeless awareness which does not accumulate nor discard, which does not stimulate nor delude. I create a field without self or centre, a field where even death becomes only analogy. I desire no results. I merely permit this field which has no goals nor desires, no perfections nor even visions of achievements. In that field, omnipresent primal awareness is all. It is the light which pours through the windows of my universe.

—**The Stolen Journals**

The sun came up, sending its harsh glare across the dunes. Leto felt the sand beneath him as a soft caress. Only his human ears, hearing the abrasive rasp of his heavy body, reported otherwise. It was a sensory conflict which he had learned to accept.

He heard Siona walking behind him, a lightness in her tread, a gentle spilling of sand as she climbed to his level atop a dune.

The longer I endure, the more vulnerable I become, he thought.

This thought often occurred to him these days when he went into his desert. He peered upward. The sky was cloudless with a blue density which the old days of Dune had never seen.

What was a desert without a cloudless sky? Too bad it could not have Dune's silvery hue.

Ixian satellites controlled this sky, not always to the perfection he might desire. Such perfection was a machine-fantasy which faltered under human management. Still, the satellites held a sufficiently steady grip to give him this morning of desert stillness. He gave his human lungs a deep breath of it and listened for Siona's approach. She had stopped. He knew she was admiring the view.

Leto felt his imagination like a conjurer calling up everything which had produced the physical setting for this moment. He *felt* the satellites. Fine instruments which played the music for the dance of warming and cooling air masses, perpetually monitoring and adjusting the powerful vertical and horizontal currents. It amused him to recall that the Ixians had thought he would use this exquisite machinery in a new kind of hydraulic despotism—withholding moisture from those who defied their ruler, punishing others with terrible storms. How surprised they had been to find themselves mistaken!

My controls are more subtle.

Slowly, gently, he began to move, swimming on the sand surface, gliding down off the dune, never once looking back at the thin spire of his tower, knowing that it would vanish presently into the haze of daytime heat.

Siona followed him with an uncharacteristic docility. Doubt had done its work. She had read the stolen journals. She had listened to the admonitions of her father. Now, she did not know what to think.

"What is this test?" she had asked Moneo. "What will he do?"

"It is never the same."

"How did he test you?"

"It will be different with you. I would only confuse you if I told you my experience."

Leto had listened secretly while Moneo prepared his daughter, dressing her in an authentic Fremen stillsuit with a dark robe over it, fitting the boot-pumps correctly. Moneo had not forgotten.

Moneo had looked up from where he bent to adjust her boots. "The Worm will come. That is all I can tell you. You must find a way to live in the presence of the Worm."

He had stood then, explaining about the stillsuit, how it recycled her body's own waters. He made her pull the tube from a catchpocket and suck on it, then reseal the tube.

"You will be alone with him on the desert," Moneo had said. "Shai-Hulud is never far away when you're on the desert."

"What if I refuse to go?" she asked.

"You will go . . . but you may not return."

This conversation had occurred in the ground-level chamber of the Little Citadel while Leto waited in the aerie. He had come down when he knew Siona was ready, drifting down in the pre-dawn darkness on his cart's suspensors. The cart had gone into the ground-level room after Moneo and Siona emerged. While Moneo marched across the flat ground to his 'thopter and left in a whispering of wings, Leto had required Siona to test the sealed portal of the ground-level chamber, then look upward at the tower's impossible heights.

"The only way out is across the Sareer," he said.

He led her away from the tower then, not even commanding her to follow, depending on her good sense, her curiosity and her doubts.

Leto's swimming progress took him down the dune's slip-face and on to an exposed section of the rocky basement complex, then up another sandy face at a shallow angle, creating a path for Siona to follow. Fremen had called such compression tracks "God's gift to the weary". He moved slowly, giving Siona plenty of time in which to recognize that this was his domain, his natural habitat.

He came out atop another dune and turned to watch her progress. She held to the track he had provided and stopped only when she reached the top. Her glance went once to his face then she turned a full circle to examine the horizon. He heard the sharp intake of her breath. Heat haze hid the spire's top. The base might have been a distant outcropping.

"This is how it was," he said.

There was something about the desert which spoke to the eternal soul of people who possessed Fremen blood, he knew. He had chosen this place for its desert impact—a dune slightly higher than the others.

"Take a good look at it," he said, and he slipped down the dune's other side to remove his bulk from her view.

Siona took one more slow turn, looking outward.

Leto knew the innermost sensation of what she saw. Except for that insignificant, blurred *blip* of his tower's base, there was not the slightest lift of horizon—flat, everywhere flat. No plants, no living movement. From her vantage, there was a limit of approximately eight kilometres to the line where the planet's curvature hid everything beyond.

Leto spoke from where he had stopped, just below the dune's crest. "This is the real Sareer. You only know it when you're down here afoot. This is all that's left of the *bahr bela ma*."

"The ocean without water," she whispered.

Again, she turned and examined the entire horizon.

There was no wind and, Leto knew, without wind, the silence ate at the human soul. Siona was feeling the loss of all familiar reference points. She was abandoned in dangerous space.

Leto glanced at the next dune. In that direction, they would come presently to a low line of hills which originally had been mountains but now were broken into remnant slag and rubble. He continued to rest quietly, letting the silence do his work for him. It was even pleasant to imagine that these dunes went on, as they once had, without end completely around the planet. But even these few dunes were degenerating. Without the original coriolis storms of Dune, the Sareer saw nothing stronger than a stiff breeze and occasional heat vortices which had no more than local effect.

One of these tiny "wind devils" danced across the middle distance to the south. Siona's gaze followed its track. She spoke abruptly: "Do you have a personal religion?"

Leto took a moment composing his reply. It always astonished him how a desert provoked thoughts of religion.

"You dare ask me if I have a personal religion?" he demanded.

Betraying no surface sign of the fears he knew she felt, Siona turned and stared down at him. Audacity was always an Atreides hallmark, he reminded himself.

When she didn't answer, he said: "You are an Atreides for sure."

"Is that your answer?" she asked.

"What is it you really want to know, Siona?"

"What *you* believe!"

"Ho! You ask after my faith. Well, now—I believe that something cannot emerge from nothing without divine intervention."

His answer puzzled her. "How is that an . . ."

"Natura non facit saltus," he said.

She shook her head, not understanding the ancient allusion which had sprung to his lips. Leto translated:

"Nature makes no leaps."

"What language was that?" she asked.

"A language no longer spoken anywhere else in my universe."

"Why did you use it then?"

"To prod your ancient memories."

333

"I don't have any! I just need to know why you brought me here."

"To give you a taste of your past. Come down here and climb on to my back."

She hesitated at first, then seeing the futility of defiance, slid down the dune and clambered on to his back.

Leto waited until she was kneeling atop him. It was not the same as the old times, he knew. She had no maker hooks and could not stand on his back. He lifted his front segments slightly off the surface.

"Why am I doing this?" she asked. Her tone said she felt silly up there.

"I want you to taste the way our people once moved proudly across this land, high atop the back of a giant sandworm."

He began to glide along the dune just below the crest. Siona had seen holos. She knew this experience intellectually, but the pulse of reality had a different beat and he knew she would resonate to it.

Ahhh, Siona, he thought, *you do not even begin to suspect how I will test you.*

Leto steeled himself then. *I must have no pity. If she dies, she dies. If any of them dies, that is a required event, no more.* And he had to remind himself that this applied even to Hwi Noree. It was just that *all* of them could not die.

He sensed it when Siona began to enjoy the sensation of riding on his back. He felt a faint shift in her weight as she eased back on to her legs to lift her head.

He drove outward then along a curving barracan, joining Siona in enjoyment of the old sensations. Leto could just glimpse the remnant hills at the horizon ahead of him. They were like a seed from the past waiting there, a reminder of the self-sustaining and expanding force which operated in a desert. He could forget for a moment that on this planet where only a small fraction of the surface remained desert, the Sareer's dynamism existed in a precarious environment.

The illusion of the past was here, though. He felt it as he

334

moved. Fantasy, of course, he told himself, a vanishing fantasy as long as his enforced tranquillity continued. Even the sweeping barracan which he traversed now was not as great as the ones of the past. None of the dunes were that great.

This whole *maintained* desert struck him suddenly as ridiculous. He almost stopped on a pebbled surface between the dunes, continuing but more slowly as he tried to conjure up the necessities which kept the whole system working. He imagined the planet's rotation setting up great air currents which shifted cold and heated air to new regions in enormous volume—everything monitored and ruled by those tiny satellites with their Ixian instruments and heat-focusing dishes. If the high monitors *saw* anything, they saw the Sareer partly as a "relief desert" with both physical and cold-air walls girdling it. This tended to create ice at the edges and required even more climatic adjustments.

It was not easy and Leto forgave the occasional mistakes for that reason.

As he moved once more out on to dunes, he lost that sense of delicate balance, put aside memories of the pebbly wastelands outside the central sands, and gave himself up to enjoyment of his "petrified ocean" with its frozen and apparently immovable waves. He turned southward, parallel to the remnant hills.

He knew that most people were offended by his infatuation with desert. They were uneasy and turned away. Siona, however, could not turn away. Everywhere she looked, the desert demanded recognition. She rode silently on his back, but he knew her eyes were full. And the old, old memories were beginning to churn.

He came within three hours to a region of cylindrical whaleback dunes, some of them more than one hundred and fifty kilometres long at an angle to the prevailing wind. Beyond them lay a rocky corridor between dunes and into a region of star dunes almost four hundred metres high. Finally, they entered the braided dunes of the central erg where the general high pressure and electrically charged air gave his spirits a lift. He knew the same magic would be working on Siona.

"Here is where the songs of the Long Trek originated," he said. "They are perfectly preserved in the Oral History."

She did not answer, but he knew she heard.

Leto slowed his pace and began to speak to Siona, telling her about their Fremen past. He sensed the quickening of her interest. She even asked questions occasionally, but he could also feel her fears building. Even the base of his Little Citadel was no longer visible here. She could recognize nothing man-made. And she would think he engaged now in small talk, unimportant things to put off something portentous.

"Equality between our men and women originated here," he said.

"Your Fish Speakers deny that men and women are equal," she said.

Her voice, full of questioning disbelief, was a better locator than the sensation of her crouched on his back. Leto stopped at the intersection of two braided dunes and let the venting of his heat-generated oxygen subside.

"Things are not the same today," he said. "But men and women do have different evolutionary demands upon them. With the Fremen, though, there was an interdependence. That fostered equality out here where questions of survival can become immediate."

"Why did you bring me here?" she demanded.

"Look behind us," he said.

He felt her turn. Presently, she said: "What am I supposed to see?"

"Have we left any tracks? Can you tell where we've been?"

"There's a little wind now."

"It has covered our tracks?"

"I guess so . . . yes."

"This desert made us what we were and are," he said.

"It's the real museum of all our traditions. Not one of those traditions has really been lost."

Leto saw a small sandstorm, a *ghibli*, moving across the southern horizon. He noted the narrow ribbons of dust and sand moving out ahead of it. Surely, Siona had seen it.

"Why won't you tell me why you brought me here?" she asked. Fear was obvious in her voice.

"But I have told you."

"You have not!"

"How far have we come, Siona?"

She thought about this. "Thirty kilometres? Twenty?"

"Farther," he said. "I can move very fast in my own land. Didn't you feel the wind on your face?"

"Yes." Sullen. "So why ask *me* how far?"

"Come down and stand where I can see you."

"Why?"

Good, he thought. *She believes I will abandon her here and speed off faster than she can follow.*

"Come down and I'll explain," he said.

She slid off his back and came around to where she could look into his face.

"Time passes swiftly when your senses are full," he said. "We have been out almost four hours. We have come about sixty kilometres."

"Why is *that* important?"

"Moneo put dried food in the pouch of your robe," he said. "Eat a little and I will tell you."

She found a dried cube of protomor in the pouch and chewed on it while she watched him. It was the authentic old Fremen food even to the slight addition of melange.

"You have felt your past," he said. "Now, you must be sensitized to your future, to the Golden Path."

She swallowed. "I don't believe in your Golden Path."

"If you are to live, you will believe in it."

"Is *that* your test? Have faith in the Great God Leto or die?"

"You need no faith in me whatsoever. I want you to have faith in yourself."

·"Then why is it important how far we've come?"

"So you'll understand how far you still have to go."

She put a hand to her cheek. "I don't . . ."

"Right where you stand," he said, "you are in the unmistakable midst of infinity. Look around you at the meaning of infinity."

She glanced left and right at the unbroken desert.

"We are going to walk out of my desert together," he said. "Just the two of us."

"You don't walk," she sneered.

"A figure of speech. But *you* will walk. I assure you of that."

She looked in the direction they had come. "So that's why you asked me about tracks."

"Even if there were tracks, you could not go back. There is nothing at my Little Citadel that you could get to and use for survival."

"No water?"

"Nothing."

She found the catchpocket tube at her shoulder, sucked at it and restored it. He noted the care with which she sealed the end, but she did not pull the face flap across her mouth, although Leto had heard her father warning her about this. She wanted her mouth free for talking!

"You're telling me I can't run away from you," she said.

"Run away if you want."

She turned a full circle, examining the wasteland.

"There is a saying about the open land," he said, "that one direction is as good as another. In some ways, that's still true, but I would not depend on it."

"But I'm really free to leave you if I want?"

"Freedom can be a very lonely estate," he said.

She pointed to the steep side of the dune on which they had stopped "But I could just go down there and . . ."

"Were I you, Siona, I would not go down where you are pointing."

She glared at him. "Why?"

338

"On the dune's steep side, unless you follow the natural curves, the sand may slide down upon you and bury you."

She looked down the slope, absorbing this.

"See how beautiful words can be?" he asked.

She returned her attention to his face. "Should we be going?"

"You learn to value leisure out here. And courtesy. There's no hurry."

"But we have no water except the . . ."

"Used wisely, that stillsuit will keep you alive."

"But how long will it take us to . . ."

"Your impatience alarms me."

"But we have only this dried food in my pouch. What will we eat when . . ."

"Siona! Have you noticed that you are expressing our situation as mutual. What will *we* eat? *We* have no water. Should *we* be going? How long will it take *us*?"

He sensed the dryness of her mouth as she tried to swallow.

"Could it be that we're interdependent?" he asked.

She spoke reluctantly. "I don't know how to survive out here."

"But I do?"

She nodded.

"Why should I share such precious knowledge with you?" he asked.

She shrugged, a pitiful gesture which touched him. How quickly the desert cut away previous attitudes.

"I will share my knowledge with you," he said. "And you must find something valuable that you can share with me."

Her gaze traversed his length, paused a moment at the flippers which once were his legs and feet, then came back to his face.

"Agreement bought with threats is no agreement," she said.

"I offer you no violence."

"There are many kinds of violence," she said.

"And I brought you out here where you may die?"

"Did I have a choice in it?"

"It is difficult to be born an Atreides," he said. "Believe me, I know."

"You didn't have to do it this way," she said.

"And there you are wrong."

He turned away from her and set off in a sinusoidal track down the dune. He heard her slipping and stumbling as she followed. Leto stopped well into the dune shadow.

'We'll wait out the day here," he said. "It uses less water to travel by night."

> *One of the most terrible words in any language is* Soldier.
> *The synonyms parade through our history: yogahnee,*
> *trooper, hussar, kareebo, cossack, deranzeef, legionnaire,*
> *sardaukar, fish speaker . . . I know them all. They stand*
> *there in the ranks of my memory to remind me:* Always make
> sure you have the army with you.

> **—The Stolen Journals**

Idaho found Moneo at last in the long underground corridor which connected the Citadel's eastern and western complexes. Since daybreak two hours before, Idaho had been prowling the Citadel seeking the majordomo and there he was, far off down the corridor, talking to someone concealed in a doorway, but Moneo was recognizable even at this distance by his stance and that inevitable white uniform.

The corridor's plastone walls were amber here fifty metres below the surface and lighted by glowstrips keyed to the daylight hours. Cool breezes were drawn into these depths by a simple arrangement of free-swinging wings which stood like gigantic robed figures on perimeter towers at the surface. Now that the sun had warmed the sands, all of the wings pointed northward for the cool air pouring into the Sareer. Idaho smelled the flinty breeze as he walked.

He knew what this corridor was supposed to represent. It

did have some characteristics of an ancient Fremen sietch. The corridor was wide, big enough to take Leto on his cart. The arched ceiling *looked* like rock. But the twin glowstrips were discord. Idaho had never seen glowstrips before coming to the Citadel; they had been considered impractical in *his day,* requiring too much energy, too costly to maintain. Glowglobes were simpler and easily replaced. He had come to realize, however, that Leto considered few things impractical.

What Leto wants, someone provides.

The thought had an ominous feeling as Idaho marched down the corridor toward Moneo.

Small rooms lined the corridor sietch-fashion, no doors, only thin hangings of russet fabric which swayed in the breeze. Idaho knew that this area was mostly quarters for the younger Fish Speakers. He had recognized an assembly chamber with attendant rooms for weapons storage, kitchen, a dining hall, maintenance shops. He had also seen other things behind the inadequate privacy of the hangings, things which fed his rage.

Moneo turned at Idaho's approach. The woman to whom Moneo had been talking retreated and let the hanging drop, but not before Idaho glimpsed an older face with an air of command about it. Idaho did not recognize that particular commander.

Moneo nodded as Idaho stopped two paces away.

"The guards say you've been looking for me," Moneo said.

"Where is he, Moneo?"

"Where is who?"

Moneo swept his gaze up and down Idaho's figure, noting the old-fashioned Atreides uniform, black with a red hawk at the breast, the high boots glistening with polish. There was a *ritual* look about the man.

Idaho took a shallow breath and spoke through clenched teeth: "Don't you start that game with me!"

Moneo took his attention away from the sheathed knife at Idaho's waist. It looked like a museum piece with its jewelled handle. Where had Idaho found it?

"If you mean the God Emperor . . ." Moneo said.

"Where?"

Moneo kept his voice mild. "Why are you so anxious to die?"

"They said you were with him."

"That was earlier."

"I'll find him, Moneo!"

"Not right now."

Idaho put a hand on his knife. "Do I have to use force to make you talk?"

"I would not advise that."

"Where . . . is . . . he?"

"Since you insist, he is out in the desert with Siona."

"With your daughter?"

"Is there another Siona?"

"What're they doing?"

"She is being tested."

"When will they return?"

Moneo shrugged, then: "Why this unseemly anger, Duncan?"

"What's this test of your . . ."

"I don't know. Now, why are you so upset?"

"I'm sick of this place! Fish Speakers!" He turned his head and spat.

Moneo glanced down the corridor behind Idaho, recalling the man's approach. Knowing the Duncans, it was easy to recognize what had fed his current rage.

"Duncan," Moneo said, "it's perfectly normal for adolescent females as well as males to have feelings of physical attraction toward members of their own sex. Most of them will grow out of it."

"It should be stamped out!"

"But it's part of our heritage."

"Stamped out! And that's not . . ."

"Oh, be still. If you try to suppress it you only increase its power."

Idaho glared at him. "And you say you don't know

342

what's going on up there with your own daughter!"

"Siona is being tested, I told you."

"And what's *that* supposed to mean?"

Moneo put a hand over his eyes and sighed. He lowered the hand, wondering why he put up with this foolish, dangerous *antique* human.

"It means that she may die out there."

Idaho was taken aback, some of his anger cooling. "How can you allow . . ."

"Allow? You think I have a choice?"

"Every man has a choice!"

A bitter smile flitted across Moneo's lips. "How is it that you are so much more foolish than the other Duncans?"

"Other Duncans!" Idaho said. "How did those others die, Moneo?"

"The way we all die. They ran out of time."

"You lie." Idaho spoke past gritted teeth, his knuckles white on the knife handle.

Still speaking mildly, Moneo said: "Have a care. There are limits even to what I will take, especially just now."

"This place is rotten!" Idaho said. He gestured with his free hand at the corridor behind him. "There are some things I'll never accept!"

Moneo stared down the empty corridor without seeing. "You *must* mature, Duncan. You must."

Idaho's hand tensed on the knife. "What does *that* mean?"

"These are sensitive times. Anything unsettling to him, *anything* . . . must be prevented."

Idaho held himself on the edge of violence, his anger restrained only by something puzzling in Moneo's manner. Words had been spoken, though, which could not be ignored.

"I'm not some damned immature child you can . . ."

"Duncan!" It was the loudest sound Idaho had ever heard from the mild-mannered Moneo. Surprise stayed Idaho's hand while Moneo continued: "If the demands of your flesh are for maturity, but something holds you in adolescence, quite nasty behaviour develops. Let go."

"Are . . . you . . . accusing . . . me . . . of . . ."

"No!" Moneo gestured at the corridor. "Oh, I know what you must've seen back there, but it . . ."

"Two women in a passionate kiss! You think that's not . . ."

"It's not important. Youth explores its potential in many ways."

Idaho balanced himself on the edge of an explosion, rocking forward on his toes. "I'm glad to learn about you, Moneo."

"Yes, well, I've learned about you, *several* times."

Moneo watched the effect of these words as they twisted through Idaho, tangling him. The gholas could never avoid a fascination with *the others* who had preceded them.

Idaho spoke in a hoarse whisper: "What have you learned?"

"You have taught me valuable things," Moneo said. "All of us try to evolve, but if something blocks us, we can transfer our potential into pain—seeking it or giving it. Adolescents are particularly vulnerable."

Idaho leaned close to Moneo. "I'm talking about sex!"

"Of course you are."

"Are you accusing me of adolescent . . ."

"That's right."

"I should cut your . . ."

"Oh, shut up!"

Moneo's response did not have the training nuances of Bene Gesserit Voice control, but it had a lifetime of command behind it. Something in Idaho could only obey.

"I'm sorry," Moneo said. "But I'm distracted by the fact that my only daughter . . ." He broke off and shrugged.

Idaho inhaled two deep breaths. "You're crazy, all of you! You say your daughter may be dying and yet you . . ."

"You fool!" Moneo snapped. "Have you any idea how your petty concerns appear to me! Your stupid questions and your selfish . . ." He broke off, shaking his head.

"I make allowances because you have personal

344

problems," Idaho said. "But if you . . ."

"Allowances? *You* make allowances?" Moneo took a trembling breath. It was too much!

Idaho spoke stiffly: "I can forgive you for . . ."

"You! You prattle about sex and forgiving and pain and . . . you think you and Hwi Noree . . ."

"Leave her out of this!"

"Oh, yes. Leave her out. Leave out *that* pain! You share sex with her and you *never* think about parting. Tell me, fool, how do you give of yourself in the face of *that*?"

Abashed, Idaho inhaled deeply. He had not suspected such passion smouldering in the quiet Moneo, but this attack, this could not be . . .

"You think I'm cruel?" Moneo demanded. "I make you think about things you'd rather avoid. Hah! Crueller things have been done to the Lord Leto for no better reason than the cruelty!"

"You defend him? You . . ."

"I know him best!"

"He uses you!"

"To what ends?"

"You tell me!"

"He's our best hope to perpetuate . . ."

"Perverts don't perpetuate!"

Moneo spoke in a soothing tone, but his words shook Idaho. "I will tell you this only once. Homosexuals have been among the best warriors in our history, the berserkers of last resort. They were among our best priests and priestesses. Celibacy was no accident in religions. It is also no accident that adolescents make the best soldiers."

"That's perversion!"

"Quite right. Military commanders have known about the perverted displacement of sex into pain for thousands upon thousands of centuries."

"Is *that* what the Great Lord Leto's doing?"

Still mild, Moneo said: "Violence requires that you inflict pain and suffer it. How much more manageable a military force driven to this by its deepest urgings."

345

"He's made a monster out of you, too!"

"You suggested that he uses me," Moneo said. "I permit this because I know that the price he pays is much greater than what he demands of me."

"Even your daughter?"

"*He* holds back nothing. Why should I? Ohhh, I think you understand this about the Atreides. The Duncans are always good at *that*."

"The Duncans! Damn you, I won't be . . ."

"You just haven't the guts to pay the price he's asking," Moneo said.

In one blurred motion, Idaho whipped his knife from its sheath and lunged at Moneo. As fast as he moved, Moneo moved faster—sidestepping, tripping Idaho and propelling him face down on to the floor. Idaho scrambled forward, rolled and started to leap to his feet, then hesitated, realizing that he had actually tried to attack an Atreides. Moneo was Atreides. Shock held Idaho immobile.

Moneo stood unmoving, looking down at him. There was an odd look of sadness on the majordomo's face.

"If you're going to kill me, Duncan, you'd best do it in the back by stealth," Moneo said. "You might succeed that way."

Idaho levered himself to one knee, put a foot flat on the floor, but remained there still clutching his knife. Moneo had moved so quickly and with such grace—so . . . so casually! Idaho cleared his throat. "How did you . . ."

"He has been breeding us for a long time, Duncan, strengthening many things in us. He has bred us for speed, for intelligence, for self-restraint, for sensitivity. You're . . . you're just an older model."

Do you know what guerrillas often say? They claim that their rebellions are invulnerable to economic warfare because they have no economy, that they are parasitic on those they would overthrow. The fools merely fail to assess the coin in which they must inevitably pay. The pattern is inexorable in its degenerative failures. You see it repeated in the systems of slavery, of welfare states, of caste-ridden religions, of socializing bureaucracies—in any system which creates and maintains dependencies. Too long a parasite and you cannot exist without a host.

—The Stolen Journals

Leto and Siona lay all day in the dune shadows, moving only as the sun moved. He taught her how to protect herself under a blanket of sand in the noontime heat, but it never grew too warm at the rock level between the dunes.

In the afternoon, Siona crept close to Leto for warmth, a warmth he knew he had in excess these days.

They talked sporadically. He told her about the Fremen graces which once had dominated this landscape. She probed for secret knowledge of him.

Once, he said: "You may find it odd, but out here is where I can be most human."

His words failed to make her fully conscious of her human vulnerability and the fact that she might die out here. Even when she was not talking she did not restore the face flap of her stillsuit.

Leto recognized the unconscious motivation behind this failure, but knew the futility of addressing that directly.

In the late afternoon, night's chill already starting to creep over the land, he began regaling her with songs of the Long Trek which had not been saved in the Oral History. He enjoyed the fact that she liked one of his favourites, "Liet's March".

"The tune is really ancient," he said, "a prespace thing of Old Terra."

"Would you sing it again?"

347

He chose one of his best baritones, a long-dead artist who had filled many a concert hall.

> "The wall of past-beyond-recall
> Hides me from an ancient fall
> Where all the waters tumble!
> And plays of sprays
> Carve caves in clays
> Beneath a torrent's rumble."

When he had finished, she was silent for a moment, then: "That's an odd song for marching."

"They liked it because they could dissect it," he said.

"Dissect?"

"Before our Fremen ancestors came to this planet, night was the time for storytelling, songs and poetry. In the Dune days, though, that was reserved for the false dark, the daytime gloom of the sietch. The night was when they could emerge and move about . . . just as we do now."

"But you said *dissect*."

"What does that song mean?" he asked.

"Oh. It's . . . it's just a song."

"Siona!"

She heard anger in his voice and remained silent.

"This planet is the child of the worm," he warned her, "and *I* am that worm."

She responded with a surprising insouciance: "Then tell me what it means."

"The insect has no more freedom from its hive than we have freedom from our past," he said. "The caves are there and all of the messages written in the sprays of the torrents."

"I prefer dancing songs," she said.

It was a flippant answer, but Leto chose to take it as a change of subject. He told her about the marriage dance of Fremen women, tracing the steps back to the whirling of dust devils. Leto prided himself on telling a good story. It was clear from her rapt attention that she could see the women whirling before his inner eye, long black hair thrown in the ancient movements, straggling across long-dead faces.

Darkness was almost upon them when he finished.

"Come," he said. "Morning and evening are still the times of silhouettes. Let us see if anyone shares our desert."

Siona followed him up to a dune crest and they stared all around at the darkening desert. There was only one bird high overhead, attracted by their movements. From the splayed-gap tips on its wings and the shape, he knew it was a vulture. He pointed this out to Siona.

"But what do they eat?" she asked.

"Anything that's dead or nearly so."

This hit her and she stared up at the last of the sunlight gilding the lone bird's flight feathers.

Leto pressed it: "A few people still venture into my Sareer. Sometimes, a Museum Fremen wanders off and gets lost. They're really only good at the rituals. And then there are the desert's edges and the remains of whatever my wolves leave."

At this, she whirled away from him, but not before he saw the passion still consuming her. Siona was being sorely tested.

"There's little daytime graciousness about a desert," he said. "That's another reason we travel by night. To a Fremen, the image of the day was that of wind-blown sand filling your tracks."

Her eyes glistened with unshed tears when she turned back to him, but her features were composed.

"What lives here now?" she asked.

"The vultures, a few night creatures, an occasional remnant of plant life out of the old days, burrowing things."

"Is that all?"

"Yes."

"Why?"

"Because this is where they were born and I permit them to know nothing better."

It was almost dark with that sudden glowing light his desert acquired in these moments. He studied her in that luminous moment, recognizing that she had not yet understood his other message. He knew that message would sit there, though, and fester in her.

"Silhouettes," she said, reminding him. "What did you expect to find when we came up here?"

"Perhaps people at a distance. You're never certain."

"What people?"

"I've already told you."

"What would you've done if you'd seen anyone?"

"It was the Fremen custom to treat distant people as hostile until they threw sand into the air."

As he spoke, darkness fell over them like a curtain.

Siona became ghostly movement in the sudden starlight. "Sand?" she asked.

"Thrown sand is a profound gesture. It says: 'We share the same burden. Sand is our only enemy. This is what we drink. The hand that holds sand holds no weapon.' Do you understand this?"

"No!" She taunted him with a defiant falsehood.

"You will," he said.

Without a word, she set out along the arc of their dune, striding away from him with an angry excess of energy. Leto allowed himself to fall far behind her, interested that she had instinctively chosen the right direction. Fremen memories could be felt churning in her.

Where the dune dipped to cross another, she waited for him. He saw that the face flap of her stillsuit remained open, hanging loose. It was not yet time to chide her about this. Some unconscious things had to run their natural course.

As he came up to her, she said: "Is this as good a direction as any other?"

"If you keep to it," he said.

She glanced up at the stars and he saw her identify

350

the Pointers, those Fremen Arrows which had led her ancestors across this land. He could see, though, that her recognition was mostly intellectual. She had not yet come to accept the other things working within her.

Leto lifted his front segments to peer ahead in the starlight. They were moving a little west of north on a track that once had led across Habbanya Ridge and Cave of Birds into the erg below False Wall West and the way to Wind Pass. None of those landmarks remained. He sniffed a cool breeze with flint smells in it and more moisture than he found pleasant.

Once more, Siona set off—slower this time, holding her course by occasional glances at the stars. She had trusted Leto to confirm the way, but now she guided herself. He sensed the turmoil beneath her wary thoughts, and he knew the things which were emerging. She had the beginnings of that intense loyalty to travelling companions which desert folk always trusted.

We know, he thought. *If you are separated from your companions you are lost among dunes and rocks. The lone traveller in the desert is dead. Only the worm lives alone out here.*

He let her get well ahead of him where the grating sand of his passage would not be too prominent. She had to think of his human-self. He counted on loyalty to work for him. Siona was brittle, though, filled with suppressed rage— more of a rebel than any other he had ever tested.

Leto glided along behind her, reviewing the breeding programme, shaping the necessary decisions for a replacement should she fail.

As the night progressed, Siona moved slower and slower. First Moon was high overhead and Second Moon well above the horizon before she stopped to rest and eat.

Leto was glad of the pause. Friction had set up a worm-dominance, the air around him full of the chemical exhalations from his temperature adjustments. The thing he thought of as his *oxygen supercharger* vented steadily, making him intensely aware of the protein factories and amino acid resources his worm-self had acquired to accommodate the placental relationship with his human cells. Desert quickened the movement toward his final metamorphosis.

Siona had stopped near the crest of a star dune. "Is it true that you eat the sand?" she asked as he came up to her.

"It's true."

She stared all around the moon-frosted horizon. "Why didn't we bring a signal device?"

"I wanted you to learn about possessions."

She turned toward him. He sensed her breath close to his face. She was losing too much moisture into the dry air. Still she did not remember Moneo's admonition. It would be a bitter lesson, no doubt of that.

"I don't understand you at all," she said.

"Yet, you are committed to doing just that."

"Am I?"

"How else can you give me something of value in exchange for what I give you?"

"What do you give me?" All of the bitterness was there and a hint of the spice from her dried food.

"I give you this opportunity to be alone with me, to share with me, and you spend this time without concern. You waste it."

"What about possessions?" she demanded.

He heard fatigue in her voice, the water message beginning to scream within her.

"They were magnificently alive in the old days, those Fremen," he said. "And their eye for beauty was limited to that which was useful. I never met a greedy Fremen."

"What's that supposed to mean?"

"In the old days, everything you took into the desert was a necessity and that was all you took. Your life is no longer free of possessions, Siona, or you would not have asked about a signal device."

"Why isn't a signal device necessary?"

"It would teach you nothing."

He moved out around her along the track indicated by

352

the Pointers. "Come. Let us use this night to our profit."

She came hurrying up to walk beside his cowled face. "What happens if I don't learn your damned lesson?"

"You'll probably die," he said.

That silenced her for a time. She trudged along beside him with only an occasional sideward glance, ignoring the worm-body, concentrating on the visible remnants of his humanity. After a time, she said: "The Fish Speakers told me that you ordered the mating from which I was born."

"That's true."

"They say you keep records and that you order these Atreides matings for your own purposes."

"That also is true."

"Then the Oral History is correct."

"I thought you believed the Oral History without question?"

She was on a single track, though: "What if one of us objects when you order a mating?"

"I allow a wide latitude just as long as there are the children I have ordered."

"Ordered?" She was outraged.

"That's what I do."

"You can't creep into every bedroom or follow every one of us every minute of our lives! How do you know your *orders* are obeyed?"

"I know."

"Then you know I'm not going to obey you!"

"Are you thirsty, Siona?"

She was startled. "What?"

"Thirsty people speak of water, not of sex."

Still she did not seal her mouth flap, and he thought: *Atreides passions always did run strong, even at the expense of reason.*

Within two hours they came down out of the dunes on to a wind-scoured flat of pebbles. Leto moved on to it, Siona close to his side. She looked frequently at the Pointers. Both moons were low on the horizon now and their light cast long shadows behind every boulder.

In some ways, Leto found such places more comfortable to traverse than the sand. Solid rock was a better heat conductor than sand. He could flatten himself against the rock and ease the working of his chemical factories. Pebbles and even sizeable rocks did not impede him.

Siona had more trouble here, though, and almost turned an ankle several times.

The flatland could be a very trying place for humans unaccustomed to it, he thought. If they stayed close to the ground, they saw only the great emptiness, an eerie place especially in moonlight—dunes at a distance, a distance which seemed not to change as the traveller moved— nothing anywhere except the seemingly eternal wind, a few rocks and, when they looked upward, stars without mercy. This was the desert of the desert.

"Here's where Fremen music acquired its eternal loneliness," he said, "not up on the dunes. Here's where you really learn to think that heaven must be the sound of running water and relief—any relief—from that endless wind."

Even this did not remind her of that face flap. Leto began to despair.

Morning found them far out on the flat.

Leto stopped beside three large boulders, all piled against each other, one of them taller even than his back. Siona leaned against him for a moment, a gesture which restored Leto's hopes somewhat. She pushed herself away presently and clambered up on to the highest boulder. He watched her turn up there, examining the landscape.

Without even looking at it, Leto knew what she saw: blowing sand like fog on the horizon obscured the rising sun. For the rest, there was only the flat and the wind.

The rock was cold beneath him with the chill of a desert morning. The cold made the air much drier and he found it more pleasant. Without Siona, he would have moved on, but she was visibly exhausted. She leaned against him once more when she came down from the rock and it was almost a minute before he realized that she was listening.

"What do you hear?" he asked.

She spoke sleepily. "You rumble inside."

"The fire never goes completely out."

This interested her. She pushed herself away from his side and came around to look into his face. "Fire?"

"Every living thing has a fire within it, some slow, some very fast. Mine is hotter than most."

She hugged herself against the chill. "Then you're not cold here?"

"No, but I can see that you are." He pulled his face partly into its cowl and created a depression at the bottom arc of his first segment. "It's almost like a hammock," he said, looking down. "If you curl up there you will be warm."

Without hesitating, she accepted his invitation.

Even though he had prepared her for it, he found the trusting response touching. He had to fight against a feeling of pity far stronger than any he had experienced before knowing Hwi. There could be no room for pity out here, though, he told himself. Siona was betraying clear signs that she would more than likely die here. He had to prepare himself for disappointment.

Siona shielded her face with an arm, closed her eyes and went to sleep.

Nobody has ever had as many yesterdays as I have had, he reminded himself.

From the popular human viewpoint, he knew that the things he did here could only appear cruel and callous. He was forced now to strengthen himself by retreating into his memories, deliberately selecting *mistakes of our common past.* First-hand access to human mistakes was his greatest strength now. Knowledge of mistakes taught him long-term corrections. He had to be constantly aware of consequences. If consequences were lost or concealed, lessons were lost.

But the closer he came to being a sandworm, the harder he found it to make decisions which others would call inhuman. Once, he had done it with ease. As his humanity slipped away, though, he found himself filled with more and more human concerns.

> *In the cradle of our past, I lay upon my back in a cave so shallow I could penetrate it only by squirming, not by crawling. There, by the dancing light of a resin torch, I drew upon walls and ceiling the creatures of the hunt and the souls of my people. How illuminating it is to peer backward through a perfect circle at that ancient struggle for the visible moment of the soul. All time vibrates to that call: "Here I am!" With a mind informed by artist-giants who came afterward, I peer at handprints and flowing muscles drawn upon the rock with charcoal and vegetable dyes. How much more we are than mere mechanical events! And my anticivil self demands: "Why is it that they do not want to leave the cave?"*

> —**The Stolen Journals**

The invitation to attend Moneo in his workroom came to Idaho late in the afternoon. All day, Idaho had sat upon the sling couch of his quarters, thinking. Every thought radiated outward from the ease with which Moneo had spilled him on to the corridor floor that morning.

"You're just an older model."

With every thought, Idaho felt himself diminished. He sensed the will to live as it faded, leaving ashes where his anger had burned itself out.

I am the conveyance of some useful sperm and nothing more, he thought.

It was a thought which invited either death or hedonism. He felt himself impaled on a thorn of chance with irritating forces pecking at him from all sides.

The young messenger in her neat blue uniform was merely another irritation. She entered at his low-voiced response to her knock and she stopped under the arched portal from his anteroom, hesitating until she had assessed his mood.

How quickly the word travels, he thought.

356

He saw her there framed in the portal, a projection of Fish Speaker essence—more voluptuous than some, but no more blatantly sexual. The blue uniform did not conceal graceful hips, firm breasts. He looked up at her puckish face under a brush of blonde hair—acolyte cut.

"Moneo sends me to inquire after you," she said. "He asks that you attend him in his workroom."

Idaho had seen that workroom several times, but still remembered it best from his first view of it. He had known on entering the room that it was where Moneo spent most of his time. There was a table of dark brown wood streaked by fine golden graining, about two metres by one metre and set low on stubby legs in the midst of grey cushions. The table had struck Idaho as something rare and expensive chosen for a single accent. It and the cushions—which were the same grey as floor, walls and ceiling—were the only furnishings.

Considering the power of its occupant, the room was small, no more than five metres by four, but with a high ceiling. Light came from two slender glazed windows opposite each other on the narrower walls. The windows looked out from a considerable height, one on to the north-west fringes of the Sareer and the bordering green of the Forbidden Forest, the other providing a southwest view over rolling dunes.

Contrast.

The table had put an interesting accent on this initial thought. The surface had appeared as an arrangement demonstrating the idea of *clutter*. Thin sheets of crystal paper lay scattered across the surface, leaving only glimpses of the wood grain underneath. Fine printing covered some of the paper. Idaho recognized words in Galach and four other languages, including the rare transite tongue of Perth. Several sheets of the paper revealed plan drawings and some were scrawled with black strokes of brush-script in the bold style of the Bene Gesserit. Most interesting of all had been four rolled white tubes about a metre long—tri-D printouts from an illegal computer. He had suspected the terminal lay concealed behind a panel in one of the walls.

The young messenger from Moneo cleared her throat to awaken Idaho from his reverie. "What response shall I return to Moneo?" she asked.

Idaho focused on her face. "Would you like me to impregnate you?" he asked.

"Commander!" She was obviously shocked not so much by his suggestion as by its *non sequitur* intrusion.

"Ahhh, yes," Idaho said. "Moneo. What shall we tell Moneo?"

"He awaits your reply, Commander."

"Is there really any point in my responding?" Idaho asked.

"Moneo told me to inform you that he wishes to confer with both you and the Lady Hwi together."

Idaho sensed a vague arousal of interest. "Hwi is with him?"

"She has been summoned, Commander." The messenger cleared her throat once more. "Would the Commander wish me to visit him here later tonight?"

"No. Thank you anyway. I've changed my mind."

He thought she concealed her disappointment well, but her voice came out stiffly formal: "Shall I say that you will attend Moneo?"

"Do that." He waved her away.

After she had gone, he considered just ignoring the summons. Curiosity grew in him, though. Moneo wanted to talk to him with Hwi present? Why? Did he think this would bring Idaho running? Idaho swallowed. When he thought of Hwi, the emptiness in his breast became full. The message of that could not be ignored. Something of terrible power bound him to Hwi.

He stood up, his muscles stiff after their long inaction. Curiosity and this binding force impelled him. He went out into the corridor, ignored the curious glances of guards he passed, and followed that compelling inner force up to Moneo's workroom.

Hwi was already there when Idaho entered the room. She was across the cluttered table from Moneo, her feet in red slippers tucked back beside the grey cushion on which she sat. Idaho saw only that she wore a long brown gown with a braided green belt, then she turned and he could look at nothing except her face. Her mouth formed his name without speaking it.

Even she has heard, he thought.

Oddly, this thought strengthened him. The thoughts of this day began to form new shapes in his mind.

"Please sit down, Duncan," Moneo said. He gestured to a cushion beside Hwi. His voice conveyed a curious, halting tone, a manner that few people other than Leto had ever observed in him. He kept his gaze directed downward at the cluttered surface of his table. The late afternoon sunlight cast a spidery shadow across the jumble from a golden paperweight in the shape of a fanciful tree with jewelled fruit, all mounted on a flame-crystal mountain.

Idaho took the indicated cushion, watching Hwi's gaze follow him until he was seated. She looked at Moneo then and he thought he saw anger in her expression. Moneo's usual plain white uniform was open at the throat revealing a wrinkled neck and a bit of dewlap. Idaho stared into the man's eyes, prepared to wait, forcing Moneo to open the conversation.

Moneo returned the stare, noting that Idaho still wore the black uniform of their morning encounter. There was even a small trace of grime down the front, memento of the corridor floor where Moneo had spilled him. But Idaho no longer wore the antique Atreides knife. That bothered Moneo.

"What I did this morning was unforgivable," Moneo said. "Therefore, I do not ask you to forgive me. I merely ask that you try to understand."

Hwi did not appear surprised by this opening, Idaho noted. It revealed much about what the two of them had been discussing before Idaho's arrival.

When Idaho did not respond, Moneo said: "I had no

right to make you feel inadequate."

Idaho found himself undergoing a curious response to Moneo's words and manner. There was still the feeling of being outmanoeuvred and outclassed, too far from his time, but he no longer suspected that Moneo might be toying with him. Something had reduced the majordomo to a gritty substratum of honesty. The realization put Leto's universe, the deadly eroticism of the Fish Speakers, Hwi's undeniable candour—*everything* into a new relationship, a form which Idaho felt that he understood. It was as though the three of them in this room were the last true humans in the entire universe. He spoke from a sense of wry self-deprecation:

"You had every right to protect yourself when I attacked you. It pleases me that you were so capable."

Idaho turned toward Hwi, but before he could speak, Moneo said: "You needn't plead for me. I think her displeasure toward me is quite adamant."

Idaho shook his head. "Does everyone here know what I'm going to say before I say it, what I'm going to feel before I feel it?"

"One of your admirable qualities," Moneo said. "You do not conceal your feelings. We . . ." he shrugged, ". . . are necessarily more circumspect."

Idaho looked at Hwi. "Does he speak for you?"

She put her hand in Idaho's. "I speak for myself."

Moneo craned to peer at the clasped hands, sank back on his cushion. He sighed. "You must not."

Idaho clasped her hand more tightly, felt her equal response.

"Before either of you asks," Moneo said, "my daughter and the God Emperor have not yet returned from the testing."

Idaho sensed the effort Moneo had required to speak calmly. Hwi heard it, too.

"Is it true what the Fish Speakers say?" she asked. "Siona dies if she fails?"

Moneo remained silent, but his face was a rock.

"Is it like the Bene Gesserit test?" Idaho asked. "Muad'Dib said the Sisterhood tests to try to find out if you are human."

Hwi's hand began to tremble. Idaho felt it and looked at her. "Did they test you?"

"No," Hwi said, "but I heard the young ones talking about it. They said you must pass through agony without losing your sense of self."

Idaho returned his attention to Moneo, noting the start of a tic beside the majordomo's left eye.

"Moneo," Idaho breathed, overcome by sudden realization. "He tested you!"

"I do not wish to discuss tests," Moneo said. "We are here to decide what must be done about you two."

"Isn't that up to us?" Idaho asked. He felt Hwi's hand in his grow slippery with perspiration.

"It is up to the God Emperor," Moneo said.

"Even if Siona fails?" Idaho asked.

"Especially then!"

"How did he test you?" Idaho asked.

"He showed me a small glimpse of what it's like to be the God Emperor."

"And?"

"I saw as much as I'm capable of seeing."

Hwi's hand tightened convulsively in Idaho's.

"Then it's true that you were a rebel once," Idaho said.

"I began with love and prayer," Moneo said. "I changed to anger and rebellion. I was transformed into what you see before you. I recognize my duty and I do it."

"What did he do to you?" Idaho demanded.

"He quoted to me the prayer of my childhood: 'I give my life in dedication to the greater glory of God.'" Moneo spoke in a musing voice.

Idaho noted Hwi's stillness, her stare fixed on Moneo's face. What was she thinking?

"I admitted that this had been my prayer," Moneo said. "And the God Emperor asked me what I would give up if my life were not enough. He shouted at me: 'What is your

361

life when you hold back the greater gift?'"

Hwi nodded, but Idaho felt only confusion.

"I could hear the truth in his voice," Moneo said.

"Are you a Truthsayer?" Hwi asked.

"In the power of desperation, yes," Moneo said. "But only then. I swear to you he spoke truth to me."

"Some of the Atreides had the power of Voice," Idaho muttered.

Moneo shook his head. "No, it was truth. He said to me: 'I look at you now and if I could shed tears, I would. Consider the wish to be the act!'"

Hwi rocked forward, almost touching the table. "He cannot cry?"

"Sandworms," Idaho whispered.

"What?" Hwi turned toward him.

"Fremen killed sandworms with water," Idaho said. "From the drowning they produced the spice essence for their religious orgies."

"But the Lord Leto is not yet a sandworm entire," Moneo said.

Hwi rocked back on to her cushion and looked at Moneo.

Idaho pursed his lips in thought. Did Leto have the Fremen prohibition against tears, then? How awed the Fremen had always been about such a waste of moisture! *Giving water to the dead.*

Moneo addressed himself to Idaho: "I had hoped you could be brought to an understanding. The Lord Leto has spoken. You and Hwi must separate and never see each other again."

Hwi removed her hand from Idaho's. "We know."

Idaho spoke with resigned bitterness: "We know his power."

"But you do not understand him," Moneo said.

"I want nothing more than that," Hwi said. She put a hand on Idaho's arm to silence him. "No, Duncan. Our private desires have no place here."

"Maybe you should *pray* to him," Idaho said.

She whirled and looked at him, staring and staring until Idaho lowered his gaze. When she spoke, her voice carried a lilting quality that Idaho had never heard there before. "My Uncle Malky always said the Lord Leto never responded to prayer. He said the Lord Leto looked on prayer as attempted coercion, a form of violence against the chosen god, telling the immortal what to do: *Give me a miracle, God, or I won't believe in you!*"

"Prayer as hubris," Moneo said. "Intercession on demand."

"How can he be a god?" Idaho demanded. "By his own admission, he's not immortal."

"I will quote the Lord Leto on that," Moneo said. "'I am all of God that need be seen. I am the word become a miracle. I am all of my ancestors. Is that not miracle enough? What more could you possibly want? Ask yourself: Where is there a greater miracle?'"

"Empty words," Idaho sneered.

"I sneered at him, too," Moneo said. "I threw his own words from the Oral History back at him: 'Give to the greater glory of God!'"

Hwi gasped.

"He laughed at me," Moneo said. "He laughed and asked how I could give what already belonged to God?"

"You were angry?" Hwi asked.

"Oh, yes. He saw this and said he would tell me how to give to that glory. He said: 'You may observe that you are every bit as great a miracle as I am.'" Moneo turned and looked out of the window on his left. "I'm afraid my anger made me deaf and I was totally unprepared."

"Ohhh, he is clever," Idaho said.

"Clever?" Moneo looked at him. "I don't think so, not in the way you mean. I think the Lord Leto may be no more clever than I am in that way."

"Unprepared for what?" Hwi asked.

"The risk," Moneo said.

"But you risked much in your anger," she said.

"Not as much as he. I see in your eyes, Hwi, that you

363

understand this. Does his body revolt you?"

"No more," she said.

Idaho ground his teeth in frustration. "He disgusts me!"

"Love, you must not say such things," Hwi said.

"And you must not call him love," Moneo said.

"You'd rather she learned to love someone more gross and evil than any Baron Harkonnen ever dreamed of being," Idaho said.

Moneo worked his lips in and out, then: "The Lord Leto has told me about that evil old man of your time, Duncan. I don't think you understood your enemy."

"He was a fat, monstrous . . ."

"He was a seeker after sensations," Moneo said. "The fat was a side effect, then perhaps something to experience for itself because it offended people and he enjoyed offending."

"The Baron only consumed a few planets," Idaho said. "Leto consumes the universe."

"Love, please!" Hwi protested.

"Let him rant," Moneo said. "When I was young and ignorant, even as my Siona and this poor fool, I said similar things."

"Is that why you let your daughter go out to die?" Idaho demanded.

"Love, that's cruel," Hwi said.

"Duncan, it has always been one of your flaws to seek hysteria," Moneo said. "I warn you that ignorance thrives on hysteria. Your genes provide vigour and you may inspire some among the Fish Speakers, but you are a poor leader."

"Don't try to anger me," Idaho said. "I know better than to attack you, but don't push me too far."

Hwi tried to take Idaho's hand, but he pulled away.

"I know my place," Idaho said. "I'm a useful follower. I can carry the Atreides banner. The green and black is on my back!"

"The undeserving maintain power by promoting hysteria," Moneo said. "The Atreides art is the art of ruling without hysteria, the art of being responsible for the uses of power."

Idaho pushed back and heaved himself to his feet. "When has your damned God Emperor ever been responsible for anything?"

Moneo looked down at his cluttered table and spoke without looking up. "He is responsible for what he has done to himself." Moneo looked up then, his eyes frosty. "You haven't the guts, Duncan, to learn why he did that to himself!"

"And you have?" Idaho asked.

"When I was most angry," Moneo said, "and he saw himself through my eyes, he said: 'How dare you be offended by me?' It was then . . ." Moneo swallowed, ". . . that he made me look into the horror . . . that he had seen." Tears welled from Moneo's eyes and ran down his cheeks. "And I was only glad that I did not have to make his decision . . . that I could content myself with being a follower."

"I have touched him," Hwi whispered.

"Then you know?" Moneo asked her.

"Without seeing it, I know," she said.

In a low voice, Moneo said: "I almost died of it. I . . ." He shuddered, then looked up at Idaho. "You must not . . ."

"Damn you all!" Idaho snarled. He turned and dashed from the room.

Hwi started after him, her face a mask of anguish. "Ohhh, Duncan," she whispered.

"You see?" Moneo asked. "You were wrong. Neither you nor the Fish Speakers have gentled him. But you, Hwi, you have only contributed to his destruction."

Hwi turned her anguish toward Moneo. "I will not see him again," she said.

For Idaho, the passage down to his quarters became one of the most difficult times in his memory. He tried to imagine that his face was a plasteel mask held immobile to hide the turmoil within. None of the guards he passed could

365

be permitted to see his pain. He did not know that most of them made accurate guesses about his emotion and shared a compassion for him. All of them had sat through briefings on the Duncans and had learned to read them well.

In the corridor near his quarters, Idaho encountered Nayla walking slowly toward him. Something in her face, a look of indecision and loss, stopped him briefly and almost brought him out of his internal concentration.

"Friend?" he said, speaking when she was only a few paces from him.

She looked at him, abrupt recognition obvious on her square face.

What an odd looking woman, he thought.

"I am no longer Friend," she said and passed by him down the corridor.

Idaho turned on one heel and stared at her retreating back—those heavy shoulders, that plodding sense of terrible muscles.

What was she bred for? he wondered.

It was only a passing thought. His own concerns returned more strongly than before. He strode the few paces to his door and into his quarters.

Once inside, Idaho stood a moment with clenched fists at his sides.

I have no more ties to any time, he thought. And how odd that this was not a liberating thought. He knew, though, that he had done the thing which would begin freeing Hwi from her love for him. He was diminished. She would think of him soon as a small, petulant fool, a subject only of his own emotions. He could feel himself fading from her immediate concerns.

And that poor Moneo!

Idaho sensed the shape of the things which had formed the pliant majordomo. *Duty and responsibility.* What a safe haven those were in a time of difficult decisions.

I was like that once, Idaho thought. *But that was in another life, another time.*

366

The Duncans sometimes ask if I understand the exotic ideas of our past? And if I understand them, why can't I explain them? Knowledge, the Duncans believe, resides only in particulars. I try to tell them that all words are plastic. Word images begin to distort in the instant of utterance. Ideas embedded in a language require that particular language for expression. This is the very essence of the meaning within the word exotic. *See how it begins to distort? Translation squirms in the presence of the exotic. The Galach which I speak here imposes itself. It is an outside frame of reference, a particular system. Dangers lurk in all systems. Systems incorporate the unexamined beliefs of their creators. Adopt a system, accept its beliefs, and you help strengthen the resistance to change. Does it serve any purpose for me to tell the Duncans that there are no languages for some things? Ahhhh! But the Duncans believe that all languages are mine.*

—**The Stolen Journals**

For two full turns of days and nights, Siona failed to seal her face mask, losing precious water with every breath. It had taken the Fremen admonition to children before Siona remembered her father's words. Leto had spoken to her finally on the cold third morning of their traverse when they stopped within a rock shadow on the windswept flat of the erg.

"Guard every breath for it carries the warmth and moisture of your life," he said.

He had known they would be three more days on the erg and three more nights beyond that before they reached water. Now, it was the fifth morning from the Little Citadel's tower. They had entered shallow drifts of sand during the night—not dunes, but dunes could be glimpsed ahead of them and even the remnants of Habbanya Ridge were a thin broken line in the distance if you knew where to look. Now, Siona took down the mouth flap of her stillsuit only to speak clearly. And she spoke through black and bleeding lips.

She has the thirst of desperation, he thought, as he let his senses probe their surroundings. *She will reach the moments of crisis soon*. His senses told him that they were still alone here at the edge of the flat. Dawn lay only minutes behind them. The low light created barriers of dust reflection which twisted and lifted and dipped in the unceasing wind. His senses filtered out the wind that he might hear other things—Siona's heaving breaths, the tumble of a small sandspill from the rocks beside them, his own gross body grating in the thin sand cover.

Siona peeled her face mask aside but held it in her hand for quick restoration.

"How much longer until we find water?" she asked.

"Three nights."

"Is there a better direction to go?"

"No."

She had come to appreciate the Fremen economy with important information. She sipped greedily at a few drops in her catchpocket.

Leto recognized the message of her movements—familiar gestures for Fremen *in extremis*. Siona was now fully aware of a common experience among her ancestors —*patiyeh*, the thirst at the edge of death.

The few drops in her catchpocket were gone. He heard her sucking air. She restored the mask and spoke in a muffled voice.

"I won't make it, will I?"

Leto looked into her eyes, seeing there the clarity of thought brought on by the nearness of death, a penetrating awareness seldom otherwise achieved. It amplified only that which was required for survival. Yes, she was well into the *tedah ri-agrimi*, the agony which opens the mind. Soon, she would have to make that ultimate decision which she yet believed she had already made. Leto knew by the signs that he was required to treat Siona now with extreme courtesy. He would have to answer every question with candour for in every question lurked a judgment.

"Will I?" she insisted.

There was still a trace of hope in her desperation.

"Nothing is certain," he said.

This dropped her into despair.

That had not been Leto's intention, but he knew that it often happened—an accurate, though ambiguous, answer was taken as confirmation of one's deepest fears.

She sighed.

Her mask-muffled voice probed at him once more. "You had some special intention for me in your breeding programme."

It was not a question.

"All people have intentions," he told her.

"But you wanted my full agreement."

"That is true."

"How could you expect agreement when you know I hate everything about you? Be honest with me!"

"The three legs of the agreement-tripod are desire, data and doubt. Accuracy and honesty have little to do with it."

"Please don't argue with me. You know I'm dying."

"I respect you too much to argue with you."

He lifted his front segments slightly then, probing the wind. It already was beginning to bring the day's heat but there was too much moisture in it for his comfort. He was reminded that the more he ordered the weather controlled the more there was that required control. Absolutes only brought him closer to vagueries.

"You say you're not arguing, but . . ."

"Argument closes off the doors of the senses," he said, lowering himself back to the surface. "It always masks violence. Continued too long, argument always leads to violence. I have no violent intentions toward you."

"What do you mean—desire, data and doubt?"

"Desire brings the participants together. Data sets the limits of their dialogue. Doubt frames the questions."

She moved closer to stare directly into his face from less than a metre away.

How odd, he thought, that hatred could be mingled so completely with hope and fear and awe.

"Could you save me?"

"There is a way."

She nodded and he knew she had leaped to the wrong conclusion.

"You want to trade *that* for my agreement!" she accused.

"No."

"If I pass your test . . ."

"It is not my test."

"Whose?"

"It derives from our common ancestors."

Siona sank to a sitting position on the cold rock and remained silent, not yet ready to ask for a resting place within the lip of his warm front segment. Leto thought he could hear the soft scream waiting in her throat. Now, her doubts were at work. She was beginning to wonder if he really could be fitted into her image of Ultimate Tyrant. She looked up at him with that terrible clarity he had identified in her.

"What makes you do what you do?"

The question was well framed. He said: "My need to save the people."

"What people?"

"My definition is much broader than that of anyone else—even of the Bene Gesserit who think they have defined what it is to be human. I refer to the eternal thread of all humankind by whatever definition."

"You're trying to tell me . . ." Her mouth became too dry for speaking. She tried to accumulate saliva. He saw the movements within her face mask. Her question was obvious, though, and he did not wait.

"Without me there would have been by now no people anywhere, none whatsoever. And the path to that extinction was more hideous than your wildest imaginings."

"Your *supposed* prescience," she sneered.

"The Golden Path still stands open," he said.

"I don't trust you!"

"Because we are not equals?"

"Yes!"

"But we're interdependent."

"What need have you for me?"

Ahhh, the cry of youth unsure of its niche. He felt the strength within the secret bonds of dependency and forced himself to be hard. *Dependency fosters weakness!*

"You are the Golden Path," he said.

"Me?" It was barely a whisper.

"You've read those journals you stole from me," he said. "I am in them, but where are you? Look at what I have created, Siona. And you, you can create nothing except yourself."

"Words, more tricky words!"

"I do not suffer from being worshipped, Siona. I suffer from never being appreciated. Perhaps . . . No, I dare not hope for you."

"What's the purpose of those journals?"

"An Ixian machine records them. They are to be found on a far away day. They will make people think."

"An Ixian machine? You defy the Jihad!"

"There's a lesson in that, too. What do such machines really do? They increase the number of things we can do without thinking. Things we do without thinking—there's the real danger. Look at how long you walked across this desert without thinking about your face mask."

"You could have warned me!"

"And increased your dependency."

She stared at him a moment, then: "Why would you want me to command your Fish Speakers?"

"You are an Atreides woman, resourceful and capable of independent thought. You can be truthful just for the sake of truth as you see it. You were bred and trained for command—which means freedom from dependence."

The wind whirled dust and sand around them while she weighed his words. "And if I agree, you'll save me?"

"No."

She had been so sure of the opposite answer that it was several heartbeats before she translated that single word. In that time, the wind fell slightly, exposing a vista across the dunescape to the remnants of Habbanya Ridge. The air was suddenly chilled with that cold which did as much to rob the flesh of moisture as did the hottest sunlight. Part of Leto's awareness detected an oscillation in weather control.

"No?" She was both puzzled and outraged.

"I do not make bloody bargains with people I must trust."

She shook her head slowly from side to side, but her gaze remained fixed on his face. "What will make you save me?"

"Nothing will make me do it. Why do you think you could do to me what I will not do to you? That is not the way of interdependence."

Her shoulders slumped. "If I cannot bargain with you or force you . . ."

"Then you must choose another path."

What a marvellous thing to observe the explosive growth of awareness, he thought. Siona's expressive features hid nothing of it from him. She focused on his eyes and glared at him as though seeking to move completely into his thoughts. New strength entered her muffled voice.

"You would have me know everything about you—even every weakness?"

"Would you steal what I would give openly?"

The morning light was harsh on her face. "I promise you nothing!"

"Nor do I require that."

"But you will give me . . . water if I ask?"

"It is not just water."

She nodded. "And I am Atreides."

The Fish Speakers had not withheld the lesson of that special susceptibility in the Atreides genes. She knew where the spice originated and what it might do to her. The teachers in the Fish Speaker schools never failed him. And the gentle additions of melange in Siona's dried food had done their work, too.

"These little curled flaps beside my face," he said. "Tease one of them gently with a finger and it will give up

372

drops of moisture heavily laced with spice essence."

He saw the recognition in her eyes. Memories which she did not know as memories were speaking to her. And she was the result of many generations in which the Atreides sensitivity had been increased.

Even the urgency of her thirst would not yet move her.

To ease her through the crisis, he told her about Fremen children poling for sandtrout at an oasis edge, teasing the moisture out of them for quick vitalization.

"But I am Atreides," she said.

"The Oral History tells it truthfully," he said.

"Then I could die of it."

"That's the test."

"You would make a real Fremen out of me!"

"How else can you teach your descendants to survive here after I am gone?"

She pulled away her mask and moved her face to within a handsbreadth of his. A finger came up and touched one of the curled flaps of his cowl.

"Stroke it gently," he said.

Her hand obeyed not his voice but something from within her. The finger movements were precise, eliciting his own memories, a thing passed from child to child to child . . . the way so much information and misinformation survived. He turned his face to its limit and looked sideways at her face so close to his. Pale blue drops began to form at the flap's edge. Rich cinnamon smells enveloped them. She leaned toward the drops. He saw the pores beside her nose, the way her tongue moved as she drank.

Presently, she retreated—not completely satisfied, but driven by caution and suspicion much the way Moneo had been. *Like father like daughter.*

"How long before it begins to work?" she asked.

"It is already working."

"I mean . . ."

"A minute or so."

"I owe you nothing for this!"

"I will demand no payment."

373

She sealed her face mask.

He saw the milky distances enter her eyes. Without asking permission, she tapped his front segment, demanding that he prepare the warm hammock of his flesh. He obeyed. She fitted herself to the gentle curve. By peering sharply downward, he could see her. Siona's eyes remained opened, but they no longer saw this place. She jerked abruptly and began to tremble like a small creature dying. He knew this experience, but could not change the smallest part of it. No ancestral presences would remain in her consciousness, but she would carry with her forever afterward the clear sights and sounds and smells. The seeking machines would be there, the smell of blood and entrails, the cowering humans in their burrows aware only that they could not escape . . . while all the time the mechanical movement approached, nearer and nearer and nearer . . . louder . . . louder!

Everywhere she searched it would be the same. No escape anywhere.

He felt her life ebbing. *Fight the darkness, Siona!* That was one thing the Atreides did. They fought for life. And now she was fighting for lives other than her own. He felt the dimming, though . . . the terrible outflow of vitality. She went deeper and deeper into the darkness, far deeper than any other had ever gone. He began to rock her gently, a cradle movement of his front segment. That or the thin hot thread of determination, perhaps both together, prevailed. By early afternoon, her flesh had trembled its way into something approaching real sleep. Only an occasional gasp betrayed the vision's echoes. He rocked her gently, rolling from side to side.

Could she possibly come back from those depths? He felt the vital responses reassuring him. The strength in her!

She awakened in the late afternoon, a stillness coming over her abruptly, the breathing rhythm changed. Her eyes snapped open. She peered up at him, then rolled out of the hammock to stand with her back to him for almost an hour of silent thinking.

Moneo had done that same thing. It was a new pattern in these Atreides. Some of the preceding ones had ranted at him. Others had backed away from him, stumbling and staring, forcing him to follow, squirming and grating over the pebbles. Some of them had squatted and stared at the ground. None of them had turned their backs on him. Leto took this new development as a hopeful sign.

"You are beginning to have some concept of how far my family extends," he said.

She turned, her mouth a prim line, but did not meet his gaze. He could see her accepting it, though, the realization which few humans could share as she had shared it: his singular multitude made all of humankind his family.

"You could have saved my friends in the forest," she accused.

"You, too, could have saved them."

She clenched her fists and pressed them against her temples while she glared at him. "But you know *everything*!"

"Siona!"

"Did I have to learn it that way?" she whispered.

He remained silent, forcing her to answer the question for herself. She had to be made to recognize that his primary consciousness worked in a Fremen way and that, like the terrible machines of that apocalyptic vision, the predator could follow any creature who left tracks.

"The Golden Path," she whispered. "I can *feel* it." Then, glaring at him. "It's so cruel!"

"Survival has always been cruel."

"They couldn't hide," she whispered. Then loud: "What have you done to me?"

"You tried to be a Fremen rebel," he said. "Fremen had an almost incredible ability to read signs on the desert. They could even read the faint tracery of windblown tracks in sand."

He saw the beginnings of remorse in her, memories of her dead companions floating in her awareness. He spoke quickly, knowing that guilt would follow quickly and then anger against him. "Would you have believed me if I had merely brought you in and told you?"

Remorse threatened to overwhelm her. She opened her mouth behind the mask and gasped with it.

"You have not yet survived the desert," he told her.

Slowly, her trembling subsided. The Fremen instincts he had set to work in her did their usual tempering.

"I will survive," she said. She met his gaze. "You read us by our emotions, don't you?"

"The igniters of thought," he said. "I can recognize the slightest behavioural nuance for its emotional origins."

He saw her accept her own nakedness the way Moneo had accepted it, with fear and hate. It was of little matter. He probed the time ahead of them. Yes, she *would* survive his desert because her tracks were in the sand beside him . . . but he saw no sign of her flesh in those tracks. Just beyond her tracks, though, he saw a sudden opening where things had been concealed. Anteac's death shout echoed though his prescient awareness . . . and the swarming of Fish Speakers attacking!

Malky is coming, he thought. *We will meet again, Malky and I.*

Leto opened his outer eyes and saw Siona still there glaring at him.

"I still hate you!" she said.

"You hate the predator's necessary cruelty."

She spoke with venomous elation: "But I saw another thing! You can't follow my tracks!"

"Which is why you must breed and preserve this."

Even as he spoke, it began to rain. The sudden cloud darkness and the downpour came upon them simultaneously. In spite of the fact that he had sensed weather control's oscillations, Leto was shocked by the onslaught. He knew it rained sometimes in the Sareer, a rain quickly dispersed as the water ran off and vanished. The few pools would evaporate as the sun returned. Most times, the downpour never touched the ground; it was ghost rain, vaporized when it hit the superheated air layer just above

376

the desert's surface, then dispersing on the wind. But this rainfall drenched him.

Siona pulled back her face flap and lifted her face greedily to the falling water, not even noticing the effect on Leto.

As the first drenching swept in from behind the sandtrout overlappings, he stiffened and curled into a ball of agony. Separate drives of sandtrout and sandworm produced a new meaning for the word *pain*. He felt that he was being ripped apart. Sandtrout wanted to rush to the water and encapsulate it. Sandworm felt the drenching wash of death. Curls of blue smoke spurted from every place the rain touched him. The inner workings of his body began to manufacture the true spice essence. Blue smoke lifted around him from where he lay in puddles of water. He writhed and groaned.

The clouds passed and it was a few moments before Siona sensed his disturbance.

"What's wrong with you?"

He was unable to answer. The rain was gone but water remained on the rocks and in puddles all around and beneath him. There was no escape.

Siona saw the blue smoke rising from every place the water touched him.

"It's the water!"

There was a slightly higher bulge of land off to the right where the water did not stay. Painfully, he made his way toward it, groaning at each new puddle. The bulge was almost dry when he reached it. The agony subsided slowly and he grew aware that Siona stood directly in front of him. She probed at him with words of false concern.

"Why does water hurt you?"

Hurt? What an inadequate word! There was no evading her questions, though. She knew enough now to go searching for the answer. That answer could be found. Haltingly, he explained the relationship of sandtrout and sandworm to water. She heard him out in silence.

"But the moisture you gave me . . ."

"Is buffered and masked by the spice."

"Then why do you risk it out here without your cart?"

"You can't be a Fremen in the Citadel or on a cart."

She nodded.

He saw the flame of rebellion return to her eyes. She did not have to feel guilty or dependent. She no longer could avoid belief in his Golden Path, but what difference did that make? His cruelties could not be forgiven! She could reject him, deny him a place in her family. He was not a human, not like her at all. And she possessed the secret of his undoing! Ring him with water, destroy his desert, immobilize him within a moat of agony! Did she think she hid her thoughts from him by turning away?

And what can I do about it? he wondered. *She must live now while I must demonstrate non-violence.*

Now that he knew something of Siona's nature, how easy it would be to surrender, to sink blindly into his own thoughts. It was seductive, this temptation to live only within his memories, but his *children* still required another lesson-by-example if they were to escape the last threat to the Golden Path.

What a painful decision! He experienced a new sympathy for the Bene Gesserit. His quandary was akin to the one they had experienced when they had confronted the fact of Muad'Dib. *The ultimate goal of their breeding programme —my father—they could not contain him, either.*

Once more unto the breach, dear friends, he thought, and he suppressed a wry smile at his own histrionics.

> Given enough time for the generations to evolve, the predator produces particular survival adaptations in its prey which, through the circular operation of feedback, produce changes in the predator which again change the prey, etcetera, etcetera, etcetera . . . Many powerful forces do the same thing. You can count religions among such forces.

> —The Stolen Journals

"The Lord has commanded me to tell you that your daughter lives."

Nayla delivered the message to Moneo in a singsong voice, looking down across the workroom table at his figure seated there amidst a chaos of notes and papers and communications instruments.

Moneo pressed his palms together firmly and looked down at the elongated shadow drawn on his table by late afternoon sunlight across the jewelled tree of his paperweight.

Without looking up at Nayla's stocky figure standing at proper attention in front of him, he asked: "Both of them have returned to the Citadel?"

"Yes."

Moneo looked out of the window to his left, not really seeing the flinty borderline of darkness hanging on the Sareer's horizon nor the greedy wind collecting sand grains from every dunetop.

"That matter which we discussed earlier?" he asked.

"It has been arranged."

"Very well." He waved to dismiss her, but Nayla remained standing in front of him. Surprised, Moneo actually focused on her for the first time since she had entered.

"Is it required that I personally attend this . . ." she swallowed, ". . . wedding?"

"The Lord Leto has commanded it. You will be the only one there armed with a lasgun. It is an honour."

She remained in position, her gaze fixed somewhere over Moneo's head.

"Yes?" he prompted.

Nayla's great lantern jaw worked convulsively, then: "He is God and I am mortal." She turned on one heel and left the workroom.

Moneo wondered vaguely what was bothering that hulking Fish Speaker, but his thoughts turned like a compass arrow to Siona.

She has survived as I did. Siona now had an inner sense which told her that the Golden Path remained unbroken.

As I have. He found no sense of sharing in this, nothing to make him feel closer to his daughter. It was a burden and it would inevitably curb her rebellious nature. No Atreides could go against the Golden Path. Leto had seen to that!

Moneo remembered his own rebel days. Every night a new bed and the constant urge to run. The cobwebs of his past clung to his mind, sticking there no matter how hard he tried to shake away troublesome memories.

Siona has been caged. As I was caged. As poor Leto was caged.

The tolling of the nightfall bell intruded on his thoughts and activated his workroom's lights. He looked down at the work still undone in preparation for the God Emperor's wedding to Hwi Noree. So much work! Presently, he pressed a call button and asked the Fish Speaker acolyte who appeared at the summons to bring him a tumbler of water and then call Duncan Idaho to the workroom.

She returned quickly with the water and placed the tumbler near his left hand on the table. He noted the long fingers, a lute-player's fingers, but did not look up at her face.

"I have sent someone for Idaho," she said.

He nodded and went on with his work. He heard her leave and only then did he look up to drink the water.

Some live lives like summer moths, he thought. *But I have burdens without end.*

The water tasted flat. It weighed down his senses, making his body feel torpid. He looked out at the sunset colours on the Sareer as they shaded away into darkness, thinking that he should recognize beauty in that familiar scene, but all he could think was that the light changed in its own patterns. *It is not moved by me at all.*

With the full darkness, the light level of his workroom increased automatically, bringing a clarity of thought with it. He felt himself quite prepared for Idaho. This one had to be taught the necessities, and quickly.

Moneo's door opened, the acolyte again. "Will you eat now?"

"Later." He raised a hand as she started to leave. "I would like the door left open."

She frowned.

"You may practise your music," he said. "I want to listen."

She had a smooth, round, almost childlike face which became radiant when she smiled. The smile still on her lips, she turned away.

Presently, he heard the sounds of a biwa lute in the outer office. Yes, that young acolyte had a talent. The bass strings were like rain drumming on a rooftop, a whisper of middle strings underneath. Perhaps she could move up to the baliset someday. He recognized the song: a deeply humming memory of autumn wind from some far away planet where they had never known a desert. Sad music, pitiful music, yet marvellous.

It is the cry of the caged, he thought. *The memory of freedom.* This thought struck him as odd. Was it always the case that freedom required rebellion?

The lute fell silent. There came the sound of low voices. Idaho entered the workroom. Moneo watched him enter. A trick of the light gave Idaho a face like a grimacing mask with pitted eyes. Without invitation, he sat down across from Moneo and the trickery was gone. *Just another Duncan.* He had changed into a plain black uniform without insignia.

"I have been asking myself a peculiar question," Idaho said. "I'm glad you summoned me. I want to ask this question of you. What is it, Moneo, that my predecessor did *not* learn?"

Stiff with surprise, Moneo sat up straight. What an un-Duncan question! Could there be a peculiar Tleilaxu difference in this one after all?

"What prompts this question?" Moneo asked.

"I've been thinking like a Fremen."

"You weren't a Fremen."

"Closer to it than you think. Stilgar the Naib once said I

381

was probably born Fremen without knowing it until I came to Dune."

"What happens when you think like a Fremen?"

"You remember that you should never be in company that you wouldn't want to die with."

Moneo put his hands palms down on the surface of his table. A wolfish smile came over Idaho's face.

"Then what are you doing here?" Moneo asked.

"I suspect that you may be good company, Moneo. And I ask myself why Leto would choose you as his closest companion?"

"I passed his test."

"The same one your daughter passed?"

So he has heard they are back. It meant some of the Fish Speakers were reporting things to him . . . unless the God Emperor had summoned the Duncan . . . *No, I would have heard.*

"The tests are never identical," Moneo said. "I was made to go alone into a cavern maze with nothing but a bag of food and a vial of spice essence."

"Which did you choose?"

"What? Oh . . . if you are tested you will learn."

"There's a Leto I don't know," Idaho said.

"Have I not told you this?"

"And there's a Leto you don't know," Idaho said.

"Because he's the loneliest person this universe has ever seen," Moneo said.

"Don't play mood games trying to arouse my sympathy," Idaho said.

"Mood games, yes. That's very good." Moneo nodded. "The God Emperor's moods are like a river—smooth where nothing obstructs him, foaming and violent at the least suggestion of a barrier. He is not to be obstructed."

Idaho looked around at the brightly lighted workroom, turned his gaze to the outside darkness and thought about the tamed course of the *Idaho* River somewhere out there. Bringing his attention back to Moneo, he asked: "What do you know of rivers?"

"In my youth I travelled for him. I have even trusted my life to a floating shell of a vessel on a river and then on a sea whose shores were lost in the crossing."

As he spoke, Moneo felt that he had brushed against a clue to some deep truth in the Lord Leto. The sensation dropped Moneo into reverie, thinking of that far planet where he had crossed a sea from one shore to another. There had been a storm on the first evening of that passage and, somewhere deep within the ship, an irritating non-directional "sug-sug-sug-sug-sug" of labouring engines. He had stood on deck with the captain. His mind had kept focusing on the engine sound, retreating and coming back to it like the oversurging of the watery green-black mountains which passed and came, repeating and repeating. Each down crash of the keel opened the sea's flesh like a fist smashing. It was insane motion, a sodden shaking, up . . . up, down! His lungs had ached with repressed fear. The lunging of the ship and the sea trying to put them down—wild explosions of solid water, hour after hour, white blisters of water spilling off the decks, then another sea and another . . .

All of this was a clue to the God Emperor.

He is both the storm and the ship.

Moneo focused on Idaho seated across the table from him in the workroom's cold light. Not a tremor in the man, but a hungering was there.

"So you will not help me learn what the other Duncan Idahos did not learn," Idaho said.

"But I will help you."

"Then what have I always failed to learn?"

"How to trust."

Idaho pushed himself back from the table and glared at Moneo. When Idaho's voice came, it was harsh and rasping: "I'd say I trusted too much."

Moneo was implacable. "But how do you trust?"

"What do you mean?"

Moneo put his hands in his lap. "You choose male companions for their ability to fight and die on the side of

right as you see it. You choose females who can comple-
ment this masculine view of yourself. You allow for no
differences which can come from good will."

Something moved in the doorway to Moneo's workroom. He looked up in time to see Siona enter. She
stopped, one hand on her hip.

"Well, father, up to your old tricks, I see."

Idaho jerked around to stare at the speaker.

Moneo studied her, looking for signs of the change. She
had bathed and put on a fresh uniform, the black and gold
of Fish Speaker command, but her face and hands still
betrayed the evidence of her desert ordeal. She had lost
weight and her cheekbones stood out. Unguent did little to
conceal cracks in her lips. Veins stood out on her hands.
Her eyes looked ancient and her expression was that of
someone who had tasted bitter dregs.

"I've been listening to you two," she said. She dropped
her hand from her hip and moved farther into the room.
"How dare you speak of good will, father?"

Idaho had noted the uniform. He pursed his lips in
thought. *Fish Speaker command? Siona?*

"I understand your bitterness," Moneo said. "I had
similar feelings once."

"Did you really?" She came closer, stopping just beside
Idaho who continued to regard her with a look of specu-
lation.

"I am filled with joy to see you alive," Moneo said.

"How gratifying for you to see me safely into the God
Emperor's service," she said. "You waited so long to have
a child and look! See how successful I am." She turned
slowly to display her uniform. "Commander of the Fish
Speakers. A commander with a troop of one, but nonethe-
less a commander."

Moneo forced his voice to be cold and professional. "Sit
down."

"I prefer to stand." She looked down at Idaho's upturned face. "Ahhh, Duncan Idaho, my intended mate.
Don't you find this interesting, Duncan? The Lord Leto

tells me I will be *fitted into* the command structure of the Fish Speakers in time. Meanwhile, I have one attendant. Do you know the one called Nayla, Duncan?"

Idaho nodded.

"Really? I think perhaps I *don't* know her." Siona looked at Moneo. "Do I know her, father?"

Moneo shrugged.

"But you speak of trust, father," Siona said. "Who does the powerful minister, Moneo, trust?"

Idaho turned to see the effect of these words on the majordomo. The man's face appeared brittle with repressed emotion. *Anger? No . . . something else.*

"I trust the God Emperor," Moneo said. "And, in the hope that it will teach both of you something, I am here to convey his wishes to you."

"His *wishes*!" Siona taunted. "Hear that, Duncan? The God Emperor's commands are now *wishes*."

"Speak your piece," Idaho said. "I know we have little choice in whatever it is."

"You always have a choice," Moneo said.

"Don't listen to him," Siona said. "He's full of tricks. They expect us to fall into each other's arms and breed more like my father. Your descendant, my father!"

Moneo's face went pale. He gripped the edge of his worktable with both hands and leaned forward. "You are both fools! But I will try to save you. In spite of yourselves, I will try to save you."

Idaho saw Moneo's cheeks tremble, the intensity of the man's stare, and felt oddly moved by this. "I'm not his stud, but I'll listen to you."

"Always a mistake," Siona said.

"Be still, woman," Idaho said.

She glared at the top of Idaho's head. "Don't address me that way or I'll wrap your neck around your ankles!"

Idaho stiffened and started to turn.

Moneo grimaced and waved a hand for Idaho to remain seated. "I caution you, Duncan, that she could probably do it. I am no match for her and you do recall your attempt at

385

violence against me?"

Idaho inhaled a deep, quick breath, let it out slowly, then: "Say what you have to say."

Siona moved to perch at the end of Moneo's table and looked down at both of them. "Much better," she said. "Let him have his say but don't listen."

Idaho pressed his lips tightly together.

Moneo released his grip on the edge of his desk. He sat back and looked from Idaho to Siona. "I have almost completed the arrangements for the God Emperor's wedding to Hwi Noree. During those festivities, I want you both out of the way."

Siona turned a questioning look on Moneo. "Your idea or his?"

"Mine!" Moneo returned his daughter's glare. "Have you no sense of honour and duty? Have you learned nothing from being with him?"

"Oh, I learned what you learned, father. And I gave my word, which I will keep."

"Then you'll command the Fish Speakers?"

"Whenever he *trusts* me with command. You know, father, he's ever so much more devious than you are."

"Where are you sending us?" Idaho asked.

"Provided we agree to go," Siona said.

"There is a small village of Museum Fremen at the edge of the Sareer," Moneo said. "It is called Tuono. The village is relatively pleasant. It's in the shadow of the Wall with the river just beyond the Wall. There is a well and the food is good."

Tuono? Idaho wondered. The name sounded familiar. "There was a Tuono Basin on the way to Sietch Tabr," he said.

"And the nights are long and there's no entertainment," Siona said.

Idaho shot a sharp glance at her. She returned it. "He wants us breeding and the Worm satisfied," she said. "He wants babies in my belly, new lives to warp and twist. I'll see him dead before I'll give him that!"

Idaho looked back at Moneo with a bemused expression. "And if we refuse to go?"

"I think you'll go," Moneo said.

Siona's lips twitched. "Duncan, have you ever seen one of these little villages? No comforts, no . . ."

"I have seen Tabur Village," Idaho said.

"I'm sure that is a metropolis beside Tuono. Our God Emperor would not celebrate his nuptials in any cluster of mud hovels! Oh, no. Tuono will be mud hovels and no amenities, as close to the original Fremen as possible."

Idaho kept his attention on Moneo while speaking: "Fremen did not live in mud huts."

"Who cares where they conducted their cultish games?" she sneered.

Still looking at Moneo, Idaho said: "Real Fremen had only one cult, the cult of personal honesty. I worry more about honesty than about comfort."

"Don't expect comfort from me!" Siona snapped.

"I don't expect anything from you," Idaho said. "When would we leave for this Tuono, Moneo?"

"You're going?" she asked.

"I am considering an acceptance of your father's kindness," Idaho said.

"Kindness!" She looked from Idaho to Moneo.

"You would leave immediately," Moneo said. "I have detailed a detachment of Fish Speakers under Nayla to escort you and provide for you at Tuono."

"Nayla?" Siona asked. "Really? Will she stay with us there?"

"Until the day of the wedding."

Siona nodded slowly. "Then we accept."

"Accept for yourself!" Idaho snapped.

Siona smiled. "Sorry. May I formally request that the great Duncan Idaho join me at this primitive garrison where he will keep his hands off my person?"

Idaho peered up at her from under his brows. "Have no fears about where I will put my hands." He looked at

Moneo. "Are you being kind, Moneo? Is that why you're sending me away?"

"It's a question of trust," Siona said. "Who does he trust?"

"Will I be forced to go with your daughter?" Idaho insisted.

Siona stood. "We either accept or the troopers will bind us and carry us out there in a most uncomfortable fashion. You can see it in his face."

"So I really have no choice," Idaho said.

"You have the choice anyone has," Siona said. "Die now or later."

Still, Idaho stared at Moneo. "Your real intentions, Moneo? Won't you satisfy my curiosity?"

"Curiosity has kept many people alive when all else failed," Moneo said. "I am trying to keep you alive, Duncan. I have never done that before."

> *It required almost a thousand years before the dust of Dune's old planet-wide desert left the atmosphere to be bound up in soil and water. The wind called* sandblaster *has not been seen on Arrakis for some twenty-five hundred years. Twenty billion tons of dust could be carried suspended in the wind of just one of those storms. The sky often had a silvery look to it then. Fremen said: "The desert is a surgeon cutting away the skin to expose what's underneath." The planet and the people had layers. You could see them. My Sareer is but a weak echo of what was. I must be the* sandblaster *today.*

> **—The Stolen Journals**

"You sent them to Tuono without consulting me? How surprising of you, Moneo! You've not done such an independent thing in a long while."

Moneo stood about ten paces from Leto in the gloomy centre of the crypt, head bowed, using every artifice he knew to keep from trembling, aware that even this could be

388

seen and interpreted by the God Emperor. It was almost midnight. Leto had kept his majordomo waiting and waiting.

"I pray I have not offended my Lord," Moneo said.

"You have amused me, but take no heart from that. Lately, I cannot separate the comic from the sad."

"Forgive me, Lord," Moneo whispered.

"What is this forgiveness you ask? Must you always require judgment? Can't your universe merely *be*?"

Moneo lifted his gaze to that awful cowled face. *He is both ship and storm. The sunset exists in itself.* Moneo felt that he stood on the brink of terrifying revelations. The God Emperor's eyes bored into him, burning, probing. "Lord, what would you have of me?"

"That you have faith in yourself."

Feeling that something might explode in him, Moneo said: "Then the fact that I did not consult you before . . ."

"How enlightened of you, Moneo! Small souls who seek power over others first destroy the faith those others might have in themselves."

The words were shattering to Moneo. He sensed accusation in them, confession. He felt his hold on a fearsome but infinitely desirable thing weakening. He tried to find words to call it back but his mind remained blank. Perhaps if he asked the God Emperor . . .

"Lord, if you would but tell me your thoughts on . . ."

"My thoughts vanish on contact!"

Leto stared down at Moneo. How strange were the majordomo's eyes perched there above that hawkish Atreides nose—free verse eyes in a metronome face. Did Moneo hear that rhythmic pulse beat: *Malky is coming! Malky is coming! Malky is coming!*?

Moneo wanted to cry out in anguish. The thing he had felt—all gone! He put both hands over his mouth.

"Your universe is a two-dimensional hourglass," Leto accused. "Why do you try to hold back the sand?"

Moneo lowered his hands and sighed. "Do you wish to

hear about the wedding arrangements, Lord?"

"Don't be tiresome! Where is Hwi?"

"The Fish Speakers are preparing her for . . ."

"Have you consulted her about the arrangements?"

"Yes, Lord."

"She approved?"

"Yes, Lord, but she accused me of living for the quantity of activity and not for the quality."

"Isn't she marvellous, Moneo? Does she see the unrest among the Fish Speakers?"

"I think so, Lord."

"The idea of my marriage disturbs them."

"It's why I sent the Duncan away, Lord."

"Of course it is, and Siona with him to . . ."

"Lord, I know you have tested her and she . . ."

"She senses the Golden Path as deeply as you do, Moneo."

"Then why do I fear her, Lord?"

"Because you raise reason above all else."

"But I do not know the reason for my fear!"

Leto smiled. This was like playing bubble dice in an infinite bowl. Moneo's emotions were a marvellous play performed only on this stage. How near the edge he walked without ever seeing it!

"Moneo, why do you insist on taking pieces out of the continuum?" Leto asked. "When you see a spectrum, do you desire one colour there above all the others?"

"Lord, I don't understand you!"

Leto closed his eyes, remembering the countless times he had heard this cry. The faces were an unseparated blend. He opened his eyes to erase them.

"As long as one human remains alive to see them, the colours will not suffer a linear *mortis* even if you die, Moneo."

"What is this thing of colours, Lord?"

"The continuum, the never-ending, the Golden Path."

"But you see things which we do not, Lord!"

"Because you refuse!"

Moneo sank his chin to his chest. "Lord, I know you have evolved beyond the rest of us. That is why we worship you and . . ."

"Damn you, Moneo!"

Moneo jerked his head up and stared at Leto in terror.

"Civilizations collapse when their powers outrun their religions!" Leto said. "Why can't you see this? Hwi does."

"She is Ixian, Lord. Perhaps she . . ."

"She's a Fish Speaker! She has been from birth, born to serve me. No!" Leto raised one of his tiny hands as Moneo tried to speak. "The Fish Speakers are disturbed because I called them my brides, and now they see a stranger not trained in Siaynoq who knows it better than they."

"How can that be, Lord, when your Fish . . ."

"What are you saying? Each of us comes into being knowing who he is and what he is supposed to do."

Moneo opened his mouth but closed it without speaking.

"Small children know," Leto said. "It's only after adults have confused them that children hide this knowledge even from themselves. Moneo! Uncover yourself!"

"Lord, I cannot!" The words were torn from Moneo. He trembled with anguish. "I do not have your powers, your knowledge of . . ."

"Enough!"

Moneo fell silent. His body shook.

Leto spoke soothingly to him. "It's all right, Moneo. I ask too much of you and I can see your fatigue."

Slowly, Moneo's trembling subsided. He drew in deep, gulping breaths.

Leto said: "There will be some change in my Fremen wedding. We will not use the water rings of my sister, Ghanima. We will use, instead, the rings of my mother."

"The Lady Chani, Lord? But where are her rings?"

Leto twisted his bulk on the cart and pointed to the intersection of two cavernous spokes on his left where the dim light revealed the earliest burial niches of the Atreides on Arrakis. "In her tomb, the first niche. You will remove those rings, Moneo, and bring them to the ceremony."

Moneo stared across the gloomy distance of the crypt. "Lord . . . is it not a desecration to . . ."

"You forget, Moneo, who lives in me." He spoke then in Chani's voice: "I can do what I want with my water rings!"

Moneo cowered. "Yes, Lord. I will bring them with me to Tabur Village when . . ."

"Tabur Village?" Leto asked in his usual voice. "But I have changed my mind. We will be wed at Tuono Village!"

> *Most civilization is based on cowardice. It's so easy to civilize by teaching cowardice. You water down the standards which would lead to bravery. You restrain the will. You regulate the appetites. You fence in the horizons. You make a law for every movement. You deny the existence of chaos. You teach even the children to breathe slowly. You tame.*
>
> **—The Stolen Journals**

Idaho stood aghast at his first close glimpse of Tuono Village. *That* was the home of Fremen?

The Fish Speaker troop had taken them from the Citadel at daybreak, Idaho and Siona bundled into a large ornithopter accompanied by two smaller guard ships. And the flight had been slow, almost three hours. They had landed at a flat, round plastone hangar almost a kilometre from the village, separated from it by old dunes locked in shape with plantings of poverty grasses and a few scrubby bushes. As they came down, the wall directly behind the village had seemed to grow taller and taller, the village shrinking beneath such immensity.

"The Museum Fremen are kept generally uncontaminated by off-planet technology," Nayla had explained as the escort sealed the 'thopters into the low hangar. One of the troop already had been sent trotting off toward Tuono with the annoucement of their arrival.

Siona had remained mostly silent all during the flight, but she had studied Nayla with covert intensity.

For a time during the march across the morning-lighted dunes, Idaho had tried to imagine that he was back in the old days. Sand was visible in the plantings and, in the valleys between dunes, there was parched ground, yellow grass, the stick-like shrubs. Three vultures, their gap-tipped wings spread wide, circled in the vault of sky—"the soaring search", Fremen had called it. Idaho had tried to explain this to Siona walking beside him. You worried about the carrion-eaters only when they began to descend.

"I have been told about vultures," she said, her voice cold.

Idaho had noted the perspiration on her upper lip. There was a spicy smell of sweat in the troop pressed close around them.

His imagination was not equal to the task of defocusing the differences between the past and this time. The issue stillsuits they wore were more for show than for efficient collection of the body's water. No true Fremen would have trusted his life to one of them, not even here where the air smelled of nearby water. And the Fish Speakers of Nayla's troop did not walk in Fremen silence. They chattered among themselves like children.

Siona trudged beside him in sullen withdrawal, her attention frequently on the broad muscular back of Nayla who strode along a few paces ahead of the troop.

What was between these two women? Idaho wondered. Nayla appeared devoted to Siona, hanging on Siona's every word, obeying every whim Siona uttered . . . except that Nayla would not deviate from the orders which brought them to Tuono Village. Still, Nayla deferred to Siona and called her "Commander". There was something deep between those two, something which aroused awe and fear in Nayla.

They came at last to a slope which dropped down to the village and the wall behind it. From the air, Tuono had been a cluster of glittering rectangles just outside the shadow of the wall. From this close vantage, though, it had been reduced to a cluster of decaying huts made even more pitiful by attempts to decorate the place. Bits of shiny materials and scraps of metal picked out scroll designs on the building walls. A tattered green banner fluttered from a metal pole atop the largest structure. A fitful breeze brought the smell of garbage and uncovered cesspools to Idaho's nostrils. The central street of the village extended out across the sparsely planted sand toward the troop, ending in a ragged edge of broken paving.

A robed delegation waited near the building of the green flag, standing there expectantly with the Fish Speaker messenger Nayla had sent on ahead. Idaho counted eight in the delegation, all men in what appeared to be authentic Fremen robes of dark brown. A green headband could be glimpsed beneath the hood on one of the delegation—the Naib, no doubt. Children waited to one side with flowers. Black-hooded women could be seen peering from side-streets in the background. Idaho found the whole scene distressing.

"Let's get it over with," Siona said.

Nayla nodded and led the way down the slope on to the street. Siona and Idaho stayed a few paces behind her. The rest of the troop straggled along after them, silent now and peering around with undisguised curiosity.

As Nayla neared the delegation, the one with the green headband stepped forward and bowed. He moved like an old man but Idaho saw that he was not old, barely into his middle years, the cheeks smooth and unwrinkled, a stubby nose with no scars from breath-filter tubes, and the eyes! The eyes revealed definite pupils, not the all-blue of spice addiction. They were brown eyes. Brown eyes in a Fremen!

"I am Garun," the man said as Nayla stopped in front of him. "I am Naib of this place. I give you a Fremen welcome to Tuono."

Nayla gestured over her shoulder at Siona and Idaho who had stopped just behind her. "Are quarters prepared for your guests?"

"We Fremen are noted for our hospitality," Garun said. "All is ready."

Idaho sniffed at the sour smells and sounds of this place. He glanced through open windows of the flag-topped building on his right. The Atreides banner flying over that? The window opened into an auditorium with low ceiling, a bandshell at the far end enclosing a small platform. He saw rows of seats, maroon carpeting on the floor. It had all the look of a stage setting, a place to entertain tourists.

The sound of shuffling feet brought Idaho's attention back to Garun. Children were pressing forward around the delegation, extending clumps of garish red flowers in their grimy hands. The flowers were wilted.

Garun addressed himself to Siona, correctly identifying the gold piping of Fish Speaker Command in her uniform.

"Will you wish a performance of our Fremen rituals?" he asked. "The music, perhaps? The dance?"

Nayla accepted a bunch of flowers from one of the children, sniffed them and sneezed.

Another urchin extended flowers toward Siona, lifting a wide-eyed stare toward her. She accepted the flowers without looking at the child. Idaho merely waved the children aside as they approached him. They hesitated, staring up at him, then scurried around him toward the rest of the troop.

Garun spoke to Idaho. "If you give them a few coins they will not bother you."

Idaho shuddered. Was this the training for Fremen children?

Garun returned his attention to Siona. With Nayla listening, Garun began explaining the layout of his village.

Idaho moved away from them down the street, noting how glances flicked toward him and then avoided his gaze. He felt deeply offended by the surface decorations on the buildings, none of it disguising the evidence of decay. He stared in through an open doorway at the auditorium. There was a harshness in Tuono, a struggling *something* behind the wilting flowers and the servile tone of Garun's voice. In another time and on another planet, this would have been a donkey-in-the-street village—rope-belted peasants pressing forward with petitions. He could hear the whine of supplication in Garun's voice. These were not Fremen! These poor creatures lived on the margins, trying to retain parts of an ancient wholeness. And all the while, that lost reality slipped farther and farther from their grasp. What had Leto created here? These *Museum* Fremen were lost to everything except a bare existence and the rote mouthing of old words which they did not understand and which they did not even pronounce correctly!

Returning to Siona, Idaho bent to study the cut of Garun's brown robe, seeing a tightness in it dictated by a need to conserve fabric. The grey slick of a stillsuit could be seen underneath, exposed to sunlight which no real Fremen would ever have let touch his stillsuit that way. Idaho looked at the rest of the delegation, noting an identical parsimonious treatment of fabric. It betrayed their emotional bent. Such garments allowed no expansive gestures, no freedom of movement. The robes were tight and confining in the way of these entire people!

Disgust propelling him, Idaho strode forward abruptly and parted Garun's robe to look at the stillsuit. Just as he had suspected! The suit was another sham—no arms on it, no boot-pumps!

Garun pulled back, putting a hand to the knife hilt Idaho had exposed at the man's belt. "Here! What're you doing?" Garun demanded, his voice querulous. "You don't touch a Fremen thus!"

"You, a Fremen?" Idaho demanded. "I lived with Fremen! I fought by their sides against Harkonnens! I died with Fremen! You? You're a sham!"

Garun's knuckles went white on the knife haft. He addressed himself to Siona. "Who is this man?"

Nayla spoke up: "This is Duncan Idaho."

"The ghola?" Garun turned to look at Idaho's face. "We have never seen your like here before."

Idaho felt himself almost overcome by a sudden desire to cleanse this place even if it cost him his life, this diminished life which could be repeated endlessly by people who had no real concern for him. *An older model, yes!* But this was no Fremen.

"Draw that knife or take your hand off it," Idaho said.

Garun jerked his hand away from the knife. "It is not a real knife," he said. "Only for decoration." His voice became eager. "But we have real knives, even crysknives! They are kept locked in the display cases to preserve them."

Idaho could not help himself. He threw his head back in laughter. Siona smiled, but Nayla looked thoughtful and the rest of the Fish Speaker troop drew into a close, watchful circle around them.

The laughter had an odd effect on Garun. He lowered his head and clasped his hands tightly together, but not before Idaho saw them trembling. When Garun peered upward once more, it was to look at Idaho from beneath heavy brows. Idaho felt abruptly sobered. It was as though some terrible boot had crushed Garun's ego into fearful subservience. There was watchful waiting in the man's eyes. And for no reason he could explain, Idaho remembered a passage from the Orange Catholic Bible. He asked himself: *Are these the meek who will outwait us all and inherit the universe?*

Garun cleared his throat, then: "Perhaps the ghola Duncan Idaho will witness our ways and our ritual and judge them?"

Idaho felt ashamed by the plaintive request. He spoke without thinking: "I will teach you anything Fremen that I know." He looked up to see Nayla scowling at him. "It will help to pass the time," he said. "And who knows? It may return something of the true Fremen to this land."

Siona said: "We've no need to play old cultish games! Take us to our quarters."

Nayla lowered her head in embarrassment and spoke without looking at Siona. "Commander, there is a thing I have not ventured to tell you."

"That you must make sure we stay in this filthy place," Siona said.

"Oh, no!" Nayla looked up at Siona's face. "Where could you go? The Wall cannot be climbed and there is only the river beyond it, anyway. And in the other direction, it is the Sareer. Oh, no . . . it is something else." Nayla shook her head.

"Out with it!" Siona snapped.

"I am under the strictest orders, Commander, which I dare not disobey." Nayla glanced at the other members of the troop then back to Siona. "You and the . . . Duncan Idaho are to be quartered together."

"My father's orders?"

"Lady Commander, they are said to be the orders of the God Emperor himself and we dare not disobey."

Siona looked full at Idaho. "You will remember my warning, Duncan, when last we spoke at the Citadel?"

"My hands are mine to do with as I wish," Idaho snarled. "I don't think you have any doubts about my wishes!"

She turned away from him after a curt nod and looked at Garun. "What does it matter where we bed in this disgusting place? Take us to our quarters."

Idaho found Garun's response fascinating—a turning of the head toward the ghola, shielding the face behind the Fremen hood, then a secret conspiratorial wink. Only then did Garun lead them away down the dirty street.

What is the most immediate danger to my stewardship? I will tell you. It is a true visionary, a person who has stood in the presence of God with the full knowledge of where he stands. Visionary ecstasy releases energies which are like the energies of sex—uncaring for anything except creation. One act of creation can be much like another. Everything depends upon the vision.

—The Stolen Journals

Leto lay without his cart on the high, sheltered balcony of his Little Citadel tower, subduing a fretfulness which he

398

knew came from the necessary delays putting off the date of his wedding to Hwi Noree. He stared toward the south-west. Somewhere off there beyond the darkening horizon, the Duncan, Siona and their companions had been six days in Tuono Village.

The delays are my own fault, Leto thought. *I am the one who changed the place for the wedding, making it necessary for poor Moneo to revise all of his preparations.*

And now, of course, there was the matter of Malky.

None of these necessities could be explained to Moneo, who could be heard stirring about within the central chamber of the aerie, worrying about his absence from the command post where he directed the *festive* preparations. Moneo was such a worrier!

Leto looked toward the setting sun. It floated low to the horizon, faded a dim orange by a recent storm. Rain crouched low in the clouds to the south beyond the Sareer now. In a prolonged silence, Leto had watched the rain there for a time which had stretched out with no beginning or end. The clouds had grown out of a hard grey sky, rain walking in visible lines. He had felt himself clothed in memories that came unbidden. The mood was hard to shake off and, without even thinking, he muttered the remembered lines of an ancient verse.

"Did you speak, Lord?" Moneo's voice came from close beside Leto. By merely turning his eyes, Leto could see the faithful majordomo standing attentively waiting.

Leto translated into Galach as he quoted: "The night-ingale nests in the plum tree, but what will she do with the wind?"

"Is that a question, Lord?"

"An old question. The answer is simple. Let the night-ingale keep to her flowers."

"I don't understand, Lord."

"Stop mouthing the obvious, Moneo. It disturbs me when you do that."

"Forgive me, Lord."

"What else can I do?" Leto studied Moneo's downcast

features. "You and I, Moneo, whatever else we do, we provide good theatre."

Moneo peered at Leto's face. "Lord?"

"The rites of the religious festival of Bacchus were the seeds of Greek theatre, Moneo. Religion often leads to theatre. They will have fine theatre out of us." Once more, Leto turned and looked at the southwest horizon.

There was a wind there now piling up the clouds. Leto thought he could hear driven sand blustering along the dunes, but there was only resonant quiet in the tower aerie, a quiet with the faintest of wind hiss behind it.

"The clouds," he whispered. "I would take a cup of moonlight once more, an ancient sea marge at my feet, thin clouds clinging to my darkling sky, the blue-grey cloak around my shoulders and horses neighing nearby."

"My Lord is troubled," Moneo said. The compassion in his voice wrenched at Leto.

"The bright shadows of my pasts," Leto said. "They never leave me in peace. I listened for a soothing sound, the bell of a country town at nightfall, and it told only that I am the sound and soul of this place."

As he spoke, darkness enclosed the tower. Automatic lights came on around them. Leto kept his attention directed outward where a thin melon slice of First Moon drifted above the clouds with orange planet-light revealing the satellite's full circle.

"Lord, why have we come out here?" Moneo asked. "Why won't you tell me?"

"I wanted the benefit of your surprise," Leto said. "A Guild lighter will land beside us out here soon. My Fish Speakers bring Malky to me."

Moneo inhaled a quick breath and held it a moment before exhaling. "Hwi's . . . uncle? That Malky?"

"You are surprised that you had no warning of this," Leto said.

Moneo felt a chill all through his body. "Lord, when you wish to keep things secret from . . ."

"Moneo?" Leto spoke in a softly persuasive tone. "I

400

know that Malky offered you greater temptations than any other . . ."

"Lord! I never . . ."

"I know that, Moneo." Still in that soft tone. "But surprise has shocked your memories alive. You are armed for anything I may require of you."

"What . . . what does my Lord . . ."

"Perhaps we will have to dispose of Malky. He is a problem."

"Me? You want me to . . ."

"Perhaps."

Moneo swallowed, then: "The Reverend Mother . . ."

"Anteac is dead. She served me well, but she is dead. There was extreme violence when my Fish Speakers attacked the . . . *place* where Malky lay hidden."

"We are better off without Anteac," Moneo said.

"I appreciate your distrust of the Bene Gesserit, but I would that Anteac had left us in another way. She was faithful to us, Moneo."

"A Reverend Mother was . . ."

"Both the Bene Tleilax and the Guild wanted Malky's secret," Leto said. "When they saw us move against the Ixians, they struck ahead of my Fish Speakers. Anteac . . . well, she could only delay them a bit, but it was enough. My Fish Speakers invested the place . . ."

"Malky's *secret,* Lord?"

"When a thing vanishes," Leto said, "that is as much of a message as when a thing suddenly appears. The empty spaces are always worthy of our study."

"What does my Lord mean, *empty* . . ."

"Malky did not die! Certainly I would have known that. Where did he go when he vanished?"

"Vanished . . . from you, Lord? Do you mean that the Ixians . . ."

"They have improved upon a device they gave me long ago. They improved it slowly and subtly, hidden shells within hidden shells, but I noted the shadows. I was surprised. I was pleased."

Moneo thought about this. *A device which concealed . . . Ahhhh!* The God Emperor had mentioned a thing on several occasions, a way of concealing the thoughts he recorded. Moneo spoke:

"And Malky brings the secret of . . ."

"Oh, yes! But that is not Malky's real secret. He holds another thing in his bosom which he does not think that I suspect."

"Another . . . but, Lord, if they can hide even from you . . ."

"Many can do that now, Moneo. They scattered when my Fish Speakers attacked. The secret of the Ixian device is spread far and wide."

Moneo's eyes went wide with alarm. "Lord, if anyone . . ."

"If they learn to be clever, they will leave no tracks," Leto said. "Tell me, Moneo, what does Nayla say about the Duncan? Does she resent reporting directly to you?"

"Whatever my Lord commands . . ." Moneo cleared his throat. He could not fathom why his God Emperor spoke of hidden tracks, the Duncan and Nayla in the same breath.

"Yes, of course," Leto said. "Whatever I command, Nayla obeys. And what does she say of the Duncan?"

"He has not tried to breed with Siona, if that is my Lord's . . ."

"But what does he do with my puppet Naib, Garun, and the other Museum Fremen?"

"He speaks to them of the old ways, of the wars against the Harkonnens, of the first Atreides here on Arrakis."

"On Dune!"

"Dune, yes."

"It's because there's no more Dune that there are no more Fremen," Leto said. "Have you conveyed my message to Nayla?"

"Lord, why do you add to your peril?"

"Did you convey my message?"

"The messenger has been sent to Tuono, but I could still call her back."

"You will *not* call her back!"

"But, Lord . . ."

"What will she say to Nayla?"

"That . . . that it is your command for Nayla to continue in absolute and unquestioning obedience of my daughter except insofar . . . Lord! This is dangerous!"

"Dangerous? Nayla is a Fish Speaker. She will obey me."

"But Siona . . . Lord, I fear that my daughter does not serve you with all of her heart. And Nayla is . . ."

"Nayla must not deviate."

"Lord, let us hold your wedding in some other place."

"No!"

"Lord, I know that your vision has revealed . . ."

"The Golden Path endures, Moneo. You know that as well as I."

Moneo sighed. "Infinity is yours, Lord. I do not question the . . ." He broke off as a monstrous shuddering roar shook the tower, louder and louder.

Both of them turned toward the sound—a descending plume of blue-orange light filled with swirling shockwaves came down to the desert less than a kilometre away to the south.

"Ahhh, my guest arrives," Leto said. "I will send you down on my cart, Moneo. Bring only Malky back with you. Tell the Guildsmen this has earned my forgiveness, then send them away."

"Your for . . . yes, Lord. But if they have the secret of . . ."

"They serve my purpose, Moneo. You must do the same. Bring Malky to me."

Obediently, Moneo went to the cart which lay in shadows at the far side of the aerie chamber. He clambered on it, watched a mouth of night appear in the wall. A landing lip extruded into the night. The cart drifted outward, feather-light, and floated at an angle to the sand beside a Guild lighter which stood upright like a distorted miniature of the Little Citadel's tower.

Leto watched from the balcony, his front segments lifted slightly to provide him a better viewing angle. His acute eyesight identified the white movement of Moneo standing on the cart in the moonlight. Long-legged Guild servitors came out with a litter which they slid on to the cart, standing there a moment in conversation with Moneo. When they left, Leto closed the cart's bubble cover and saw moonlight reflected from it. At his beckoning thought, the cart and its burden returned to the landing lip. The Guild lighter lifted in its noisy rumbling while Leto was bringing the cart into the chamber's lights, closing the entrance behind it. Leto opened the bubble cover. Sand grated beneath him as he rolled to the litter and lifted his front segments to peer in at Malky who lay as though sleeping, lashed into the litter by broad grey elastic bindings. The man's face was ashen under dark grey hair.

How he has aged, Leto thought.

Moneo stepped down off the cart and looked back at the litter's occupant. "He is injured, Lord. They wanted to send a medical . . ."

"They wanted to send a spy."

Leto studied Malky—the dark wrinkled skin, the sunken cheeks, that sharp nose at such contrast with the rounded oval of his face. The heavy eyebrows had turned almost white. There but for a lifetime of testosterone . . . yes.

Malky's eyes opened. Such a shock to find evil in those doe-like brown eyes! A smile twitched Malky's mouth.

"Lord Leto." Malky's voice was little more than a husky whisper. His eyes turned right, focusing on the major-domo. "And Moneo. Forgive me for not rising to the occasion."

"Are you in pain?" Leto asked.

"Sometimes." Malky's eyes moved to study his surroundings. "Where are the houris?"

"I'm afraid I must deny you that pleasure, Malky."

"Just as well," Malky husked. "I don't really feel up to

their demands. Those were not houris you sent after me, Leto."

"They were professional in their obedience to me," Leto said.

"They were bloody hunters!"

"Anteac was the hunter. My Fish Speakers were merely the clean-up crew."

Moneo shifted his attention from one speaker to the other, back and forth. There were disturbing undertones in this conversation. Despite the huskiness, Malky sounded almost flippant . . . but then he had always been that way. A dangerous man!

Leto said: "Just before your arrival, Moneo and I were discussing infinity."

"Poor Moneo," Malky said.

Leto smiled. "Do you remember, Malky? You once asked me to demonstrate infinity."

"You said no infinity exists to be demonstrated." Malky swept his gaze toward Moneo. "Leto likes to play with paradox. He knows all the tricks of language that have ever been discovered."

Moneo put down a surge of anger. He felt excluded from this conversation, an object of amusement by two superior beings. Malky and the God Emperor were almost like two old friends reliving the pleasures of a mutual past.

"Moneo accuses me of being the sole possessor of infinity," Leto said. "He refuses to believe that he has just as much of infinity as I have."

Malky stared up at Leto. "You see, Moneo? You see how tricky he is with words?"

"Tell me about your niece, Hwi Noree," Leto said.

"Is it true, Leto, what they say? That you are going to wed the gentle Hwi?"

"It is true."

Malky chuckled, then grimaced with pain. "They did terrible damage to me, Leto," he whispered, then: "Tell me, old worm . . ."

Moneo gasped.

Malky took a moment to recover from pain, then: "Tell me, old worm, is there a monster penis hidden in that monster body of yours? What a shock for the gentle Hwi!"

"I told you the truth about that long ago," Leto said.

"Nobody tells the truth," Malky husked.

"You often told me the truth," Leto said. "Even when you didn't know it."

"That's because you're cleverer than the rest of us."

"Will you tell me about Hwi?"

"I think you already know it."

"I want to hear it from you," Leto said. "Did you get help from the Tleilaxu?"

"They gave us knowledge, nothing more. Everything else we did for ourselves."

"I thought it was not the Tleilaxu's doing."

Moneo could no longer contain his curiosity. "Lord, what is this of Hwi and Tleilaxu? Why do you . . ."

"Here there, old friend Moneo," Malky said, rolling his gaze toward the majordomo. "Don't you know what he . . ."

"I was never your friend!" Moneo snapped.

"Companion among the houris then," Malky said.

"Lord," Moneo said, turning toward Leto, "why do you speak of . . ."

"Shhhh, Moneo," Leto said. "We are tiring your old companion and I have things to learn from him yet."

"Did you ever wonder, Leto," Malky asked, "why Moneo never tried to take the whole shebang away from you?"

"The *what*?" Moneo demanded.

"Another of Leto's old words," Malky said. "She and bang—shebang. It's perfect. Why don't you rename your Empire, Leto? The Grand Shebang!"

Leto raised a hand to silence Moneo. "Will you tell me, Malky? About Hwi?"

"Just a few tiny cells from my body," Malky said. "Then the carefully nurtured growth and education—everything an exact opposite to your old friend, Malky. We did it all in

406

the no-room where you cannot see!"

"But I notice when something vanishes," Leto said.

"No-room?" Moneo asked, then as the import of Malky's words sank home. "You? You and Hwi . . ."

"That is the shape I saw in the shadows," Leto said.

Moneo looked full at Leto's face. "Lord, I will call off the wedding. I will say . . ."

"You will do nothing of the kind!"

"But Lord, if she and Malky are . . ."

"Moneo," Malky husked. "Your Lord commands and you must obey!"

That mocking tone! Moneo glared at Malky.

"The exact opposite of Malky." Leto said. "Didn't you hear him?"

"What could be better?" Malky asked.

"But surely, Lord, if you now know . . ."

"Moneo," Leto said, "you are beginning to disturb me."

Moneo fell into abashed silence.

Leto said: "That's better. You know, Moneo, once tens of thousands of years ago when I was another person, I made a mistake."

"You, a mistake?" Malky mocked.

Leto merely smiled. "My mistake was compounded by the beautiful way in which I expressed it."

"Tricks with words," Malky taunted.

"Indeed! This is what I said: 'The present is distraction; the future a dream; only memory can unlock the meaning of life.' Aren't those beautiful words, Malky?"

"Exquisite, old worm."

Moneo put a hand over his mouth.

"But my words were a foolish lie," Leto said. "I knew it at the time, but I was infatuated with the *beautiful* words. No—memory unlocks no meanings. Without anguish of the spirit, which is a wordless experience, there are no meanings anywhere."

"I fail to see the meaning of the anguish caused me by your bloody Fish Speakers," Malky said.

"You're suffering no anguish," Leto said.

"If you were in this body you'd . . ."

"That's just physical pain," Leto said. "It will end soon."

"Then when will I know the anguish?" Malky asked.

"Perhaps later."

Leto flexed his front segments away from Malky to face Moneo. "Do you really serve the Golden Path, Moneo?"

"Ahhh, the Golden Path," Malky taunted.

"You know I do, Lord," Moneo said.

"Then you must promise me," Leto said, "that what you have learned here must never pass your lips. Not by word or sign can you reveal it."

"I promise, Lord."

"He promises, Lord," Malky sneered.

One of Leto's tiny hands gestured at Malky, who lay staring up at the blunt profile of a face within its grey cowl. "For reasons of old admiration and . . . many other reasons, I cannot kill Malky. I cannot even ask it of you . . . yet he must be eliminated."

"Ohhh, how clever you are!" Malky said.

"Lord, if you will wait at the other end of the chamber," Moneo said. "Perhaps when you return Malky no longer will be a problem."

"He's going to do it," Malky husked. "Gods below! He's going to do it."

Leto squirmed away and went to the shadowed limit of the chamber, keeping his attention on the faint arc of a line which would become an opening into the night if he merely converted the wish into a thought-of-command. What a long drop that would be out there—just roll off the landing lip. He doubted that even his body would survive it. But there was no water in the sand beneath his tower and he could feel the Golden Path winking in and out of existence merely because he allowed himself to think of such an end.

"Leto!" Malky called from behind him.

Leto heard the litter grating on the wind-scattered sand which peppered the floor of his aerie.

Once more, Malky called: "Leto, you are the best! There's no evil in this universe which can surpass . . ."

A sodden thump shut off Malky's voice. *A blow to the throat,* Leto thought. *Yes, Moneo knows that one.* There came the sound of the balcony's transparent shield sliding open, the rasping of the litter on the rail, then silence.

Moneo will have to bury the body in the sand, Leto thought. *There is as yet no worm to come and devour the evidence.* Leto turned then and looked across the chamber. Moneo stood leaning over the railing, peering down . . . down . . . down . . .

I cannot pray for you, Malky, nor for you, Moneo, Leto thought. *I may be the only religious consciousness in the Empire because I am truly alone . . . so I cannot pray.*

> *You cannot understand history unless you understand its flowings, its currents and the ways leaders move within such forces. A leader tries to perpetuate the conditions which demand his leadership. Thus, the leader requires the out-sider. I caution you to examine my career with care. I am both leader and outsider. Do not make the mistake of assuming that I only created the Church which was the State. That was my function as leader and I had many historical models to use as pattern. For a clue to my role as outsider, look at the arts of my time. The arts are barbaric. The favourite poetry? The Epic. The popular dramatic ideal? Heroism. Dances? Wildly abandoned. From Moneo's viewpoint, he is correct in describing this as dangerous. It stimulates the imagination. It makes people feel the lack of that which I have taken from them. What did I take from them? The right to participate in history.*

> —The Stolen Journals

Idaho, stretched out on his cot with his eyes closed, heard a weight drop on to the other cot. He sat up into the mid-afternoon light which slanted through the room's single window at a sharp angle, reflecting off the white-tiled floor on to the light yellow walls. Siona, he saw, had come in and stretched herself on her cot. She already was reading one of the books she carried around with her in a green fabric pack.

Why books? he wondered.

He swung his feet to the floor and glanced around the room. How could this high-ceilinged, spacious *box* be considered even remotely Fremen? A wide table/desk of some dark brown local plastic separated the two cots. There were two doors. One led directly outside across a garden. The other admitted them to a luxurious bath whose pale blue tiles glistened under a broad skylight. The bath contained, among its many functional services, a sunken tub and a shower, each at least two metres square. The door to this sybaritic space remained open and Idaho could hear water running out of the tub. Siona appeared oddly fond of bathing in an excess of water.

Stilgar, Idaho's Naib of the ancient days on Dune, would have looked on that room with scorn. "Shameful!" he would have said. "Decadent! Weak!" Stilgar would have used many scornful words about this entire village which dared to compare itself with a true Fremen sietch.

Paper rustled as Siona turned a page. She lay with her head propped on two pillows, a thin white robe covering her body. The robe still revealed clinging wetness from her bath.

Idaho shook his head. What was it on those pages which held her interest this way? She had been reading and re-reading since their arrival at Tuono. The volumes were thin but numerous, bearing only numbers on their black bindings. Idaho had seen a number *nine*.

Swinging his feet to the floor, he stood and went to the window. There was an old man out there at a distance digging in flowers. The garden was protected by buildings on three sides. The flowers bore large blossoms—red on the outside but, when they unfolded, white in the centre. The old man's uncovered grey hair was a kind of blossom waving among the floral white and jewelled buds. Idaho smelled mouldering leaves and freshly turned dirt against a

410

background of pungent floral perfume.

A Fremen tending flowers in the open!

Siona volunteered nothing about her strange reading matter. *She's taunting me*, Idaho thought. *She wants me to ask.*

He tried not to think about Hwi. Rage threatened to engulf him when he did. He remembered the Fremen word for that intense emotion: *kanawa*, the iron ring of jealousy. *Where is Hwi? What is she doing at this moment?*

The door from the garden opened without a knock and Teishar, an aide to Garun, entered. Teishar had a dead-coloured face full of dark wrinkles. His eyes were sunken with pale yellow around the pupils. Teishar wore a brown robe. He had hair like old grass that had been left out to rot. He seemed unnecessarily ugly, like a dark and elemental spirit. Teishar closed the door and stood there looking at them.

Siona's voice came from behind Idaho. "Well, what is it?"

Idaho noticed then that Teishar seemed strangely excited, vibrating with it.

"The God Emperor . . ." Teishar cleared his throat and began again. "The God Emperor will come to Tuono!"

Siona sat upright on the bed, folding her white robe over her knees. Idaho glanced back at her, then once more at Teishar.

"He will be wed here, here in Tuono!" Teishar said. "It will be done in the ancient Fremen way! The God Emperor and his bride will be guests of Tuono!"

Full in the grip of *kanawa*, Idaho glared at him, fists clenched. Teishar bobbed his head briefly, turned and let himself out, shutting the door hard.

"Let me read you something, Duncan," Siona said.

Idaho was a moment understanding her words. Fists still clenched at his sides, he turned and looked at her. Siona sat on the edge of her cot, a book in her lap. She took his attention as agreement.

"Some believe," she read, "that you must compromise

411

integrity with a certain amount of dirty work before you can put genius to work. They say the compromise begins when you come out of the *sanctus* intending to realize your ideals. Moneo says my solution is to stay within the *sanctus*, sending others to do my dirty work."

She looked up at Idaho. "The God Emperor—his own words."

Slowly, Idaho relaxed his fists. He knew he needed this distraction. And it interested him that Siona had emerged from her silence.

"What is that book?" he asked.

Briefly, she told him how she and her companions had stolen the Citadel charts and the copies of Leto's journals.

"Of course you knew about that," she said. "My father has made it plain that spies betrayed our raid."

He saw the tears latent in her eyes. "Nine of you killed by the wolves?"

She nodded.

"You're a lousy commander!" he said.

She bristled but before she could speak, he asked: "Who translated them for you?"

"This is from Ix. They say the Guild found the key."

"We already knew our God Emperor indulged in expedience," Idaho said. "Is that all he has to say?"

"Read it for yourself." She rummaged in her pack beside the cot and came up with the first volume of the translation which she tossed across to his cot. As Idaho returned to the cot, she demanded: "What do you mean I'm a lousy commander?"

"Wasting nine of your friends that way."

"You fool!" She shook her head. "You obviously never saw those wolves!"

He picked up the book and found it heavy, realizing then that it had been printed on crystal paper. "You should have armed yourselves against the wolves," he said, opening the volume.

"What arms? Any arms we could get would've been useless!"

"Lasguns?" he asked, turning a page.

"Touch a lasgun on Arrakis and the Worm knows it!"

He turned another page. "Your friends got lasguns eventually."

"And look what it got them!"

Idaho read a line, then: "Poisons were available."

She swallowed convulsively.

Idaho looked at her. "You did poison them after all, didn't you?"

Her voice was almost a whisper: "Yes."

"Then why didn't you do that in advance?" he asked.

"We . . . didn't . . . know . . . we . . . could."

"But you didn't test it," Idaho said. He turned back to the open volume. "A lousy commander."

"He's so devious!" Siona said.

Idaho read a passage in the volume before returning his attention to Siona. "That hardly begins to describe him. Have you read all of this?"

"Every word! Some of them several times."

Idaho looked at the open page and read aloud: "I have created what I intended—a powerful spiritual tension throughout my Empire. Few sense the strength of it. With what energies did I create this condition? I am not that strong. The only power I possess is the control of individual prosperity. That is the sum of all the things I do. Then why do people seek my presence for other reasons? What could lead them to certain death in the futile attempt to reach my presence? Do they want to be saints? Do they think that *thus* they gain the vision of God?"

"He's the ultimate cynic," Siona said, tears apparent in her voice.

"How did he test you?" Idaho asked.

"He showed me a . . . he showed me his Golden Path."

"That convenient . . ."

"It's real enough, Duncan." She looked up at him, her eyes glistening with unshed tears. "But if it was *ever* a reason for our *God* Emperor it is not reason for what he has become!"

Idaho inhaled deeply, then: "The Atreides come to this!"

"The Worm must go!" Siona said.

"I wonder when he's arriving?" Idaho said.

"Garun's little rat friend didn't say."

"We must ask," Idaho said.

"We have no weapons," Siona said.

"Nayla has a lasgun," he said. "We have knives . . . rope. I saw rope in one of Garun's storage rooms."

"Against the Worm?" she asked. "Even if we could get Nayla's lasgun, you know it won't touch him."

"But is his cart proof against it?" Idaho asked.

"I don't trust Nayla," Siona said.

"Doesn't she obey you?"

"Yes, but . . ."

"We will proceed one step at a time," Idaho said. "Ask Nayla if she would use her lasgun against the Worm's cart."

"And if she refuses?"

"Kill her."

Siona stood, tossing her book aside.

"How will the Worm come to Tuono?" Idaho asked. "He's too big and heavy for an ordinary 'thopter."

"Garun will tell us," she said. "But I think he will come as he usually travels." She looked up at the ceiling which concealed the Sareer's perimeter wall. "I think he will come on peregrination with his entire crew. He will come along the Royal Road and drop down to here on suspensors." She looked at Idaho. "What of Garun?"

"A strange man," Idaho said. "He wants most desperately to be a real Fremen. He knows he is not anything like what they were in my day."

"What were they like in your day, Duncan?"

"They had a saying which describes it," Idaho said. "You should never be in the company of anyone with whom you would not want to die."

"Did you say this to Garun?" she asked.

"Yes."

"And his response?"

414

"He said I was the only such person he had ever met."

"Garun may be wiser than any of us," she said.

> *You think power may be the most unstable of all human achievements? Then what of the apparent exceptions to this inherent instability? Some families endure. Very powerful religious bureaucracies have been known to endure. Consider the relationship between faith and power. Are they mutually exclusive when each depends upon the other? The Bene Gesserit have been reasonably secure within the loyal walls of faith for thousands of years. But where has their power gone?*

—**The Stolen Journals**

Moneo spoke in a petulant tone: "Lord, I wish you had given me more time."

He stood outside the Citadel in the short shadows of noon. Leto lay directly in front of him on the Imperial Cart, its bubble hood retracted. He had been touring the environs with Hwi Noree who occupied a newly installed seat within the bubble cover's perimeter and just beside Leto's face. Hwi appeared merely curious about all the bustle which was beginning to increase around them.

How calm she is, Moneo thought. He repressed an involuntary shudder at what he had learned of her from Malky. The God Emperor was right. Hwi was exactly what she appeared to be—an ultimately sweet and sensible human being. *Would she really have mated with me?* Moneo wondered.

Distractions drew his attention away from her. While Leto had toured Hwi around the Citadel on the suspensor-borne cart, a great troop of courtiers and Fish Speakers had been assembled here, all the courtiers in celebration finery, brilliant reds and golds dominant. The Fish Speakers wore their best dark blues distinguished only by the different colours in the piping and hawks. A baggage caravan on suspensor sleds had been drawn up at the rear with Fish Speakers to pull it. The air was full of dust and the sounds and smells of excitement. Most of the courtiers had reacted with dismay when told their destination. Some had immediately purchased their own tents and pavilions. These had been sent on ahead with the other impedimenta piled now on the sand just outside Tuono's view. The Fish Speakers in the entourage were not taking this in a festive mood. They had complained loudly when told they could not carry lasguns.

"Just a *little* more time, Lord," Moneo was saying. "I still don't know how we will . . ."

"There's no substitute for time in solving many problems," Leto said. "However, you can place too much reliance on it. I can accept no more delays."

"We will be three days just getting there," Moneo complained.

Leto thought about that time—the swift walk-trot-walk of a peregrination . . . one hundred and eighty kilometres. Yes, three days.

"I'm sure you've made good arrangements for the way-stops," Leto said. "Plenty of hot water for the muscle cramps."

"We'll be comfortable enough," Moneo said, "but I don't like leaving the Citadel in these times! And you know why!"

"We have communications devices, loyal assistants. The Guild is suitably chastened. Calm yourself, Moneo."

"We could hold the ceremony in the Citadel!"

For answer, Leto closed the bubble cover around him, isolating Hwi with him.

"Is there danger, Leto?" she asked.

"There's always danger."

Moneo sighed, turned and trotted toward where the Royal Road began its long climb eastward before turning south around the Sareer. Leto set his cart in motion behind the majordomo, heard his motley troop fall into step behind them.

"Are we all moving?" Leto asked.

Hwi glanced backward around him. "Yes." She turned toward his face. "Why was Moneo being so difficult?"

"Moneo has discovered that the instant which has just left him is forever beyond his reach."

"He has been very moody and distracted since you returned from the Little Citadel. He's not the same at all."

"He is an Atreides, my love, and you were designed to please an Atreides."

"It's not that. I would know if it were that."

"Yes . . . well, I think Moneo has also discovered the reality of death."

"What's it like at the Little Citadel when you're there with Moneo?" she asked.

"It's the loneliest place in my Empire."

"I think you avoid my questions," she said.

"No, love. I share your concern for Moneo, but no explanation of mine will help him now. Moneo is trapped. He has learned that it is difficult to live in the present, pointless to live in the future and impossible to live in the past."

"I think it's you who have trapped him, Leto."

"But he must free himself."

"Why can't you free him?"

"Because he thinks my memories are his key to freedom. He thinks I am building our future out of our past."

"Isn't that always the way of it, Leto?"

"No, dear Hwi."

"Then how is it?"

"Most believe that a satisfactory future requires a return to an idealized past, a past which never in fact existed."

"And you with all of your memories know otherwise."

Leto turned his face within its cowl to stare at her, probing . . . remembering. Out of the multitudes within him, he could form a composite, a genetic suggestion of Hwi, but the suggestion fell far short of the living flesh. That was it, of course. The past became row on row of eyes staring outward like the eyes of gasping fish, but Hwi was vibrant life. Her mouth was set in Grecian curves designed for a Delphic chant, but she hummed no prophetic syllables. She was content to live, an opening person like a flower perpetually unfolding into fragrant blossom.

"Why are you looking at me like that?" she asked.

"I was basking in the love of you."

"Love, yes." She smiled. "I think that since we cannot share the love of the flesh, we must share the love of the soul. Would you share that with me, Leto?"

He was taken aback. "You ask about my soul?"

"Surely others have asked."

He spoke shortly: "My soul digests its experiences, nothing more."

"Have I asked too much of you?" she asked.

"I think that you cannot ask too much of me."

"Then I presume upon our love to disagree with you. My Uncle Malky talked about your soul."

He found that he could not respond. She took his silence as an invitation to continue. "He said that you were the ultimate artist at probing the soul, your own soul first."

"But your Uncle Malky denied that he had a soul of his own!"

She heard the harshness in his voice, but was not deterred. "Still, I think he was right. You are the genius of the soul, the brilliant one."

"You need only the plodding perseverance of duration," he said. "No brilliance."

They were well on to the long climb to the top of the Sareer's perimeter wall now. He lowered his cart's wheels and deactivated the suspensors.

Hwi spoke softly, her voice barely audible above the grating sound of the cart's wheels and the running feet all around them. "May I call you Love, anyway?"

He spoke around a remembered tightness in a throat which was no longer completely human. "Yes."

"I was born an Ixian, Love," she said. "Why don't I share their mechanical view of our universe? Do you know my view, Leto my love?"

He could only stare at her.

"I sense the supernatural at every turning," she said.

Leto's voice rasped, sounding angry even to him: "Each person creates his own supernatural."

"Don't be angry with me, Love."

Again, that awful rasping: "It is impossible for me to be angry with you."

"But something happened between you and Malky once," she said. "He would never tell me what it was, but he said he often wondered why you spared him."

"Because of what he taught me."

"What happened between you two, Love?"

"I would rather not talk about Malky."

"Please, Love. I feel that it's important for me to know."

"I suggested to Malky that there might be some things men should not invent."

"And that's all?"

"No." He spoke reluctantly. "My words angered him. He said: 'You think that in a world without birds men would not invent aircraft! What a fool you are! Men can invent anything!'"

"He called you a fool?" There was shock in Hwi's voice.

"He was right. And although he denied it, he spoke the truth. He taught me that there was a reason for running away from inventions."

"Then you fear the Ixians?"

"Of course I do! They can invent catastrophe."

"Then what could you do?"

"Run faster. History is a constant race between invention and catastrophe. Education helps but it's never enough. You also must run."

"You are sharing your soul with me, Love. Do you know that?"

Leto looked away from her and focused on Moneo's back, the motions of the majordomo, the tucked-in pretences of secrecy so apparent there. The procession had come off the first gentle incline. It turned now to begin the climb on to Ringwall West. Moneo moved as he had always moved, one foot ahead of another, aware of the ground where he would place each step, but there was something new in the majordomo. Leto could feel the man drawing away, no longer content to march beside his Lord's cowled face, no longer trying to match himself to his master's destiny. Off to the east, the Sareer waited. Off to the west there was the river, the plantations. Moneo looked neither left nor right. He had seen another destination.

"You do not answer me," Hwi said.

"You already know the answer."

"Yes. I am beginning to understand something of you," she said. "I can sense some of your fears. And I think I already know where it is that you live."

He turned a startled glance on her and found himself locked in her gaze. It was astonishing. He could not move his eyes away from her. A profound fear coursed through him and he felt his hands begin to twitch.

"You live where the fear of being and the love of being are combined, all in one person," she said.

He could only blink.

"You are a mystic," she said, "gentle to yourself only because you are in the middle of that universe looking outward, looking in ways that others cannot. You fear to share this, yet you want to share it more than anything else."

"What have you seen?" he whispered.

"I have no inner eye, no inner voices," she said. "But I have seen my Lord Leto whose soul I love and I *know* the only thing that you truly understand."

He broke from her gaze, fearful of what she might say. The trembling of his hands could be felt all through his front segment.

"Love, that is what you understand," she said. "Love, and that is all of it."

His hands stopped trembling. A tear rolled down each of his cheeks. When the tears touched his cowl, wisps of blue smoke erupted. He sensed the burning and was thankful for the pain.

"You have faith in life," Hwi said. "I know that the courage of love can reside only in this faith."

She reached out with her left hand and brushed the tears from his cheeks. It surprised him that the cowl did not react with its ordinary reflex to prevent the touch.

"Do you know," he asked, "that since I have become thus, you are the first person to touch my cheeks?"

"But I know what you are and what you were," she said.

"What I was . . . ahhh, Hwi. What I was has become only this face, and all the rest is lost in the shadows of memory . . . hidden . . . gone."

"Not hidden from me, Love."

He looked directly at her, no longer afraid to lock gazes. "Is it possible that the Ixians know what they have created in you?"

"I assure you, Leto, love of my soul, that they do not know. You are the first person, the only person to whom I have ever completely revealed myself."

"Then I will not mourn for what might have been," he said. "Yes, my love, I will share my soul with you."

> Think of it as plastic memory, this force within you which trends you and your fellows toward tribal forms. This plastic memory seeks to return to its ancient shape, the tribal society. It is all around you—the feudatory, the diocese, the corporation, the platoon, the sports club, the dance troupe, the rebel cell, the planning council, the prayer group . . . each with its master and servants, its host and parasites. And the swarms of alienating devices (including these very words!) tend eventually to be enlisted in the argument for a return to "those better times". I despair of teaching you other ways. You have square thoughts which resist circles.

> —The Stolen Journals

Idaho found he could manage the climb without thinking about it. This body grown by the Tleilaxu remembered things the Tleilaxu did not even suspect. His original youth might be lost in the eons, but his muscles were Tleilaxu-young and he could bury his childhood in forgetfulness while he climbed. In that childhood he had learned survival by flight into the high rocks of his home planet. It did not matter that these rocks in front of him now had been brought here by men, they also had been shaped by ages of weather.

The morning sun was hot on Idaho's back. He could hear Siona's efforts to reach the relatively simple support position of a narrow ledge far below him. The position was virtually useless to Idaho, but it had been the argument which had brought Siona finally into agreement that they should attempt this climb.

They.

She had objected that he might try it alone.

Nayla, three of her Fish Speaker aides, Garun and three chosen from his Museum Fremen waited on the sand at the foot of the barrier wall which enclosed the Sareer.

Idaho did not think about the wall's height. He thought only about where he would next put a hand or a foot. He thought about the coil of light rope around his shoulders. That rope was the *tallness* of this wall. He had measured it out on the ground, triangulating across the sand, not counting his steps. When the rope was long enough it was long enough. The wall was as high as the rope was long. Any other way of thinking could only dull his mind.

Feeling for handholds which he could not see, Idaho groped his way up the sheer face . . . well, not quite sheer. Wind and sand and even some rain, the forces of cold and heat, had been at their erosive work here for more than three thousand years. For one full day, Idaho had sat on the sand below the wall and he had studied what had been accomplished by Time. He had fixed certain patterns in his mind—a slanting shadow, a thin line, a crumbling bulge, a tiny lip of rock here and another over there.

His fingers wriggled upward into a sharp crack. He tested his weight gently on the support. Yes. Briefly, he rested, pressing his face against warm rock, not looking up or down. He was simply *here*. Everything was a matter of the pacing. His shoulders must not be allowed to tire too soon. Weight must be adjusted between feet and arms. Fingers took inevitable damage, but while bone and tendons held, the skin could be ignored.

Once more, he crept upward. A bit of rock broke away from his hand; dust and shards fell across his right cheek but he did not even feel it. Every bit of his awareness concentrated on the groping hand, the balance of his feet on the tiniest of protrusions. He was a mote, a particle which defied gravity . . . a fingerhold here, a toehold there, clinging to the rock surface at times by the sheer power of his will.

Nine makeshift pitons bulged one of his pockets, but he resisted using them. The equally makeshift hammer dangled from his belt on a short cord whose knot his fingers had memorized.

Nayla had been difficult. She would not give up her lasgun. She had, however, obeyed Siona's direct order to accompany them. A strange woman . . . strangely obedient.

"Have you not sworn to obey me?" Siona had demanded.

Nayla's reluctance had vanished.

Later, Siona had said: "She always obeys my direct orders."

"Then we may not have to kill her," Idaho had said.

"I would rather not attempt it. I don't think you have even the faintest idea of her strength and quickness."

Garun, the Museum Fremen who dreamed of becoming a "true Naib in the old fashion", Garun had set the stage for this climb by answering Idaho's question: "How will the God Emperor come to Tuono?"

"In the same way he chose for a visit during my great-grandfather's time."

"And that was?" Siona had prompted him.

They had been sitting in the dusty shadows outside the guest house, sheltering from the afternoon sun on the day of the announcement that the Lord Leto would be wed in Tuono. A semicircle of Garun's aides squatted around the doorstep where Siona and Idaho sat with Garun. Two Fish Speakers lounged nearby, listening. Nayla was due to arrive momentarily.

Garun pointed to the high wall behind the village, its rim glistening distant gold in the sunlight. "The Royal Road runs there and the God Emperor has a device which lowers him gently from the heights."

"It's built into his cart," Idaho said.

"Suspensors," Siona agreed. "I've seen them."

"My great-grandfather said they came along the Royal Road, a great troop of them. The God Emperor glided down to our village square on his device. The others came down on ropes."

Idaho spoke thoughtfully: "Ropes."

"Why did they come?" Siona asked.

"To affirm that the God Emperor had not forgotten his Fremen, so my great-grandfather said. It was a great honour, but not as great as this wedding."

Idaho arose while Garun was still talking. There was a clear view of the high wall from nearby—straight down the central street, a view from the base in the sand to the top in the sunlight. Idaho strode to the corner of the guest house and out into the central street. He stopped there, turned and looked at the wall. The first look told why everyone said it was not possible to climb that face. Even then, he resisted thinking about a measurement of the height. It could be five hundred metres or five thousand. The important thing lay in what a more careful study revealed— tiny transverse cracks, broken places, even a narrow ledge about twenty metres above the drifting sand at the bottom . . . and another ledge about two thirds of the way up the face.

He knew that an unconscious part of him, an ancient and dependable part, was making the necessary measurements, scaling them to his own body—so many Duncan-lengths to that place, a handgrip here, another there. His own hands.

He could already feel himself climbing.

Siona's voice came from near his right shoulder as he stood in that first examination. "What're you doing?" She had come up soundlessly, looking now where he looked.

"I can climb that wall," Idaho said. "If I carried a light rope, I could pull a heavier rope. The rest of you could climb it easily then."

Garun joined them in time to hear this. "Why would you climb the wall, Duncan Idaho?"

Siona answered for him, smiling at Garun. "To provide a suitable greeting for the God Emperor."

This had been before her doubts, before her own eyes and the ignorance of such a climb, had begun to erode that first confidence.

With that first elation, Idaho asked: "How wide is the Royal Road up there?"

"I have never seen it," Garun said. "But I am told it is very wide. A great troop can march abreast along it, so they say. And there are bridges, places to view the river and . . . and . . . oh, it is a marvel."

"Why have you never gone up there to see it for yourself?" Idaho asked.

Garun merely shrugged and pointed at the wall.

Nayla arrived then and the argument about the climb had begun. Idaho thought about that argument as he climbed. How strange, the relationship between Nayla and Siona! They were like two conspirators . . . yet not conspirators. Siona commanded and Nayla obeyed. But Nayla was a Fish Speaker, the *Friend* who was trusted by Leto to make a first examination of the new ghola. She admitted that she had been in the Royal Constabulary since childhood. Such strength in her! Given that strength, there was something awesome about the way she bowed to Siona's will. It was as though Nayla listened for secret voices which told her what to do. *Then* she obeyed.

Idaho groped upward for another handhold. His fingers wriggled along the rock, up and outward to the right, finding at last an unseen crack where they might enter. His

425

memory provided the natural line of ascent, but only his body could learn the way by following that line. His left foot found a toehold . . . up . . . up . . . slowly, testing. Left hand up now . . . no crack but a ledge. His eyes, then his chin lifted over the high ledge he had seen from below. He elbowed his way on to it, rolled over and rested, looking only outward, not up or down. It was a sand horizon out there, a breeze with dust in it limiting the view. He had seen many such horizons in the Dune days.

Presently, he turned to face the wall, lifted himself on to his knees, hands groping upward, and he resumed the climb. The picture of the wall remained in his mind as he had seen it from below. He had only to close his eyes and the pattern lay there, fixed the way he had learned to do it as a child hiding from Harkonnen slave raiders. Fingertips found a crack where they could be wedged. He clawed his way upward.

Watching from below, Nayla experienced a growing affinity for the climber. Idaho had been reduced by distance to such a small and lonely shape upon the wall. He must know what it was like to be alone with momentous decisions.

I would like to have his child, she thought. *A child from both of us would be strong and resourceful. What is it that God wants from a child of Siona and this man?*

Nayla had awakened before dawn and had walked out to the top of a low dune at the village edge to think about this thing that Idaho proposed. It had been a lime dawn with a familiar winding cloth of dust in the distance, then steel day and the baleful immensity of the Sareer. She knew then that these matters certainly had been anticipated by God. What could be hidden from God? Nothing could be hidden, not even the remote figure of Duncan Idaho groping for a pathway up to the edge of heaven.

As she watched Idaho climb, Nayla's mind played a trick on her, tipping the wall to the horizontal. Idaho became a child crawling across a broken surface. How small he looked . . . and growing smaller.

An aide offered Nayla water which she drank. The water brought the wall back into its true perspective.

Siona crouched on the first ledge, leaning out to peer upward. "If you fall, I will try it," Siona had promised Idaho. Nayla had thought it a strange promise. Why would both of them want to try the impossible?

Idaho had failed to dissuade Siona from the impossible promise.

It is fate, Nayla thought. *It is God's will.*

They were the same thing.

A bit of rock fell from where Idaho clutched at it. That had happened several times. Nayla watched the falling rock. It took a long time coming down, bounding and rebounding from the wall's face, demonstrating that the eye did not report truthfully when it said the wall was sheer.

He will succeed or he will not, Nayla thought. *Whatever happens, it is God's will.*

She could feel her heart hammering, though. Idaho's venture was like sex, she thought. It was not passively erotic, but akin to rare magic in the way it seized her. She had to keep reminding herself that Idaho was not for her.

He is for Siona. If he survives.

And if he failed, then Siona would try. Siona would succeed or she would not. Nayla wondered, though, if she might experience an orgasm should Idaho reach the top. He was so close to it now.

Idaho took several deep breaths after dislodging the rock. It was a bad moment and he took the time to recover, clinging to a three-point hold on the wall. Almost of its own accord, his free hand groped upwards once more, wriggling past the rotten place into another slender crack. Slowly, he shifted his weight on to that hand. Slowly . . . slowly. His left knee felt the place where a toehold could be achieved. He lifted his foot to that place, tested it. Memory told him the top was near, but he pushed the memory aside. There was only the climb and the knowledge that Leto would arrive tomorrow.

Leto and Hwi.

He could not think about that, either. But it would not go away. *The top . . . Hwi . . . Leto . . . tomorrow.*

Every thought fed his desperation, forced him into the immediate remembrance of the climbs of his childhood. The more he remembered consciously, the more his abilities were blocked. He was forced to pause, breathing deeply in the attempt to centre himself, to go back to the *natural* ways of his past.

But were those days *natural*?

There was a blockage in his mind. He could sense intrusions, a finality . . . the *fatality* of what might have been and now would never be.

Leto would arrive up there tomorrow.

Idaho felt perspiration run down his face around the place where he pressed a cheek against the rock.

Leto.

I will defeat you, Leto. I will defeat you for myself, not for Hwi, but only for myself.

A sensation of cleansing began to spread through him. It was like the thing which had happened in the night while he prepared himself mentally for this climb. Siona had sensed his sleeplessness. She had begun to talk to him, telling him the smallest details of her desperate run through the Forbidden Forest and her oath at the edge of the river.

"Now I have given an oath to command his Fish Speakers," she said. "I will honour that oath, but I hope it will not happen in the way he wants."

"What does he want?" Idaho asked.

"He has many motives and I cannot see them all. Who could possibly understand *him*? I only know that I will never forgive him."

This memory brought Idaho back to the sensation of the wall's rock against his cheek. His perspiration had dried in the light breeze and he felt chilled. But he had found his centre.

Never forgive.

Idaho felt the ghosts of all his other selves, the gholas who had died in Leto's service. Could he believe Siona's

428

suspicions? Yes. Leto was capable of killing with his own body, his own hands. The rumour which Siona recounted, had a feeling of truth in it. And Siona, too, was Atreides. Leto had become something else . . . no longer Atreides, not even human. He had become not so much a living creature as a brute fact of nature, opaque and impenetrable, all of his experiences sealed off within him. And Sonia opposed him. The real Atreides turned away from him.

As I do.

A brute fact of nature, nothing more. Just like this wall.

Idaho's right hand groped upward and found a sharp ledge. He could feel nothing above the ledge and tried to remember a wide crack at this place in the pattern. He could not dare to allow himself into the belief that he had reached the top . . . not yet. The sharp edge cut into his fingers as he put his weight on it. He brought his left hand up to that level, found a purchase and pulled himself slowly upward. His eyes reached the level of his hands. He stared across a flat space which reached outward . . . outward into blue sky. The surface where his hands clutched showed ancient weather cracks. He crawled his fingers across that surface, one hand at a time, seeking out the cracks, dragging his chest up . . . his waist . . . his hips. He rolled then, twisting and crawling until the wall was far behind him. Only then did he stand and tell himself what his senses reported.

The top. And he had not required pitons or hammer.

A faint sound reached him. Cheering?

He walked back to the edge and looked down, waving to them. Yes, they were cheering. Turning back, he strode to the centre of the roadway, letting elation still the trembling of his muscles, soothe the aching of his shoulders. Slowly, he turned full circle, examining the top while he let his memories at last estimate the height of that climb.

Nine hundred metres . . . at least that.

The Royal Roadway interested him. It was not like what he had seen on the way to Onn. It was wide, wide

. . . at least five hundred metres. The roadbed was a smooth, unbroken grey with its edge some one hundred metres from each lip of the wall. Rock pillars at man height marked the road's edge, stretching away like sentinels along the path Leto would use.

Idaho walked to the far side of the wall opposite the Sareer and peered down. Far away in the depths, a hurtling green flow of river battered itself into foam against buttress rocks. He looked to the right. Leto would come from there. Road and wall curved gently to the right, the curve beginning about three hundred metres from the place where Idaho stood. Idaho returned to the road and walked along its edge, following the curve until it made a returning "S" and narrowed, sloping gently downward. He stopped and looked at what was revealed for him, seeing the new pattern take shape.

About three kilometres away down the gentle slope, the roadway narrowed and crossed the river gorge on a bridge whose faery trusses appeared insubstantial and toylike at this distance. Idaho remembered a similar bridge on the road to Onn, the substantial feel of it beneath his feet. He trusted his memory, thinking about bridges as a military leader was forced to think about them—passages or traps.

Moving out to his left, he looked down and outward to another high wall at the far anchor of the faery bridge. The road continued there, turning gently until it was a line running straight northward. There were two walls along there and the river between them. The river glided in a man-made chasm, its moisture confined and channelled into a northward wind-drift while the water itself flowed southward.

Idaho ignored the river then. It was there and it would be there tomorrow. He fixed his attention on the bridge, letting his military training examine it. He nodded once to himself before turning back the way he had come, lifting the light rope from his shoulders as he walked.

It was only when she saw the rope come snaking down that Nayla had her orgasm.

> *What am I eliminating? The bourgeois infatuation with peaceful conservation of the past. This is a binding force, a thing which holds humankind into one vulnerable unit in spite of illusionary separations across parsecs of space. If I can find the scattered bits, others can find them. When you are together you can share a common catastrophe. You can be exterminated together. Thus, I demonstrate the terrible danger of a gliding, passionless mediocrity, a movement without ambitions or aims. I show you that entire civilizations can do this thing. I give you eons of life which slips gently toward death without fuss or stirring, without even asking why? I show you the false happiness and the shadow-catastrophe called Leto, the God Emperor. Now, will you learn the real happiness?*

> **—The Stolen Journals**

Having spent the night with only one brief catnap, Leto was awake when Moneo emerged from the guest house at dawn. The Royal Cart had been parked almost in the centre of a three-sided courtyard. The cart's cover had been set on one-way opaque, concealing its occupant, and was tightly sealed against moisture. Leto could hear the faint stirring of the fans which pulsed his air through a drying cycle.

Moneo's feet scratched on the courtyard's cobbles as he approached the cart. Dawn light edged the guest house roof with orange above the majordomo.

Leto opened the cart's cover as Moneo stopped in front of him. There was a yeasting dirt smell to the air and the accumulation of moisture in the breeze was painful.

"We should arrive at Tuono about noon," Moneo said. "I wish you'd let me bring in 'thopters to guard the sky."

"I do not want 'thopters," Leto said. "We can go down to Tuono on suspensors and ropes."

Leto marvelled at the plastic images in this brief exchange. Moneo had never liked peregrinations. His youth as a rebel had left him with suspicions of everything he could not see or label. He remained a mass of latent judgments.

"You know I don't want 'thopters for transport," Moneo said. "I want them to guard . . ."

"Yes, Moneo."

Moneo looked past Leto at the open end of the courtyard which overlooked the river canyon. Dawnlight was frosting the mist which arose from the depths. He thought of how far down that canyon dropped . . . a body twisting, twisting as it fell. Moneo had found himself unable to go to the canyon's lip last night and peer down into it. The drop was such a . . . such a temptation.

With that insightful power which filled Moneo with such awe, Leto said: "There's a lesson in every temptation, Moneo."

Speechless, Moneo turned to stare directly into Leto's eyes.

"See the lesson in my life, Moneo."

"Lord?" It was only a whisper.

"They tempt me first with evil, then with good. Each temptation is fashioned with exquisite attention to my susceptibilities. Tell me, Moneo, if I choose the good, does that make me good?"

"Of course it does, Lord."

"Perhaps you will never lose the habit of judgment," Leto said.

Moneo looked away from him once more and stared at the chasm's edge. Leto rolled his body to look where Moneo looked. Dwarf pines had been cultured along the lip of the canyon. There were hanging dewdrops on the damp needles, each of them sending a promise of pain to Leto. He longed to close the cart's cover, but there was an immediacy in those jewels which attracted his memories even while they repelled his body. The opposed synchrony threatened to fill him with turmoil.

"I just don't like going around on foot," Moneo said.

"It was the Fremen way," Leto said.

Moneo sighed. "The others will be ready in a few minutes. Hwi was breakfasting when I came out."

Leto did not respond. His thoughts were lost in memories of night—the one just past and the millennial others which crowded his pasts—clouds and stars, the rains and the open blackness pocked with glittering flakes from a shredded cosmos, a universe of nights, extravagant with them as he had been with his heartbeats.

Moneo suddenly demanded: "Where are your guards?"

"I sent them to eat."

"I don't like them leaving you unguarded!"

The crystal sound of Moneo's voice rang in Leto's memories, speaking things not cast in words. Moneo feared a universe where there was no God Emperor. He would rather die than see such a universe.

"What will happen today?" Moneo demanded.

It was a question directed not to the God Emperor but to the prophet.

"A seed blown on the wind could be tomorrow's willow tree," Leto said.

"You know our future! Why won't you share it?" Moneo was close to hysteria . . . refusing anything his immediate senses did not report.

Leto turned to glare at the majordomo, a gaze so obviously filled with pent-up emotions that Moneo recoiled from it.

"Take charge of your own existence, Moneo!"

Moneo took a deep, trembling breath. "Lord, I meant no offence. I sought only . . ."

"Look upward, Moneo!"

Involuntarily, Moneo obeyed, peering into the cloudless sky where morning light was increasing. "What is it, Lord?"

"There's no reassuring ceiling over you, Moneo. Only an open sky full of changes. Welcome it. Every sense you possess is an instrument for reacting to change. Does that tell you nothing?"

"Lord, I only came out to inquire when you would be ready to proceed."

"Moneo, I beg you to be truthful with me."

"I am truthful, Lord!"

"But if you live in bad faith, lies will appear to you like the truth."

"Lord, if I lie . . . then I do not know it."

"That has the ring of truth. But I know what you dread and will not speak."

Moneo began to tremble. The God Emperor was in the most terrible of moods, a deep threat in every word.

"You dread the imperialism of consciousness," Leto said, "and you are right to fear it. Send Hwi out here immediately!"

Moneo whirled and fled back into the great house. It was as though his entrance stirred up an insect colony. Within seconds, Fish Speakers emerged and spread around the Royal Cart. Courtiers peered from the guest house windows or came out and stood under the deep eaves, afraid to approach him. In contrast to this excitement, Hwi emerged presently from the wide central doorway and strode out of the shadows, moving slowly toward Leto, her chin up, her gaze seeking his face.

Leto felt himself becoming calm as he looked at her. She wore a golden gown he had not seen before. It had been piped with silver and jade at the neck and the cuffs of its long sleeves. The hem, almost dragging on the ground, had heavy green braid to outline deep red crenellations.

Hwi smiled as she stopped in front of him.

"Good morning, Love." She spoke softly. "What have you done to get poor Moneo so upset?"

Soothed by her presence and her voice, he smiled. "I did what I always hope to do. I produced an effect."

"You certainly did. He told the Fish Speakers you were in an angry and terrifying mood. Are you terrifying, Love?"

"Only to those who refuse to live by their own strengths."

434

"Ahhh, yes." She pirouetted for him then, displaying her new gown. "Do you like it? Your Fish Speakers gave it to me. They decorated it themselves."

"My love," he said, a warning note in his voice, "decoration! That is how you prepare the sacrifice."

She came up to the edge of the cart and leaned on it just below his face, a mock-solemn expression on her lips. "Will they sacrifice me then?"

"Some of them would like to."

"But you will not permit it."

"Our fates are joined," he said.

"Then I shall not fear." She reached up and touched one of his silver-skinned hands, but jerked away as his fingers began to tremble.

"Forgive me, Love. I forget that we are joined in soul and not in flesh," she said.

The sandtrout skin still shuddered from Hwi's touch. "Moisture in the air makes me overly sensitive," he said. Slowly, the shuddering subsided.

"I refuse to regret what cannot be," she whispered.

"Be strong, Hwi, for your soul is mine."

She turned at a sound from the guest house. "Moneo returns," she said. "Please, Love, do not frighten him."

"Is Moneo your friend, too?"

"We are friends of the stomach. We both like yogurt."

Leto was still chuckling when Moneo stopped beside Hwi. Moneo ventured a smile, casting a puzzled glance at Hwi. There was gratitude in the majordomo's manner and some of the subservience he was accustomed to show to Leto he now directed at Hwi. "Is it well with you, Lady Hwi?"

"It is well with me."

Leto said: "In the time of the stomach, friendships of the stomach are to be nurtured and cultivated. Let us be on our way, Moneo. Tuono awaits."

Moneo turned and shouted orders to the Fish Speakers and courtiers.

435

Leto grinned at Hwi. "Do I not play the impatient bride-groom with a certain style?"

She leaped lightly up to the bed of his cart, her skirt gathered in one hand. He unfolded her seat. Only when she was seated, her eyes level with Leto's, did she respond, and then it was in a voice pitched for his ears alone.

"Love of my soul, I have captured another of your secrets."

"Release it from your lips," he said, joking in this new intimacy between them.

"You seldom need words," she said. "You speak directly to the senses with your own life."

A shudder flexed its way through the length of his body. It was a moment before he could speak and then it was in a voice she had to strain to hear above the hubbub of the assembling cortège.

"Between the superhuman and the inhuman," he said, "I have had little space in which to be human. I thank you, gentle and lovely Hwi, for this little space."

In all of my universe I have seen no law of nature, unchanging and inexorable. This universe presents only changing relationships which are sometimes seen as laws by short-lived awareness. These fleshy sensoria which we call self are ephemera withering in the blaze of infinity, fleetingly aware of temporary conditions which confine our activities and change as our activities change. If you must label the absolute, use its proper name: Temporary.

—The Stolen Journals

Nayla was the first to glimpse the approaching cortège. Perspiring heavily in the midday heat, she stood near one of the rock pillars which marked the edges of the Royal Road. A sudden flash of distant reflection caught her attention.

She peered in that direction, squinting, realizing with a thrill of awareness that she saw sun-dazzle on the cover of the God Emperor's cart.

"They come!" she called.

She felt hunger then. In their excitement and singleness of purpose, none of them had brought food. Only the Fremen had brought water and that because "Fremen always carry water when they leave sietch". They did it by rote.

Nayla touched one finger to the butt of the lasgun holstered at her hip. The bridge lay no more than twenty metres ahead of her, its faery structure arching across the chasm like an alien fantasy joining one barren surface to another.

This is madness, she thought.

But the God Emperor had reinforced his command. He required his Nayla to obey Siona in all things.

Siona's orders were explicit, leaving no way for evasions. And Nayla had no way here to query her God Emperor. Siona had said: "When his cart is in the middle of the bridge—then!"

"But why?"

They had been standing well away from the others in the chill dawn atop the barrier wall, Nayla feeling precariously isolated here, remote and vulnerable.

Siona's grim features, her low, intense voice, could not be denied. "Do you think you can harm God?"

"I . . ." Nayla could only shrug.

"You *must* obey me!"

"I must," Nayla agreed.

Nayla studied the approach of the distant cortège, noting the colours of the courtiers, the thick masses of blue marking her sisters of the Fish Speakers . . . the shiny surface of her Lord's cart.

It was another test, she decided. The God Emperor would know. He would know the devotion in His Nayla's heart. It was a test. The God Emperor's commands must be obeyed in all things. That was the earliest lesson of her Fish

Speaker childhood. The God Emperor had said that Nayla must obey Siona. It was a test. What else could it be?

She looked toward the four Fremen. They had been positioned by Duncan Idaho directly in the roadway and blocking part of the exit from this end of the bridge. They sat with their backs to her and looked out across the bridge, four brown-robed mounds. Nayla had heard Idaho's words to them.

"Do not leave this place. You must greet him from here. Stand when he nears you and bow low."

Greet, yes.

Nayla nodded to herself.

The three other Fish Speakers who had climbed the barrier wall with her had been sent to the centre of the bridge. All they knew was what Siona had told them in Nayla's presence. They were to wait until the Royal Cart was only a few paces from them, then they were to turn and dance away from the cart, leading it and the procession toward the vantage point above Tuono.

If I cut the bridge with my lasgun, those three will die, Nayla thought. *And all the others who come with our Lord.*

Nayla craned her neck to peer down into the gorge. She could not see the river from here, but she could hear its distant rumblings, a movement of rocks.

They would all die!

Unless He performs a miracle.

That had to be it. Siona had set the stage for a holy miracle. What else could Siona intend now that she had been tested, now that she wore the uniform of Fish Speaker Command? Siona had given her oath to the God Emperor. She had been tested by God, the two of them alone in the Sareer.

Nayla turned only her eyes to the right, peering at the architects of this greeting. Siona and Idaho stood shoulder to shoulder in the roadway about twenty metres to Nayla's right. They were deep in conversation, looking at each other occasionally, nodding.

Presently, Idaho touched Siona's arm—an oddly possessive gesture. He nodded once and strode off toward the bridge, stopping at the buttress corner directly in front of Nayla. He peered down, then crossed to the other near corner of the bridge. Again, he peered downward, standing there for several minutes before returning to Siona.

What a strange creature, that ghola, Nayla thought. After that awesome climb, she no longer thought of him as quite human. He was something else, a demiurge who stood next to God. But he could breed.

A distant shout caught Nayla's attention. She turned and looked across the bridge. The cortège had been in the familiar trot of a Royal peregrination. Now, they were slowing to a sedate walk only a few minutes away from the bridge. Nayla recognized Moneo marching in the van, his uniform brilliant white, the even, undeviating stride with his gaze straight ahead. The cover of the Emperor's cart had been sealed. It glittered in mirror-opacity as it rolled behind Moneo on its wheels.

The mystery of it all filled Nayla.

A miracle was about to happen!

Nayla glanced to the right at Siona. Siona returned her gaze and nodded once. Nayla drew the lasgun from its holster and rested it against the rock pillar as she sighted along it. The cable on the left first, then the cable on the right, then the faery trellis of plasteel on the left. The lasgun felt cold and alien against Nayla's hand. She took a trembling breath to restore calm.

I must obey. It is a test.

She saw Moneo lift his gaze from the roadway and, not changing stride, turn to shout something at the cart or the ones behind it. Nayla could not make out the words. Moneo faced front once more. Nayla steadied herself, a part of the rock pillar which concealed most of her body.

A test.

Moneo had seen the people on the bridge and at the far end. He identified Fish Speaker uniforms and his first thought was to wonder who had ordered these greeters. He turned and shouted a question at Leto, but the God Emperor's cart cover remained opaque, hiding Hwi and Leto within it.

He was well on to the bridge, the cart rasping in blown sand behind him, before he recognized Siona and Idaho standing well back from the far end. He identified four Museum Fremen seated on the roadway. Doubts began squirming through Moneo's mind, but he could not change the pattern. He ventured a glance down at the river—a platinum world there caught in the noonday light. The sound of the cart was loud behind him. The flow of the river, the flow of the cortège, the sweeping importance of these things in which he played a role—all of it caught up his mind in a dizzying sensation of the inevitable.

We are not people passing this way, he thought. *We are primal elements linking one piece of Time to another. And when we have passed, everything behind us will drop off into no-sound, a place like the no-room of the Ixians, yet never again the same as it was before we came.*

A bit from one of the lute-player's songs wafted through Moneo's memory and his eyes went out of focus in the remembrance. He knew that song for its wishfulness, a wish that all of this were ended, all past, all doubts banished, tranquillity returned. The plaintive song drifted through his awareness like smoke, twisting and compelling:

> *"Insect cries in roots of pampas grass."*

Moneo hummed the song to himself:

> *"Insect cries mark the end.*
> *Autumn and my song are the colour*
> *Of the last leaves*
> *In roots of pampas grass."*

Moneo nodded his head to the refrain:

> *"Day is ended,*
> *Visitors gone.*
> *Day is ended.*
> *In our sietch,*
> *Day is ended.*
> *Storm wind sounds.*
> *Day is ended.*
> *Visitors gone."*

Moneo decided that the lute-player's song had to be a really old one, an old Fremen song, no doubt of it. And it told him something about himself. He wished the visitors truly gone, the excitements ended, peace once more. Peace was so near . . . yet he could not leave his duties. He thought of all that impedimenta piled out there on the sand just beyond visibility range from Tuono. They would see it all soon—tents, food, tables, golden plates and jewelled knives, glowglobes fashioned in the arabesque shapes of ancient lamps . . . everything rich and full of expectations from completely different lives.

They will never be the same in Tuono.

Moneo had spent two nights in Tuono once on an inspection tour. He remembered the smells of their cooking fires—aromatic bushes kindled and flaming in the dark. They would not use sunstoves because "that is not the most ancient way".

Most ancient!

There was little smell of melange in Tuono. A sweet acridity and the musky oils of oasis shrubs, these dominated the odours. Yes . . . and the cesspools and the stink of rotting garbage. He recalled the God Emperor's comment when Moneo had finished reporting on that tour.

"These *Fremen* do not know what is lost from their lives. They think they keep the essence of the old ways. This is a failure of all museums. Something fades; it dries out of the exhibits and is gone. The people who administer the museum and the people who come to bend over the cases

441

and stare—few of them sense this missing thing. It drove
the engine of life in earlier times. When the life is gone, it is
gone."

Moneo focused on the three Fish Speakers who stood
just ahead of him on the bridge. They lifted their arms high
and began to dance, whirling and skipping away from him
only a few paces distant.

How odd, he thought. *I've seen other people dance in the
open, but never Fish Speakers. They only dance in the
privacy of their quarters, in the intimacy of their own
company.*

This thought was still in his mind when he heard the first
awful humming of the lasgun and felt the bridge lurch
beneath him.

This is not happening, his mind told him.

He heard the Royal Cart scrape sideways across the
roadbed, then the *snap-slap* of the cart's cover slamming
open. A bedlam of screams and cries arose from behind
him, but he could not turn. The bridge's roadbed had
tipped steeply to Moneo's right, spilling him on to his face
while he went sliding toward the abyss. He clutched a
severed strand of cable to stop himself. The cable went with
him, everything grating in the spilling film of sand which
had covered the roadbed. He clutched the cable with both
hands, turning with it. He saw the Royal Cart then. It
skewed sideways toward the edge of the bridge, its cover
open. Hwi stood there, one hand steadying her on the
folding seat while she stared past Moneo.

A horrible screaming of metal filled the air as the
roadbed tipped even farther. He saw people from the
cortège falling, their mouths open, arms waving. Something had caught Moneo's cable. His arms were stretched
out over his head as he turned once more, twisting. He felt
his hands, greased by the perspiration of fear, slipping
along the cable.

Once more, his gaze came around to the Royal Cart. It
lay jammed against the stubs of broken girders. Even as
Moneo looked, the God Emperor's futile hands groped for

442

Hwi Noree, but failed to reach her. She fell from the cart's open end, silently, the golden gown whipping upward to reveal her body stretched out as straight as an arrow.

A deep, rumbling groan came from the God Emperor.

Why doesn't he activate the suspensors? Moneo wondered. *The suspensors will support him.*

But the lasgun was still humming and, as Moneo's hands slipped from the cable's severed end, he saw lancing flame strike the cart's suspensor bubbles, piercing one after another in eruptions of golden smoke. Moneo stretched his hands over his head as he fell.

The smoke! The golden smoke!

His robe whipped upward, turning him until his face was directed downward into the abyss. With his gaze on the depths, he recognized a maelstrom of boiling rapids there, the mirror of his life—precipitous currents and plunges, all movements gathering up all substance. Leto's words wound through his mind on a path of golden smoke: *"Caution is the path to mediocrity. Gliding, passionless mediocrity is all that most people think they can achieve."* Moneo fell freely then in the ecstasy of awareness. The universe opened for him like clear glass, everything flowing in a no-time.

The golden smoke!

"Leto!" he screamed. "Siaynoq! I believe!"

The robe tore away from his shoulders then. He turned in the solid wind of the canyon—one last glimpse of the Royal Cart tipping . . . tipping from the shattered roadbed. The God Emperor slid out of the open end.

Something solid smashed into Moneo's back—his last sensation.

Leto felt himself sliding from the cart. His awareness held only the image of Hwi striking the river—the distant pearly fountain which marked her plunge into the myths and dreams of termination. Her last words, calm and steady, rolled through all of his memories: "I shall go on ahead, Love."

As he slipped from the cart, he saw the scimitar arc of the

river, a silver-edged thing which shimmered in its mottled shadows, a vicious blade of a river honed through eternity and ready now to receive him into its agony.

I cannot cry, nor even shout, he thought. *Tears are no longer possible. They're water. I'll have water enough in a moment. I can only moan in my grief. I am alone, more alone than ever before.*

His great ridged body flexed as it fell, twisting him about until his amplified vision revealed Siona standing at the broken brink of the bridge.

Now, you will learn! he thought.

The body continued to turn. He watched the river approach. The water was a dream inhabited by glimpses of fish which ignited an ancient memory of a banquet beside a granite pool—pink flesh dazzling his hungers.

I join you, Hwi, in the banquet of the gods!

A bursting flash of bubbles enclosed him in agony. Water, vicious currents of it, buffeted him all around. He felt the gnashing of rocks as he struggled upward to broach in a torrential cascade, his body flexing in a paroxysm of involuntary, writhing splashes. The canyon wall, wet and black, sped past his frantic gaze. Shattered spangles of what had been his skin exploded away from him, a rain of silver all around him darting away into the river, a ring of dazzling movement, brittle sequins—the scale-glitter of sandtrout leaving him to begin their own colony lives.

The agony continued. Leto marvelled that he could remain conscious, that he had a body to feel.

Instinct drove him. He clutched at a rock around which the torrent spilled him, felt a clutching finger torn from his hand before he could release his grip. The sensation of it was only a minor accent in the symphony of pain.

The river's course swept to the left around a chasm buttress and, as though saying it had enough of him, it sent him rolling on to the sloping edge of a sandbar. He lay there a moment, the blue dye of spice essence drifting away from him in the current. The agony moved him, the worm body moving of itself, retreating from the water. All the covering sandtrout were gone and he felt every touch more immediate, a lost sense restored when all it could bring him was pain. He could not see his body, but he felt the thing that would have been a worm as it made its writhing, crawling progress out of the water. He peered upward through eyes that saw everything in sheets of flame from which shapes coalesced of their own accord. At last, he recognized this place. The river had swept him to the turn where it left the Sareer forever. Behind him lay Tuono and, just a way down the barrier wall, was all that remained of Sietch Tabr—Stilgar's realm, the place where all of Leto's spice had been concealed.

Exuding blue fumes, his agonized body writhed its way noisily along a shingle of beach, dragged its blue-dyed way across broken boulders and into a damp hole which might have been part of the original sietch. It was only a shallow cave now, blocked at its inner end by a rock fall. His nostrils reported the wet dirt smell, but no hint of spice.

Sounds intruded on his agony. He turned in the confinement of the cave and saw a rope dangling at the entrance. A figure slid down the rope. He recognized Nayla. She dropped to the rocks and crouched there, staring into the shadows at him. The flame which was Leto's vision parted to reveal another figure dropping from the rope: Siona. She and Nayla scrambled toward him in a rattle of rocks and stopped, peering in at him. A third figure dropped off the rope: Idaho. He moved with frantic rage, hurling himself at Nayla, screaming:

"Why did you kill her! You weren't supposed to kill Hwi!"

Nayla sent him sprawling with a casual, almost indifferent sweep of her left arm. She scrambled closer up the rocks and stopped on all fours to peer in at Leto.

"Lord? You live?"

Idaho was right behind her, snatching the lasgun from her holster. Nayla turned, astonished, as he levelled the weapon and pulled its trigger. The burning started at the top of Nayla's head. It split her, the pieces slumping apart.

A shining crysknife spilled from her burning uniform and shattered on the rocks. Idaho did not see it. A grimace of rage on his face, he kept burning and burning the pieces of Nayla until the weapon's charge was gone. The blazing arc vanished. Only wet and smoking bits of meat and cloth lay scattered among the glowing rocks.

It was the moment for which Siona had waited. She scrambled up to him and pulled the useless lasgun from Idaho's hands. He whirled toward her and she poised herself to subdue him, but all the rage was gone.

"Why?" he whispered.

"It's done," she said.

They turned and looked into the cave shadows at Leto.

Leto could not even imagine what they saw. The sandtrout skin was gone, he knew. There would be some kind of surface pocked with cilia holes from the departed skin. As for the rest, he could only look back at the two figures from a universe furrowed by sorrow. Through the vision flames he saw Siona as a female demon. The demon name came unbidden to his mind and he spoke it aloud, amplified by the cave and much louder than he had expected:

"Hanmya!"

"What?" She moved a step closer to him.

Idaho put both hands over his face.

"Look at what you've done to poor Duncan," Leto said.

"He'll find other loves." How callous she sounded, an echo of his own angry youth.

"You don't know what it is to love," he said. "What have you ever given?" He could only wring his hands then, those travesties which once had been his hands. "Gods below! What I've given!"

She scrambled closer and reached toward him, then drew back.

"I am reality, Siona. Look upon me. I exist. You can touch me if you dare. Reach out your hand. Do it!"

Slowly, she reached toward what had been his front segment, the place where she had slept in the Sareer. Her hand was touched with blue when she withdrew it.

"You have touched me and felt my body," he said. "Is that not strange beyond any other thing in this universe?"

She started to turn away.

"No! Don't turn away from me! Look at what you have wrought, Siona. How is it that you can touch me but you cannot touch yourself?"

She whirled away from him.

"*There* is the difference between us," he said. "You are God embodied. You walk around within the greatest miracle of this universe, yet you refuse to touch or see or feel or believe in it."

Leto's awareness went wandering then into a night-encircled place, a place where he thought he could hear the metal insect song of his hidden printers clacking away in their lightless room. There was a complete absence of radiation in this place, an Ixian no-thing which made it a place of anxiety and spiritual alienation because it had not connection with the rest of the universe.

But it will have a connection.

He sensed then that his Ixian printers had been set in motion, that they were recording his thoughts without any special command.

Remember what I did! Remember me! I will be innocent again!

The flame of his vision parted to reveal Idaho standing where Siona had stood. There was gesturing motion somewhere out of focus behind Idaho . . . ah, yes: Siona waving instructions to someone atop the barrier wall.

"Are you still alive?" Idaho asked.

Leto's voice came in wheezing gasps: "Let them scatter, Duncan. Let them run and hide anywhere they want in any universe they choose."

"Damn you! What're you saying? I'd have sooner let her live with you!"

"Let? I did not *let* anything."

"Why did you let Hwi die?" Idaho moaned. "We didn't know she was in there with you."

Idaho's head sagged forward.

447

"You will be recompensed," Leto husked. "My Fish Speakers will choose you over Siona. Be kind to her, Duncan. She is more than Atreides and she carries the seed of your survival."

Leto sank back into his memories. They were delicate myths now, held fleetingly in his awareness. He sensed that he might have fallen into a time which, by its very being, had changed the past. There were sounds, though, and he struggled to interpret them. *Someone scrambling on rocks?* The flames parted to reveal Siona standing beside Idaho. They stood hand in hand like two children reassuring each other before venturing into an unknown place.

"How can he live like that?" Siona whispered.

Leto waited for the strength to respond. "Hwi helps me," he said. "We had something few experience. We were joined in our strengths rather than in our weaknesses."

"And look what it got you!" Siona sneered.

"Yes, and pray that you get the same," he husked. "Perhaps the spice will give you time."

"Where is your spice?" she demanded.

"Deep in Sietch Tabr," he said. "Duncan will find it. You know the place, Duncan. They call it Tabur now. The outlines are still there."

"Why did you do it?" Idaho whispered.

"My gift," Leto said. "Nobody will find the descendants of Siona. The oracle cannot see her."

"What?" They spoke in unison, leaning close to hear his fading voice.

"I give you a new kind of time without parallels," he said. "It will always diverge. There will be no concurrent points on its curves. I give you the Golden Path. That is my gift. Never again will you have the kinds of concurrence that once you had."

Flames covered his vision. The agony was fading, but he could still sense odours and hear sounds with a terrible acuity. Both Idaho and Siona were breathing in quick, shallow gasps. Odd kinesthetic sensations began to weave their way through Leto—echoes of bones and joints which he knew he no longer possessed.

"Look!" Siona said.

"He's disintegrating." That was Idaho.

"No." Siona. "The outside is falling away. Look! The worm!"

Leto felt parts of himself settling into warm softness. The agony removed itself.

"What're those holes in him?" asked Siona.

"I think they were the sandtrout. See the shapes?"

"I am here to prove one of my ancestors wrong," Leto said (or thought he said, which was the same thing as far as his journals were concerned). "I was born a man but I do not die a man."

"I can't look!" Siona said.

Leto heard her turn away, a rattle of rocks.

"Are you still there, Duncan?"

"Yes."

So I still have a voice.

"Look at me," Leto said. "I was a bloody bit of pulp in a human womb, a bit no larger than a cherry. Look at me, I say!"

"I'm looking." Idaho's voice was faint.

"You expected a giant and you found a gnome," Leto said. "Now, you're beginning to know the responsibilities which come as a result of actions. What will you do with your new power, Duncan?"

There was a long silence, then Siona's voice: "Don't listen to him! He was mad!"

"Of course," Leto said. "Madness in method, that is genius."

"Siona, do you understand this?" Idaho asked. How plaintive, the ghola voice.

"She understands," Leto said. "It is human to have your soul brought to a crisis you did not anticipate. That's the way it always is with humans. Moneo understood at last."

"I wish he'd hurry up and die!" Siona said.

"I am the divided god and you would make me whole,"

Leto said. "Duncan? I think of all my Duncans I approve of you the most."

"Approve?" Some of the rage returned to Idaho's voice.

"There's magic in my approval," Leto said. "Anything's possible in a magic universe. *Your* life has been dominated by the oracle's fatality, not mine. Now, you see the mysterious caprices and you would ask me to dispel this? I wished only to increase it."

The *others* within Leto began to reassert themselves. Without the solidarity of the colonial group to support his identity, he began to lose his place among them. They started speaking the language of the constant IF. "If you had only . . . If we had but . . ." He wanted to shout them into silence.

"Only fools prefer the past!"

Leto did not know if he truly shouted or only thought it. The response was a momentary inner silence matched to an outer silence and he felt some of the threads of his old identity still intact. He tried to speak and knew the reality of it because Idaho said: "Listen, he's trying to say something."

"Do not fear the Ixians," he said, and he heard his own voice as a fading whisper. "They can make the machines, but they no longer can make *arafel*. I know. I was there."

He fell silent, gathering his strength, but he felt the energy flowing from him even as he tried to hold it. Once more, the clamour arose within him—voices pleading and shouting.

"Stop that foolishness!" he cried, or thought he cried.

Idaho and Siona heard only a gasping hiss.

Presently, Siona said: "I think he's dead."

"And everyone thought he was immortal," Idaho said.

"Do you know what the Oral History says?" Siona asked. "If you want immortality, then deny form. Whatever has form has mortality. Beyond form is the formless, the immortal."

"That sounds like *him*," Idaho accused.

"I think it was," she said.

450

"What did he mean about your descendants . . . hiding, not finding them?" Idaho asked.

"He created a new kind of mimesis," she said, "a new biological imitation. He knew he had succeeded. He could not see me in his futures."

"What are you?" Idaho demanded.

"I'm the new Atreides."

"Atreides!" It was a curse in Idaho's voice.

Siona stared down at the disintegrating hulk which once had been Leto Atreides II . . . and something else. The *something* else was sloughing away in faint wisps of blue smoke where the smell of melange was strongest. Puddles of blue liquid formed in the rocks beneath his melting bulk. Only faint vague shapes which might once have been human remained—a collapsed foaming pinkness, a bit of red-streaked bone which could have held the forms of cheeks and brow . . .

Siona said: "I am different, but still I am what he was."

Idaho spoke in a hushed whisper: "The ancestors, all of . . ."

"The multitude is there but I walk silently among them and no one sees me. The old images are gone and only the essence remains to light his Golden Path."

She turned and took Idaho's cold hand in hers. Carefully, she led him out of the cave into the light where the rope dangled invitingly from the barrier wall's top, from the place where the frightened Museum Fremen waited.

Poor material with which to shape a new universe, she thought, but they would have to serve. Idaho would require gentle seduction, a care within which love *might* appear.

When she looked down the river to where the flow emerged from its man-made chasm to spread across the green lands, she saw a wind from the south driving dark clouds towards her.

Idaho withdrew his hand from hers, but he appeared calmer. "Weather control is increasingly unstable," he said. "Moneo thought it was the Guild's doing."

"My father was seldom mistaken about such things," she

said. "You will have to look into that."

Idaho experienced a sudden memory of the silvery shapes of sandtrout darting away from Leto's body in the river.

"I heard the Worm," Siona said. "The Fish Speakers will follow you, not me."

Again, Idaho sensed the temptation from the ritual of Siaynoq. "We will see," he said. He turned and looked at Siona. "What did he mean when he said the Ixians cannot create *arafel*?"

"You haven't read all the journals," she said. "I'll show you when we return to Tuono."

"But what does it mean—*arafel*?"

"That's the cloud-darkness of holy judgment. It's from an old story. You'll find it all in my journals."

Excerpt from the Hadi Benotto secret summation on the discoveries at Dar-es-Balat:

Herewith the minority report. We will, of course, comply with the majority decision to apply a careful screening, editing and censorship to the Journals from Dar-es-Balat, but our arguments must be heard. We recognize the interest of Holy Church in these matters and the political dangers have not escaped our notice. We share a desire with the Church that Rakis and the Holy Reservation of the Divided God do not become "an attraction for gawking tourists".

However, now that all of the Journals are in our hands, authenticated and translated, the clear shape of the Atreides Design emerges. As a woman trained by the Bene Gesserit to understand the ways of our ancestors, I have a natural desire to share the pattern we have exposed—which is so much more than Dune to Arrakis to Dune, thence to Rakis.

The interests of history and science must be served. The Journals throw a valuable new light on to that accumulation

452

of personal recollections and biographies from the Duncan Days, the Guard Bible. We cannot be unmindful of those familiar oaths: *"By the Thousand Sons of Idaho!"* and *"By the Nine Daughters of Siona!"* The persistent Cult of Sister Chenoeh assumes new significance because of the Journals' disclosures. Certainly, the Church's characterization of Judas/Nayla deserves careful re-evaluation.

We of the Minority must remind the political censors that the poor sandworms in their Rakian Reservation cannot provide us with an alternative to Ixian Navigation Machines, nor are the tiny amounts of Church-controlled melange any real commercial threat to the products of the Tleilaxu vats. No! We argue that the myths, the Oral History, the Guard Bible, and even the Holy Books of the Divided God must be compared with the Journals from Dar-es-Balat. Every historical reference to the Scattering and the Famine Times has to be taken out and re-examined! What have we to fear? No Ixian machine can do what we, the descendants of Duncan Idaho and Siona, have done. How many universes have we populated? None can guess. No one person will ever know. Does the Church fear the occasional prophet? We know that the visionaries cannot *see* us nor predict our decisions. No death can find all of humankind. Must we of the Minority join our fellows of the Scattering before we can be heard? Must we leave the original core of humankind ignorant and uninformed? If the Majority drives us out, you know we never again can be found!

We do not want to leave. We are held here by those *pearls* in the sand. We are fascinated by the Church's use of the pearl as "the sun of understanding". Surely, no reasoning human can escape the Journals' revelations in this regard. The admittedly fugitive but vital uses of archeology must have their day! Just as the primitive machine with which Leto II concealed his Journals can only teach us about the evolution of our machines, just so, that ancient awareness must be allowed to speak to us. It would be a crime against both historical accuracy and science for us to abandon our attempts at communication with those "pearls of awareness" which the Journals have located. Is Leto II lost in his endless dream or could he be re-awakened to our times, brought to full consciousness as a storehouse of historical accuracy? How can Holy Church fear this truth?

For the Minority, we have no doubt that historians must listen to that voice from our beginnings. If it is only the Journals, we must listen. We must listen across at least as many years into our future as those Journals lay hidden in our past. We will not try to predict the discoveries yet to be made within those pages. We say only that they must be made. How can we turn our backs on our most important inheritance? As the poet, Lon Bramlis, has said: "We are the fountain of surprises!"